GOLDBRICKS WIFE

BY

NIMA GOLD

Copyright Registration Number: TXu 2-411-782 Nima Gold

Date February 8, 2024

This book is a work of fiction. Any references to real people, or real places are used fictitiously. Other names, characters, places, and events are products of the author's imagination, and any resemblances to actual events or places or persons, living or dead, is entirely coincidental.

All rights reserved, including the right to reproduce, duplicate, or transmit any part of this document in either electronic means or printed format. Recording of this publication is strictly prohibited of this book or portions thereof in any for whatsoever.

Publisher: Amazon Publishing Agency
870 N Main Street, Sheridan, WY 82801

To my Love Joel Archer Marshall

"Wherever you are"

TABLE OF CONTENTS:

CHAPTER 1……………………………………………………..10

CHAPTER 2……………………………………………………..24

CHAPTER 3……………………………………………………...35

CHAPTER 4……………………………………………………..53

CHAPTER 5……………………………………………………...69

CHAPTER 6……………………………………………………...84

CHAPTER 7……………………………………………………111

CHAPTER 8……………………………………………………127

CHAPTER 9……………………………………………………134

CHAPTER 10…………………………………………………...150

CHAPTER 11…………………………………………………...186

CHAPTER 12…………………………………………………...224

CHAPTER 13…………………………………………………...244

CHAPTER 14…………………………………………………...270

CHAPTER 15…………………………………………………...299

CHAPTER 16…………………………………………………...314

CHAPTER 17…………………………………………………...334

CHAPTER 18…………………………………………………...389

CHAPTER 19……………………………………………..407

CHAPTER 20……………………………………………..424

CHAPTER 21……………………………………………..452

CHAPTER22……………………………………………...466

CHAPTER 23…………………………………………….503

CHAPTER 24……………………………………………..522

About the Author

Nima Gold resides in New York City with her family.

Goldbricks Wife, book 2, continues the story of Lia's desperate search to find Joel.

Both end up being engulfed in the mayhem Business of Queen Elizabeth Enahoros' evil ways.

Desperate to be together, Lia and Joel take measures in their own hands never realizing what lies ahead for their future.

GOLDBRICKS WIFE

BASED ON A TRUE STORY

Book 2

"LOVE IS ETERNAL"

CHAPTER 1

August 30, 2017

LIA:

"I could not reach Joel to find out how his trip was going. He said he would call, but I heard nothing. He had disappeared and I just waited and hoped that I would hear positive news.

I did not know that Joel's partner, Queen Elizabeth Enahoro had arranged to intercept his boat ride with the police, arrest everyone, and seize all the assets aboard.

She was fully exercising her power to show Joel her importance and show him how mistaken he was trying to escape her grasp and run towards another woman.

She had dispatched her spy Hassan, Joel's translator, to contact me and try to show Joel how weak and incompetent I would be in the struggle of trying to free him in an impossible situation."

August 31, 2017

HASSAN AND LIA:

HASSAN:

"Hassan was Joel's translator whom he met upon arrival in North Cyprus. He was on the payroll of Queen Elizabeth Enahoro, as one of her confident spies. "

"Joel did not know this. Hassan became Joel's friend and tried to arrange for Joel to board the escape ship and make sure that I send him money for his trip which was confiscated and taken by Queen Elizabeth Enahoro once the boat was captured by the police.

Hasan lived with his family in a poor neighborhood in a small town and commuted by bus to Queen Enahoros' compound daily.

He was basically a good man, but his action was dictated by the fact that he was poor, he did not have any good working skills, and became interwoven in Joel's life by sheer chance. He genuinely liked Joel and enjoyed his company.

Queen Elizabeth Enahoro was his Boss, and she made sure he was well paid and was eager and ready to do her spying and watching of Joel daily.

There were times when Hasan did not like himself and his actions, especially the ones toward Joel, but he needed to feed his family, and this was his opportunity to work and show them that he could support them.

He was hoping that Joel would overcome his struggle with his contract and with Queen Elizabeth Enahoro and that he would find happiness with his wife.

He knew that Joel's face would light up every time that he spoke of Lia, and it hurt him inside a bit, to know that he was being paid to prevent this man from finding his happiness.

We continued to text and call and do our best to locate and find Joel and try to set him free. "

August 31, 2017, 3:45 PM

HASSAN:

Hassan calls Lia and tells her that Joel was arrested by the authorities, and everyone on the boat, including the Capitan, was thrown into prison.

LIA:

"I was beside myself as I learned that all his effort had failed, and he was unreachable. All the money was gone as well, and I was left to deal with his Turkish translator Hassan.

I looked on the Internet for Criminal attorneys and found Mr. Chambers in North Cyprus.
I emailed him and consulted with him as to what to do next. He needed the arrest docket and the location where Joel was taken.

Hassan told me Joel is in prison and that there is no arrest docket. He did not want to talk to my lawyer, he said he had his own, whom he knew and who had taken Joel's case over already.
Joel was taken to the secured compound, which Queen Elizabeth Enahoro owned and operated.

He was given a room and necessities and had a guard who ensured his stay in her compound.

The rest of the boat crew was sent to Nicosia jail. If you sent someone to look for Joel in that jail, they had no record of anyone with his name since Joel was at the Queen Elizabeth Enahoro compound. There was no arrest docket either because the Queen had arranged to have Joel released to her care, and she held on to all his records. "

"When my Lawyer inquired about Joel's arrest, he found no information because the jail and the courthouse did not have a record of Joel.

I did not know any of this and looked for Joel in all the right places, and so did all my other sources, but since he was not in the central jail and since he had been released to Queen Elizabeth Enahoros care, he did not exist in the North Cyprus system, jail, court and there was no paperwork of any kind with his name on it. He had completely vanished."

HASSAN AND LIA:

Lia:
"Hi Hassan, please call this Attorney! The attorney will contact you to help Joel. The Attorney is Michael Chambers, this is his number, 25819966.
Thank you so much for everything!
My email is: liaroth23@gmail.com."
Hassan:
"Thank you so much, I got the text, which has the email. Here is mine:
Hassanmehmet500@gmail.com"
Lia:
"Thank you."

September 1, 2017, 8:13 AM

Lia:
"Hi, Hassan, can you tell me where Joel is being held and what is the location and place where he is? Thank you!"

LIA:

"Hassan did not answer me regarding my Attorney which I contacted. Instead, I got an email from his Attorney who claimed that he was now representing Joel and that I needed to work with him in order to release and pay bail to free Joel.

Despite several attempts to tell Hassan to deal with my chosen Attorney, he insisted that he knew this man and he was the best choice for freeing Joel from the prison that he was sent to. "

Sep 1, 2017, at 6:59 AM

DR. RALPH YIANGOU AND LIA:

Lia:
"I received long emails from Dr. Ralph Yiangou with explanations and introductions about what happened to Joel, that he was arrested, that Dr. Ralph Yiangou was his appointed attorney, and that Joel's bail was being set already By the Court.
The original E-mail is below:"

Dr. Ralph Yiangou:

Dear Lia Roth,
"We are contacting you regarding your husband (Joel Marshall), he was arrested while trying to travel illegally, and he has been charged with tax evasion and leaving the country illegally.

We are glad to inform you that your name (Lia Roth) and that of your husband (Joel Marshall) has have been added to our New Contacts Database pending further perfection of your instructions. "

"Once your instructions are perfected, your details shall be added to our Case Management System and a client reference number will be generated for you.

Please be informed that Dr. Ralph Yiangou, is the Solicitor dealing with your matter, and all inquiries regarding your case should be addressed to him. We shall notify you if, for one reason or the another, he is unable to deal with your matter; however, in his absence, you can contact me, the Secretary, Mrs. Mary Gineri, who would be familiar with your matter.

We endeavor to deal with all new instructions within 12- 24 hours, but due to the matter of urgency required in this matter, Dr. Ralph Yiangou or someone delegated by him will be visiting the detention camp where Joel Marshall is currently held.

Upon verification, Dr. Ralph Yiangou will provide you with a status report detailing of our findings as well as how to get your husband released ASAP and relay the same to you for your firm instructions and perfection of your brief."

Thank you for choosing Dr. Ralph Yiangou, Attorney at Law, and do expect the best of our professional services. Please provide a telephone number where I can reach you."

Kind regards,

Mrs. Mary Gineri, (Legal assistant/Secretary).
Dr. Ralph Yiangou, Attorney at Law
Frosia House, 4th Floor, Corner
Evagorou & Menandrou str.1,
P.O. Box 25570, 1310
Nicosia 1066 Cyprus
Phone + 357 220 51991 E-mail: drr@counsellor.com

September 1, 2017, 7:50 AM

Dr. Ralph Yiangou:

"Dear Lia Roth,
"I have gone to the detention camp, and I have met with Joel, and officially notified the authorities that I will be representing him in this case. Also, we have filled for an Application for Bail, which the court will hear and decide on Tuesday 5th of September 2017.
Since the offense is non-bailable because he was arrested while trying to flee the country by boat, we have to move an application setting out the grounds for the grant of bail.
In case the court is convinced that bail should be granted, the order is passed after hearing the arguments.

At that stage, we have to fill in the bail bond duly signed by the surety and to be filled through us, "his advocate". In case Joel is before the court, he is set at liberty in the court itself, and in case the Joel is under detention in the jail, orders of grant of bail will be sent to the concerned jail.

We might also consider the option of getting a surety who will take the responsibility for producing Joel in the court or before the investigating agency. Any person who has the capacity, control, and competence to produce Joel in case of non-appearance or to pay the amount of the surety can be accepted by the court for the purpose. In some cases, while granting bail, the court directs for personal bond, the payment of personal bonds as well as security in cash.

The amount of every bond executed shall be fixed with due regard to the circumstances of the case. Kindly call me or provide me with a telephone number to reach you."

Yours Truly, Dr. Ralph Yiangou, Attorney at Law.

Sep 3, 2017, 9:15 PM

LIA:

"I had no choice but to work with the Attorney Dr. Ralph Yiangou to begin the process on how Joel can be freed from this sentence.

It had become a very complex situation now since my entire dealing was with third parties, which I did not know.
I had no knowledge even if Joel wanted me to deal with these people since I had not heard directly from him."

DR. RALPH YIANGOU AND LIA:

Lia:

"Dear Dr. Ralph Yiangou,

Thank you so much for taking Joel's case. As you move into litigation mode for his defense, I want to make you aware that Joel acted the way not because he wanted to but because there was no other alternative.
Joel's situation would give him a huge advantage if he could pay the taxes on his cargo and fulfil his contract.

The situation that he fell into when he first got to North Cyprus, difficult to understand and explain, forced him to have no other alternative but to leave, in order to be able to get to his bank, where he can release his funds and pay the taxes on his cargo. Due to his circumstances, his illness in the hospital, which delayed his business, lack of insurance, and inability to secure his funds, he was punished by the same people who are imposing on his contract."

"He has no funds of any kind to continue to stay in North Cyprus, the only way for him to pay his obligation is to be extradited to the USA, to release his funds and pay off his expenses. He stands to make money once they are paid, why would he avoid paying them?

This is the only way they will get his taxes paid! It's better to pay the taxes than for the Authorities to have another jail mate, which will cost the country money!

He never wanted to leave his responsibility unfinished, I must say repeatedly, he spent endless hours trying to figure out how it can be done. I spent endless hours trying to secure funds for him through loans, friends, and my own money with exhausted endings.

The amount asked for the taxes was greater than anyone could come up with, and not having collateral, we could not secure even a loan! We did try everything we knew, and Joel tried the hardest, but without the ability to secure his funds, it is impossible!

No matter what kind of bail or punishment they impose on him, if he is not released to secure his funds, his only choice will be to remain as a burden to his captors, which serves no purpose to anyone!

Thank you for contacting me! First, I want to know where Joel is being detained, which facility, and its location, exactly! Second, I want a picture taken of Joel and sent to me to be sure it's him we are talking about. Third, I am not his wife but wife-to-be, and you should not be adding me to anything without my permission! Once I receive what I asked for, we can proceed accordingly!

Thank you. Lia."

LIA:

"This entire situation with Joel had taken a great toll on me. I did not want to deal with his translator, Hassan. He seemed nice and caring, but I didn't know him, and I could not cozy up to him so fast.

I did not like Hassan appointing the Attorney for Joel.
I wanted to use my Attorney and was starting to resent the entire side of Hassan, but I had no choice since my Attorney could not find the arrest docket for Joel, and Hassan would not talk and give us details and information of about exactly where Joel was.

I began to work with them, since I wanted to find Joel, but I had a bitter taste in my mouth."

HASSAN AND LIA:

September 2, 2017, 10:04 AM

Lia:
"Hi Hassan, it's Lia, I've heard nothing from Joel? Where is he? Is he OK? Thank you for securing the Attorney! Much appreciated."

DR. RALPH YIANGOU AND LIA:

September 2, 2017, 2:21 PM

Dr. Ralph Yiangou:

"Dear Lia Roth,
I told you to send your telephone number where so I can call to explain in detail, but I wonder why you are not sending-

your telephone number. Anyway, Joel is currently in detention, and as I said, an Application for Bail has been filled, which the court will hear and decide on Tuesday, 5th September 2017. The first step is to get him out of detention on bond, and then we will proceed with the trial. I will keep you posted."
Yours Truly, Dr. Ralph Yiangou, Attorney at Law

September 5, 2017, 9:45 AM

Dr. Ralph Yiangou:

"Dear Lia Roth,
Sorry, I could not hear you over the phone, and I tried to call back several times, but there was no response."
Yours Truly,
Dr. Ralph Yiangou, Attorney at Law

September 05, 2017, at 12:42 PM

Lia:
To: rrw@counsellor.com
"Hello, Dr. Ralph Yiangou,
I have not heard from you, and I don't know what is happening with Joel and his case. Can you please explain how is Joel is doing? Have you seen him? Thank you!"

HASSAN AND LIA:

Lia:
"Hi Hassan, it's Lia, Joel was granted bail and will have a trial on 9/12/17. Please go see Joel immediately. Ask him how to contact the people who are holding his money. Also, he needs to grant me Power of Attorney to get this done."

"To make his bail and pay the attorney I need to receive the check money which came to my house, Joel knows! Without that money I would not be able to pay for anything!
We don't have time, so it must be done ASAP! Thank you!"

September 5, 2017, 8:37 PM

Lia:
"Thank you, Hassan, I wrote you an E-mail, about what the Lawyer said. Also, ask Joel if I should call his daughter?"

September 6, 2017, 9:45 PM

Lia:
"Hi, Hassan, it's Lia, can you text me the name of the jail and the place where he is?
Thank you!"

September 8, 2017, 9:43 AM

Lia:
"Dear Hassan, in order to secure a bond for bail I need to know the following: 1. Bond Number, 2. Location The location where Joel is 3. Offence The offense he is charged with, 4. Amount of offense.
I spoke to the Lawyer, he has difficulty receiving payment with credit cards, the only payment available, so I gave him a start! I have requested this information from him, but he has not replied. If I don't receive the information about where Joel is, I will be forced to secure my own people to investigate where Joel is being held. I am not sure why I have to ask so many times, and not be given simple information! Thank you!"

September 11, 2017, 9:12 AM

Lia:

"Dear Hassan, the Attorney has not provided me with the information requested. Please send information on the things I asked for so that I can apply for a loan for the bail money! Please call the Lawyer and ask him to be patient. I will try to secure his fee and as soon as I receive the information, I will apply for the loan for bail. Thank you so much, Hassan!"

September 15, 2017, 11:18 AM

Lia:

"Hello, how are you? It's Lia, how is Joel? Have you heard anything?"

LIA:

"It took a long time for any of them to answer my questions and inform me of Joel's situation.

Both Hassan and the Attorney were demanding money but did not give any information as to Joel's whereabouts. Both had thick accents and it was so difficult to understand them on the telephone and that is why I preferred email, which was so I could read and have the information when I needed to refer to it. Joel was being hidden for some reason, and no one was talking.

I did not know that Queen Elizabeth Enahoro had put Joel in one of her detention cells, which were only accessible to her spies, which meant that no one knew where he was, nor could anyone find him aside of her team. I had no knowledge of this and was trying to find him in legitimate prisons and courts. "

"Of course, no one ever heard of him in any jail or court nor his arrest because it was all done by Queen Elizabeth Enahoro and a staff of spies.

This made me question everything that any of them did because it did not add up in my head.
Joel was missing, and even though they claimed that they knew where he was, they were not telling me, and were taking their sweet time in responding, and were not allowing me contact with Joel!"

CHAPTER 2

September 15, 2017, 4:49 PM

HASSAN AND LIA:

Hassan:
"I called you twice, two days ago, but you didn't pick up. Still the same, I managed to see him. He had really lost weight."

Lia:
"Sorry, I did not see any calls from you on my phone! It will take a lot of money to get him out.
I need to find someone who has it, and I am thinking of coming to North Cyprus to sort all this out! Can he call me? Maybe he needs food, he is skinny? How can he lose more weight?   Did he complain?"

Hassan:
"Of course, there are things he needs while there. I guess he can call, but he needs to do all that and I'm down now. Well, the first thing we need is to find out a way to pay the lawyer because he has really helped Mr. Joel so much already.
I wouldn't want him to drop the case because he is a local, grew up here, and knows most people in high places. That's the first thing to do so nothing will escalate."

Lia:
"Please find a way for Joel to call me! I am very surprised that he has not done this yet! The Lawyer is appointed by the court, or did you find him?   You can download WhatsApp on your phone, we can text for free if you want! Don't be down, Hassan. Now is when you must be most positive. Don't lose Joel, whatever happens!
Please let me know the name and address of the facility where he is staying. "

"The Lawyer got a payment, but he said he does not take credit cards. No one knows him either, and he does not come up on the internet with an address and phone! How is that possible for an Attorney who has American clients?

The other Lawyer had no problems, he took PayPal and credit cards. What's all this, Hassan? Please find out what happened to Joel's money and credit card! I cancelled it because I don't know who has his stuff! Thank you, Hassan! Stay alert and positive, you are the main man!"

Hassan:
"No Lawyer takes credit cards here. I don't know who you've been talking to. I live here, and I know better."

Lia:
"Mr. Michael Chambers takes credit cards. But never mind, I will sort it out. Please see how Joel can call me! Thank you so much!"

Hassan:
"Sort what out?"

Lia:
"How to pay the Lawyer! He should give a couple of options! Like half now, half later!
What about you? You probably have spent money looking after Joel and, with your good heart, have not asked for anything! You dear man...."

September 17, 2017, 6:51 PM

LIA:

"I received a phone message from Joel, apologizing for the situation and for him being in a compromising situation again. He told me to try to cooperate with Hassan and the lawyer and do whatever I can to get him out."

HASSAN AND LIA:

Lia:
"Dear Hassan, thank you, I got a phone call from Joel! Please tell Joel that I got his message and that I love him! Please also tell him that to get bail and payment, I need to know the bail number, the location of Joel, the amount of bail, and the location of the transfer!
His Lawyer said that Joel refuses to give the information to me but if I don't have it, I cannot secure bail payment!"

September 20, 2017, 7:45 PM

Lia:
"Dear Hassan, may G-d bless you for all that you do! Be good to my Joel and keep his spirits high! Maybe by next week, I may have some money to pay the lawyer's fee. The bail amount is too high, and without all the documentation, I cannot apply to borrow it!
Maybe they can go through the trial without paying bail and see the outcome. Give my love to Joel! I hear his voice every day!"

September 25, 2017, 7:45 AM

Lia:
"Dear Hassan, I hope you are well. How is Joel? I find it very hard that I cannot speak to him.
Is there any way for him to be able to communicate? I am waiting on for money to come in, it's taking forever! I hate being in this position! Please send my love to Joel!
Thank you so much, Hassan, for being such a good man!"

September 28, 2017, 8:39 AM

Hassan:
"You need to call me!"

LIA:

"Hassan was becoming difficult. He would not answer my messages and would say he called, but I would not have it on my phone, and I felt a bit lost trying to figure things out between him and the Lawyer he had chosen for Joel."

September 28, 10:30 AM

HASSAN AND LIA:

Lia:
"Please tell Joel that I need to speak to him! Call me at 4 PM, my time if he can. Thank you!"

September 28, 2017, 11:36 AM

Lia:
"I don't need to speak to anyone but Joel! I can receive calls now!"

September 29, 2017, 5:55 AM

Hassan:
"When you are up, you need to call me, it seems your prison is my fathers' house!"
Lia:
"What?"

September 29, 2017, 9:56 AM

Lia:
"Next week, I will be getting a loan from my cousin, you will get the money. Where is Joel going to live after he gets out of jail? Is he going to need more money?
Thank you, Hassan!"

September 29, 2017, 11:27 PM

Lia:
"Did you mean the prisoner is in your father's house, in your last message? Like Joel is out of jail and in your father's house? Is that what you mean? I need to speak to Joel! Very important!
Does he have a phone?"

October 1, 2017, 4:39 AM

Hassan:
"No, Mr. Joel is not, I was being sarcastic! Just to let you know that I cannot go to prison at any time I feel like. Call me when you are up!"

October 1, 2017, 7:32 AM

Lia:
"My friends have a house on the island! I will ask if I can rent it. I might come, and then I can visit Joel with you. Send him my love! Thank you, Hassan. Send me the picture of Joel and the information, please!"

October 1, 2017, 11:29 AM

Lia:
Where and how do I send you the money?
Hassan:
"Send it to Hassan Said by Western Union."
Lia:
"Address, please?"
Hassan:
"Country-North Cyprus, Sorry I just did, l. Let me know if I did."
Lia:
"I have to insert your address on my end! Please send it. Thank you!
Hassan:
"That's all you need!"

October 1, 2017, 4:41 PM

Lia:
"Great! No address and no amount!"

October 1, 2017, 11:06 PM

Hassan:
"I already sent you all the details needed, but here it is again. Name: Hassan Said, Country, North Cyprus, Western Union, about the amount, it depends on you, however, I will need some good money to sort the warders for protection and for him to have a single better room to himself."

LIA:

"This was a huge surprise! Hassan was not asking for a specified amount and left it up to me! "

"Just when I thought everything smelled fishy, he came up with an interesting statement!"

HASSAN AND LIA:

Lia:
"Please tell Joel that next week we'll have some money for him and tell him that my number is blocked on his phone and I cannot call him back. Thank you!"

October 2, 2017, 6:44 AM

Hassan:
"Mrs. Lia, how can you call someone in prison? His phone can never be with him and must be dead. I will convey the GOOD NEWS. I'm sure he would be so glad to be out and see you.
Did you send the money yet, so it can be cashed ASAP?"
Lia:
"Let's not waste any money for now, we'll need it all for next week!"
Hassan:
"What's a waste? Do you know how prison can be rough in a third third-world country?
Anything can happen in a week. Much isn't needed, at least $500 should do!"
Lia:
"Oh...I'll see what I can do! Will text you soon."
Hassan:
"Ok, Great!"

October 2, 2017, 5:17 PM

Hassan:
"Hello, I've not heard from you all day!"

Lia:
"I am sorry, Hassan, but I had a terrible day! This morning, they called from the Hospital, my mom could not breathe, and she was admitted. I am in NJ and will be away for a couple of days. I hope she will be ok and will not be required to go to the Nursing Home. So sorry! Pray for her!!"

October 2, 2017, 9:25 PM

Hassan:
"I'm so sorry about what happened to your mom. May Allah grant her quick recovery.
Please take care of yourself!"
Lia:
"Thank you so much, Hassan!"
Hassan:
"Don't forget I will be going to check Mr. Joel at the prison tomorrow, so I need to drop the money to do the right thing!"

LIA:

"My mom, who lived in NJ, was found by her caretaker on the floor when she got to her apartment. The ambulance took her to Hospital, where she had several blood transfusions and testing done.
The payment for Joel was delayed because I was busy with my mother in the Hospital.

Several days had passed and I had no message or phone call from Joel to see how I was doing and coping or how my mom was feeling! I found it odd and was a bit hurt!

When I did receive a response, it was one of inflicted guilt and resentment as if Joel was the most important and only one in my life, and my love was equated by the amount of money I could send."

"I was beginning to tire of Hassan and his lack of care, but he was the only one who had access to Joel, and I had no choice but to dance around him."

October 5, 2017, 1:02 PM

HASSAN AND LIA:

Hassan:
"I'm sorry to say it, but it's obvious you don't care about this man!"
Lia:
"On the contrary, he has done nothing, not even call me, and you are bothering me with petty cash while you know I am in NJ with my dying Mom in the Hospital. What's the matter with you?"
Hassan:
"Hello, Good Morning. I hope you are better. I thought you had forgotten about our conversation.

I don't bother going to the prison anymore since I didn't get the money as discussed, and I don't have money on me either. Are you back home now? Mr. Joel can't call you either because he must pay with money before he can get a calling card. Enjoy your day, and please keep me updated!"

October 14, 2017, 10:31 PM

Lia:
"Hello, Hassan, my cousin Uri is away in Europe, and I hope he contacts me soon so he can bring you the money for Joel. Give Joel my love and a big hug!"

October 16, 2017, 7:13 AM

Hassan:
"Hello, Mrs. Lia, how was your weekend? How is your mom feeling? I tried reaching you a few times, but you didn't pick up. I really don't know what to do at this point anymore. Mr. Joel will be transferred to another prison with high-security next week. I went to see Mr. Joel, and he has the same message to pass across to you.

He said I should tell you that he loves you, and it's been long a long time since he heard your voice or even your laugh. He wants out of this misery. He said you shouldn't forget about him and asked me to remind you of your promises to him.

You promised not to let him die on this island. Prison here is terrible, and it has been a miracle he has survived. Mr. Joel is asking you to please honor your promise to him and don't let him rot here. You will forever remain his woman!"

Lia:
"Thank you, Hassan! Tell Joel to call me if he can! Where and what prison is he being transferred to? You told me there are only two! My cousin will call me soon, and he will meet with you. He has the money. Is his trial over? Prisons can appoint lawyers to those that who have no money for one.

My Lawyer cannot find Joel! You need to tell me exactly where he is, what jail and what place?"

Hassan:
"I really don't understand you! Call me."

Lia:
"My lawyer needs to know exactly what jail and what location Joel is at. Please text me this information. Thank you!"

Hassan:
"Like I told you, he is in Sanayi. Please, whatever happens next is none of my business, since you know better than I do. Allah knows I have tried my best!"
Lia:
"Sanayi in what town?"
Hassan:
"Nicosia. Since your lawyer is from here, he should know the place."
Lia:
"Don't worry, Hassan, I will turn the whole island upside down for Joel! I will never stop looking for him. He is my man forever and I miss hearing his voice and, and I miss hearing his voice.
I love him too!"

CHAPTER 3

LIA:

"Well, now this was strange since the town he gave me did not exist in North Cyprus.
I was frightened and knew something did not add up somehow. I looked up a Detective service in North Cyprus and I hired it to go look for Joel. I gave them all the information I had and all that had taken place and instructed them to find him.

Both services advised not to give any money to anyone anymore and their investigation led them to report that they believed that Joel was a Nigerian love scammer or a figment of my imagination.

The only other way to go forward with any other investigation was to come to North Cyprus myself in person and file a Police report and investigation report with the Attorney General.

I could not go to North Cyprus by myself to do this, it was too dangerous, and I may end up in the same position as Joel. I decided to proceed and go forward with extreme caution."

October 17, 2017, 12:07 PM

Hassan:
"Hello Madam, I went to see Mr. Joel today and I told him everything, also I left him money so he can talk."

"I'm sure he called you already, he also told me he tried calling you, but you didn't pick up. You should pick up foreign numbers that call you."
Lia:
"Thank you, Hassan! You are a good man! He keeps calling me when I'm in class or at work.
He needs to give me a time so I can be available!"
Hassan:
"This is most difficult Mrs. Lia because this prison system does not work as you may think or are used to. Please understand there is just one cell phone available to use by the prisoners in each cell block, there are many other prisoners, stronger, older, and more influenced who need to make calls at various times, Mr. Joel cannot be prioritized!
This schedule was very hard to get a hold of, let's not waste it, we might not get it again. Mrs. Lia try to make time to talk to him!"
Lia:
"I am trying but tell me next time before you go! I spoke to you yesterday. Tell me next time you are going, and I will wait!"

LIA:

"Joel was calling me during exercise class, and I never got his calls. It was becoming ridiculous.
I cannot stay all day and wait for a ring from a foreign number which I might not know.
I had to get used to having someone in jail. I did not know how to act here!"

HASSAN AND LIA:

Hassan:
"Try to answer him when he calls because it's in a phone booth they have here. "

"Ok, but I can't make a time because the phone they use is in the facility and so he is out of reach from me when he makes his calls, but I'll try to make something happen tomorrow so keep a look out, ok?
Thank you. You are a woman with a good heart!"
Lia:
"OK Hassan, thank you! Tell him not to be excited or angry, I miss him too!!"
Hassan:
"He is quite upset but I keep telling him it would soon be over as we meet the bail bond.
For now, the Lawyer keeps extending the trial date! But I understand the situation!"

October 17, 2017, 3:41 PM

Lia:
"Thank you, Hassan, we spoke and resolved a lot of issues! You are a great man!"
Hassan:
"Wow. You don't know how happy this news made me feel! I am very pleased Mrs. Lia, now I can sleep well tonight knowing Mr. Joel got to you! Thank you, I hope you are happy!"
Lia:
"Ecstatic! Thank You! I love that man so much!!"
Hassan:
"He is loving, and he loves you so much too. All he ever talks about is how he wants to be back and be with you!"
Lia:
"Thank you, Hassan."

October 18, 2017, 7:30 AM

Hassan:
"Good morning Mrs. Lia, how was your night? I'm glad I could be of great help. It's always good to be good!!"

October 18, 2017, 3:30 PM

Lia:
"I cannot talk now, I'll be free after 6 PM my time."
Hassan:
"Ok, did I call you mistakenly?"
Lia:
"No, just in the middle of something!"
Hassan:
"OK, but you texted me saying you can't talk now."

October 18, 2017, 5:03 PM

Lia:
"I made a mistake"
Hassan:
"Ok, it's fine Madam. How is your day going?"
Lia:
"Fine, thank you for asking. Hope you are well too!!"

October 22, 2017, 8:43 AM

Hassan:
"Morning! I am very well, thank you for asking but Mr. Joel isn't well. What's going on?"
Lia:
"Good morning, Hassan! Why is Joel not well? I spoke to him. In order to post bail for him they need to know where he is and what the bailment number and amount is?"

"They were not able to get this information because when they went to see the Lawyer, he was not at the address given! I have no more money of my own and just like you cannot come up with bail money, I must supply information to third parties' requirements. I am very busy with my mother and her stuff, and I don't have time to repeat myself!

Ask Joel what he wants to do and make it happen. Send him my love.

Thank you!!"

October 23, 2017, 11:49 AM

Lia:
"What name is Joel under in jail? No one can find him in jail under Joel Marshall?"
Hassan:
"Same name, I just hope you don't go doing things yourself and fall in liars' hands."
Lia:
"Dear Hassan, my friend went to pay your lawyer at his address, and he found nothing there, no office, no lawyer! He checked the Cyprus Bar Association, and he is not listed there as well, they called and there was no answer!! They called all the jails, and none have an arrest docket, or a prisoner named Joel Marshall!!

If you don't give me the exact place and address where Joel is, they will not give the money to post bail! Without a bail docket, bail cannot be determined, Got it!!"
Hassan:
"Sorry, who's your friend?"
Lia:
"My friend is Uri."
Hassan:
"I already told you where he is. Also, whatever your friend or whoever told you must be a lie and give me the number you called that told you his name isn't listed!"

Lia:
"Elides & Partners, 4th Fl. Corner, Evagorou & Menandrou St. 1, PO Box 25570, Nicosia, 1066 357 22667730"
Hassan:
"Where is the number you called the that gave such information?"
Lia:
"357-220-51951"
Hassan:
"This is not even North Cyprus number"
Lia:
"This is the number and the exact address of the Lawyer"
Hassan:
"We need to talk on the phone because, to me, you are taking the wrong direction on this issue.
To be sincere with you seems like you don't care or love this man anymore."
Lia:
"Dr. Ralph Yiangou, the number is: 357-220-51951, same address as Eliade & Partners, their number is: 357-226-67830. Same area code, same address! No one knew him there or anywhere else in the building!
Please give me the name of the prison, address, and phone number and I will double-check! Everything must match otherwise they don't give the money!"
Hassan:
"You are not making sense and you sound like a shallow-minded person.
When you want to talk on the phone let me know because right now, I don't know a thing you are saying, and I can't keep texting back and forth!"

LIA:

"My cousin Uri flew in from Israel to visit his friend in Cyprus."

"When I heard that he will be going there I asked him to do me the favor of lending me the bail money and to go to the lawyers' place and pay for everything.

When Uri and his friend got there, they went looking in the entire building for Dr. Ralph Yiangou, the lawyer, but he did not have an office at the stated address.
They called and called him, but no answer. Uri called me and was a little mad that I had sent him to a place with a lot of money for no reason at all. He called me negligent in my research because he felt I should know the person to whom I am paying a lot of money to.

Also, the Detective services that I hired came with the same assessment. They couldn't find the office and the lawyer either. They went to several other places in the same building and asked if anyone knew of this lawyer and no one did. Uri also went to the Court and jail, and no one had a record of Joel Marshall. The situation was becoming very strange."

HASSAN AND LIA:

Lia:
"I just know that if all of this information requested was clear and furnished as asked, Joel would have been bailed out many weeks ago!"

Hassan:
"I have helped Mr. Joel collect all the money you sent, and you are sounding like you don't trust me. You are saying you want to borrow money, where on earth does the bail condition stands as collateral to receive one? You are intentionally punishing this man and keeping him in prison because of your trust issue. Is that all he means to you?"

Lia:
"Please let's not do any of this. I will let you know what I decide to do. I don't have the money, so I am not doing anything! Just trying to borrow it but they have many questions!!"

October 23, 2017, 2:50 PM

Lia:
"Hi Hassan, I spoke to Joel. I apologize if I caused you any anguish! Joel said that if you can get me the name of the Court and its phone number it would help a lot! Thank you!"
Hassan:
"Courts of Kyrene."
Lia:
"Thank you!"
Hassan:
"You are welcome! I want us to talk like Family! What are you really doing?"
Lia:
"Trying to pull my hair down. It's been standing up since this morning!"
Hassan:
"Ok, I mean to get money so we can have Mr. Joel out of prison. Because the only solution here is to look for money so we can finish the case."
Lia:
"Yes. Thank you!"

QUEEN ELIZABETH ENAHORO:

"Queen Elizabeth Enahoro had arranged for Joel to be transferred to one of her compound prisons, where Joel was being watched and manipulated by her and her spies to think, know, and be advised to follow her direction and instruction."

"Joel did not even know of her scheme. He thought he was in real jail and had a real lawyer and that Hassan was his best friend and was helping him to communicate with me and helping him to escape his prison sentence.
Hassan was directed and instructed by Queen Elizabeth Enahoro to confuse and handle me and to keep Joel safe and unaware of the outside world.
Her mission was evil and selfish, and no one knew anything of her present demise or any of her future plans for any of us."

HASSAN AND LIA:

October 26, 2017, 8:12 AM

Hassan:
"Good morning Mrs. Lia. How is it going?"

November 1, 2017, 1:06 PM

LIA:

"The same pattern was repeating with Hassan. He would take several days to answer my E-mail, and hassle me for money, he knew I did not have, and I was now totally mistrusting the entire situation. There were too many things going on at the same time.
I also found it strange that no one made any comment or effort to meet with Uri and his friend and collect the money."

HASSAN AND LIA:

Hassan:
"Hello, how are you doing? I hope all is well?"

November 1, 2017, 3:50 PM

Lia:
"Thank you, Hassan. Everything is bad. My Mom is getting worse, and I cannot find money for Joel!
See if you can find someone to post bail for him. They will get it back after sentencing!"
Hassan:
"If I had that source, I would have done that a long time ago. You said something about making some payments via credit card. I found a way, ok?"
Lia:
"No one has that much credit! I borrowed 50K for his tax. Have to pay it back now. He was to be back by now!"

November 3, 2017, 12:12 PM

Lia:
"Hi, it's Lia, what is the way you found with your credit card? Which Court is the bail payment going to, Nicosia, Kyrene? Have a nice weekend!"

Nov 4, 2017, at 1:34 PM

Hassan:
"No court has an account number here, you must make the payment in cash and also, in the local currency at the cashier... Lol... So that can't just work out! "

November 4, 2017, 2:15 PM

Lia:
"Thank you so much, Hassan! You are so good! May G-d bless you forever! I am so angry that Joel and I are in this impossible and helpless situation!"

"I am so torn and upset at not being able to act immediately to get him out! My main focus is on posting that bail amount and getting him out of jail! When he gets out, he will have a plan as to how to take care of the rest! My problem lies with not being able to find the bailment number and the account of the Court where it needs to be posted!

Please Hassan find this information as soon as possible! The Court, its address, contact number, Bailment number, and their Bank Account posting information! Bail has to be posted to the Courts Bank account! Please do this as soon as you can! The rest will take be taken care of later!
Thank you, Hassan! "

Nov 4, 2017, at 8:47 AM

Hassan:
"Hello, I saw your message, I have been to the person helping Mr. Joel. I actually found a great way to charge your credit card so what I will be needing is the credit card no, ccv, ex-date, name on the card and I can get the money. Will be waiting to get the information.
Have a great day and hope your mom gets better."

LIA:

"I found someone online, who had credit available and when I asked for the amount I needed, they wanted $2500 upfront before they would give the credit. Joel said not to do it because it sounded like a scam.

I was trying so hard to come up with the money needed for Joel and by now I did not know who the scammer was and who was being scammed!"

November 6, 2017, 11:35 AM

Lia:
"Hi, it's Lia. Please send the wire transfer information for Joel's money. Thank you!"

Nov 7, 2017, 11:18 AM

Hassan:
"Oh, now I understand you need to be careful while you are trying to get the money. It's obvious there are scams, have heard of so many situations, like this, whenever a loan agency or company asks you for money upfront it's 100% scam. So, all they said about some information not matching the purpose of the loan is a lie."

Lia:
"They refused to do that as well! They asked for several thousand dollars of upfront payment before they could do the transfer! Joel told me not to do that, it's most likely a scam and I would just lose my money and get nothing! Back to square one! I hope G-d will work in a mysterious way this time! I am waiting for a miracle for Joel!"

Hassan:
"Well, I don't know where you are getting the money from, however, when you get it, you can let me know so we can have it transferred here. "

Lia:
"Hi Hassan, the bank of the third party refused the wire transfer because they cannot insure the amount and cannot verify that it will be used for its intended purpose! Let's see if I will think of another way! Maybe the best is for me to come with the money to Cyprus and take care of it!
I will see what else I can do! Thank you!"

Hassan:
"Where will the person contact me? I need to know the day so I can be available. "
Lia:
"Just remember that if someone contacts you for any information about the transfer, please answer them quickly! Elgin Guler has an address?"
Hassan:
"Hi Mrs. Lia, how was your night? I'm glad you spoke with him, I clearly understand your point. None of us can afford to make any mistake and that's why I gave you a trustworthy close relative of mine who works in the government and his account can receive such an amount of money. You have nothing to worry about, I believe Mr. Joel trusts me in handling the situation so well since I have always been the person helping him to receive all his money. I just need to know when you are sending it so the bank can be informed. Enjoy the rest of your day. "
Lia:
"Hi Hassan, I got to speak to Joel, thank you! I must tell you that nothing can go wrong with any of the money this time!

Nov 6, 2017, at 1:03 PM

Hassan:
"Hi Mrs. Lia, here are the account details:

Account Holder: Elgin Guler
Bank name: turkiye is bankasi
Customer number: 179621033
IBAN: TR460006400000268180272480
Branch/Swift code: ISBKTRIS-6814
Bank Address: Arasta - Lefkosa – KKTC

I wouldn't be able to tell him to call you today, as it's not a visit day. "

"Besides, the time is gone but I hope he calls you because I bought him some calling units to use in calling you. I will also make sure I get some blankets and sweaters across to him.
I'm sure he would be glad when he hears this good news. Enjoy the rest of your day."

LIA:

SENDS $1500 TO ELGIN GULER FOR JOELS RELEASE

Nov 8, 2017, 12:58 PM

Hassan:
"Hello Mrs. Lia, how has your day been?"

November 8, 2017, 2:15 PM

Lia:
Hi Hassan,
"Thank you for asking! Hectic and somewhat productive! How are you doing?"

Nov 10, 2017, at 9:46 AM

Hassan:
"Thanks, I'm doing good, please give me any good updates?"

Nov 10, 2017, 10:19 AM

Hassan:
"Okay no problem, how do we get to pay the lawyer now that's one problem we need to sort out. "

"We can pay it with your credit card details like I told you."
Lia:
"As soon as I pay off the balance, I will do Hassan! Thank you!"
Hassan:
"When do you pay your balance because I have given the lawyer some money already and I'm broke, and I need my money back also to make it complete.

Okay no problem, how do we get to pay the lawyer now that's one problem we need to sort out. We can pay it with your card details like I told you."
Lia:
"I am afraid I cannot! Cannot get any more funding until I pay off the one, I took already! I am so upset, I am besides myself! It's unbelievable that all of this can happen this way! My Joel is in such a place! Give him my love!
Thank you, Hassan, so much!"

Nov 10, 2017, at 8:44 PM

Hassan:
"Well, I can't wait that long. I need to get the money, I have already paid him anyway. I have things to sort out with my money and I regret ever getting myself involved with any of you guys' problems.

You claim you love this man, yet you can get a loan, lying that you can't get any more loans. Who told you that.? You are indeed a great liar, who tells you one can only get one loan when it's not from the same agency. "

November 11, 2017, 9:56 AM

Lia:
"Most likely at the end of this month, I hope!"

November 11, 2017, 3:12 PM

Lia:
"Dear Hassan,
I want to send you some money, so you are not stressed! Please take care of yourself! Will send WU in North Cyprus to Hassan Saidu for $500. tomorrow! G-d bless you and thank you!"

November 12, 2017, 3:24 PM

Lia:
"Wire transfer to:
Hassan Said,
WU #707 999 601 $512.00.
Tracking # 691 984 2351

Mon, Nov 13, 2017, 10:23 AM

Hassan:
"Hello Mrs. Lia,

"I'm sorry for the late response, I hope you are doing okay and well. I didn't get the reason why you wanted to send me the money. That is why I haven't responded yet. I'm not stressed about myself, I have just been too worried and stressed about Mr. Joel's condition and how he is fairing there. He had been there for close to 3 months now and that's why I might have sounded rude to you and telling told you what to do.

I'm very sorry because it seems like I'm in the only person in this alone, and I have basically taken care of him and I don't know how long I can keep up. "

"All I want is Mr. Joel's happiness and yours too. And I only care for both of you and how you both can be together and leave all these problems behind.

I also saw your email in which has the WU details, as soon as I get it tomorrow, I will make sure to go give Mr. Joel some money to hold so he can have decent meals, more calling cards, and other basic things he will need. While I also will buy him some blankets, and winter clothing so he can always change his wears since it will be difficult for him to do his laundry because there aren't washing machines for them in the cell."

LIA:

"This entire period between Hassan, Joel's friend and translator, and Dr. Ralph Yiangou, the lawyer, was a stressful affair. Hassan did not disclose any information regarding where Joel was exactly, and he was difficult to understand since he spoke English with a heavy accent.

Uri and his friend went to see the Attorney in Nicosia only to find that he did not exist at the address given on in his email. They were not able to find him or get in touch with him by phone.

I hired two detective services, one on the South side and one on the North side of Cyprus.

Their investigation concluded that this was a Nigerian scammer partnership, and I should stay away from them. The evidence they both got was not based on true visual facts but on internet research and assumed facts. Again, it was not beyond a reasonable doubt, and I continued waiting and searching for Joel by contacting a Lawyer's Office on the Island, recommended by a friend."

"The worst conclusion came from the Lawyers Office, Attorney Alon and his comment, that Joel was a figment of my imagination and the only way to solve and investigate the situation was for me to personally go to North Cyprus and file a police report.

It was unbelievable, not even the Attorney General of a half an island, North Cyprus, could investigate and find one man.

I had invested a tremendous amount of emotion, energy, and money into this relationship, and it was not easy to give it up so quickly. Plus, the uncertainty of things kept moving me along to find out the next step."

CHAPTER 4

ALON AND LIA:

November 13, 2017, 11:11 AM

LIA:

"I contacted an attorney which was recommended by a friend to investigate the entire case and tell me what to do since I still did not what the truth was and how to find Joel."
Lia:
(Contacts the Attorney's office and asks to open up an investigation to find Joel.)

Hello Mr. Alon,

"You were recommended by a friend. I need someone to find out where my friend Joel Marshall is. I need someone to go to Gonyeli Prison and see if Joel Marshall is there!
I have no ID on him. I have a third party, Hassan Said, who recommended a lawyer for him, but I cannot find him at the Cyprus bar association.
Hassan Said, +905488493106, who is his friend and translator, may be involving him in a scam with a lawyer, Dr. Ralph Yiangou, +35722051951, whom no one knows, my friends went to his office, but he did not exist there, and now I am not sure that if bail money is sent, to either of them, that it will go for bailing him out! Hassan told me that his bailment is at Kyrene District Court. I have a picture of Joel and nothing else. He was arrested for leaving the country illegally!
He is British but lives in NYC!
Thank you so much!
Lia.

Alon:
(E-Mail correspondence)

Dear Lia,
"I will try to get as much information about the below below-mentioned person as possible.
Do you know exactly when he was arrested? If yes, how long is he in detention?"

Nov 13, 2017, 9:11 AM

Lia:
"Hi Alon,
Thank you so much! His arrest took place at the end of August and the beginning of Sept. I do not know how long the detention is."

November 15, 2017, 1:10:14 PM

Lia:
"Hello Alon,
He just called and said something about wanting to proceed with a new lawyer, but he is not sure if that would benefit or hurt his case!
He is very afraid to shake the boat and now his sentencing is postponed until 11/21/17. Have you gone to Gonyeli Prison to see Joel Marshall?"

Nov 16, 2017, 4:39 AM

Alon:
"Dear Lia,
As per your email below, I went to central prison but there is no person named Joel Marshall there. I believe that there is a misunderstanding regarding your friends' situation. "

"Is he on bail or he has just been released on bail? Please confirm."
Lia:
"Hello Alon, Thank you for your response.
He told me he is in jail, and he has this lawyer that we could not find, which says he has bail of $31,500. which needs to be paid in order for Joel to be released from prison.
I think this may confirm that this is a scam. Did the Court have a bailment under his name?
The answer to your question is that he is on bail!"

Nov 16, 2017, at 8:28 AM

Alon:
"Dear Lia,
I now understand that this is a scam which I suggest you refrain from. I confirm that there is no one under the name of Joel Marshall in prison.
For bailment, the amount which you have stated is absurdly high.
Please do not proceed or agree with any payment requests from third parties."

Nov 17, 2017, at 4:24 AM

Alon:
"Dear Lia,
Do you have the details of the persons involved in this scam? More specifically, to whom and when it was the last time you made a money transfer?"
Regards,
Alon

Nov 19, 2017, at 5:23 PM

Lia:
"Hello Alon,
Please make sure that someone has called the Court and inquired if there is a bailment or postponed trial for Joel or Jo Marshall. I want to be 1000% sure before I proceed.
I have all the research from two detective services one in the South and one in the North.

I needed an Attorney who can enter Gonyeli Prison and confirm their finding!

I know that I sound stupid with this request, but I go back with Joel to NYC, and I cannot understand how a Senior Designer at Aedes, and graduate of Brighton University in the UK, and an Oil contractor can go and become a scammer in North Cyprus!"

Nov 20, 2017, at 5:30 PM

Lia:
"Dear Alon,
I just spoke to Joel. He told me he is being sentenced tomorrow and he is petrified as to the fact that you could not locate him! He thinks that they are hiding him for a reason, (I know it sounds crazy), but he is in jail for tax evasion and for leaving the country illegally and they want to get the money, (which he does not have), out of him!

Tomorrow, he will tell me exactly where they are taking him to be sentenced and will give me his exact location so that you will be able to find him! I hope they don't kill him!"

Nov 22, 2017, at 3:39 PM

Lia:
"Dear Alon,
Today Joel called and said that he had his hearing for sentencing, he argued for himself, and he got a fine of 2500 euros and 4 more months in jail! What do you say about this event?"

Nov 22, 2017, at 5:16 PM

Alon:
"Dear Lia,
At this stage, I do not want to make any further comments because all of these statements are untrue and false statements. There is no one being sentenced at the courts under the name of Joel Marshall.
I confirmed this with the court and also with the central prison.
Hope this helps. Have a nice day."

LIA:

"This finding by the Attorney hit me very hard. Alon was saying that Joel did not exist in jail or the Court system and all that had transpired between us was a fraud of some sort.

The investigators that I hired also had given me reports that I had been scammed and robbed by Nigerian love scammers. On the other hand, Joel was telling me frightful stories of his jail existence and Hassan was confirming it.

I was confused and uncertain and did not know what I had gotten myself into. I had to explain the entire connection to Alon so he would understand me better and perhaps take it more seriously."

QUEEN ELIZABETH ENAHORO:

"No one knew the plan of Queen Elizabeth Enahoro. She had Joel in a detention cell where he was being held and manipulated and demeaned every day. She was taking great pleasure in showing him, how not having money, could impact his life and my weakness of not having the means to release him and set him free.
Neither Joel nor I knew any of this!"

LIA:

Nov 26, 2017, at 1:04 AM

Lia:
"Hi Alon,
"Enclosed is an explanation and investigation of this whole case so you will be able to let me know if we can submit it to any authorities!

I have held on to this fearing that maybe Joel is the one being scammed by the two other scammers the whole time, I have been trying to explain in my head how a guy like Joel can become a scammer! The investigations show different things! Lol!

Joel Marshall and I met on OK Cupid, a dating site online, and talked for a few months before he came to North Cyprus. He said he lived in Staten Island, NY, and was working for a Development Design Company Aedes as a Senior Design Engineer!

We were both business-minded people and had a lot in common. We talked for hours about everything in our lives and got along very well! "

"He raved about his daughter Dion, who lives in London, England and he had to go visit her because she had gotten ill.

He came back two weeks later, we were to go out and meet, but he called and said he had fainted in the shower and had to go to the Hospital because he did not feel well.

They gave him some pills, for stress to calm him down and sent him home.
Couple days later he landed in North Cyprus and according to him had passed out at the airport and was sent to the Near East University Hospital in Nicosia +90 3924440535, diagnosed with a walking pneumonia in its very advanced stages!

He had told me that he suffered from asthma before he got there! He was in the hospital for about 4 weeks where emotions were high, and we got very close!
He said that someone had tried to extract funds from his account and all his assets were frozen and he had to go back to the USA in person to release it. Therefore, he needed someone to pay his hospital bill and get him out of there! I gave him 7K via wire transfer to WU to pay that bill!

When he got out, he needed money to live and he told me that the reason he was there in the first place was because he had secured a contract with Socar Oil, and his cargo had arrived 4 weeks prior and was now being taxed for sitting in the bay for 4 weeks.

He sent me the contract and the bank account at Credit Suisse, of money he was going to get if he delivered this oil to his client in Spain. His friend Donald Wood gave him 30K and 7K to live on and I gave him 50K to pay the tax bill. He also asked for numerous iPhone cards for his phone and cash for his housing and food via Western Union."

"Just as I thought it was over, he announced that his contract demanded that he pay the late payment for failure to discharge cargo in a reasonable time. This was going to cost $450K!

The excuse was that because he had gone to take care of his daughter and had to come back to the States for one week before he went to North Cyprus to take care of the contract, he had not had time to secure insurance, because it was for one week only to release it and he did not think he needed it! This was hard to understand because no one could believe that a cargo shipment would not have insurance!!

No one could come up with the amount he needed! His friend Donald did manage after a long time to secure $160K for a $450K payment but Joel said it was not enough and did not take it! Not sure if Donald Wood, 1416700865, dowoos003@gmail.com, was his friend and actually, gave him money or if he was the pawn to get me to give him money!

Since no one could get a hold of that kind of money, I told him that the only way he would be able to take care of his business was to come home, release his funds, and go back to pay the cargo shipment!

He needed 18K for the boat back home and I gave him that as well. He attempted to leave by boat and there he was caught, arrested, and returned, charged with tax evasion, and leaving the country illegally!
Hassan Said, +90 548 849 3106, hassanmehmet@gmail.com, who was his translator in the Hospital and developed a friendship with him, called me to tell me that Joel was in jail, and he needed a small amount of money, $500 to pay the guards, to give Joel his own cell and make him more comfortable!"

"He told me that he hired a local lawyer who secured bail for Joel, and they needed the money for bail, $31,707K, and the lawyer's fee of $7,563K!

When I checked out his intended lawyer he did not exist on the internet! The lawyer called as well and sent many emails requesting the money! That is when I hired the Investigator to find out what was going on!"

Below is a copy of the lawyers' email to me:

On Tue, Sep 5, 2017, at 9:52 AM,

Dr. Ralph Yiangou, Attorney at Law <rrw@counsellor.com> wrote:
Payment request email from the Dr. Ralph Yiangou, his non-existing lawyer:
Dear Lia Roth,
Bailed has been granted to Joel for 109,000 Turkish Lira, $31,707 in USD equivalent.
Also, our retainer fee is also 26,000 Turkish Lira, $ 7,563 in USD equivalent.
Total: 135,000 Turkish Lira, $39,270.45 in USD equivalent. Meanwhile, Joel has been returned to detention pending when he will be able to meet up with this bail condition. However, his trial will be beginning on 12th September 2017, there is a need to get him released from jail pending the trial.
Kindly get back to us to enable us to provide wire details where the required $39,270.45 will be wired.
Yours Truly,
Dr. Ralph Yiangou, Attorney at Law
Frosia House, 4th Floor,
Corner Evagorou & Menandrou str.1,
P.O. Box 25570, 1310 Nicosia 1066 Cyprus 472
Phone + 357 220 51955

E-mail: rrw@counsellor.com

Investigator # 1

IBRIC in South Cyprus:
Zoe Lazarou Soteriou
International Business Risk Intelligence Company
Members of W.A.D., I.W.W.A., I.A.R.L.I.
Email: zlazarou@ibriccy.com
Website: www.ibriccy.com

Investigator # 2
Wilson Detectives in North Cyprus

The Attorney which I contacted:
Attorneys' findings on Joel's arrest:

Michael Chambers <info@cypruslawfirm.com> wrote:
Dear Lia:
The police have no record of such an arrest. Please provide more information.
Kind Regards
Michael Chambers,
Tel: +357 25819966
www.cypruslawfirm.com

Money given to Joel Marshall:

All the bank deposits went to:

Bank name:
BANK NAME: TURKEYE IS BANKASI
TITLE: SALAHI SAHINER
SWIFT CODE: ISBKTRIS
IBAN NO: TR580006400000268040062838

ACCT NO: TR580006400000268040062838
BANK ADDRESS: CEBECI SOKAK NO:19
YENIKENT GONYELI/K.K. T.C. O,01400

ADDRESS OF ACCT HOLDER:
Cebeci sokak Sokak No.
Apartment 3B Guppa
Homes, Hamitkoy.
K.K.T.C. 01400
11/17/2017
$50K & $18K

The Bank details given recently given by Hassan Saidu, hassanmehmet500@gmail.com, for the payment of his so-called lawyer is:

Account Holder: Engin Guler
Bank name: turkiye is bankasi
Customer number: 179621033
IBAN: TR460006400000268180272480
Branch/Swift code: ISBKTRIS-6814
Bank Address: Arasta - Lefkosa - KKTC
$1.5K

WU payments to Joel Marshall:

Western Union # 707 999 601 was sent on numerous occasions:
11/12/17, tracking no:6919842351, $500. picked up by Hassan Saidu
12/6/17, tracking no: 0838773811, $1500 picked up by Hassan Saidu
12/11/2017, MTCN) is: 5308677498, $1500, picked up by Hassan Saidu
8/4/17, tracking number (MTCN) is: 5636372300, $1000. picked up by Benazir Umar Jada

8/20/17, tracking number (MTCN) 5418994673, $ 2000. picked up by Benazir Umar Jada
iTunes cards bought periodically, totalling $1000.

Last amount given by loan:

Bunyamin Korkmaz
Sudore Tekstil Sanayi, LLC
Halide Edip Adivar 20/4,
Istanbul, Turkey
011 90 212 224 1055
ACCOUNT NAME: SUDORE TEKSTIL SANAYI LTD.STI
ACCOUNT NUMBER: 74238913-5002
IBAN NUMBER: TR51-0001-0007-5774-2389-13-5002
BANK NAME:
TC. ZIRAAT BANKASI/MECIDIYEKOY SUBESI
BANK ADDRESS:
MECIDIYEKOY MAH. BUYUK DERE CAD NO: 83 SISLI/ISTANBUL
BENEFICIARY ADDRESS:
HALIDE EDIP ADIVAR MH.
BALCI SK. NO:20/4 SISLI-ISTANBUL
US DOLLAR SWIFT CODE: TCZBTR2AXXX
25K for Joel's exit

Lia:
"The reason why Joel went to North Cyprus was to release his contract cargo with Socar Oil.
I have all the documentation on all these above. Please let me know if anything can be done."
"I think WU is very helpful, they have cameras and if they can provide a picture ID of who picked up, they can apprehend them!
Thank you!"

Nov 29, 2017, 9:33 AM

Alon:
"Dear Lia,
Thank you for the information provided.
I will liaise with the Attorney General in this regard and obtain their opinion on this matter.
Further investigation of these documents reveals that there is a serious fraud present on in this matter. I will let you know once I get the information."
Thank you.
Best regards, Alon

December 20, 2017, 6:06 PM

Lia:
Hello Alon,
"Has anything happened with the Attorney General on this matter? Thank you!

Dec 25, 2017, at 2:25 AM

Alon:
"Dear Lia,
I hope this email finds you well.

Please kindly be informed that I had a meeting with the Attorney General on this matter and explained everything in detail.

While every detail proves that this matter is linked to a serious fraud on the face of it, the Attorney General advised that you should come to North Cyprus in person and make a complaint to the Nicosia Police regarding this matter."

"This is the only way to move forward as a file of complaint should be opened for initial investigation purposes and if only there are grounds of suspicion of any person involved, then, it is for the Attorney General to bring an action against the person/s involved.

Hence, your complaint is of utmost importance for resolving this matter.

Awaiting to hear from you."

Kind regards,

Alon

December 29, 2017, 4:01 AM

Lia:
"Meanwhile, the last time I spoke to Joel he was being held by some people whom he did not know, and they fined him $3000, and in prison until April. He was negotiating with them for a quicker release. He did not know where he was being held nor the identity of the people, perhaps he does not want me involved in it, not sure but the last time I spoke to him was 12/10/17 and he has vanished since then.
What am I to do now?"

Alon:
"I am afraid that there is no other way to file a police report. You should personally come and explain the situation in detail. Hope that this helps."

December 29, 2017, 1:22 AM

Lia:
"Is there a way to file the Police report from here, I am not sure I can come to Cyprus!"

Dec 29, 2017, 1:53 AM

Alon:
"I explained to you how to proceed. Joel is a fictitious character. Please do not wait anymore and let the authorities chase this matter. You should come to Cyprus at your earliest convenience."
Kind regards,
Alon

December 31, 2017, 11:59 PM

LIA:

"It was a disappointing end of the year having gone through so much with individuals whom I did not know and whose sole purpose was to get me closer to finding out where Joel had gone.

It was so confusing to decide what was right and what was wrong, but it seemed to me at the time that there was no right or wrong, there was only finding a way to locate and find the man I had fallen in love with.

New Years was coming, and I was alone. It felt very alone because I had not been able to rescue Joel and he was still somewhere hidden. I stayed positive telling myself that it would work out somehow and put my best face forward and celebrated New Years alone again!"

"I did not know what had happened to Joel. I had no choice but to wait and see if he would contact me. I also decided that if he did, I would be more vigilant, and will would be questioning his intentions and need for money. It was the strangest relationship that had ever happened to me! "

QUEEN ELIZABETH ENAHORO:

"Queen Elizabeth Enahoro was relieved that despite all my searches and all the investigators praying, no one was able to get to the truth of where Joels was being held and who he really was.

She was able to hold on to him and manipulate him to think that I did not care for him anymore and even if I did, I had no means left to rescue and free him from all his troubles which were mounting up day by day.

Joel was still hers and she was able to see him every day and go happily forward into the New Year with new hopes and desires for their relationship."

CHAPTER 5

JOEL:

January 22, 2018, 5:07 PM

Joel:
Sends Email to Lia:
"My Wife,
Overrun with mixed emotions all over again My beautiful Queen, the first thing you will hear from me is that I love you with the deepest passion.

How are you, baby? Are you all right Lia? Is your mother and your children all right?

Dion has left me over 100 messages my love!!! Please, I beg you to tell me if you have been in contact with her at any point in at least the past two months. The final messages she left me were not very pleasant and loving. I understand, whatever she's doing is directly as a result of all the mess I'm plunged in, baby I miss her so much and I will never forget whatever befalls her.

Being solitary confined for the last month had me feeling as if the world had finally ended, it had me feeling I might finally never get to you after all we have sacrificed, it had me feeling like we had lost it all baby, I never want to lose you, I thought this world of evil ripped all we ever had with the intent to run us through the ground, I have never been so embarrassed in my whole life.

I miss you and I miss everything about you! Your voice, you're loving and caring nature, words cannot express how I feel right now or how you make me feel. "

"You are my love and still very well the one woman after my heart. I have so much to tell you, so much to talk about with you, I might just keep on writing because well, I have all night in this cafe and about 100 dollars on me, so I know that's going to take me a long way.

My life does feel like a mess right now, but I honestly confess I have never felt as happy ever in my entire life. I have learned that anger and confusion would lead only to hatred and destruction. I have given up all that ties me to this world, and I have learned truly what it means to have nothing and no one.

I would love to apologize to you for having put your heart through the misery, I have had you gone through so much emotionally, physically, and financially, and I'm sorry for all I have you gone through for me, and baby, on my life I had never forgot any promises I've made to you, I will make it all up to you when I arrive in New York, I will put all who had shamed you to shame.
The appreciations I have for you I cannot adequately express but there are a few things I want to highlight.

I appreciate your trust...the way you've trusted me to handle this all, I appreciate you for the support you have given me, forever been my pillar, forever been my savior, I had prayed for is to see the day come when I will be out of this hole, have you held up above all to stand as your pillar.

Today, it all ends, today I strip myself of all sadness and self-pity, I make this promise today, my Dear, to now look into the future and forget the past, my life is all yours and your life is mine."

"We will make it last forever. Together we will build a better one than the ones we had burned to the ground, I love you more today than I ever did yesterday, and I'll love you more tomorrow than I will ever do today.

I don't really know how to express the conflicting emotions that have surged in me like a storm through my heart all day. I only know that first and foremost in all my thoughts have been the glorious thoughts of having you in my arms as I've always dreamt, I always dream of you near me. I wish that just calling out your name when I needed you here really gets you here.

However, knowing you love me so much seemingly isn't enough, my soul weeps every night, I don't have you with me, my love, dreams of being inside you still has me losing my mind. I don't think I would ever be the same again, going through this what I've gone through, if you've been through half this shit, I've gone through, it will hurt you too, I don't pray for horrible circumstances to befall you, but I would never ever let you go through any of what I have tasted down here. I'm always praying to love you more than you love me so I can show you compassion, as you've shown me, you've loved me without effort, unconsciously, and of course, unconditionally, all I have ever thought of in my heart is you.

Baby love, I was only released a few hours ago and I'll be honest with you, I need you not to worry. Lol, as you speculated, my phone was stolen but I'll be able to work around something tomorrow and I will call you, I'll get a small phone tomorrow from the local store here. I am okay and can manage tomorrow, I'll spend the night in this cafe and see what I can do tomorrow."

"You have the greatest soul with the most noble nature, the sweetest and most loving heart I have ever known, my love and admiration for you compares exclusively to none. You are mine, you are wonderful, my pride and joy you are so perfect with such a perfect heart. Lia, my love you are supreme, your love is beyond all others. After so long of dreaming of spending our lives with each other, after all my life I have waited for someone like you, and now that I have found you, I will never let you go.

I love you so much and all that I can offer you is great happiness and a joyful relationship that can never change. With all my heart I am forever yours.
I'm so eager to get a simple hello from you, hurry and get back to me!!"

Love, Joel

LIA:

"My emotions were so conflicted after the entire Joel finding report of both Investigating Services and the Attorney himself surmised the entire adventure as a fraudulent circumstance, yet no one could prove what they said or disprove what Joel said.

What was I to do? I had invested and spent so much and so long of my funds and time. I also cared for him so much and in the end, his guilt or innocence could not be proven beyond a reasonable doubt. I answered his E-mail and continued to love him."

JOEL AND LIA:

February 2, 2018, 10:14 AM

Joel:
"Hello? Baby love. Are you getting this, my love? I miss you so much!"
Lia:
"You got your phone back? Wow! Amazing! How are you doing my Darling?
Words cannot express how I missed you! (hearts)"

February 3, 2018, 10:54 AM

Lia:
"(Heart, kisses), Sends Joel" Perfect "by Ed Sheeran, google.com"

February 3, 2018, 5:18 PM

Joel:
"Honey, I don't know why I can't make calls. It's disturbing. A week now I've been waiting to get connected."
Lia:
"You want me to call you?"
Joel:
"Calls I make just bounce back with a tone!"
Lia:
"I got your voice mail!"
Joel:
"Will it go through? Oh, you got that one?"
Lia:
"I'll try now!"
Joel:
"OK"

Lia:
"It said the call was rejected! Did you go into settings and unblock my number?"
Joel:
"I'm still waiting, you know…They've told me to just hang on and I'll be connected. I've been dormant for a long time. Sight! I don't even know if calls can come through?"
Lia:
"Go into settings, go to the phone, and unblock. How is everything, babe?"
Joel:
"But it's not blocked, babe! "
Lia:
"Ok, then your service does not work. It just rings now!"
Joel:
"Nothing!"
Lia:
"Lol…I thought you left already! You've been there for over a year! They will fix the phone when you least expect it!"
Joel:
"I wish! This is hell, literally for me!"
Lia:
"How are you Dear? More hell for me?"
Joel:
"I know, I've been worried, too worried even!"

February 3, 2018, 5:35 PM

Lia:
"When it gets warm there, I'll come with my bikini!"
Joel:
"I don't want to be selfish though, I have to ask first how you are my Darling? Ha, hah! April, I guess? You haven't lost your touch. I love that!"

"I love you even more being away from you. I'm sorry about all that's happened to you through me. I promise now, I will come to make things right for you!"
Lia:
"Without you, I cannot be up to any tricks! I cannot even hold you to any promises, there are so many, and you are still there!"
Joel:
"The money I have coming in is in chunks and I'm still needing an account though. I love you! How are you? But I don't want to talk about those things. I want to know about you?"
Lia:
"What kind of account do you need? Offshore?"
Joel:
"Not really, that's too complicated! Is the limit to your Credit card still up to 20K?"
Lia:
"I have been working mostly, No! Why can't you use the account I gave you?"
Joel:
"You reduced it? Because I could send the money there and cash it out from the ATM.
I would use the card you made me but I didn't get it back with the rest of my stuff. I hate being here, they've taken everything from me!"
Lia:
"If you put money in the account I will give it to you, I will mail you a debit card with a pin and you will be able to use the money!"
Joel:
"I don't know who owns the account you gave me Darling?"
Lia:
"The card I gave you was cancelled after your arrest. I gave you the account information."

Joel:
"I just don't want to use it without your permission my Love! Thank G-d it was."
Lia:
"Lol...what is your status now? When will you get your freedom?"
Joel:
"I have your details."
Lia:
"If I give you the account it's yours to use. If you need it again, I will resend it. It's funny what you say to me. Why would I give you someone else's account to put money in?"
Joel:
"Well, I don't know? I didn't understand what the message was about. What were you on about in the email? What happened to you?"
Lia:
"Too long and difficult to explain by text! If there is no good Bank there, I can get you another account, I will try to help you as much as I can, but you have to come forth as well!
I also met a young Turkish attorney, she will work at the UN but said that if you need anything she will take care! You are up late, where are you staying? Tomorrow is the Super Bowl!
I remember last year you wanted to come over!"

February 3, 2018, 6:16 PM

Joel:
"Super Bowl! Ah... feels like forever babe! I'm in a village here past Lefke, it's a small town at Faruk's place my Dear! It's quiet and peaceful, reminds me so much of when I was here first, and the hustle all began for me. It's far though, I don't go out to town until I need to."
Lia:
"Did you get my email on King Faruk?"

Joel:
"I've been waiting on a better connection to get these details before I go back to town.
I did not see an Email about Faruk my Love. When did you send it to me?"
Lia:
"Couple days ago. It does not matter. You are Ok in a remote village! Lol...when and how will you know if you can leave?"
Joel:
"Lol, I know. I'll be fine though! I'll leave once I can pay them off, I don't want to wait as long as it's going to take to get a bank account for me Lia, there's so much stress to that... I don't want you doing that right now my Love, you need not worry about anything really!"
Lia:
"Your text is not coming through!"
Joel:
"What do you mean Love? (Two broken hearts)".
Lia:
"How can you pay off when you said they have taken everything from you?"
Joel:
"That's why I need the details I asked for my Dear. I'll have money sent to your Credit Card, you'll then debit it and send it to me. I can have someone in the UK or elsewhere retrieve the money before sending it to me ultimately. I have most of what I need except the final 4 digits of your social."
Lia:
"You just told me not to do the account I gave you?"
Joel:
"I used to have it, but I don't anymore. Where is your bank account?
Lia:
"Here."

Joel:
"Do you use the same details you gave me when I was in the Hospital? Maiden name-Cohen, Card ending in 9939?"
Lia:
"Some yes and others no. I had the FBI contact me! They said that you are a figment of my imagination and helping you could be aiding terrorism! They searched for you everywhere and could not find you!"
Joel:
"Nah, I don't like the sound of that. I can't trust any enforcement after all I've gone through. I'm sorry, I only want you or nothing, please. Please understand you're the only constant to me in this fucking messed up world babe!"
Lia:
"I will give you a bank account and mail you a debit card to use! If you give me an address. If you want it in your name, I need a passport or drivers' license."
Joel:
"Terrorism? Is this what the world has reduced me to? Those are with the authorities here, so I won't escape again!"
Lia:
"That's for me. Can you imagine? The only thing that saved me was a WU transfer that was issued in your name and the notes on the wire transfer that had added your name to it. After that, they dropped everything and told me if I needed help to contact them!"
Joel:
"That's nonsense, what they did to you! No way did they have the right to do that. Did they show any paperwork, Lia? Why did you let them violate you? None of this should've scared you baby. Oh, what have they done to you, my Dear?"
Lia:
"I had to show all the paperwork! I am not scared but I don't want to be involved again with any third parties. I cannot take the risk and don't want to go through all that again."

"Life is short, I want to be free of stress and be happy! This has gone on for so long and I don't see the light! I will support you, I love and care what happens to you, and if I can, I will, but if I cannot then, I cannot! All of this has to have a limit and an end! If you have money coming in, you should put it in the bank account!"
Joel:
"Babe!"
Lia:
"Where is my picture of you?"
Joel:
"Calm down, this is important! I know I still owe you photos. I owe you too much right now. Let me handle this!"
Lia:
"Ok, Love cat!"
Joel:
"Okay, tell me about your bank account? What happened to your old bank account?
Suddenly, I don't get what you've been saying babe, please work with me!"
Lia:
"I can get you a bank checking account with a debit card. You put money in it and use the card to pay for your things or take cash out. My accounts are of my dealings, you need a fresh new account just for you! I got to go! Have a nice night, sweet dreams! (hearts)"
Joel:
"Okay, we'll talk tomorrow. Goodnight!"
Lia:
"(Butterfly)"

February 4, 2018, 7:24 AM

Joel:
"I believe I'll find a way. You know? Success had been defined in history by Winston Churchill as the ability to move from" Failure to failure without the loss of enthusiasm." This is my pick and motivation from last night's conversation with you.

Thank you for everything, my Love! (Hearts) You are more than a significant other to me.
To me, you are my essential other. (heart). I hope you're sleeping sweet my Love!"

(Sends Lia, "La vie en rose" by Daniela Andrade on youtube.com)
Lia:
"What a great song and positivity to wake up to! Thank you, my Love! (Heart, kiss)

February 4, 2018, 8:50 AM

Lia:
"One of my favorite melodies in the world"!

February 4, 2018, 10:41 AM

Lia:
"(Heart) Thinking of you! Cooking up a storm, chicken, and sliders. Lol, it's fun! Super Bowl!
It's 6 degrees in Minnesota, good thing the stadium is enclosed. Have a nice night!"

February 4, 2018, 12:59 PM

Joel:
"I'm still obsessed with you Honey! (hearts), Obsessed about with you! I couldn't sleep last night, so I slept during the day!"
Lia:
"Who can sleep? Lol…you have your phone back! So exciting! Obsessed, interesting!!"
(Hearts, kisses, butterflies).
Joel:
"Yes, obsessed with you, my love, it's you I'm obsessed about! When do you finish your food, Honey? I'm so starved I could do with your cooking right about now!"
Lia:
"I am done except for the chili! I'm making it now. Preston is lingering like a starved dog, he is too busy to have breakfast yet! I wish I could cook something you like babe, would do it with pleasure! Did you have a nice day? Do you feel rested now? Miss you! (kiss)"

February 4, 2018, 3:01 PM

Joel:
"So mean! (Cry face)"
Lia:
"What's so mean? That you are not here to eat the chili?"
Joel:
"Lol, Oh Preston, I miss him so much. Oh, how is his girlfriend? Lol...You have jokes, Lia baby, "Starved dog" though? No, my phone isn't fixed, my messages don't always deliver."

Lia:
"I have lots of jokes, but you seem to have won me over! What are you doing there all day and how long do you have to stay? You missed my Birthday and now yours is coming again and you are still there! Lol...how long?"
Joel:
"It's Sunday today so there was nothing to do all day baby. I slept late because I can't sleep at night and I absolutely do not know why.
I'll only stay until I get my passport and documents from them once I find a way for my lenders to send me money."
Lia:
"Because you are obsessed! You need kisses, and loving love so you can be calm and sleep well!
Who are they? Who are the lenders?"
Joel:
"I broke when I realized I had missed your Birthday. I'm never going to miss another one again.
The Company responsible for that check they had sent you earlier with my name on it baby!"
Lia:
"They said the check was fake! It had been written by someone who used their business name and made fake checks and was sent out by a person who also used a fake address for their Business.
The chili is so good! Yummy! Did you eat anything, Darling?"

February 5, 2018, 7:33 AM

Joel:
"I love you, Baby! Call me when you're up, it's working now. I had to get another phone, the one I had with me wasn't recognizable, and I needed to get a smaller one before it could fit. I so miss your voice, baby cakes! I'm listening to the song from yesterday my Love (heart)!"

Lia:
"Our song now!! When you are done call me! I just got your voicemail. You may not have international calling yet!! (Hearts and kisses) Going into an IT meeting, I will not be able to talk for several hours.

Hope you fix the service soon!"

CHAPTER 6

February 5, 2018, 11:04 AM

JOEL AND LIA:

Joel:
"Tell me when you're done? (heart)"
Lia:
"Hello, Darling! (Kisses)"
Joel:
"My Love, how are you?"
Lia:
"Fine Darling! Dying to speak to you but none of the calls went through!"
Joel:
"Tell me about it, I'm so sad I can't reach you while your voice is all I desire to hear!
I'm sorry I made you wait! I can't stop apologizing to you for my whole life!"
Lia:
"Why don't you try to call me now?"
Joel:
"Okay lovely!"
Lia:
"Were you able to get through my Love?"
Joel:
"Still trying, call failed, that's what message I get."
Lia:
"Lol... needs more work!! Is voice mail only off? It will work someday soon baby cat!
How is it going? How are you calling anyone else with this service?"

Joel:
"I don't call anyone else sugar! Who else deserves my call but you? The only ones I'm able to connect to is Verizon and that's a service direct call so it's permitted. I'll keep trying, you know how relentless I am about you."
Lia:
"You must make a serious effort to get your passport ASAP! Tell them you cannot do without an ID. Did you get the number on the iTunes card I sent before your travel?"
SENDS PICTURE OF ITUNES CARDS FOR JOEL
Joel:
"My baby, I just got the one you just sent."
Lia:
"Did you use it?"
Joel:
"Not the one you sent before my travel. I'm just about to, please hold on!"
Lia:
"Ok, perfect! I am at the Bank. Will be home in a few!"
Joel:
"Okay baby cat, I love you!"
Lia:
"Well, I will talk another time, I just called, and it goes to voicemail! Have you had something good for dinner Love?"
Joel:
"Not yet, I've been on this case. It's tough for me, I need to get out of Cyprus babe! Food isn't a priority!
Lia:
"Yes, you do! Please the faster the better!! (Kisses)"
Joel:
"Tu me manques (Heart)"
Lia:
"I miss you too babe (heart), my Darling!"

Joel:
"How is your day going Darling? Just got it loaded lol, paying this will do this time, I'm sure I had international credits loaded before I was closed down."
Lia:
"Very well for a Monday! Had a very good meeting and spent time testing each site for shipping problems and it's moving in a positively, had breakfast with my daughter, and I wish to have one day when every day is Saturday, and I can spend time growing English roses in a big garden!"
Joel:
"I love the idea of growing roses, (Flower and love), everyone will represent how much I love you!"
Lia:
"Yes! I love you more!"
Joel:
"How's the project going? No more IT guys giving you stress, are there?"
Lia:
"Project is moving forward! It has to be handled with care and direction!"
Joel:
"True, pay close attention. Don't give up on it my Love. I am so proud of you!"
Lia:
"I always stay on it. I won't give up! Thank you!"
Joel:
"It's your newest baby. Hold on to it okay?"
Lia:
"OK"
Joel:
"Are you home Love? How is Tara?"
Lia:
"Yes, Good. Kisses my Love cat Jolie! Have a wonderful night! (Hearts, kisses, butterfly)"

Joel:
"I'm not sleeping until I hear your voice tonight! My priorities are set!"
Lia:
"I am going for a long walk to freeze my bones! (Kiss faces...)"
Joel:
"Don't!"
Lia:
"Why not?"
Joel:
"I'm not there to warm you up, Honey!"
Lia:
"I miss you that way obsessively!"
Joel:
"You have no idea!"
Lia:
"Why do you say this?"
Joel:
"You're my motivation, G-d knows the reason I'm alive today is because of you!"
Lia:
"(Hearts)"
SENDS JOEL A PICTURE OF LIA
Joel:
"I don't even want you falling sick with a cold, or headache, NO!"
Lia:
"Please don't say this! It's an epidemic here!"
Joel:
"I always want you 100%, please let me take the burden of any illness and stress for you. It is? Oh, I have a story for you when we get connected. Lol...No blanket and a broken arm (Please remind me)"

Lia:
"You have done your share of heartache already, you need to get out and come back and thrive! With kisses too!! Tell me your story. How is your arm?"
Joel:
"Lol, (Hysterical laughing face) so funny, I almost got into trouble because of that!"
Lia:
"Let me hear?"
Joel:
"Oh, hey my arm's fixed, it hurts a bit, but my cast is off, but there's still a bump on it. (Love faces) NO!! Ohh!! I'm going to cry! You've just brought me joy!"
Lia:
"What? The kisses?"
Joel:
"No!! Your Face!! You just made my heart drop, it's so heavy now. My wife! (heart)"
Lia:
"I am sending you no makeup and then I will send you one with it on!!"
Joel:
"I'm not happy about how much my love for you has been robbed from you for this long!"
Lia:
"No one is happy with that one for sure!"
Joel:
"Okay, babes! Can't load your photo though, just a thumbnail version is killing me today!!"
Lia:
"Ok, not bad, better than nothing. It's a beautiful day! How is it up in the mountains now? Cold? I'm so lucky I can enjoy this time!"
Joel:
"Freezing, I can feel the sea around me. Smells fresh though! But I don't want that, I want you!"

Lia:
"I love that! I just want you! (Heart) Good night sweet Darling!"
Joel:
"Baby, I'm here! Gosh, I miss you so much about you! Has it really been forever?"
Lia:
"YES"
Joel:
"Ha-ha!! Jokes, you forget I have my ways, Darling! Seeing you is just a must. My heart thrives off it. So, you mentioned no makeup and a make up?
Lol… I grabbed my screen and zoomed it in! Yes!! I'm that desperate. I love you!!"
Lia:
"Now you are being silly!!"
Joel:
"Anyways, back to your photos, I don't see a difference, I love you either way!"
Lia:
"Great! Thank you! What would it take to get your passport back?"
Joel:
"You're the most beautiful woman I have ever laid eyes on and through everything still believe me when I say I have not yet seen anyone more beautiful!"
Lia:
"Thank you, Love."
Joel:
"Still no luck Honey!"
Lia:
"I appreciate it so much that you tried so hard! Maybe tomorrow! (Kiss face) Rest and relax and have a nice night!"
Joel:
"(Broken heart) I'm not happy!"

Lia:
"It will be better tomorrow!"
Joel:
"I hope so baby! Though if I'm to be honest, I'm heartbroken and disappointed!
The longer this takes the worse I feel and I have so much we need to discuss."
Lia:
"Why don't you text me what we have to discuss or e-mail me?"

February 5, 2018, 9:06 PM

Joel:
"I love you and I thank you for the support through this. I know it's not as easy holding down and suppressing what negativity my heart crawls up the heart. We've tried so hard at such a cost to keep our hearts together through this and I am proud of you. All things considered, I know you're a really patient woman, Lia, honestly, wars have been started for less and I am surprised you've not started one with these people already!"
Lia:
"I did start a war with the entire island! In the South and the North! The Attorney General and the Police are waiting for me and my staff, but you must appear and be ready to fight next to me!
I cannot fight for a ghost by myself! I told you the Law Office is waiting for you. You only need to appear!"
Joel:
"So they lock me up again? We were all friends with them when I reported my case to them. Powerful influence had overturned me. Be careful with these people, be careful with putting your trust in them, Hassan sold me off, lawyers can be paid as we have both seen, I cannot risk my life or our Love for anybody but you Lia."

"I'm pleased to know you fought valiantly for me. I want nothing more from you. I have not forgotten anything and will not forget anything you've done for me. With all my life I will forever be good to you, you will not know sadness in my name."

Lia:
"Babe, my attorney is part of a religious organization, which is worldwide! They will do no harm to you of any kind!"

Joel:
"Please, I don't want to hear about this. Neither will I talk about it again. I am sorry, my Love."

Lia:
"OK! I just wanted you to know that I did turn the place upside down for you! You always have a safe haven with these people. What you need to do now is up to you!

The place, where you are telling me you are, is not safe for you! It's one of the oldest cities on the island with people who will sell you in a minute!

You need to be vigilant and make every effort to get your passport and get out. I thought that my attorney could have the Attorney General get your passport."

Joel:
"My everyday life since I arrived here has been nothing but unsafe. Every day I spend here has my heart bleeding out. I don't need to be reminded of where I am or the conditions which I'm in. Oh yeah!! I missed this too, baby girl!"

Lia:
"Why the resistance of going to a legitimate attorney and the Attorney General?"

Joel:
"I've just got out of a 4-month jail stay baby, forgive me for mistrusting their system."

Lia:
"Why are they keeping your passport after your jail sentence?"

Joel:
"Listen, do me a favor and cut ties with these people, will you? Everything is suddenly so simplified and confusing, too many stories flying around, I've told you I don't want anyone but you in this. Why do you keep up with this?? I still owe them their money in taxes, that was what got me into this sticky situation in the first place."
Lia:
"But we paid 80K in taxes?"
Joel:
"There's no way they'll let me just up and leave Lia, baby! This was for the port, keeping my shipment logged in since I was in the Hospital. And it was for only one shipment, the final one of three."
Lia:
"Can you tell me exactly what you need to do in order to be released, get your passport, and be free to leave?"
Joel:
"I had paid off and cleared the two before I fell sick with my lung disease. How am I still not clear on this?
You did not know why I was locked up all this while Lia? We should've been clear on this a while ago!"
Lia:
"I know but you did go to jail for it! Does it not count?"
Joel:
"And you listen to me and cut off the ties with these people, I don't want any more trouble with any one in or around that, please! "
Lia:
"OK, no problem!"
Joel:
"I went to jail for attempting to flee imposed tax, babe, there was no way I could pay all 300K while staying here, I need to come back home to sort things out."

"I have to pay 45% of it before my passport is released to me. It's less but it's still much and I don't want to trouble you with this anymore.
My whole time in there I knew this was coming, had a hunch they weren't going to let me go off with their money on me, I'm in contact with a financier who's helping me put together money for me. That's why I had been asking for your bank details so I can work with him in getting everything together at once."
Lia:
"OK, I'm glad you have help on this one! How would it work?"
Joel:
"I'm also trying to reach Donald, I'm dying to reach him, I haven't lost hope."
Lia:
"I e-mailed him 100 times and texted him but have not received anything! Do you want me to try again?"
Joel:
"I have! And I'm not even angry with him. I just lost hope and my trust for him."
Lia:
"Sorry babe, he was funny!"
Joel:
"Please do. Though I see no reason why he'll not answer just one of us?"
Lia:
"OK. You owe him money, why would he not want to stay in touch?"
Joel:
"Exactly, I know as someone who goes off the grid for a long but not this long and you could always reach him on by E-mail. I just hope he's fine and well!"
Lia:
"OK, I opened an account in the bank, you can use it if you want.!"

Joel:
"Lol, in my name?"
Lia:
"I cannot, unless you send me a copy of your driver's license!"
Joel:
"It's all right, I can't use it for now anyways but keep it at hand, put a few dollars in it for activity. I had proposed when you mentioned the account to me back when you were in Florida, he preferred me to get an account with a little history on it, the process involved for my financier to send the money into the new account is time time-consuming, and I cannot afford to be paying him for overtime right now!"

February 5, 2018, 10:05 PM

Lia:
"They are very strict at the Banks now even with checking accounts due to aiding terrorism. This is a basic checking account and must always have a balance of $1500. The next level is 10K and the third is 15K! Can you imagine, and you have to always keep this amount in them or you get fined? The only bank which is not restricted is my bank, the account I gave you is good for any amount! They should wire transfer to my bank account. My bank only charges $40 to receive any amount of money!"
Joel:
"I'll ask him tomorrow if he could work with this. I'll get back to you with a response.
I feel relieved to hear this. You are such a wife. (Heart)"
Lia:
"Jolie, you are my Man, my Heart! Anything that I can do, I will do for you!"
Joel:
"I have no words for you right now!"

Lia:
"(Hearts and kisses)"
Joel:
"You make me want to cry!"
Lia:
"Baby boy!"
Joel:
"I have never experienced love like this, I love you so much sugar! (Heart and love face) What are you doing? Where's Preston? He's doing alright yeah? He's being a good man at home, yeah?"
Lia:
"I want our love to last until I take my last breath! I am going first because I can never bear to be without you!"
Joel:
"So deep, I cannot tarnish it by saying anything."
Lia:
"Preston is a very nice person. You will get along with him perfectly! He has a big heart and warm soul and despite his huge ego, he is a sweetie!"
Joel:
"Nothing can top this. He takes after you! A little less of a gut description is all I could imagine when reading, lol..."
Lia:
"I am waiting till he tells me that he found an apartment and is moving out. Lol…will give have a huge party! But I will miss him because he is so sweet!"
Joel:
"I'm not surprised considering his mother is literally the most anointed woman walking the face of the earth. Ha-ha! You've been waiting so long for that."
Lia:
"You are killing me!"

Joel:
"I hope you wouldn't be surprised when you ask him to stay with you because you miss him so much! I had meant to write "a little less of your description" …earlier.
Thick fingers, small keys, life is hard being me, lol…"
Lia:
"No, I will not do that but will miss him. He is a fun guy with great interests!"
Joel:
"Aw…You love him!"
Lia:
"Always."
Joel:
"I wish my mother had loved me as you love Preston! I would've turned out Prime Minister of England, Baby!"
Lia:
"Your Mother loved you just as much. Not too late to be Prime Minister!"
Joel:
"How can you tell? Ha-ha! With you by my side, I'm aiming to be King! Baby Love, I want to try to catch some sleep. It's so early down here and I'm exhausted!"
Lia:
"Because you've become a creative, interesting entrepreneur who is not done yet! Look how much you've endured! With me, you will always be my King!"
Joel:
"Your words are so kind to me, I love you so much and I'm so glad you love me despite my flaws. You are forever tattooed in my heart! Why I'm so glad to say those words to you is because of all the sweet words I've come across my entire life on earth, those combinations are the one combination you've exposed me to you that's unique to you and you alone. I love you!"

Lia:
"We all have flaws! But you are tattooed in my heart and so that is that! Please get some sleep, you've been up all night! I love you more!" (Heart, kiss, kiss)."

February 5, 2018, 10:34 PM

Joel:
"(Hearts) Nothing! No one can ever replace you. "
Lia:
"(Kiss faces)"
Joel:
"Dream of nothing but me and you, lying in a bed with gold sheets and purple covers wrapped around us. I love you! He, he...I can't get enough of you, babe!!"
Lia:
"Gold and purple sheets are hard to find, but I'm looking! I only care that I am wrapped around you!" (Crazy face, heart, kiss)
Joel:
"(Hearts) fire that lights my soul! My sun and my moon, I love you, sleep tight."
Lia:
"You too my Darling! Kisses! All over! "(Hearts, kisses)

February 6, 2018, 7:16 AM

Joel:
"Call me when you're awake! Please send me some money for my basics, please!!"
Lia:
"OK, let me know where to send it!"

February 6, 2018, 8:19 AM

Joel:
"Can't reach Jada, the cell number I have can't be reached."
Lia:
"OK"
Joel:
"Mr. Faruk, though, has someone else for me so please hold on! His sales boy, we're going into town so I can do everything before the banks shut!"
Lia:
"OK"
Joel:
"Here is the contact Love,
Given names: Kennedy Main Anson surname: Magma Main Anson is the middle name; I have a few minutes before the Banks close."
Lia:
"The full name is: Kennedy Main Anson Magma"?
Joel:
"Yes, my Love."
Lia:
"I'm sending it Western Union?"
Joel:
"Yes"
Lia:
"North Cyprus?"
Joel:
"Yes, baby girl! Baby, I got 10 min. waiting on details?"
Lia:

SENS JOEL PICTURE OF 1.5K CONFIRMATION FROM WU

February 6, 2018, 10:10 AM

Joel:
"Did not make it babe, I would just try tomorrow. Are you Okay?"
Lia:
"Baby cat! Will you be OK?"

February 6, 2018, 3:52 PM

Lia:
"(Funny face, crazy face, heart, kiss)
Joel:
"This one is so in love. I miss you, I had fallen asleep…"
Lia:
"Now you are not going to sleep all night! (Kiss face) Good time to Email everyone!
You don't need an account to pay your tax. Ask them if they accept a certified check, which can be sent to you with the exact amount and the name of the facility. You are very cute sometimes! (Heart, kiss)"
Joel:
"Ha-ha…but it's alright, I know. You'll be with me! (heart)
I have no problem with being cute once you like it, what are you doing babe?"
Lia:
"Going home to have dinner!"

SENDS JOEL A PICTURE OF A HEART IN A WINDOW

February 7, 2018, 7:37 AM

Joel:
"My Love, how are you?"

Lia:
"Good Darling!! How is your Day?"
Joel:
"Good morning my Love, how was your night? Did you enjoy your night?"
Lia:
"I slept well, thank you! Are you making progress with your financier?"
Joel:
"I was able to get the money you sent last night, Love. Thank you!
Yes, I have, we're still exchanging emails. I'll call you soon and give you a rundown."
Lia:
"Please try hard, I am worried about my Man!"
Joel:
"Your Man is trying so much to be with you!"
Lia:
"Best The best thing you can do for yourself! (Kiss)"
Joel:
"You do know that if a man wants you, nothing can keep him away. So it is that if he doesn't want you, there's nothing that can make him stay. Not the seven seas, the frozen mountains, or the desert, I'm in, nothing can keep me from you. I love you with all my heart, you're what's good for me my Love!"
Lia:
"Exactly! Why are you still there then? I am not worried about this my Love but your state of being! I want you to succeed and feel good about this event in the end!"
Joel:
"I love that you're the one for me, I've always resulted in being by myself and strong for me because I had no one. "

"Though deep down I've always known indeed that I need someone, I needed a woman but I need one who is different in all ways that matter, a confident woman who can be my confidant, a woman strong in faith and strong at heart standing alongside me.

I'm glad I've got you, you remind me that I'm not in this alone and I am totally in love with that my dear.

I love you and it makes me happy but there's no one I'd rather be in love with but you despite being in a world this large. I love you with all my heart babe, I let it out because, with all the strength in me, I have tried and failed to hold it within me.

You're always on my mind, I'm always thinking about you, even now I am. (heart)"

Lia:
"You have found your woman who is all of this and much more I am afraid, but in a real good way! I think that being together with you will broaden my world and make it extraordinary, just for you being there. You are my anchor and my man and I await your presence.
Love must have action. I love you and I want you!"

February 7, 2018, 12:30 PM

Joel:
"What are you up Lover?"
Lia:
"Working! Missing you! (heart)
Joel:
"Miss you even more."
Lia:
"(Kisses)"

Joel:
"What are you working on? Is it going fine? When do you finish?"
Lia:
"It's going! Will be working forever!! Did you have a good dinner Love?"
Joel:
"Forever is so long!! How about when I need your attention?"
Lia:
"I'm here baby! You are my first attention! You don't compare yourself with anything else. You come first!"
Joel:
"I love you!"
Lia:
"(Hearts, kisses)'
Joel:
"It goes without saying that you're first to everything in my life. You are my Life! (Love face),
I will kiss you forever, that's work I would want to do forever baby!"
Lia:
"Clever Man! Please do!!"
Joel:
"Lol...I love it! Okay focus, I'm here for whenever you need me. I did have a good dinner tonight my Love!"
Lia:
"What did you have?"
Joel:
"Some lamb chops, spaghetti, and salad babe. Very delicious, I wish you would eat these foods with me."
Lia:
"Wonderful!"
Joel:
"I've gotten so used to Turkish food now babe!"

Lia:
"It's good cuisine. Glad you enjoyed it!"
Joel:
"I just got a message from my financier, my Love. What he wants is an old account, one with history on it, not a new one. Do you have to meet this requirement?"
Lia:
"The bank account. I have it perfect! If he does not like it, I have another account he can use as well, but the first bank is better, much less expensive."
Joel:
"Don't worry about the expense."
Lia:
"So, which do you want?"
Joel:
"Which one is older?"
Lia:
"The first one."
Joel:
"OK. Give me the details to it Baby."
Lia:
"I am out now, will do it in an hour, Honey!"
Joel:
"Okay, my Love. Take your time, okay?"
Lia:
"(Heart, kiss)"
Joel:
"I love you, I miss you! When you're back, I'll call you and we will talk, okay?"
Lia:
"(Sends Joel the Bank Account Information)"
Joel:
"Okay baby, I want them too! Do you have the Credit card details?"

Lia:
"Bank has to send the CC for you! Once you wire transfer the money you will get a debit card which you can take money out of the account!
I'm going out now and will be back after several hours. Give them the account to place the money in. Debit The debit card I can send you when the money is there."

LIA:

"Joel had come out of jail and became adamant again about getting himself out of North Cyprus.

I was used to the foreplay of sweet words exchanged between the two of us and then he would come with the punchline of wanting money or some other banking.

The news was that he had backers who were going to give him the big money which he needed to pay his taxes and expenses, but he needed a bank account in which they could deposit his money and then I would send it to him for payment.

It was starting to look like a banking situation and talking about money all the time, but this is what had to be if Joel was going to pay off his tax and get himself home."

QUEEN ELIZABETH ENAHORO AND JOEL:

"Queen Elizabeth Enahoro held on to Joel for as long as she could, but Joel fought her back and used his charms to soothe her and give her renewed hope for the two of them. He was trying to calm her anger and put her in a mood where she could be reasoned with."

"He convinced her that executing their contract would benefit them both, since even though the contract was in his name, everyone knew that she had awarded it to him and therefore her reputation was on the line as well.

He made her understand that they were in this contract together and assured her that he would contact his sources and get the money for the overdue taxes and expenses, and they would both be the beneficiaries of this act.

He asked to be released and allowed to work on his mission to raise the money, and to get this completed and be done with. There were additional opportunities that had been open to them if this contract was completed.

Fortunately for Joel, Queen Elizabeth Enahoro agreed, and she allowed him to be free to execute and finish his job. Her spies would be watching carefully to make sure Joel obliges and does what he set out to do."

February 7, 7:06 PM

JOEL AND LIA:

Lia:
"(Heart, kiss)"
Joel:
"You're back baby. Missed you, babe!
Lia:
"Miss you too Honey! Sleeping yet?"
Joel:
"I've got the details you sent, do you have the logins for the online banking babe? I personally would need. Have you got the answers to the security questions for the account too? Might need to know the account limit as well. Stuff that is generally like that."

Lia:
"I don't have online banking for this account but tomorrow I will go to the Bank and arrange it for you."
Joel:
"No, I'm not sleeping! I'm actually up sending and responding to emails I had from those I'm in contact with. Alright, do that, please. How long has the account been up for?"
Lia:
"The account limit will be the money your financier put in. It's no problem to do it online, I will take care of it tomorrow. Long time, It's the best account and bank!"
Joel:
"I'm asking because I need to know if 100K can be transferred into the account and please ask for the limit of the account to be raised up!"
Lia:
"This bank is good because they let you transfer as much as you want as long as the money is in the account. 100k is not a problem."
Joel:
"Okay, get me the remainder of the details I need. Fingers crossed this works now!"
Lia:
"OK, you need about 150K?"
Joel:
"I cannot pull it all out, my Dear! I am scared."
Lia:
"Don't be scared!! Stay Positive. They sent a check to my house for 170K, so they can do it!
The stock market has been having a roller coaster ride the past few days and everyone is on hold. Give it a day or so for everyone to catch their breath!"

Joel:
"Okay, my Love! It's scary cus I don't have that time, my Love! (Kiss face) I would've loved to wait, I need all the pressure I can get."
Lia:
"Keep pressing and get enough and more to get out of there and then you can do what you want."
Joel:
"Okay my Love, Thank you. I will try!"
Lia:
"You must be my Darling! There is no other way! Please! I love you!" "(Love face)
Joel:
"I love you more! What are you doing babe? I know it's cold now, are you taking care of yourself?"
Lia:
"Reading and waiting for the dryer to dry the Laundry! There is an epidemic of the flu in NYC! Everyone is sniffling and coughing! It's impossible. So far, so good, but you never know! I am hoping to escape it this year!"

February 8, 2018, 6:40 AM

Joel:
"My Love, Good morning(heart)"
Lia:
"(Heart, kiss)"

February 8, 2018, 8:35 AM

Lia:
"Call me!"

February 8, 2018, 10:58 AM

Lia:
"You are having a nice day?"
Joel:
"Yes my Love, I am. How are you doing? "
Lia:
"All is well here!" (Crazy face)
Joel:
"I love you dearly! Don't forget to eat lunch whilst running your errands! So thoughtful of you!
Lia:
"I love you dearly too! I ate already because I was starved! I have two sets of appointments after 2 PM and will get no food till much later. Had a good meeting downtown. They will send me pictures of things they have to sell. Going well so far this morning. So many people trust me!
I have to learn to do the same myself."
Joel:
"Okay. Glad your meeting was good, babe. I also want to see what your online store looks like! You have no idea how excited any news about that makes me. I wish you so much luck with this (Heart)"
Lia:
"Thank you! They are not ready yet, but you can see if you want! Hope it's not too overwhelming Love!"
Joel:
"Lol...Nope, I have all the time for you!"
Lia:
"You are the bastes!"
Joel:
"It's more exciting than overwhelming, honestly!"
Lia:
"Then ENJOY!"

Joel:
"(Smiley face) Oh Baby! I'm loving them already! I see your concept!"
Lia:
"I want to finish my testing on them soon so we can go forward! Thank you!"

February 8, 2018, 6:19 PM

Joel:
"Honey"

February 8, 2018, 7:30 PM

Lia:
"(Heart, kiss)"
Joel:
"How are you doing my Love? Did you have dinner?"
Lia:
"Excellent! My friend's daughter is visiting, spending time with her!"
Joel:
"Okay, have fun, my Love, (Heart, happy face) Take care of her, lol...I trust you will anyway! (Heart), I'll go to sleep, only have a few hours before sunrise."
Lia:
"Kisses."
Joel:
"My heroine, my Queen!"
Lia:
"(Heart)"
Joel:
"None compares and nothing will ever compare. I must go now, (Heart, Crazy face, high heel shoe, Star), I'll be with you in your dreams Love! Ha-ha! That's how you make me feel you know!!"

Lia:
"Ok, sleep well! Dream away, my Love! (hearts)"

CHAPTER 7

LIA:

"I wanted to help Joel in every way that I could. I wanted to do it with an open heart full of love and trust. Deep down I had a lot of reservations about his doings and for banking he was asking for. I could not understand why he did not have his own banking account for his deposits and needs.

I also remembered the findings of the Detectives and the warning of the attorney and always proceeded with caution and took my time before I did anything that I was not sure about doing.

I hated doing banking for him, it was complex to understand, and it always involved a third party, which I did not know, and Joel did not know the difference between a debit card and a credit card, and I couldn't understand how that was actually possible, but because Joel needed the funding, I had to help him with the transactions.

This behavior from me frustrated Joel because I did not tell him how I felt and despite all the love and hope I had for us, I always threaded carefully and asked many questions from him which did not sit well with Joel.

He was getting it from Queen Elizabeth Enahoro and he was getting it from me as well and it was becoming difficult for Joel to handle all of it in a pleasant and happy manner.

He was desperate for money since he had very little for food and his stay. He moved in with one of his Business friends, Farouk, and stayed in his house for a while."

JOEL AND LIA:

Joel:
"What are you doing? How are you entertaining your guests?"
Lia:
"Wonderful!"
Joel:
"Okay (Heart), I want details for the card you've got honey!"
Lia:
"Tomorrow"
Joel:
"Your bank card, just take photos of the back and the front. Yeah, I know it's late now.
I tried logging in, but I don't have access. I don't know why, but I'll try again tomorrow!!
We might have to raise the limit on the card as well to maybe 20K or more if possible.
I might be needing to pay by punching it out with a machine! Everything now, it's just so complicated!!"
Lia:
"You are making me crazy! What card? The card is a debit card, it gives you only the money you already have in the account. You'll have to try to log in tomorrow!"
Joel:
"Why are you going crazy?"
Lia:
"I'll talk to you tomorrow!"
Joel:
"I'd like to have everything with me so there's no hook up later.
You know this. OK"!
Lia:
"OK."

Joel:
"Goodnight Love! (Flowers and kiss face)"
Lia:
"Good night (Sunflower)"

February 9, 2018, 6:41 AM

Joel:
"(Hearts) My Queen!"
Lia:
(**"Sends Gianluca Vacchi's song, "Love"**)
Good morning!"
Joel:
"Good morning babe! How was your night?"
Lia:
"Wonderful, thank you! Are you having a good day?"
Joel:
"It's early in the day and you have me wondering what it is I've done, who it was I fooled to find a woman like you as mine, you're too good, I don't deserve you (Heart)!"
Lia:
"What should we do then? Should we stay together or not?"
Joel:
"I can't live without you! Why would you even say such a thing?"
Lia:
"Then from this moment forward we never have to question it! (Heart, kiss)"
Joel:
"I'm constantly in adoration of the woman that you are, you brighten up my life, how can I not be cute? Lol...you make me feel special (heart), (kiss face)"
Lia:
"You are! My Man is the best there is!"

Joel:
"I'm only as good as my Queen is. I'm the best because my Queen is divine and the best there is!"
Lia:
"Love you! (Heart, kiss)"
Joel:
"I love you!"
Lia:
"Kiss"

February 9, 2018, 2:05 PM

Joel:
"(Hearts, Flower), Thinking of you!"
Lia:
"(Love faces, kisses)"

SENDS JOEL PICTURE OF NEW JERSEY VIEW OF THE STATUE OF LIBERTY
Lia:
"Love cat (Love cat)! How was your day my Love? Lol... I am tired!"
Joel:
"You should be sweetheart! You've had a busy day. How was it? Were you able to at least have something to eat, Baby?" (Hearts)
Lia:
"Great day! Went to a home furnishing showroom in NJ, then back in the city for lunch!
Just dropped her off at the Buying service. And I went shopping at "hanky panky!"

SENDS JOEL A PICTURE OF LIA WITH HER NEW MASK

Joel:
"Oh, you had a beautiful day baby, I always get jealous of you honestly!"

February 10, 2018, 8:22 AM

Joel:
"(Heart, flower), My dear, how are you?"
Lia:
"Good morning! (Kiss face), (sober face), How was your night?"
Joel:
"I'm dying to know what the story is with that photo? You know how I get when I see you in masks, Sugar (Heavy faces), now it's your fault I hadn't been able to control myself all day long!"
Lia:
"Good babe! What are you up to? I can share a little sugar with you, my Love!"
Joel:
"This is a wonderful thing, (heart), Thank G-d that I have you!"
Lia:
"What do you do when you lose control?"
Joel:
"You know just the right amount of sugar for me!"
Lia:
"I want to share some sunshine with you! (Sunshine, rose)"
Joel:
"I want to share more with you!"
Lia:
"Wow...this weekend before your Birthday!! I am getting excited!!" (Crazy face)
Joel:
"Sunshine would only be the start of it. Ha-ha baby (heart)!"

Lia:
"How old are we now??"
Joel:
"I wish I had you with me for it!"
Lia:
"Nothing more I would like!"
Joel:
"That's all I care about the most. Spending time with you (Heart). Spend real time! What are you doing my love?"
Lia:
"Yes, babe. Would be so amazing! Talking to you! I cannot get out of bed this morning!"
Joel:
"Stay in bed. I just got comfortable! In the mood for you! Hope you don't have a stressing or demanding day today babe?"
Lia:
"Buy something you like for yourself babe for your Birthday! Treat yourself from me!"
Joel:
"I want you resting, I need you with me. You know, right?"
Lia:
"Ok Darling, will do!"
Joel:
"You always know how to get me, baby!"
Lia:
"(Hearts, kisses)"

February 10, 2018, 9:47 AM

Lia:
"Baby cat! (Love cat)"
Joel:
"Yes baby, I missed your call, I'm sorry! (Heart)"
Lia:
"Are you feeling OK?"

Joel:
"Yes, baby cakes, I'm perfect, thank you! I was going through the multitudes of emails, you and I have sent and there are a lot, all of them magical, I have all the emotions in me blooming. I really do Love you, with you I have no reason not to feel okay my Love!"
Lia:
"That is promising then! (Love cat)"
Joel:
"It's everything!! (Love faces), You are everything! You've not left the bed, I'm sure? Lol…"
Lia:
"I have left it! I am all ready for the day's action. Just had a yummy breakfast and now enjoying my coffee!"
Joel:
"Oh, I want some. Mmm… What did you have?"
Lia:
"You are almost on dinner! Coffee should be very good where you are!
Good cheese and raspberry rugelach! Opposite tastes, one sweet one salty but sometimes I like that combo! It leaves an undescribed flavor in my mouth that lasts!"
Joel:
"You always have the best stuff baby! Lol, you know how far I have to go to get an English breakfast? Lol..."
Lia:
"Scones and cream?"
Joel:
"It's a 45-minute drive for me to the nearest shop. Tastes, tastes, tastes. You have my mind running wild already!! "
Lia:
"Why don't you get some eggs and cheese and jam and make breakfast for yourself? Save your money!"
Joel:
"Oh, I do that, potatoes, and bread too. I just mean if I wanted one from a restaurant!"

Lia:
"Your cooking is better than the restaurant!"
Joel:
"Ha-ha! Always hyping me up! I love that! (Heart, Smile faces), Yes baby, it's far…"
Lia:
"I know that already!"
Joel:
"I'm a better chef than most of the places I've eaten food from here in Cyprus! Definitely the prison chef, lol…that was the worst!"
Lia:
"You could probably run the restaurant and improve the menus! The kitchen is yours!"
Joel:
"I want you with me though."
Lia:
"I work at the cash register and greet customers! That's my specialty! (Angel face)"
Joel:
"(Heart) So humble, Yes! I need you there. I'll be back in the kitchen when you'll periodically come to me for a kiss and tease!"
Lia:
"OK, will have a kitchen collaboration spark up!! (All vegetables and fruit dancing)"
Joel:
"Ha-he. Okay, that's nice. I love it! Ha-he. You actually do the most love! Love that too!!"
Lia:
"(Kisses)"
Joel:
"What do you have doing today baby cats? (Heart)"

Lia:
"Removing the old rug from my bedroom and putting the new one down! Lol…there is so much stuff here! But it has to be done!"

Joel:
"Hahh...get someone to help you please. How are you planning on moving stuff?"

Lia:
"I have help!"

Joel:
"This should be when I help you with this stuff!"

Lia:
"I have been telling you to hurry up! You are missing a lot of fun!"

Joel:
"(Hearts) I will, baby! I love you!"

February 10, 2018, 12:52 PM

Joel:
"How is it going, babe?"

Lia:
"Lol...the rug is a different shade from the one I ordered! Now they have to come and take it back and I have to get another rug. Lovely day I'm having. I'll go to the movies better! (Mad face)"

February 10, 2018, 7:58 PM

Joel:
"Baby! Lol...are you feeling better now?"

Lia:
"Have to wait till Tuesday now. It will be my Valentine's Special Affair, a new rug in the bedroom! (Heart)"

Joel:
"Special Affair though, lovely! What shade did they get? What one did you want initially, baby?"
Lia:
"You are up so late Darling?"
Joel:
"I need to be with you through the night! (Heart)"
Lia:
"I always get into trouble when I choose something more complex but it was not my fault this time! It was to be ivory and light blue with pale yellow and they sent brown tan and misty antique blue which was awful! It's going back and I got the black, grey cream pebble wool rug which goes with everything!"
Joel:
"Wow, ivory, light blue, and pale yellow though, please make them bring this one!

They can have their tan brown whatever back. We don't want it, lol.

Anyway, which one are you having instead babes? Aw, but it's fine Lia. Don't worry I'm here now."
Lia:
"It was lovely in the picture but the one they delivered the rug color is so different. What are you going to do tomorrow?"
Joel:
"It's a weekend, but I'll go around to the market myself to get a few things I need.

Market runs here every Sunday, food stuff is good and cheap here."
Lia:
"Great! I love those markets. Everything is so fresh!"
SENDS PICTURE OF THE DIFFERENT RUG COLORS

Lia:
"The lighter picture is what I ordered, the darker is what they sent! The winter Olympics are on. Ice dancing, my favorite is on!"
Joel:
"Lol...no way baby, don't take the one they sent! You're following the Olympics?"
Lia:
"I am not. They are picking it up!"
Joel:
"Lol"
Lia:
"Yes. The Olympics is the Best!!"
Joel:
"I'm not. The world is enjoying itself and I'm not!"
Lia:
"There's no TV there?"
Joel:
"I'm not interested so I never checked if it's showing!"
Lia:
"OK"
Joel:
"It's showing everywhere, isn't it?"
Lia:
"Yes. It is bringing North and South Korea under one roof!"
Joel:
"Something I never thought I would witness".
Lia:
"Things are happening! Israel was attacked by an Iranian drone via Syria yesterday, 3 Israeli pilots were hit, and no one is talking!"
Joel:
"I read about the Israel pilots earlier today. The whole thing is becoming an even bigger mess. War crimes alert coming up from US troops."

"Russia being as involved as it is. The whole lot baby, it's hard not to follow up on that piece being that I'm right next door to Syria."
Lia:
"Big mess indeed! They are all getting ready for something!"
Joel:
"There's North Korea on the side as well. We're not forgetting those."
Lia:
"Yup! That is why I love Hawaii!"
Joel:
"Ha-he. So chilled, I know, let's go there! When all this starts just go and don't wait for me.
I'll paddle myself through this shit all the way to Hawaii".
Lia:
"Far away from everything! I will wait for you!"
Joel:
"(Heart) My everything! I love you!"
Lia:
"I love you more! (Kisses)"
Joel:
"I'll have to go back to sleep now, Honey! I'm a bit drowsy!"
Lia:
"Sleep well, Love! I kiss your face a thousand times! (Kisses)"
Joel:
"And a thousand more. I love you!"
Lia:
"(Hearts) (Kiss face) (Gennie)"
Joel:
"Ha-ha, I love that!"
Lia:
"I knew you would! Enjoy! (heart)"
Joel:
"(Love cat<3 Love face)"

Lia:
"Kisses"
Joel:
"I feel them from 1000 miles away".
Lia:
"If you were only 1000 miles away, I'd be there in person!"
Joel:
"(Hearts)"

February 11, 2018, 8:28 AM

Lia:
"(Gennie, Kisses)"
Joel:
"Sugar, (Flower)"
Lia:
"What did you get at the market?"
Joel:
"Good morning my Angel!".
Lia:
"Good morning for me and Good day to you!"
Joel:
"My clock is your clock, I'm just doing overtime, lol..."
Lia:
"Ok, Love!"

February 11, 2018, 12:04 PM

Lia:
"(Fun mojos)"
Joel:
"Hello pumpkin (Flower, heart), How are you doing?"
Lia:
"Good babe! What are you up to?"

Joel:
"I'm just out for fresh air, go sit by the bar, listen to my mind on things. Trying to be positive for tomorrow, hoping it brings with its goodness for me. I'm just sipping everything, Babe.
You? What are you up to?"
Lia:
"Bar is not a great place to sit! Your head gets muddled and strange people pick you up!"
Joel:
"I don't know, I just don't want to be alone babe, I'm sorry!"
Lia:
"Invite destiny within you. Open up to receiving what you really want in life. The stars are aligned for you, make your request now! You are not alone! You should not feel that way, it will make you do stupid things!"
Joel:
"Okay. I love you! I'm not going to do stupid things though."
Lia:
"I say this to you, so you don't feel alone and sorry. I had a Birthday too while you were away, but it is at these times that you must believe in yourself and persevere. Be strong and determined and embrace the beginning of your freedom. I love you and believe and trust in you and I want you to be deserving of all that will come your way. (Heart, kiss)."
Joel:
"(Hearts) I need you, I want you! I'm strong but I cannot do this without you. Beginning of my freedom, I love that."
Lia:
"I can pack my bag and come and join you!"
Joel:
"(Heart) Wouldn't that be a Birthday treat I can't forget! I love you!"

February 11, 2018, 12:54 PM

Lia:
"Why did you never ask me to come to you?"
Joel:
"A million times I did! Everything else came up instead! There's no way now that I'll let you get mixed up further in this though".
Lia:
"OK, my Love! (Heart, kiss)"
Joel:
"Thank you for tonight though, you've never failed at supporting me through everything! (Hearts) (Kiss face)"
Lia:
SENDS A HAPPY BIRTHDAY CARD TO JOEL
Joel:
"I was waiting for that, I'm back indoors now."

February 11, 2018, 2:57 PM

Lia:
LIA SENDS A PICTURE OF A CAKE AND BIRTHDAY CARD TO JOEL
Joel:
"I love these, is that one from you Darling?"
Lia:
"Yes"
Joel:
"Souls do tend to go back to who feels like home (Heart), Oh my...I killed me the more...
You really have my heart baby!"
Lia:
"(Kisses), For love! (Sends Synchronized Fireworks show on youtube.com").
 "Give your heart and soul to me and life will be "La Vien en Rose! Je t'aime!"

February 12, 2018, 6:28 AM

Lia:
"Happy Birthday to you!! (Sends instrumental song for Happy Birthday)!"

SENDS JOEL A PICTURE OF FLOWERS AND HAPPY BIRTHDAY CARD

Joel:
"I love you, Honey! Let me know when you're up baby? Thank you for these, I'm so pleased today. I keep going over them!"

LIA:

"Joel's Birthday was February 12, so he said, and I wanted him to feel special after his entire ordeal. He was deep into trying to find all the money necessary to pay off his debt and was setting up his banking credentials.

I was helping him with everything he wanted but I had no knowledge of what he was exactly going to do and accomplish with all the banking. He had many requests all the time but most of them he never used, he just demanded this and that and sometimes I did not take him seriously because it was a lot of work and I didn't want to do it.

I just wanted all his problems to be gone and for him to come home so we can meet and be together. I did have a feeling that something was going to take place and I had to be careful not to miss it!"

CHAPTER 8

JOEL AND LIA:

Joel:
"Thank you so much for everything, my love, you're making my Birthday so much more colorful. Just got in, my cell had been dead the whole time! I'll call you in a few, I want to boost some charge on it. Is that Ok, my Love?"
Lia:
"I am on my way home from downtown. Will call when I get home, Darling! (Heart, kiss)"
Joel:
"OK, (heart)"

February 12, 2018, 11:43 AM

Joel:
"Are you alright baby? It's been an hour plus since, and I miss you!"
Lia:
"I am juicing the phone. I will call you soon."
Joel:
"(Hearts), about to have dinner! Can I call you when I'm done instead?"
Lia:
"OK, Enjoy!"
Joel:
"Just wanted to know you're doing fine, my love. All my Love!"
Lia:
"Everything is OK. Had to go downtown for a doctor's appointment. Did some shopping and now I am back. Enjoy your Birthday dinner, babe! Kisses(heart)"

Joel:
"Babe, a doctor's appointment? What for? You're Okay, aren't you, babe?"
Lia:
"I am OK, as long as you are mine! "(Love face)
Joel:
"Forever, I promise I'll remain yours, my Love!"
Lia:
"(Hearts, kisses)".
Joel:
"I'm always here with you, and I'm proud of you, my Darling. Don't you worry, we will be fine, and well after this all ends, baby! I love you!"
Lia:
"Enjoy! Missing being without you! I want to celebrate with you! You are so strong and amazing! Love you! "(heart)
Joel:
"My life and strength all come directly from you, my Darling. In our hearts, we are together and will celebrate forever. This is only a day out of a long life we are going to share together, thank you for your love, my Dear!"
Lia:
"Sounds like a wonderful dream that I am looking forward to sharing with you!"
Joel:
"It's US!" (Love faces)
Lia:
"Yes!"
Joel:
"Lol, we keep this up, and I might never just eat dinner!"
Lia:
"Go eat dinner, babe! Enjoy!"

Joel:
"Okay babe, (flower, rose), You're beautiful, you're strong, gorgeous, wonderful, you sweeter to all and to me, you give me life, you are life, and right now I want you to please take a deep breath and remember I'm here for you and I love you. Baby, you have a wonderful life and I want to be part of it, and I want to be part of it and be in it with you." (heart)
Lia:
"OK, Honey. I know, Honey, and I appreciate you!" (Kiss)

February 12, 2018, 3:00 PM

Lia:
"What are you having for Dinner Darling?"
Joel:
"I sent you an email, baby!"
Lia:
"Gorgeous! Glad you have good people around you to celebrate with!" (Heart, love face)
Joel:
"If only I was with you (Heart), You are my life (Heart) being with you beats any feeling in the world, baby! I feel you in my heart, though!"
Lia:
"Wonderful! I wish nothing more but to be able to celebrate all occasions with you, my love!" (Heart)
Joel:
"(Heart), you're too much baby!"

February 13, 2018, 7:37 AM

Joel:
"Good Morning, Lover!"
Lia:
"Good Morning, Sweetness!" (Heart!)
LIA SENDS PICTURE OF HERSELF TO JOEL

February 13, 2018, 2:00 PM

Joel:
"My wife (Heart), You're so gorgeous! I love the hair and your glasses (Love cats), I want a baby!"
Lia:
"(Heart, kiss)"
Joel:
"I love you. Where are you? I had a good Popeyes today, my Love".
Lia:
"Shopping for food! Yes. Kisses!"
Joel:
"Oh, good. You're alone? Or do you have any one with you? Kisses, my Love! Let me know when you are done." (Hearts)
Lia:
"OK"
Joel:
"Take care of yourself for me."
Lia:
"I will babe! You as well!"
Joel:
"Okay, Honey!"
Lia:
"What are you going to dream about tonight (Love cat)?"
Joel:
"Gold! (Red heart, gold heart), You?"
Lia:
"How did you know that I am thinking of you this minute? (Kiss face), Very sweet, thank you!"
Joel:
"It's easy, you and I are very connected. It's unlike anything I've ever seen in my life. You drive me crazy!!"
Lia:
"How does it happen? I cannot understand?"

Joel:
"I want to spend every day of my life in your arms, Honey, I wish I was not here, I'm so drawn to you, and I lose concentration from all other things when I turn to you!"
Lia:
"They had a building party downstairs, and the lady Sheila on the 11th floor was reading cards.
I had to pick one card. WOW!! Unbelievable! She said you already have a partnership with your man!"
Joel:
"You really are my first Love!"
Lia:
"What are you saying?"
Joel:
"She told you nothing but the truth."
Lia:
"I just want to kiss you every day for some time! (Kiss)"
Joel:
"Hold on to her words, mine too! I've taken so long but I'll come to you as I have promised. Sometime? Why not the rest of our lives? You really think I wouldn't be into that? You really are my first love ... that was what I meant to write Honey!"
Lia:
"Sometime in my day, every day! I cannot keep you chained all day!! You are so cute! Amazingly sweet. I appreciate it so much, and I am so grateful that I found you and that you let me in. I love that about you the most! You are so kind! (Heart, Love face)."
Joel:
"But you own me, I'm yours. I have been, and I will always be. This you know, and I have told you repeatedly."
Lia:
"I know, Love, but I want you to hear it anyway!"
Joel:
"I love you, baby girl! I just love you!"

Lia:
"I love you, baby boy!" (Heart)
Joel:
"(Gold hearts)"
Lia:
"Love the Gold Hearts".

February 14, 20, 11:04 AM

Lia:
"You know what kind of cake this is!" (heart)
SENDS JOEL A PICTURE OF VALENTINES DAY FLOWERS AND RED VELVET CAKE

Joel:
"My wife!" (Sends Valentine Lyrics)."

(Joel writes an Email to Lia:)

"All my love, My Valentine. At this point, I am lost. Lost for all the right reasons.
I struggled with these words more than understanding my own existence.
See, a material gift will never match what I feel within. I could give you the world, but it will not be enough. So, I drift ever into the night, wishing upon the moon and the stars…that this overwhelming feeling that they call love will never lose a hold on us.
I've learned that a writer is not a writer without its their muse. So, I think of how far we have come to only realize we have just begun.
My always, my forever. I love you, my ray of sun."
Lia:
"Thank you, my Love! Same here!" (Heart, Kiss, Rose)

February 14, 2018, 3:18 PM

Joel:
(Calls to wish Lia a Happy Valentine's Day, which they say at the same time to each other)
Lia:
" I love you, my love cat!"

February 15, 2018, 7:54 AM

Lia:
"(Heart)"

February 15, 2018, 8:55 AM

Joel:
"(Hearts)"

LIA:

"Our talks had taken a very romantic and loving tone. It was the most exciting time of my day to spend time talking to Joel. When he was in a good mood, he was the most amazing human.

He was loving, charming, and supportive! He became my everything, and I forgot all the past struggles and pain, his disappearances, lawyers, and past problems."

CHAPTER 9

February 15, 2018, 10:32 AM

Lia:
"Baby cat! How are you? Have you got a response and commitment from your financier?"
Joel:
"Send me photos of the back and front of the Bank card, I personally need them."
Lia:
"OK, will do!"
Joel:
"I'm in talks with him, my Love, he's Chinese, and today is New Year's Eve or something, but we're working on it together. Okay, baby (Heart). What are you doing?"
Lia:
"Going to an appointment."
Joel:
"Don't take forever. What appointment is it, babes?"
Lia:
"Lol... Chinese New Year is a whole week and some more! How did he become Chinese?"
"Why does this whole financier thing sound strange? I can send you the card, so you have it. What are you going to do with a picture of it?"
Joel:
"I don't need the card physically, though it's fine if you want to send it. Right now, I need only a picture of it. Anyways, I don't personally know how the Chinese New Year thing worked, how is its "New Year" now, when we're in mid-February? And babe, if he says it's Chinese New Year and he's preparing for the celebrations and says that's why he's been delaying me, what can I do, babe?"

"I'll have to take it and his word because I know he has no reason to tell me anything other than the truth."
Lia:
"Chinese New Year begins 2/16 this year and lasts for a week. Year of the Dog.
Will send you a copy when I get home! China news service next door to my appointment, office empty of all employees! Lol...."
Joel:
"Sad, they'll all be having spareribs tonight, lol...and not news!"
Lia:
"I worked with them for many years. If you succeed with them, you will be a real hero!"
Joel:
"I usually like to leave them out of my way except if I really can't!"
Lia
"There are a few restaurants downtown that offer Chinese New Year spreads and it's something like a food feast!"
Joel:
"Okay, baby."
Lia:
"You might want to consider putting on the escort to the US on the table, with you to pay this mission and be done."
Joel:
"Lol, food feast? Lol...they're always so extra though".
Lia:
"It is incredible! I used to go with the Chinese staff every year!"
Joel:
"Babe, they had refused that offer of having an escort to follow me home from me way before I had gone into prison. Unless you want me to try again, then I would."

Lia:
"You might run out of choices. You need a Greek tycoon or an escort!
I'm not sure the Chinese will deliver unless they are desperate to get money out. I would look for more options while you are waiting. There has to be someone else with a lot of money looking to do the same deal as the Chinese!"
Joel:
"Be careful, anything around this circle worries me. Honestly!"
Lia:
"I only look after you! (heart) Let me ask the famous question? What happens if you cannot get the money to pay them?"
(Sends Joel the copy of the front and back of the bank debit card.)

February 15, 2018, 4:15 PM

Lia:
"Hi, did you get everything I sent you?"
Joel:
"Hey, Honey. No. What did you send?"
Lia:
"A copy of the card, front and back."
Joel:
"I did not get it, honey. E-mail or text it".
Lia:
"You have to download the WeChat app on your phone if you are going to text with China.
They are forbidden to use anything else. Did you get it now?"

February 16, 2018, 7:00 AM

Joel:
"I love you! Good morning, my Angel! I cannot believe I have actually found you, and honestly, babe, the feelings I have for you are so subtle!

I've found out that the first thing I wake up to every day is to see if I have anything from you, and this has been a feeling that's been there since I had first woken up with you in mind.

You drive me so crazy, and you're sweet, so romantic, you're independent, and you're considerate, you saved me from myself and the darkness I had plunged myself in the loneliness and isolation.

I've locked my heart up with your wonderful character, you're very noble, and I've decided that with you, I'll just follow my heart and let nothing else determine what I feel for you. My heart is true, and it has fallen deeply in love with you.

I'll let it happen and, I just hope you do, too (heart). It's so amazing to be with you. I think you're sunny and, sweet and romantic, and it always melts me down.
I love you, you mean the world to me. I'm forever yours."
Lia:
"Good morning, my Poet! Very sweet! Now, get Skype, I want to see and be with you every day!"
Joel:
"Good morning to you too, Princess! Lol, Skype? I don't have a phone or laptop for that, honestly, I wish I did. If you could get me a laptop or phone for that I'll be really grateful! Talking to you and Facetime with you would be everything."
Lia:
"What happened to your laptop?"

Joel:
"Probably with the authorities if they still know where it is."
Lia:
"What authorities?"
Joel:
"I never got it back from the police when I was caught.
I can't fight for such things when my life is at stake!"
Lia:
"Baby, why did the US financier not come through for you?"
Joel:
"I am still working on it."
Lia:
"How can you communicate and get yourself out without your laptop? Ridiculous!"
Joel:
"Honestly, it's so annoying but I have faith that all of this would be in the past, too.
Those things are too little to worry me, honestly."
Lia:
"I hope so, too."
Joel:
"I have bigger problems than a laptop. Yes, baby!"
Lia:
"Kisses."
Joel:
"How are you today?"
Lia:
"I am just dragging myself out of bed. Wishing for breakfast in bed this morning! Can you sneak in and warm me up?"
Joel:
"Ha-ha, if I sneak in, we wouldn't be going anywhere today!"
Lia:
"That would be wonderful! (Heart, love face), Paradise! (Butterfly)"

February 16, 2018, 9:10 AM

Joel:
"Ha-ha... I know, baby!"
Lia:
"I hate leaving in this hidden relationship, though, I must admit! I want to see you! I need a visual of you! I cannot take the darkness anymore, I need to see you!"
Joel:
"Me too, love, all this would be over pretty soon."
Lia:
"Ok, Love."

February 16, 2018, 4:46 PM

Joel:
"With all my heart, I swear I love you!"
Lia:
"(Heart, kiss)"
Joel:
"What are you doing? Are you alright?"
Lia:
"Everything is OK!"
Joel:
"I understand, everything will be alright".
Lia:
"Did you read the news about the Russian investigation?"
Joel:
"Did you have lunch, babe, or were you too busy to have anything? I did not read anything close to that. Let me check now."
Lia:
"I am waiting to eat dinner. Very stormy out tonight, will stay in. Tomorrow, a snowstorm is coming! Special Counsel Muller indicted 13 Russians for election meddling!"

Joel:
"Oh my, please take care of yourself and stay baby indoors. The weather here is peaceful. Beautiful, if only it had you in it! 13 Russians? Baby, wow! Meddling in the American elections? (Laughing faces) if that's that, then I really was expecting it!"

Lia:
"I will, Darling. Glad it's ok by with you! Enjoy your evening and have a good rest."

Joel:
"I shall, Honey! You'll be ok?"

Lia:
"Then there is the FBI, which did not follow up and resolve the tip on the FL shooter, which killed 17 people! Not good at all. Very lame!!

I will be Ok but missing you enormously! Please forgive me! (Heart, mermaid, kiss)"

Joel:
"Forgive you for what Love (Flower)?"

Lia:
"For missing you so much!"

Joel:
"I am sorry you have to miss me this way!"

Lia:
"Heart"

Joel:
"I will love you forever (heart). Mark my words, babe, I will love you forever!"

Lia:
"Kiss."

Joel:
"Go have dinner, okay? I'll rest from the day."

Lia:
"(Kiss face) Ok, thank you!"

February 17, 2018, 7:33 AM

Joel:
"Thank you for being the angel that guards my life. I love you, Good Morning, honey pot,
how was your night?"

February 17, 2018, 9:02 AM

Lia:
"So sweet, Good Morning!"

February 17, 2018, 11:36 AM

Joel:
"Good morning, my Love. Your morning going on well?"
Lia:
"So busy today! All is well, Darling. Getting ready to go away for a few days!" (Love cat)
Joel:
"Ha-ha... Okay, can I come with you? You'll just put me in your pockets."
Lia:
"Sure."
Joel:
"Ha-ha, I love you! I'm glad I've heard from you. I always want you, alright. I always want you!"
Lia:
"You are the sweetest!" (flowers)
Joel:
"How are your children, babe? They're alright?"
Lia:
"Yes, they are fine, thank you! What are you up to?"
Joel:
"I was reading some news from all around. "

Lia:
"Anything exciting?"
Joel:
"Nah, just news about the school shooting and the Russians. Nothing else is eye eye-catching."
Lia:
"You already know this! You like the hat?"
SENDS JOEL A PICTURE OF LIAS RED COWBOY HAT
Joel:
"Babe, the card to the bank account you sent me earlier, does it have anything on it?
If it does, what's the limit on it?
I love it! (Love face, heart), Ow, you look mean... Where did you get that from?
I love it! Ha-ha... I'll make you wear it all around."
Lia:
"I am going to tell you this once again about the card. It is a debit card and can only give you the money that you put in your account. If there is no money in the account, you will not be able to get any.
What are you going to do with this account and a copy of the debit card?"

February 18, 2018, 9:49 AM

Joel:
"My Love!"
Lia:
"You are my Love!"

February 18, 2018, 11:36 AM

Joel:
"Missed your call, Honey! I'm out in town, that's why, it's pretty noisy where I am. I'm also trying to help in whatever way I can!"
Lia:
"OK, love."
Joel:
"I'm trying not to put too much faith in the financier and my debtors. Time just keeps flying by and I'm losing it by the day. Staying here has taken its toll on me, and I cannot take it anymore. I am tired!"
Lia:
"You told me that you will handle it! What happened to the money from the two previous
containers that you told me you released before you became ill? Try hard, babe, to make this happen! There is no other way!"

February 19, 2017, 7:47 AM

Joel:
"Baby, I miss you!"
Lia:
"(Hearts, kisses)"
Joel:
"How are you?"
Lia:
"Good babe! Another week. Having a big lunch today, Tara's boyfriend is coming over to meet me! How was your weekend, Darling?"
Joel:
"Horrible. I spent all of it thinking about how I could leave. How is she? Is she alright?
He should come to meet you. It's the proper way!"

Lia:
"You need to be patient, Dear! She is great, and I cannot wait to meet him. What happens if you cannot pay them?"

Joel:
"We don't need to go there. I'm terrified of thinking about it. I'm afraid I might need you again."

Lia:
"Can you call your bank and release your money to do banking online? You have an account they can transfer money into?"

Joel:
"(Broken hearts), I'm losing so bad, baby."

Lia:
"You told me all of this was going to be OK, why does it get so complex and difficult all of a sudden? Your Chinese connection will not be able to speak until next week.
Try to be patient!"

Joel:
"Hmm, Okay. You know how tense I get when things I have here aren't working out fine! I despise feeling this way!"

Lia:
"Relax and take it easy, extra stress will not help you!"

Joel:
"I need you, emotionally. I love you!"

Lia:
"Baby, you and I are really good. I just need you to be strong and smart thinking and to figure this puzzle out! I love you!"

QUEEN ELIZABETH ENAHORO:

"She was watching Joel very carefully. He had spent an entire year in her confinement cente and now he was free to tend to his business."

"She had not given him any of his money, and he was peddling and trying to find business sources that would help him pay off his debt.

I did not know any of this, and I tried to help him as much as I could without being the person that would do it all."

February 19, 2018, 10:17 AM

Joel:
"I love you too, baby! Everything would be okay, I promise."
Lia:
"(Heart, kiss)"

February 19, 2018, 1:17 PM

Joel:
"I love you!"
Lia:
"I love you! In the middle of lunch with a new boyfriend!"

SENDS PICTURE OF LEA AND HER FRIENDS DOG

Joel:
"Oh, lol, so sweet, how is he, baby?"

February 19, 2018, 3:07 PM

Joel:
"Didn't want to disturb your lunch with the new boyfriend, lol…How was it?"

February 19, 2018, 4:45 PM

Lia:
"Just ended! They are getting ready to leave. Very nice young man!"

February 20, 2018, 7:47 AM

Joel:
"(Heart, kiss face) My heart and a kiss to carry and protect you through this lovely day. I love you.
Honey, if you get any code, relay it to me. How are you this morning? I've missed you. Wake up (heart)."
Lia:
"Good morning! (heart), What code? Where are you?"
Joel:
"My Love, I'm here now. I love you! Your voice and your kind words make me feel like everything is okay!"
Lia:
"(Heart, kisses)"
Joel:
"Thank you for that. I remain yours forever. Tattooed on your heart."
Lia:
"You are so sweet! Tattooed in my heart! (heart)."

February 20, 2018, 1:54 PM

Lia:
"Hi, babe! (flower) Sunshine mode! Preston went to the Bank today and got his account separated from mine but it will take a few days to reflect. All is good."
Joel:
"Okay, my Love".

Lia:
"Love cat"
Joel:
"Thank you!"
Lia:
"You are welcome!"
Joel:
"How's your day going, sweetheart?"
Lia:
"Wonderful"
Joel:
"I'm glad! Lunch, baby?"
Lia:
"It is so warm! Tomorrow, it's supposed to hit 70 degrees in February, go figure?
Leftovers from yesterday. Quiche and berries. Made a lot of food yesterday! How did your day go, babe?"
Joel:
"Hey, I'm ready for bed now. Oh, how much do I want to eat your food! >3
Lia:
"Ready for bed with you! (Kiss)"
Joel:
"I wish I could have some sent to me. (Smiley faces) Oh...I love you!"
Lia:
"I have an extra one! Will put it in the freezer! Let's see who gets it first! You or me?
Have a good sleep, Love!" (Heart, kiss, Love cat)

February 21, 2018, 7:44 AM

Joel:
"Good morning, baby cats (hearts). I love you so much!"
Lia:
"Hearts, champagne, strawberries!"

Joel:
"Out hustling for things. Lol… How did you sleep?"
Lia:
"Wonderful! (Heart, kiss)".
Joel:
"I'll text you if anything, in about 10 or 15 min. max, Okay?"
Lia:
"OK, babe! Lots of Luck!"
Joel:
"Had this chance to say hello!" (Heart)
Lia:
"10 to 15 min. Ok for what?" (Kiss's face)
Joel:
"Before I get another free time to talk to you. This love and bond between us keeps us strong, and I know it's everlasting because this chemistry with you feels divine.

I have never felt this way in my life before, and even in this sad time, it's you I have, only you! You're really an angel! You know, I've told you a million times and more, baby, I'm your man, your Prince, and you and I will have a bright future together."
Lia:
"(Heart, flower)"

February 22, 2018, 6:34 AM

Joel:
"I dream. Sometimes! You're beautiful, you're strong, gorgeous, wonderful, you're sweet to all and to me, you give me life, you are life, and right now, I want you to please take a deep breath and remember I'm here for you, and I love you."

February 22, 2018, 8:31 AM

Lia:
"Good morning, Love cat!"

LIA:

"I enjoyed having Joel back. Our cute chatting and teasing were something I looked forward to every day.

He was trying to get financiers that would lend him the money which he needed for his contract payments.

I was skeptical about everything he was doing since I was not sure it would amount to success. I needed time to defrost from the previous shock of Joel in jail.

He was doing banking, something I did not like, and I was looking forward to someone rescuing him and all of it going away.

I was waiting to see what would come next, I knew how Joel used sweet words to warm me up and then hit me with the surprise of needing more money for his payment.

It wasn't that I didn't want to help him, I knew I couldn't without losing everything I had. It was also aggravating me that his stay there was prolonged, and the actual plan of his return was not revealed."

CHAPTER 10

February 22, 2018, 11:53 AM

Joel:
Sends an E-mail to Lia:

"I am stuck. Stuck between this stone and a pillow. I am in chaos. My mind overthinks, and my soul is detached from my weak body. I want to rest, I want to get tired just to distract myself, but I feel my bones are being under construction, all I do is destruction. A sucker for pain, a paper that gains no written words all at once.

I can't go on, my mindset wants to see the future as reality. Reality with you and only you in it. None of this BS, I hate being myself now, but one thing I know is that I would uphold what I have with you and what promises I have made to you.

I promise now that I, Joel, will be the man that you hope for a future with and that you desire Lia. I love you with all my heart. I can't have anything happen to you. I'll get out of this, day by day, your love and support is all I require.

All my love, Joel."

Lia:
"I want my dream to be the same as yours! (Butterfly, hearts)"

Lia writes an Email to Joel:

"You see, it's not how we get along during this ride that I am questioning! I know that despite many difficult moves we have turned it around to be positive and have managed to reconnect and move forward!

What I am questioning is your collaboration with third parties and the truth of your situation, which I have no knowledge of or am privy to!

You disappeared for two months, twice, and I had no clue as to where you were or if you would ever reappear again!

This situation may be advantageous to you, no one knows where you are, no one has a visual of you, and no one has a copy of any record that states who you are!

You have received a lot of money through third parties, all of them who are unknown, and are planning on more!

My situation is to watch and assist whenever you ask without any guarantee that you will make it through or not vanish again!

My prize is not that one day you will appear in NY, it will be my joy if it takes place, but coming back here is your escape and prize, I am already here! My prize is the relationship and love with you!

Whatever feelings and joys we exchange between us is one thing, but my questions and the darkness I live in with you every day remain unchanged!"

February 22, 2018, 6:44 PM

Lia:
"Sends Joel, **"Perfect"** –Ed Sheeran on youtube.com, I love you!"
Joel:
Writes an Email to Lia:

"Patience is an important key to having a wonderful life. It was only after I met you that I realized that my life had absolutely no purpose. My days, weeks, months, and years were melded into nothingness. I was lost, and you saved me. I finally opened my eyes and saw that you are my purpose in life.

Baby, you are my dream come true. It is very rare for dreams to ever come true, my dream of a perfect cherub has been far surpassed by you. You have altered my being into something better and worthy to be presented to you, my Queen. Everything I am and ever will be, I pledge to you.

You are the holder of my heart, and you really have indeed ruined me for anyone else, my angel.

I am yours, and you are my baby. If I could turn back the hands of time, baby you know I would go back and make sure that I would have met you earlier on in my life.

Going to a time before we had gone through any of the pain we had to endure before we met.
However, our past is what determines how we are now, and I wouldn't have you any other way.

It may have taken us a long time to find each other, but a higher power had already planned for us to be together."

"There is nothing anyone can do to stop us from being together.

I love you forever and ever. In all honesty, I have never fallen for anyone so deeply. I don't want to think about the future without you. You have tattooed me on your heart, and I yours, our souls are bound.

You captured me from the first time you responded to me. My Jasmine, I cherish you and support you in all that you do, just like you are supporting me. It makes me feel so much better inside that I am leaving knowing where exactly we stand, and that I have you in on our team.

I live for the day that I can finally touch you, hold you, and show you how much you mean to me. Perhaps, one day, we will leave our own love lock on the Ponte Milvio, (hopefully, they still allow that), before we head home to make love under the stars and moon.

Until that day comes, I will hold every conversation we have ever had close to my heart.

I hope you get to stay around things that make you happy, make you truly smile, and remind you of me! Know that my mind is on you only, and that is the reason why I'm never lonely. I have gotten used to us. I have never been the same since the first time I met you. We have lots of conversations, and lovely memories to share when we are together.

I keep on loving you more and more every day. I feel content each time we talk every day, and I believe that it will be physically so amazing and beautiful. I am now impatient for us.

All my love, Joel. "

February 23, 2018, 6:45 AM

Joel:
"Thanks for the song, Love. I'm not well these past few days. I'm sorry for the lack of communication. I hope I'll be better soon, babe!"
Lia:
"What's happened? Are you ill? You see why I'm upset and crazy? If something serious happens to you, I don't even know where you are or have someone who can find and take care of you.
Here it is now! Therefore, I'm wild! Feel better soon!" (Heart, kiss)

February 24, 2018, 8:22 AM

Joel:
"(Gold hearts), Good Morning, Honey!"
Lia:
"Hi! How do you feel? What was wrong?"
Joel:
"I feel so weak, but I'm feeling better, so don't worry. I've not been able to keep anything down in the past two nights now. Got more serious yesterday but now I'm not as bad Honey!
I'm trying to conjure up the energy for a shower, though! It's 3 PM, and I've been lying here all night all day! How are you, baby?"
Lia:
"I'm fine, but mad at you! When you feel better, we will get into it! Now, hope you feel better!"
Joel:
"Okay, I'm sorry. I would've informed you, but it really felt like it was nothing at first, just a stomach upset. But I promise I'm taking care of myself, just as I had told you I was going to take care of myself, Baby! I promise that I am."

Lia:
"Yes, you should make every effort to get better!"
Joel:
"Okay, Honey. How are you?"
Lia:
"I am fine, thank you. Have a good day!" (Butterfly, flower)
Joel:
"Thank you, baby! You are really mad at me. I'm sorry. What did I do to hurt you, baby?"
Lia:

"You are ignoring what I want to know. Silence is not going to work. I want to know exactly where you are and I want to know how to reach Dion or someone else who knows your whereabouts. If something happens to you, we should be able to trace you and find you. If you want to remain silent, then you are on your own. I can be in your world only with knowledge!"

Joel:

"OK, I'm sorry, love! I understand, and I will do exactly as you have asked. Have a good day" (heart)
Lia:
"Feel better, Honey!" (Heart, Kisses)"
Joel:
"I love you! Okay, honey, I will. You're, Okay?"
Lia:
"I love you so much!" (Love face)
Joel:
"(flower) You're wonderful!"

February 24, 2018, 2:52 PM

Joel:
"Honey, you know what? I was thinking about you and figured, in this life, I don't want anything but you, I'm thinking that I have you, and that is enough. I'll give up everything else. I will give you my all, I will show you my flaws, I want to be lost in you. I have found you, and I want nothing else because nothing in this crazy universe matters. I love you".
Lia:
"(Heart)"

February 25, 2018, 8:15 AM

Lia:
"Hi, how do you feel, Sunshine? Are you better today?" (kiss)

February 25, 2018, 4:43 PM

Joel:
"Hey, Sunshine! How are you, my Love?"
Lia:
"I am fine, thank you. How are you doing?"
Joel:
"I'm not bad, getting better. Want to go to the clinic or a hospital tomorrow. I still need a check-up. I'm scared it's not just a fever, baby, my throat is sore, I can't talk, can't swallow. I've been drinking only for the past day."
Lia:
"You said you are better!"
Joel:
"I am, I'm able to text and walk to the bathroom."

Lia:
"Oh good, you should see a doctor, but be careful of the Hospital!"
Joel:
"Yes, Honey!", I'm going tomorrow. Thank you, baby! How are you? I still have $200 from what you had sent earlier, so I'm going to use that on there".
Lia:
"Hope all is well with you. Email me how it went. I'm going out of town for a while."
Joel:
"I've sent you an email already. Check it, Honey. I love you! Where are you going? Can I not reach you on by text?"
Lia:
"I am going to Toronto! Phone The phone does not work well up there."
Joel:
"How long? What's in Toronto? I've been so far from you, my heart just broke!"
Lia:
"Week-10 days, I have friends and Family there."
Joel:
"Everything is alright? Okay, Okay, Honey!"
Lia:
"You are unfortunately taking too long to get your stuff together!"
Joel:
"If wishes were horses, Lia. I am just a man and because I haven't raised what I need now, and because I haven't raised what I need now, it does not mean I'm failing! You, of all people, should know I wouldn't fail! Not now that I have a clear chance at freedom. Why are you upset?"
Lia:
"I said nothing. I am looking at the whole picture from the outside! Your health is fragile and staying there for so long does not benefit you."

"I am so mad that your financier has not come through with what you need. Why can't they send you the money they sent here?
I still have the check. Lol...I'm not mad at you, babe! I just hate what you are into."
Joel:
"I love you, and I will get out of this. You mean the world to me, and the journey to you, though tough and uneasy, hasn't got me backing down or slowing up, you're my goal, baby, having you tattooed in me seemingly does not just cut it for me."
Lia:
"Ok. I'll hold you to this because I need you to do it. I love you too" (hearts, kiss).

February 25, 2018, 6:25 PM

Joel:
"(hearts) When do you leave, baby?"
Lia:
"Tomorrow morning."
Joel:
"Okay, That's nice. I'm actually happy. I always love it when you're out traveling!"
Lia:
"Why?"
Joel:
"Traveling is good, lol...I could use some myself (happy face), it eases the mind!"
Lia:
"Yes"
Joel:
"You'll be fine. I wish you a wonderful night tonight, baby!"
Lia:
"Thank you, babe! You take care of yourself and be strong. I love you to pieces!" (Heart, love cat)

Joel:
"And your trip tomorrow is going to be a blast, my Love. I love you more!"
Lia:
"Thank you!" (heart)
Joel:
"I trust you without question. I love you without hesitation. Keep these close to your heart and at the forefront of your mind for me."
Lia:
"I keep you in my heart all the time, and believe it or not, I am trying so hard to get myself next to you, babe! I dream of this all the time. But will do what you ask!" (Kiss faces)

February 26, 2018, 5:32 PM

Joel:
"I love you," (Flower, heart) so much."

February 27, 2018, 12:38 PM

Joel:
Writes an Email to Lia:

"I dream, sometimes, I think that's the only right thing to do, people have always told me that poetry existed in places other than the space between pen and paper, but I never truly believed them, until I met you.

Your eyes contained the most extraordinary constellations and lit up in the most beautiful way when talking of the things you're passionate about, your mind so complex and more potent than any drug, and your laugh, oh G-d, your laugh could replace my obsession with the stars. "

"Something as simple as trailing your fingertips along my collarbones causes my skin to set fire and my world to blur.

Through these things, I realized they were completely right, poetry does exist in places other than words, poetry exists within you.
I miss you so much, my love, tell me what's happening."
Joel

Lia:
Writes an E-mail back:

"My Dearest Darling,
Everything is very good! I do love Toronto, it is a mini Manhattan, and it has everything but the enormity and clog of a huge city!"
They did overbuild around the lake and now there are so many condos and people, but its core remains the same. Polite Canadians and British British-based coolness abound everywhere!
All my friends here are so nice, and I always have a good time!
You are being so poetic all the time, thank you for all your beautiful words. I love you so!
Please tell me something about your health and, what is happening with your supporters, and why are they taking so long to release and set you free? I hate being stuck in an infinite dream, I like reality and am looking forward to it! Do you think it will ever happen?"

March 2, 2018, 9:53 AM

LIA:

"I realized that my trips to visit friends and places had become a sort of escape therapy for me."

"Joel and I would go through a long stretch of conversations about some mishap or another, and as soon as our conversation became heated and sweet, he would come up with something and ask for money. It became a constant repetition of a certain pattern, and I started to recognize it.

I would try to prolong the conversations so it would take longer to get to the money-asking part.

His pursuit was constant and on target, like a pro. I was exhausted from his asking for more money and constant phone calls and, emails, and texts. I had never spoken so much and so often to another human being in my life.

He was patient but controlled in his speaking with me. If he did not want to answer, he would just ignore the question and go on to the next thing, which I hated, because I did not get the answers to my specific questions. I did not know what to do.

I didn't know that Queen Elizabeth Enahoro was putting pressure on him and challenging the state of how his contract was proceeding.

He was challenging her back and was standing his ground and he informed her that he would not be leaving North Cyprus without transferring his money from the contract. He had told her that he did not care what she would do to him, that he was going to get his money, and that he was going to marry his girl, too.

He was the only one who knew the entire story of events and carefully played between the woman he loved and the woman he hated."

JOEL AND LIA:

Joel:
"You have become the fiber of my soul, the very reason for my existence, I miss you so much, Honey(heart)
I have no other words to describe the way you make me feel! No words, No words, No action could even come close. (Love face, Heart)"
Lia:
"Twinkle, twinkle little star, how I wonder what you are, up above the sky like a diamond in the sky, twinkle little star, how I wonder where you are! (Star)"
"Why don't you answer the phone? I love you! (Heart, kiss)"

March 4, 2018, 2:44 PM

Lia:
"Baby cat, where are you? (heart)"

March 4, 2018, 4:22 PM

Lia:
"I need you! (Kiss faces)"

March 5, 10:30 AM

Joel:
"Baby cats, I was recovering, how are you, my Dear?"
Lia:
"Real good! Are you OK, my Love?"
Joel:
"I'm alive, I'm getting better, Honey!"
Lia:
"What did you have?"

Joel:
"Meds? A lot!"
Lia:
"You had the flu?"
Joel:
"I was down with a fever first, then couldn't keep just anything down, kept throwing up, and the cough started, that was exactly what paralyzed me, really."
Lia:
"Wow! You didn't tell me the severity of the situation. How are you now? It's 70 degrees in North Cyprus, how did you get so sick? Something you ate? Cannot get the flu in this temperature! What can this be? Coughing comes from where? You had the AC on?"
Joel:
"No AC, I think it's just stress from the whole thing happening! It hit my lungs again, and that really brought me down. It's not 70 degrees, I'm in the middle of the Mediterranean, baby, weather and temperatures turn with the tide."
Lia:
"How did you hit your lungs?"
Joel:
"Not physically, babe, I mean the flu!"
Lia:
"Then you need to cuddle up in bed with yourself, drink plenty of fluids, and eat something, and ride it out, baby cat! (Love cat) I was thinking about your situation. Had a thought about it, so I will share it with you. I am not sure why you are enduring this situation in North Cyprus if you have money in an account here in NY.
Why don't you call your bank and authorize them to release the exact amount of money which that you need, then send me a power of attorney, you can do it online and send it to me as an authorized pick up, and they can issue a bank check which is insured, and I can deposit it or send it to you."

"It would get out much faster. Worst scenario, I can get on a plane and bring it to you. Can you make this happen for yourself?"

March 5, 2018, 5:12 PM

Lia:
"Feeling better?" (Heart, kiss, flower)
Joel:
"Thank you, love, I'll call you tomorrow. You're back in NY?"
Lia:
"Yes, Darling!"
Joel:
"Okay. How was your trip, Love?"
Lia:
"Wonderful! I want to take you there with me next time to see Toronto!"
Joel:
(Heart)
Lia:
"Kisses"

March 6, 2018, 12:37 PM

Lia:
"How are you my Darling? Did you eat something today?"
Joel:
"Hey, Honey, I did try to eat some noodles. Was able to eat some of it and not much!"
Lia:
"OK, so rest and eat some more later! (heart)"
Joel:
"I did. It's cold now and tastes nasty. Food tastes nasty whenever I'm not well. How are you?"

"I got your mail, baby. I was able to read it today. I am sorry. I promise I am working here to get myself out. I should be able to present you with something positive next week."
Lia:
"You must try to eat as much as you can!"
Joel:
"It's not easy raising 160K down in this hell hole. I try to baby love, but it's not easy. It just disturbs me and comes back out afterwards."
Lia:
"The test of a solid relationship is when both of us eat a year's worth of salt. We've done that, so the rest should be easy!"
Joel:
"Wow, you are so poetic!"
Lia:
"Your health is most important! (Heart, kiss)"
Joel:
"I'll need a librarian's brain to decipher what you just wrote to me. I know, but I'm trying to get out of Cyprus quickly and in good faith."
Lia:
"You know it's the truth! They have a lot of eggplants in Cyprus? The green handles on top of the eggplant, dried in the sun, makes tea when boiled in water.
It clears the bacteria in the stomach lining which rejects normal interactions with food. It may help you if you can get a hold of it!"
Joel:
"I don't think it's eggplant season, my Love, plus, I don't have time and energy to dry it, Honey!"
Lia:
"I have it at home."
Joel:
"Dried one? Lol, OK, keep them for me."

Lia:
"Yes! I actually saved a life, that's why I know about it. It was a long time ago, but she had the same where she couldn't keep any food down. All the meds and Doctors eventually gave up.
A Turkish woman, who knew my mother, called me in and gave me the eggplant handles for the tea. After a couple of days of drinking it, she was able to digest and process all her food intake and gain herself back to health. Are you Ok otherwise? Is the house comfortable? Are you alone or do you have help?"
Joel:
"Okay, Love, I'll try the eggplant when I'm home."
Lia:
"Love you (Love cat)"
Joel:
"Yeah, I'm okay, Love. This house is Okay, it's just that I fear that I'm becoming a liability to this family. I really wished I could move out!"
Lia:
"Have a nice conversation with Faruk and tell him that you need some more time. He will understand. You cannot make yourself more stressed than you already have.
That is why I told you that you are taking too long to get this done because you are living on someone else's expense. Let's see what will happen in the next couple weeks. I've given you all the ideas I have until now."
Joel:
"I'm honestly still waiting on my lenders."
Lia:
"Ok"
Joel:
"I'm hoping something positive comes out of it. How are you?"
Lia:
"It must be Darling. I am good. Missing you!"

Joel:
"I miss you too, my Love. So much!"
Lia:
"Remember you are the man who told me to always stay positive. I am trying to make you proud of me (heart)"
Joel:
"You are so sweet Lia, I admire the shape of your heart, its content makes me so jealous. I will for your sake make more effort to get out of this hell hole baby as soon as possible. I love you so much!"
Lia:
"Baby cat, I love you! (kisses)."

March 7, 2018, 6:58 AM

Joel:
"Hello Lover, <3"
Lia:
"Good morning baby cat, how do you feel today my Love?"
Joel:
"How was your night? I have good news!! I'm okay, so happy and I am just filled with joy!
I woke up to an Email from my financier containing a slip confirming a transfer to me.
We succeeded!! Wait, I'll send it to you Honey!"
(Sends Lia the HSBC wire transfer information to E –mail:)

HSBC Receipt:
Sender: Wei Chun
11201 77th Ave.
Forest Hills, NY 11375
Recipient:
HSM KARGO INSAAT SANAYI VE TICA
GENCTURK CADDESI OMUR
LALELI FATIH
Pick up location:

Turkiye is Bankasi
Customer Code:
U3u37z
Date Available:
March 13
Transfer Amount:
$120,000
Transfer fee:
$30
Receiver:
Marshall
Account:
TR680006400000 Routing: ISBKTRISXXX

Lia:
"Fantastic! I'm so happy for you! (heart)"
Joel:
"For me? Why not for us? Oh no, I'm happy for us!"
Lia:
"Us! I love it baby cats! You did it! Is this payment enough for you?"
Joel:
"You managed to elude me for this long. Well, I am coming for you! Lol finally!
I am so glad though, something is happening! I feel like I can almost jump out of this bed and dance, Oh my!!"
Lia:
"Me too! I'm dancing already!"
Joel:
"Ha-ha!! Oh no baby! Wait until I arrive please! We will dance and rejoice together. I am afraid it's not enough Honey!"
Lia:
"It's the 7th today, your luck begins! Just so you know the Bank is renewing their online system and will be ready by the end of this week."

Joel:
"Okay good. Update me on the Bank Honey!"
Lia:
"I cannot believe it, I just woke up and my daughter arrived from LA as your messages came through. I am so excited to hear your beautiful voice. I am so happy that this day has arrived. I love you so much!" (Heart, kiss)
Joel:
"I have the whole family here, I'll call once they are done. You'll have to pardon my cough, Honey! I am happy with myself. I can't wait to hold you really! This has taken the longest time."
Lia:
"I am breathless but concerned about your health. I cannot wait to hold you and be near you baby! Oh... you made me be in ecstasy! I love you! "(Hearts)
Joel:
"I'm here alone, I have nothing and nobody but you right now. You are what's keeping me going every day. I wake up and think about you, it gives me the motivation to do my best in whatever I lay my hands on. All I've got is you! You're my woman, someone I can proudly call mine, I am so proud of you.
I hope that we are never strangers to each other, I hope we're never pretenders, what I have for you is real and I can't imagine being in a world without you."
Lia:
"I feel the same with you my Darling"
Joel:
"You and your words keep resounding in my mind" I've always loved you. You are my baby girl, Oh, how I miss you!"
Lia:
"(Hearts, kisses)"

Joel:
"What are you doing Honey? Honey, there will never be disguises and unfamiliarity between us, I believe we will at all times be the truest version of ourselves, we will be happy every day for the rest of our lives."
Lia:
"Working on my stuff, hanging out with Tara, she starts a new job on Monday, going to my friend's house for a gathering, her daughter made the National Olympic ski team so we have exciting news all around! I am talking with you, I am your biggest fan!"
Joel:
"Exciting news all around! Oh, I'm so excited my Love! You are awesome! You rock!! "
Lia:
"You are awesome!"
Joel:
"Lol...Well, you get the idea!"
Lia:
"And amazing!"
Joel:
"I am?"
Lia:
"Yes! To me, you are the most amazing, awesome man and my heart was tattooed with you!"
Joel:
"Ha-ha!! I love hearing that!! I love it, I love it!!"
Lia:
"You are going to be hearing it for me till my last breath! I am going to have a smile on my face the whole time until I see you!"
Joel:
"(Gold heart) that That just made me confident!
Very confident! Thank you, you're the best, my Love!"
Lia:
"Don't ever forget you are always in my heart!"

Joel:
"No baby, I won't ever forget!"
Lia:
"Nothing can go wrong now, you've been through so much, I cannot wait to have you in my arms." (Heart, Love cat)
Joel:
"(Love faces, flower)"

LIA:

"Joel had received a transfer from his Chinese source. I was very skeptical about the entire thing. I went to Queens myself to check out the address on the transfer slip, but I couldn't find the address on it.
I went to the bank to verify the transfer, and the agent said that it looked like their transfer but couldn't confirm if it was real or fake.

Again, there was doubt in my head. I also knew that the money was not enough and that Joel would be asking me for the rest, which was 40K. I did not want to give him any more money, I had none left, and whatever I had, I wanted to keep for myself.

It was a selfish way to look at this situation, but I had already given him so much, and it seemed that his situation had not changed, and he was still there repeating the same pattern over again.

I wanted him to come home so we could meet and make a life together. I wanted to love him and to be able to speak to him, flirt with him, and have him by my side forever. I was so fond of him!
I just was not certain that he was telling me everything, and I always processed everything he said with caution."

"Joel knew that Queen Elizabeth Enahoro and her spies were watching him carefully, and he wanted to keep me as far away from their grasp as he could."

JOEL AND LIA:

March 7, 2018, 1:34 PM

Joel:
"Hey Bunny, (Heart)"
Lia:
"I feel like a lioness today! (genie)"
Joel:
"Oh, do you now?"
Lia:
"Hmm…I do!"
Joel:
"You're a lioness. My lioness, I am your lion! (Gold heart) I love you!"
Lia:
"You bet! (heart), Snowstorm in NY today!"
LIA SENDS JOEL A PICTURE OF THE CITY IN THE SNOWSTORM
Lia:
"You know what the lioness does to the lion? She gets on his back and grabs his tail and then asks him to go forward, while she flips the tail back and forth, so he goes faster! Miao!!"
Joel:
"Lol…I don't know how we could apply that to our everyday life together, babes, but I'm with you if you are with me. I love you. How are you? Don't go anywhere today, my Love, you should be indoors, keeping safe. Where are your children?"

Lia:
"We are all home safe and snug! Must have fun whenever I can with you. I love you! (Cat love)"
Joel:
"(Hearts), Yes, baby! I'm okay now since I know where you are. My heart is calm now.
I love today! It's been a wonderful day!"
Lia:
"You are my wonderful, awesome Man! It has been a great day! (Magic Star)"
Joel:
"Yes, it has Honey! You've been faithful. (heart), I love you. Thank you, Honey!"
Lia:
"(Hearts)"
Joel:
"What are you up to?"
Lia:
"Working and talking to you. What are you doing?"
Joel:
"I'm laying down, baby, there's nothing much that I can do, baby. I just remembered that colorful dog you had seen on the sidewalk one time. Lol… Hope you see another! (Heart) Oh, that was long ago, and you still feel the same way you feel for me."
Lia:
"How do you feel, babe? I want that dog for myself! When you come back, we are getting him!"
Joel:
"I feel like I need you. My heart is stubborn, but even it needs your warmth!"
Lia:
"I am here, baby, feeling you!"
Joel:
"I love you so much, my lover! Thank you for your love. I remember those photos." (Laughing face)

Lia:
SENDS JOEL A PICTURE OF HER FRIENDS WEARING FUNNY TEE SHIRTS
Joel:
"Oh, I remember, babe! That's yours? Ha-ha…I'm dead! Where did you get these? You always do the most!"
Lia:
"Long time ago!"
Joel:
"You are out of this world (laughing face), Ha-ha! Oh, baby, we already have so many memories! I'm so happy!"
Lia:
"Well, let's just say I keep everyone laughing for a long time!"
Joel:
"I feel so close to you. I feel I can almost reach out to you."
Lia:
"You can, Honey! Same here! (Kiss)"
Joel:
"I love your body more, Honey!"
Lia:
"(Kisses, love cat)"
Joel:
"You done working?"
Lia:
"What do you mean, babe?"
SENDS PICTURE OF JOEL AND LIA'S FAVORITE DOG
Joel:
"I am blown away, ha-ha! You know how to make me happy. I keep smiling!"
Lia:
"Baby cat!!"

March 8, 2018, 9:14 AM

Joel:
"Loving you is easy because…you're the one for me. I trust you, I need you, I want you, and I know I have you. I love you! My Muse. Your King!"
Lia:
"I love you! (Love cat)"
Joel:
"How are you?"
Lia:
"Good! How do you feel today? (Crowns, flowers, sun, world)."

March 8, 2018, 12:56 PM

Joel:
"Hey Honey!" (hearts)
Lia:
"Hi baby!" (Love cat, hearts)"

March 8, 2018, 3:00 PM

Lia:
"There is no circumstance, fate, or situation that can hinder the unstoppable power of the human soul."

March 8, 2018, 9:11 PM

Joel:
"(Heart), I am holding on by the skin of my teeth here. You have no idea how much confidence you give me to pull through this!"
Lia:
"Baby! Please, please try to get all the money you need! Please!!"

March 9, 2018, 7:48 AM

Joel:
"I trust you without question. I love you without hesitation. I cannot wait until I touch you. That would be the moment where stars and everything falls in place, then nothing can shake how perfect that moment will feel! That moment will be that moment that gives us purpose. Good morning my Darling, these are words I'll keep saying till I breathe my last breath! I love you!"

March 9, 2018, 9:10 AM

Lia:
"I adore these words, keep repeating them forever! My dearest Darling, I wish you a day of greatness and I give you all my love and many kisses."

March 9, 2018, 11:55 AM

Lia:
"Sweetness, (Kisses)".
Joel:
"Gorgeous, how are you? Lia baby! (hearts)"
Lia:
"Splendid my Dear! How are you feeling, better, I hope?? I hope you are feeling better. (Kiss faces, flower)"
Joel:
"You know? I'm getting better by the day. What's your day been like?"
Lia:
"I am so glad that you feel better! Best news! (Flowers), Today is a bit hectic, I have so much to do and not enough time."

"But will keep on plugging until its done. Have dinner guests coming, friends of Tara's whom I look forward to seeing again. Just must get it all together and have some time for me!"
Joel:
"Please do everything quickly and make sure you keep time for your stuff. Where are you now?"
Lia:
"Will do Love. I am home getting everything done!"
Joel:
"Ha-he. How many guests are you expecting?"
Lia:
"Two."
Joel:
"Oh, hush! And you made it seem as if it were an emergency! You are good, you can handle this!"
Lia:
"I can, Darling!"
Joel:
"I believe in you! I wished I was helping you, though!"
Lia:
"You are so sweet! The kitchen is yours!"
Joel:
"I'll come in my apron."
Lia:
"Will the apron be see-through? I had a dream last night that you and I were working in an office together, and I was bothering you every 10 minutes with this, and that and some other things which I won't mention, and it was very entertaining! "
Joel:
"Impossible!! You and I in one office? We'd never get any work done!"
Lia:
"It was something like that, but you were very happy with it, and you put up with all my calls!"

Joel:
"Ha-ha! Being with you is all I live for! I would do anything for you, and I would most definitely put up with all your calls, Honey!"
Lia:
"It's a very funny dream. I've had it several times, I don't know why?"
Joel:
"Thank you for ALWAYS thinking about me. I wish we were together right this second, sipping on champagne and eating a shrimp cocktail! I hate the fact that you are halfway across the world away from me, m. My heart aches for you every second of every day.
I need you, Lia, I'm not as strong as you think, or as much as you give me credit for. I'm so weak without you!"
Lia:
"Well, I was thinking about this very thing, and I decided that for whatever reason, we are tested to prove our own self-worth to ourselves, these are the kind of times where we must overcome and endure to higher standards and prove ourselves worthy of what we achieve in the now and future.
I did say that if you say the word and think it's a good idea, I will pack a bag and come to you ASAP!"
Joel:
"I love you dearly!"
Lia:
"Me too!" (heart)"
Joel:
"Appreciate the love and care you put into me and take care of me! Thank you!"
Lia:
"(Heart, flower)"
Joel:
"You are divine! None will ever compare!"
Lia:
"Thank you, Darling!" (Kiss face)

Joel:
"You have everything under control?"
Lia:
"I am trying!"
Joel:
"Can I get you a drink?"
Lia:
"I drink champagne and good red wine, do you have them?"
Joel:
"Here? Oh, No! I can't drink alcohol with my meds, Honey! I stayed off anything alcohol!
When I come through?"
Lia:
"Baby, you asked me if I wanted a drink, and I told you what I like to drink. How can we have drinks together? You are just wishing for that moment and I so appreciate it and look forward to it. My favorite of all is water!"
Joel:
"My favorite is you! Every time, every day! I miss you!"
Lia:
"I made chicken in the oven with chickpeas and golden beets! Then I made beef in red wine sauce with pine nuts rice and salmon with orange curry sauce and asparagus and carrots. Is it enough?"
Joel:
"I want some"
Lia:
"With pleasure my Love."
Joel:
"But you'll be nice and serve me my food in my mouth? I am after all your baby boy?"
Lia:
"Don't worry about this, y. You just get here, and I will make sure you are so spoiled that you will just smile all day long! (Kiss face)"

March 9, 2018, 5:40 PM

Lia:
"Now I have seven guests coming, happy?" (flower)

March 10, 12:04 PM

Joel:
"Hi, Honey!"
Lia:
SENDS JOEL A PICTURE OF LIA AT DAVID BOWIE EXHIBIT
Joel:
"Ha-ha..."
Lia:
"Hello, Darling! How are you, baby? Feeling better?"
Joel:
"Didn't know you were a fan? Thought you were my number 1 Fan? You're cheating on me!!"

March 10, 2018, 12:07 PM

Lia:
"I am not, but don't mind him, but my friend is! No, you are cheating on me if you think that way!!"
Joel:
"(broken heart) Oh Lia! Lol…
Lia:
"Love you, baby cats! (Heart, kiss), You are my Man! I see no one else!"
Joel:
"I love you, so deeply!"
Lia:
"Sends **"Viento"** by Gianluca Vachhi on youtube.com
Joel:
"How are you feeling today, my Love?"

Lia:
"Splendid! You?"
Joel:
"What was that video?"
Lia:
"New song out! Can you see videos on your phone?"
Did I tell you that hearing from you makes my whole day so much brighter and happier!?"
(Flowers)

March 10, 2018, 3:08 PM

Joel:
"(Hearts) No, you did not, though you've never failed at expressing how you feel."
Lia:
"You are my heart and Honey!"
Joel:
"You always bathe me with these words(heart)."
Lia:
"At last…I've given you a bath…ahh…(butterfly)"
Joel:
"Thank you. Lol...at last, she says… Someone's been waiting!"
Lia:
"My favorite song!"
Joel:
"(laughing face) You're impossible! (Hearts)
Lia:
"Sends **"At Last" by Etta James** on youtube.com, Impossible…. impossible…"
Joel:
"(Heart) What are you doing?"
Lia:
"Why are you up so late?"

Joel:
"I see you're in a good mood! (Love face), Messages woke me up!"
Lia:
"I am!"
LIA SENDS JOEL A PICTURE OF LIA WITH A MASK
Joel:
"I love the photo, you are so sexy!"
Lia:
"So sorry to wake you!"
Joel:
"And honestly, I still cannot take my mind off you! Your heart and body! I still need you badly!
I still want to fuck you bad! Love the mask. Love the red bra. You're my fine wine.
Did you just take it? You are so fair and beautiful! Gosh, I can't stop looking at your glowing skin!"
Lia:
"Thank you. Are you talking to me as if you don't know me or have seen me before?"
Joel:
"Well, I never could take my mind off you! These feelings, these urges! I never really got the opportunity to express them to you!"
Lia:
"You are my sweet, loving Man! (heart)"
Joel:
"Did it feel that way because I said I want to fuck you, Baby girl? I can't hide that, no matter how hard I try! I can't not say it either because every day, my Love, I want to!"
Lia:
"No, we have a lot of fucking to do and catching up too. I am hoping it will be soon! But I should be on your mind all the time, just like you are on mine!"

"I am just a simple girl who is trying to put a smile on your face in the middle of the night!
What better time after all!! Baby cat!" (Kisses)
Joel:
"(Uncertain face), You sure, baby? Because you're putting more than a smile on me!"
Lia:
"Well, I do have to be polite! I want to be on top of you right now, and I want my lips to move all over you until you cannot control yourself!
My hands want to gently rub every part of your body slowly, then harder, and I will mount you, or you can straddle me, and we can ride until I am breathless and wet all over!"
Joel:
"I am losing my mind!"
Lia:
"But, first a bath and some massaging with a fragrant soap! I want you so much in my arms tonight! I just want you to know that I do all the time and miss you to pieces! (Heart, kisses)"
Joel:
"Oh Honey, all I want and wish for it's just for you to be in my arms right now!"
Lia:
"I wish and pray that you are done there soon and come back as you promised. Do not shatter my heart!"
Joel:
"I wish I have had a way I can to prove to you that all I want is for you to be happy with me.
My prayers remain to finish up here. Get them what they want! I really need you on me!"
Lia:
"I love you, baby cat!"
Joel:
"Losing control like you just described."

Lia:
"Come to me I am here waiting. I am here waiting for and wanting you!"
Joel:
"You know I have done all I can, all my best. Did the time. I just want you!"
Lia:
"Yes baby, I know, you've endured like a hero. You have me!"
"You just need to find a way to leave and get out of there, it's been so long, and I am going to scream! I am the masked heroine in your movie! Hah…"
Joel:
"Don't! I'll be back and we are going to be okay. I Love you!"
Lia:
"I love you (kiss), Getting back to the fetish, I like interesting and variety and have high energy so you may find yourself making distinct memories in many different places! Got to have some fun, No!"
Joel:
"Well, sure, have fun with me around"
Lia:
"Looking forward to it!"

LIA:

"Our conversations were so intimate and frequent. Not only on by text but he was calling me on the telephone and staying on for hours, teasing me and talking about our future.

I was very fueled by all of this but always kept a reserved eye because I was very uncertain where it was going. His plan and wish for coming back were constant, but I did not hear the plan that would actually bring him back."

"He was exciting to flirt with and responsive to all the crazy conversations that came from me, and we went on and had a great time making each other laugh and comforted each other from a great distance.

He did get funding from a source, but I knew that the amount was not enough for his payment and I was not hearing from Joel that he had any other sources for more.

I had this fear the entire time we were talking and I had a hard time letting my feelings go freely when I knew I was going to hear the punchline very soon.

Meanwhile, throughout all of this, his coming back kept prolonging and taking a backseat.

I felt as if we were two grown grown-up people who were totally insane with different needs and wants who needed entertainment and someone by their side to alleviate their loneliness and their true desire to love and be loved back by their soulmate."

QUEEN ELIZABETH ENAHORO:

"Queen Elizabeth Enahoro had seized all the important documents relating to Joel's ownership of the contract.

Joel had no way of proving to any of the lenders that he was the owner and he was trying his best to persuade her to release the documentation and enable him to receive the transfer of funds and deposit it in the bank for payment.

It became a very difficult tug of war between them.
Did Joel tell me anything about this? Not one word!"

CHAPTER 11

JOEL AND LIA:

March 10, 2018, 9:29 PM

Joel:
"(Heart, happy face), I love how you put those words together, conversing with you make conversing with others as basic. Your sentences always have the most eccentric wordings! I love It!"
Lia:
"What others do you converse with like this?"
Joel:
"Not like this silly! (Confused face), Converse, in general! And that's me excluding Turks!"
Lia:
"I got it! I just wanted to see what you'll say!"
Joel:
"Lol...I know, you know where my heart is! Where my loyalty lies. Oh, how I love you!"
Lia:
"I know, babe! (Hearts)"
Joel:
"What are you doing, sugar?"
Lia:
"Looking at all the pictures I've taken. I should be a photographer!"
Joel:
"Can I look with you Honey? Is low resolution on my phone but it gives me an idea!"
Lia:
"I sent some good ones tonight! I have to get the stick that holds that phone. Very hard to pose and click."

Joel:
"Well, was that all? That was only some good ones. Lol...Not even all the good ones!! Oh yes!
Get the stick tomorrow!"
Lia:
"Ok, will do!"
Joel:
"Any later and I might be there to take them myself thus making the stick redundant!"
Lia:
"True!" I will dress you and take portraits of you and then jazz you up and take some more!"
Joel:
"Only The only stick you'll have to play with us is one that came factory factory-fitted on me (Happy face)."
Lia:
"I will make collage works with all your soul and heart, heart, and fetish on canvas!
That will be my full concentration and desire!"
Joel:
"I'll dress up to be whatever you want me to be, I could be your Elvis or Roger Moore!
Lia:
"I'm going for Tarzan tonight!"
Joel:
"Tonight? I want in!"
Lia:
"You gave me a choice of Elvis or Roger! I want Tarzan! (Crazy faces) I promise to behave from now on! I am sorry for waking you up like this!"
Joel:
"I love you!! You've always behaved yourself. I trust you!"
Lia:
"(Kisses)"
Joel:
"But wow! Tarzan tonight! You are on Fire my wild one!!"

Lia:
"You are my Tarzan!! I am definitely for sure on definitely on fire for you! We must find a place with a lot of tall trees! As Tarzan, you must learn how to swing from one tree to the next! Who knows where I'll be in the forest?!! (Hysterical laughing faces)"

March 10, 2018, 10:06 PM

Joel:
"(Apprehensive face), I'm King! King of the jungle!! You'll be my Jane!" (heart)
Lia:
"Ok, then you know how to swing!"
Joel:
"Ha-ha... (Monkey), You said it?"
Lia:
"I am your Jane, we had this conversation established before."
Joel:
"Call and put my name "Tarzan" and I'll be swinging down from tree to tree! Ha-ha! You're my everything!!
I just like a repetition!!"
Lia:
"So funny!"
Joel:
"Never get tired of you! Always in the mood for you! My Flower, even now I want more of you! Way more I'm sure than you can offer at this moment!"
Lia:
"Go get some rest baby! I am keeping you up! I'll soon come up with something else.
Tell me some fetishes you like?"

Joel:
"You're like a falling star, a rare sight to catch, behold, I have you in my sight, baby. I am staying up all night for you!"
Lia:
"I wish we could go for a walk together now by the beach, and we can sneak and find a safe place and make love in the moonlight!"
Joel:
"A walk in the park, late night with you!"
Lia:
"Then we will go swimming and have breakfast! I am starving! I don't know what to have!"
Joel:
"Wait! I'm still looking for a safe place to make love, baby!"
Lia:
"There is a park where you are? I thought you were by the beach? There are not many safe places in a park to make love!"
Joel:
"We mustn't make love in the park my Love! We could find another place or park our car in a corner somewhere!"
Lia:
"You are hysterical!"
Joel:
"Well? Just suggesting!"
Lia:
"You like the car?"
Joel:
"I love the car, a Range? I still have that in mind, you know! I never break my promises!!
Not until Cyprus, that is… (Broken heart)"
Lia:
"Ok, good to know, then we can give it a workout!"
Joel:
"You'll love it, I know!! Just hang in there a little longer!"

Lia:
"Can you imagine if they catch you making love on the beach in North Cyprus!?
Lol... They will stone me to death!!"
Joel:
"You will finally feel my cum gushing inside you! (Laughing faces) Honestly, they might stone us both. They are ruthless!"
Lia:
"True, and I will pay with my life! Hysterics!"

March 10, 2018, 10:22 PM

Joel:
"Yet, too many homosexuals amidst them!"
Lia:
"I heard! Do you have a twin brother?"
Joel:
"I wouldn't let you pay with your life! I will give my life for you! Over and over again!"
Lia:
"I wouldn't let you pay with your life"
Joel:
"You said you will pay with your life."
Lia:
"OHH...OK!"
Joel:
"If we were ever caught making love in Cyprus!"
Lia:
"That's my Tarzan!!"
SENDS JOEL A PICTURE OF LIA WEARING A RED TOP
"If I could only find a red bikini?"
Joel:
"(Broken heart), This just broke me!"

Lia:
"Kiss"
Joel:
"I want you so bad, Lia! Come wearing that, and I will tear you from limb to limb!!"
Lia:
"You know what has to be done. I'm ready!!"
Joel:
"This escalated quickly! I'm worried now that you don't mind being torn from limb to limb!"
Lia:
"I don't like to take the chains off too often, it's not fair to you or me but it sure is fun to do this occasionally!"
Joel:
"(Little devil) By me."
Lia:
"I said I am ready! You need to get here and do it!"
Joel:
"You have total control of me there, and it's exhilarating to be in this position!! I love you!"
Lia:
"Yes! Exhilarating is the word!! I love you!!"
Joel:
"Ok, back to the photos, Honey! You sure you don't have any more of them hidden up somewhere?"
Lia:
"Yes, Dear! Which ones?"
Joel:
"I like the feeling they give me. I love the feeling you give me! Ones you keep teasing me with all through the night!"
Lia:
"I know! But I must save some for another time!"
Joel:
"Why save when you can just take more of those other times?"

Lia:
"Tonight was perfect, no one is home but me, I can be a little creative!"
Joel:
"Wild!"
Lia:
"Wild, that's me!"
Joel:
"(Little devil), that's the more appropriate word to use!"
Lia:
"But I'm good wild most of the time!"
Joel:
"Just how I like it!"
Lia:
"Good to know."
Joel:
"So, are there more?"
Lia:
"Thank you for remembering the Range. I'm not sure I've had the pleasure of the car yet! Yes, there are, but I've given you the best ones!"
Joel:
"Not yet seen the best of it, yes! Just yet!"
Lia:
"What do you mean?"
Joel:
"Was talking about the Range Rover, Honey!"
Lia:
"Oh...ok! You are very quick tonight! Keeping me on my toes here!"
Joel:
"Lol...I'm all for you! And that's evident I'm getting better! My mind needs to get sharper, though!"
Lia:
"I am so happy!"

Joel:
"Did you know, I've yet to get the money from the bank that was sent! Don't panic, it's safe and in safe hands but the bank, I'm keeping tabs until it's available, and I can leave my sickie bed."
Lia:
"How are you going to get your mind sharper? Your money is available on 3/13, it said on the slip. This financier did not have the entire amount for you babe?"
Joel:
"Yes, it is, you remember. Though however, it may get here earlier! You know they give so much time to cut themselves some slack so they can do whatever with our money.
The financier couldn't get the entire amount, I was lucky to get this much! Think of how long I personally have been trying to get this myself! I think this is a miracle, 120 K takes us so far from the ground!"
Lia:
"Yes!! All transactions take a long time. They are watching everything!"
Joel:
"Not enough, sadly, but fair!"
Lia:
"It is a miracle for sure! If only Donald would appear!"
Joel:
"Frankly, I've been continually losing my mind as I keep thinking of how and where to pull the remaining money out. I have nowhere! Nothing! And with what I have, I can't let myself go back to square one!! I can't have that happen! I won't survive it!
It's been months and, and there has been no word about Donald! You'll be amazed I checked the obituary lists!! Didn't want to leave any stone unturned! I am in shock that he just left!"

Lia:
"I texted him and e-mailed him, but nothing!! Where would he go?"
Joel:
"That's my life story! That's why I used to panic every time I thought about me and you!
I've always thought you would leave too, like everyone else! (Broken heart)"
Lia:
"Please never tell me this again!"
Joel:
"This isn't from today!"
Lia:
"They will let you have your passport after you have paid what amount?"
Joel:
"These thoughts were from a year ago. You have cleared me of all of that. I'm rid of that, my Love!"
Lia:
"Good!"

March 10, 2018, 11:13 PM

Joel:
"I remain strong with you, and I know you're solid with me! Tattooed in our hearts. That's not easy to do!"
Lia:
"You bet!"
Joel:
"I've never heard of it being done before. We're unique!"
Lia:
"Yes!! Will they let you have your passport after you have paid?"

Joel:
"After I've paid half of the initial fee, which is 320K. They call it a pardon, but I still think 160K is high!! I can't complain to no one here, so I'm forced to carry my cross with me. But 160K is half of 320K, honey!"

Lia:
"So, the fine is 160K and then they give your passport back. Yes?"

Joel:
"Yes!! Signed and stamped!"

Lia:
"So, you need maybe another 50K to get out!"

Joel:
"And the rest of my stuff, they have a bag of stuff! Documents and all, literally all I travelled with. I only was left with my clothes and shoes! Yes, thereabout!! That's ripping my heart out!

Good thing I have a real heart safe with you! Yes, I do need to pay them 40K, baby, not 50K. "

Lia:
"50K should not be so hard to get from a financier! Try to get it. I wish I could help, but I cannot do anything, I am tied up here with all the payments from last year, taxes, and expenses. I'm going to jump from the terrace!"

Joel:
"You must be joking! Please tell me you are joking!"

Lia:
"40K plus you need some money for your pocket and expenses, etc. Joking about what?"

Joel:
"The terrace? What will I do then? Surely, you know I'll just jump after you! Please stop thinking about these! My heart breaks! I don't have another financier. This is it, this man had worked for me sometime before all this mess, that's how I was able to get a hold of him!"

Lia:
"I don't know what to tell you. I am torn in opposite directions every day! I cannot do anything for your sake, and I don't know where the money will come from for all the expenses. I am tied in chains!"
Joel:
"He had only responded to me on a lucky count. You know he did this for free for me? Not a penny! Because he understood taking a penny off me in this situation would devastate me!"
Lia:
"It's amazing, you'll have to thank him in a special way, but ask him if he may know someone else that can lend you the rest, even with interest!"
Joel:
"I have no more debtors to demand my money from."
Lia:
"So, what is your plan then?"
Joel:
"Those who remain will never pay, I know, even if it is hit with a lawsuit. It's sad that it's taken this long for me to realize this. We worked on this with him for months, he knows more, he has tried for me!"
Lia:
"Lol…"
Joel:
"There were no holes we could dig from, nothing we could do!! I had almost given up hope and then this came through!! That's why I need to hold on!!"
Lia:
"You need to think of someone else. You cannot hold on forever, or something else!!"
Joel:
"Yes, my Love!"

Lia:
"Let me go to sleep and dream of all this and see what happens in the morning. Rest up, darling! Something will turn up!"
Joel:
"I love you. Thank you."
Lia:
"Love you more! (Heart)"
Joel:
"(Flower, gold heart), Sleep well, my Angel!"
Lia:
"Thank you! You too! Rest up! (Kiss, flower)".

March 11, 2018, 8:07 AM

JOEL:

"Joel's partner, Queen Elizabeth Enahoro, had finally released Joel from her detention center since I discovered that the entire Hassan and lawyer set up was fake.

I told Joel when he was allowed to make a call and warned him that the entire story of his disappearance was fabricated and used only as a collection of money for someone's pocket.

Joel understood all of this and demanded his release and warned her to stay away. She did stay away from him, knowing that his contract tankers had come into port and had accrued taxes and fees that were astronomical.

She knew that Joel, being in the situation he was in, could not pay such large fees and left him unfunded and alone, as a punishment, to pay his own way through the entire mess so that he could realize that his girlfriend would not be able to fund him and set him free. "

"She was determined to ruin him and show him that she was the only one he should be with.

She seized all of his ownership documents to his contract and left him to beg agencies and banks to recognize him as the owner without his legitimate paperwork in a foreign country.

I didn't know any of this myself and only knew what he would tell me.

I also knew that I could never come up with the amount of money he needed, nor could I borrow from anyone else or the bank. My options were exhausted, and I didn't know how he would get out and accomplish his contract mission successfully.

He knew his dilemma, and I knew mine."

JOEL AND LIA:

Lia:
"Good morning, Love! (heart), Can you send me the signed and stamped contract of your payment due?"
Joel:
"Morning, Honey! What's up? Did you sleep well?"
Lia:
"Yes, baby, but I am missing you! (Heart, kiss)"
Joel:
"Me more, too much to say! What do you need, my Love?"
Lia:
"Your payment due invoice! Do you have it?"

March 11, 2018, 9:54 AM

Joel:
"I need to make a call to see if someone can prepare it for me on your request, Honey! (heart).
Yet again (Pray hands) thank you!"
Lia:
"You don't have a copy of it, Honey?"
Joel:
"OH no, not at all!"
Lia:
"Lol...how can you claim a contract without having it in your hand?"
Joel:
"Never got one. I was released and the term was expressly made clear to me when I asked for my passport and other documents back.
Well, I wasn't really asking that having just been let out of a 4+ month stay and locked up for apparently no lawful reason.
Lol... I was scared any wrong move would've cost me my head!"
Lia:
"You must get a copy of the contract tomorrow, immediately, before the transfer is available on Tuesday."
Joel:
"Okay, my transfer of 120K?"
Lia:
"Yes!"
Joel:
"Because even now, I am a little lost now."

QUEEN ELIZABETH ENAHORO:

"Queen Elizabeth Enahoro had taken all the required paperwork for the contract cargo and held onto it, knowing that it was required for Joel to receive any kind of loan or funding for it.

She held the insurances for the project and Joel could not prove ownership despite everyone's request and his need for this paperwork to secure and deposit funding.

How did Joel think he could accomplish all the deposits and payments without invoicing and proper ownership paperwork?"

JOEL AND LIA:

Lia:
"Once they get the money, if you are not holding the signed contract, they can deposit elsewhere and screw you up! Tomorrow, first thing!! You have the right to have a copy of your invoice for the contract. Otherwise, we are just talking here!"

Joel:
"Okay, okay! But you know, I wouldn't be paying even if the money arrives and I clear it, right?"

Lia:
"Now you are shocking me. You chose to handle the matter by yourself? You know you need paper to make a claim. Please!"

Joel:
"I'll need the complete funds before showing up to claim my passport!"

Lia:
"You need a copy of that contract no matter what. Even to borrow money you need a contract! Must have it! How can you go to pay something without your contract or invoice?"
Joel:
"It's when I have the complete funds that I'll go first to the police to collect all necessary documents before any payment! I'm not letting anyone cheat or take advantage of me to calm down!"
Lia:
"You need a receipt or an invoice to make that payment!"
Joel:
"Before and after I make the payment, Yes!! But I'll need to get the money up first.
What's the point of having those receipts without any of the money?"
Lia:
"I understand, but you need the paper that states how much you owe in the first place.
This is what I want. Please email it to me."
Joel:
"Showing 360K? It's all with the police. They've kept all of what I had."
Lia:
"Lol...so you don't have it in writing!"
Joel:
"Either way, Honey, I'll need to make those calls!"
Lia:
"Ok, Honey, I know you can do it. I love you!"
Joel:
"Yes! They have all the documents, sensitive ones, and the non-sensitive ones! Whatever I had packed into my briefcase when I was on the boat, they have it! You don't think they'd let me walk with those, do you? After all they've done to me?"

Lia:
"I just really feel like you need a copy of the pardon contract!"
Joel:
"You know how to get my blood flowing! (Heart, Rose), I love you, my Love!"
Lia:
"Kiss."
Joel:
"Ok, though saying that would land me more, lol…I was able to eat some food honey, I really am officially getting better!"
Lia:
"I am so happy you are getting better! Love it!!" (Happy face)
Joel:
"Well, thanks to you. You keep empowering me."
Lia:
"Good! That was my aim!"
Joel:
"Your aim?"
Lia:
"To make you feel better!" (Flower)
Joel:
"You've always had good intentions for me!"
Lia:
"Yes, I do!"

LIA:

"I wanted him to know what the investigators and my lawyer came up with, and I needed to open up and be straight with him. I also wanted him to know that I did everything I knew to try to find him and help him. I sent Joel an email explaining the entire ordeal."

Lia sends an E-mail to Joel:

"I feel so close to you now my darling, that I am going to tell you all of the things that have transpired and all of my feelings that are bottled in my heart! I love you so much and want you to consider all that I am going to tell you with angel patience and love!

I've waited a long time to tell you what happened while you were away, when you left on the boat, when you disappeared, when you went to prison. I am telling you all of this information because I want you to know how it affected both of us and how I feel each moment as I travel with you in this situation.

The only clear thought that I refer back to is that when you left North Cyprus and vanished. I was the one who texted you to see what had happened to you, this is important because I looked for you, you did not drag me into this yourself!

Anyway, when Hassan called me to let me know that you had been returned from the boat, I contacted a Lawyer and asked him to trace your arrest and see what can could be done. He could not find your arrest docket and did not want to go further because I did not have sufficient information on your whereabouts and Hassan did not respond to his calls. I was then contacted by Hassan and his Lawyer. Hassan insisted on having his Lawyer and I finally gave in and let him handle it!

Our communication was weak and dependent on Hassan's direction, and I was very uncertain how to proceed and it did not sit well with me. He would not disclose the location of where you were located. "

"After I sent my friend and cousin to pay your Lawyer, they found no one at the designated address. I hired two detective services to try to locate you.

I feared that you had fallen into the hands of the wrong people. Given all the information I had, Hassan's name, phone, e-mail, same as same with the Lawyer, your phone and e-mail and name, they searched all areas on the Island that may have you, including Police Stations, Detention centers, Jails, all Courts and record Departments, in the South and North and they did not find anyone named Joel Marshall anywhere!

The report of their investigations was that you were a Nigerian love scammer who preys on women whom you scam for money! This included Hassan and the Lawyer! Both services came with the same report!

I remained neutral, I could not speak to you, and I needed time for myself to process the information. Your email was traced to a College Dormitory Canter where you advertised ads for rentals!

I then called my friend who gave me another Lawyer in North Cyprus, their office was with the Attorney General. I also had him do an investigation as well and he could not find anyone named Joel Marshall in any jail, detention center or in any Courthouse in North Cyprus!
He finally told me that you are a figment of my imagination! Needless to say, this cost me a huge fortune as well!

I felt very down after I got all of these reports. I hadn't met you before you left but I opened up my heart to help you as a human being in need and our relationship had developed and I could do it. "

"I had given you money to help you out in a situation that was extremely hard to explain and validate, since you chose to stay so hidden!

My heart cares for you and I want to believe that you are the Man that I can trust, because this is what I must learn to do! If this trust is broken my heart will shatter and it will all end!

Once I processed everything, I realized that if you are the scammer, then I have been scammed and I will never see my money again! If you are a scammer, you have done your job well! I have been good with you, so be good with me and let me go and let it be.

I am not sure at this point what's what and I don't have much choice either way, I have spent all my money and have no more to give to anyone, you have chosen again not to use Counsel to resolve the situation you are in!

I have you tattooed in my heart, and I can never think of you as a scammer, you are my love, my Man whom I adore!

If you are my Man and you are in this crazy situation, open up and validate your payment with a receipt, with another person, with Counsel, so when payment is made you will not be giving all your money to scammers of North Cyprus whatever, who will not let you go and will steal all you have and throw you in jail to die. No one will be able to help you then! If these are not legitimate court-appointed officials, you will lose handling it all by yourself! Witnessing any crime is the best defense!

You remain hidden, not one picture shared of you in a year, hiding behind pictures of someone else, giving out safety information only when I ask, it's not very fair in a relationship as ours!"

"Don't you think I would like to know and see who I am in love with?
Let's see if you can handle it like a man with heart and soul and will try to find a way to do the smart thing which will benefit all!

I love and care about you no matter who or what you are, I just want you to open up and let me come in, because as long as you remain hidden, I cannot come into your heart, your action is blocking me and I remain an observer from the outside looking in and if your actions do not validate and explain this situation you will break my heart and most of all my trust which you will not be able to gain back again.

I am here, but I need to know whom I am with, only then can I stay or move forward!
It has to be mutual, one sided cannot be a relationship!"
All my love, Lia

March 13, 2018, 9:09 AM

Joel:
"Hi, baby!"
Lia:
"Hi, Love! How are you?"
Joel:
"I'm alright, how are you?"
Lia:
"Good! Did you have a nice day?"

March 13, 2018, 2:29 PM

LIA:

"Joel did not say anything about the information in the email I sent him. I wanted him to know that I did look for him and that I did not abandon him. I wanted him to open up to me because deep inside I knew he was not telling me everything. It was irritating to have to guess all of his actions and to have patience for actions that I was not sure would ever happen. A conversation about coming back was gone, the only conversation going forward was about the more money he needed for his payments."

JOEL AND LIA:

Joel:
"Yes Honey, I did have a nice day. Are you having a good day? I hope you're home today. The storm, I heard about it!"
Lia:
"Another one but it did not hit NYC, it went east into the ocean and then North. We got some snow and rain this morning but nothing serious. It is still a little cold outside!"

March 13, 2018, 3:40 PM

Joel:
"Can't eat it so I'm giving it to you! (heart)"
Lia:
"What can't you eat?"
Joel:
"The chocolate" (Hearts)
Lia:
"I'll take it if it's dark or white chocolate!"

Joel:
'Of course, it's dark chocolate Honey! I would always bear you the most perfect gifts!"
Lia:
"Then bring it on! Thank you! (heart)."
Joel:
SENDS LIA A PICTURE OF A HUGE CHOCOLATE HEART
Lia:
"Beautiful. How nice! Where did you find this heart?"
Joel:
"Got the chocolate from a local roadside market babe!"
Lia:
"This is chocolate I eat, or it's chocolate I put all over me, and you get to eat it?"

March 13, 2018, 6:37 PM

Joel:
"(Happy face), second option! Definitely the second option!"
Lia:
"Where are you now?"
Joel:
"Still where I was, never moved, never left the bed. How about your day? Tell me about it."
Lia:
"We had a hurricane, rain and snow mix the entire day. I went to a study group and the gym in the morning, and in the afternoon, I had a meeting with a merchandiser who is going to review my e-commerce sites. Now I am resting and doing some laundry and studying things in my head with you in mind all the time!"

Joel:
"I so love the last part. You are so sweet Lia. I'm glad you met the merchandiser, try all you can to take advantage of having him around. This is exactly how these opportunities come through! Don't worry, soon you'll be done with all that's stressing you, and you'll be looking down at the live report and all you've created, progressing!"
Lia:
"Thank you!"
Joel:
"I'm proud of you!"
Lia:
"Thank you! You are such a positive force in my life! (Heart)"
Joel:
"I'll always encourage you to strive for more! You have so much potential!"
Lia:
"Thank you!"
Joel:
"Despite all that's happened to you, you're never relentless."
Lia:
"What do you mean?"
Joel:
"Thinking through life, generally! You're strong and a survivor, you're my mentor and motivator. You've moved me so much through the times you've been in my life, baby!"
Lia:
"That is always the challenge, to be stronger and better each day for the next!
Preparation makes us achieve and enjoy the prize!"
Joel:
"(Hearts) y You're just perfect, y. You continue to inspire me!"

Lia:
"Endless, extraordinary, and impossible, traits I strive for! You are so sweet and amazing my Dear Man!"
Joel:
"Thank you, my Dear Woman (heart), I will put myself in a box and mail myself to you!" (Heart Face and flower)
Lia:
"If you don't soon, I will become impossible only! (Kiss face, flower)."
Joel:
"How's Tara and Preston?"
Lia:
"Real good, thank you for asking. Have you spoken to Dion?"
Joel:
"Yes, she occasionally lets me off the hook when she misses me! Kids, lol…I wish I had more!"
Lia:
"I have her on my emergency list. I cannot stress her out more. Don't get anyone pregnant!!"
Joel:
"I can't! You have my heart and my dick! You are the only one I'll happily shove it into!"
Lia:
"I will have to hold you to your words then! I don't want to shock Dion!"
Joel:
"Ha-ha!! Please. Trust me on this! I have many flaws, but I will never cheat on you! On my life, I won't!!"
Lia:
"I love you so much!"
Joel:
"(Heart), With you, I can stay up and survive!
Lia:
"You bet!"

Joel:
"You rock, baby!"
Lia:
"Thank you!"
Joel:
"Don't just give up on me, this just might be the best thing to happen to us, the best Union.
Do remember that this is only the beginning. (heart)"
Lia:
"I am not worried. I just like to know where I stand! You seem in such a good mood. I love you this way!"
Joel:
"Right in my heart, you know that, and you don't need a team of investigators to tell you that. You would never have stayed with me this long if you didn't know where you stand!"
Lia:
"Absolutely! But I did get wrinkled and ironed smooth again!"
Joel:
"Don't let your heart sway, you're mine and I am yours forever!"
Lia:
"Stand is not what I worry about, I just want to know what you look like!"
Joel:
"Without you there's no Me, I can't do this on my own!"
Lia:
"You will. You have no choice! You've decided the way!"
Joel:
"Bad things happen, bad things have happened, we both are alive and still together, that's what we should thank G-d the most for and not worry about the lesser things Life throws at us."

Lia:
"Just give me what I want and the rest you can have!"
Joel:
"When you see me in your heart, what do you see? Do you see me? Do you just see a figure, or do you see a masked mural? Tell me baby, do you really know what you want?"
Lia:
"Listen, I am visual! I have to see you! Yes, I do!"
Joel:
"What do you want?"
Lia:
"A picture of you!"
Joel:
"You are visual! Yes! I know that about you. You have pictures of me!"
Lia:
"No! I have pictures of Gianluca Vacchi. It's not you!"
Joel:
"Okay Lia baby!"
Joel:
SENDS LIA SONG "EVERYTHING GONNA BE ALRIGHT" by Bob Marley
Lia:
"I love Bob Marley. Thank you!"
Joel:
"I'm listening to him now! One love is playing. Let's get together and feel alright."
Lia:
"Love his style so much"
Joel:
"Yes! He is truly amazing!!
Lia:
"Enjoy"

Joel:
"Possessed a gift though which he could touch hearts from far and wide. One other person I know with this ability is you my Dear!"
Lia:
"Sweet of you to say!"
Joel:
"You're welcome, always. You're okay? I sense a change in your mood?
Lia:
"Where is Joel Marshall?"
Joel:
"Calm down! What's wrong with you? Why all this nonsense? Are you losing your mind?
Get yourself together Lia, Come on. Stop it, you'll hurt. I don't want you hurting baby".
Lia:
"Ok Honey! Enjoy your music. I am folding the laundry!"
Joel:
"Okay Lover. I love you! It's too late for me to be up!"
Lia:
"Have a good sleep. (Hearts, kisses)"
Joel:
"Thank you. You too. (Hearts)"
Lia:
"Kiss"
Joel:
"We will be fine(heart)"
Lia:
"I know, babe! I got you!"

March 14, 2018, 6:07 PM

Lia:
"(Love cat, kiss, heart)"

March 15, 2018, 12:11 PM

Joel:
"Hi Love!"
Lia:
"Hi baby! You ok? Miss you! (Flower)"
Joel:
"I'm okay, baby! Stronger now, able to move about. You don't need to worry much, I'm handling things now. How are you? Are you alright, my Love?
Lia:
"Wonderful! Do you need some exercise? Yes, I am in good shape, thank you! (Heart)"
Joel:
"You're in GOOD SHAPE (heart). I love that. I always need you to be."
Lia:
"Well, so far so good!" (Kiss face)
Joel:
"So far so good... What are you doing today? You had lunch?"
Lia:
"I just had lunch and enjoyed the warm sunshine on a cold day. Now I have to work and bring everything up to par. I hate sitting for a long time. Did you have a nice day? Swimming?"

March 15, 2018, 2:56 PM

Joel:
"I never went swimming, what are you talking about?"
Lia:
"I am kidding with you! Why are you so upset?"
Joel:
"No, no I'm not upset my Love! I don't get upset anymore."

Lia:
"Ok Honey, just smile and breathe. I love you and sometimes kid around with you!"
Joel:
"I'm breathing, trust me, thanks to you, you know that!"
Lia:
"Ok, Honey!"
Joel:
"What are you up to honey cakes? I really missed talking to you!"
Lia:
"Me too"
Joel:
"You're sweet., you ease my heart no matter what."
Lia:
"Baby cats!"

LIA:

"I was beginning to be at odds with Joel. He was choosing to remain hidden and did not want to confide and show himself to me.

After everything that we had been through I felt as if we should know everything between one another. I wanted to be in with him and know his entire situation and be able to rationalize our situation and where we were heading.

He was not budging and was not explaining why, and he was beginning to irritate me because his actions were making me distrust him, and I did not understand why he wanted that to happen."

March 15, 2018, 5:24 PM

Joel:
"What are you up to? "
Lia:
"Watching a retrospective on the Highline in NYC."
Joel:
"Retrospective?"
Lia:
"You are staying up late!"
Joel:
"Interesting, how is it going?"
Lia:
"It's interesting. How and who built it!"
Joel:
"Sometimes my eyes just won't close. I had stayed off my meds today, so I'm guessing that's why. I'm just tired of swallowing pills, Honey. They remind me of my hospital days! Aww!"
Lia:
"Good decision."
Joel:
"It's just for a day or two."
Lia:
"Don't take them if you don't need them!"
Joel:
"Pills are good, but I've got to consider my kidneys".
Lia:
"And your liver! What medication did they give you?"
Joel:
"Lol...them too. Turkish mostly, but they're pain relievers and some for cold and flu.
 I'll copy the names, give me a second."

Lia:
"Antibiotics are for a certain amount of time, then you are done. What do you need pain killers for? Where do you have pain?"

Joel:
"Levopront, this one's a syrup and that's definitely for the mucus and my chest. Got regular strepsils here, Nurofen, parasol, cold away for flu and cold etc. I'm feeling better now, my throat still hurts so I take a lot of tea."

Lia:
"I will look into them but it's not good to take so many together."

Joel:
"I don't. Some are finished and some remain, I've been taking them for over the course of the illness."

Lia:
"There are natural remedies for the throat depending on the severity."

Joel:
"Don't worry much. Thanks for the help as always. Love! My heroine, (Kiss face)"

Lia:
"Ok Baby, feel good!"

March 15, 2018, 8:48 PM

Lia:
"You are so sweet in the middle of the night!"

Joel:
"It's you. I'm not even being sweet."

Lia:
"You are very funny too?"

Joel:
"Lol...Well, I don't know?"

Lia:
"Try something natural, your kidneys and liver will thank you!"
Joel:
"Hey, I've got Lia fever, and I just realized that! That's maybe why I need you, my medicine!"
Lia:
"Levopront syrup, your medicine, can be used for 7 days only. Side effects are: Severe skin reactions, uneven heart function, hypoglycaemic coma, stomach pains, vomiting!"
Joel:
"Wow!"
Lia:
"Always check before you put something in your body. That's your job!"
Joel:
"I did take it for longer than 7 days, but I haven't gotten any reactions yet. Thank you for reading this. They didn't tell me about the date."
Lia:
"No problem."
Joel:
"Okay Dear."
Lia:
"My pleasure. Are you going to sleep tonight, or are you watching the moonlight?"
Joel:
"Lol...I shall go to sleep now my Love."
Lia:
"Ok you'll be fine. We all have taken some form of medicine when we need it. Sleep and Dream big my Love! Kisses…"

March 16, 2018, 1:12 PM

Joel:
"Hi Honey!"
Lia:
"Hey baby, how are you, lover?"
Joel:
"I'm good Honey! How's your day going?"
Lia:
"Very nice! Freezing my bones every time I go out!"
Joel:
"Lol, you're no Eskimo Honey!" Don't go out…Lol…"
Lia:

"I had to call everyone in FL last night, a major bridge collapsed across the highway, they just finished building. Lol…so the students from UM can cross the Highway. It killed 4 four people, maybe more, I have to see today! I am in the mood for some warm weather and swimming in the ocean."

Joel:

"Yes! I saw it! It's horrible. You don't have anyone involved, do you? Crappy construction job. Lol…I am too in the mood for swimming. I can't guarantee that if I enter the ocean though I will remain on this island. I shall swim across."
Lia:
"No, everyone is ok in FL. I tried getting you a boat but they didn't go that far."
Joel:
"We made it all the way past Greece. Lol…I'll swim this time!"
Lia:
"Did you receive your transfer?"

Joel:
"Bounced twice now. I'm not allowing negativity to consume me though."
Lia:
"Wow! How can that be? What about the place that sent the check here? Was that your money?"
Joel:
"Bank issues, transfer info wasn't right, bank beneficiary. For many reasons, I'm just tired and stressed. I can kill myself honestly!"
Lia:
"It has to match. The bank requires it. Just rest, it will be OK."
Joel:
"Okay Honey, it's just the financier is tired of me already going back and forth. Everyone is tired of me! (Broken heart)"
Lia:
"I am aware of this issue, you somehow have to solve this situation in a different way and make your way back!"
Joel:
"I know. What do you think I'm doing? I'm on it!"
Lia:
"Ok Honey! I love you! (Heart, kiss, flower)"
Joel:
"(Hearts)"

March 17, 2018, 10:18 AM
Joel:
"Morning my Love!"

March 17, 2018, 7:25 PM

Joel:
"Are you alright?

Lia:
"As long as I have you, I am always alright!" (Heart, kiss)
Sends Joel an email with a written Poem:

ROSES ARE RED, VIOLETS ARE BLUE, I SEE YOU!
"I have not met you yet, but I look for you in every man I see,
I have not seen you yet, but I look for you in everyone I meet,
I love to hear your voice and talk, laugh, and tell you stories,
Good and sometimes bad, sad, and happy, but every time,
I learn something new and amazing, to feel, to trust and to love!
Every day I wait to hear how you are and it is exciting all the time!
The days pass and I look for you, wait for you, run after you!
You've become my reflection and my shadow, my friend, and my Love, my sweet man whom I adore, whom I miss.
You are a man of mystery, passion, brave and headstrong, and you considering best for all.
I have not met you yet, but I know you so well, all of your smiles and tears, all of your wisdom and all your pleasures.
I have not seen you yet, but I look at the moon and see you,
I look at lovers and see you, I look in my heart and I see you,
I look for your face, I feel for you, I run for you, and I pray for you, that one day you will see me too!"

Joel:
" I love you!"
Lia:
"Thank you! How are you doing my love?"
Joel:
"Thinking about you, what marrying you would love to be like? (Heart)"
Lia:
"Imagination runs wild sometimes!"

Joel:
"Yeah, but I don't let it run far off."
Lia:
"Love or life or both? I know that about you. It boils down to what we choose to be in the
end!" (Rose)
Joel:
"Both (heart), with you and you alone. I choose to be for you!" (hearts)
Lia:
"You are the sweetest and I smooch you!!" (Kisses)
Joel:
"And you alone."
Lia:
"Otherwise, it will be menage a trois, like the wine my friend brought, now I have to finish
the bottle! Lol…."
Joel:
"Lol…are you drinking again Lia? "(Laughing faces)
Lia:
"Baby cat! I miss you so much!!
I invited my friends Vicky and Janet for dinner. Janet brings a bottle of wine called Menage a trois. I looked at her and she said, don't mind the title, it's really good wine! (Hysterical laughing face).
I am going to marry you and play your song at our wedding, La Vie En Rose!"
Joel:
"You amuse me! I love you so much! What are you up to?"
Lia:
"Imagine if I was serious."
Joel:
"Lol…noo. this is just right for me."
Lia:
"I love you!" (Kiss!)

Joel:
"A few more steps and we are there. I'm hanging on with all of my life!"
Lia:
"Think of Tarzan, every time you feel this way. You are swinging from tree to tree with all your might, in your nakedness, being pursued, and you make it to Jane's port where she is ready and waiting for you!" (Happy face)
Joel:
"Ha-ha...Tarzan though baby! Right now I am in the mood for Jasmine! Jane comes off as a little soft tonight!!"
Lia:
"Jasmine has plenty of new friends now and she is very happy. Opium is eyeing you but she will not have you until you come in person! You are stuck talking to me. Ha-ha...."
Joel:
"Just what I like to hear. I have my ways of bringing them to me, you just wait…"

LIA:

"Jasmine and Opium are my plants. I teased Joel and used their names to be creative with him.

It was just for fun and between us."

CHAPTER 12

JOEL AND LIA:

Lia:
"What do you want, baby cat?"
Joel:
"You, mind, body, and soul! (Heart, Rose, Magic Star), It's not too much to ask, is it?"
Lia:
"No, it's not! You are being your wonderful self in the middle of the night, and I wish I was there to embrace all that you are, my Love cat!"

March 17, 2018, 5:30 PM

JOEL:

"I will tell you again and again you are enough. You are incredibly enough."
Sends Email to Lia:

"Hello Darling,
Everything about you is just wonderful and I really do cherish the attributes you possess, all of them including, your love, I adore you. I like how considerate you are, I appreciate all you've done for me, you've kept a good attitude while doing what needed doing, even when it was an inconvenience to you, how you don't take anything personal but you come up with your sweet, sweet voice to help me relax.

You really do know how to make me feel good, and you make me feel so loved, so special even at times when I don't feel so good about myself. "

"Being here to support me means so much to me baby, I love your continuous love and care for us, and honestly, I have to admit it does make me miss having a family and a home.

I am sorry if I have ever said anything to offend you, it was never my intent to offend you, I never intend to hurt you, ever! Baby, you mean so much to me! And personally for me, you are everything, everything, everything and more!!

Your care and concern for our physical and emotional wellbeing is admirable! Thank you for loving me so well and so powerfully.

May the luck of the Irish St Patrick's day today guide us through a beautiful path through our relationship my love.

Thank you for your prayers <3, I love you. Everyday!"
Joel.

JOEL AND LIA:

March 18, 2018, 7:50 AM

Lia:
"(Heart, kiss)"
Of course, I am more than enough Darling!"
Joel:
"Always and every day!"
Lia:
"Having a pleasant day, Love?"
Joel:
"Can't complain. What are you up to?"
Lia:
"Just waking up and enjoying our conversation!"

Joel:
"Ha-ha…Come shower with me…It would be fun! No masks!"
Lia:
"I would love to!" (Flower)
Joel:
"Hurry! I'm waiting my Love!"
Lia:
"You better have some nice soap, I like to slither with it! I get to slither you with soap all over!! Then you have to follow instructions! I love the shower!!
You are getting me excited, my Man! Lol…. Let us just have a nice shower together!! (heart)"

March 18, 2018, 2:26 PM

Joel:
"Honey, <3"
Sends Lia an E- mail:

"My Love, here's to those that inspire you and don't even know it. Because of you, I laugh a little harder, cry a little less, and smile a lot more. Baby, thank you for being the behind my smile. I am thankful to you.

If only you knew how much the little moments I get to spend with you matter to me, growing through life, the one thing I've learned is that the best things in life comprise of the people you love, the places you've seen, and the memories you've made along the way.

Thank you for all the small things and the big ones, too. lol, don't give up on me baby. "

All my love, Joel

Lia:
"Thank you too, baby!"
Joel:
"How are you, baby? You had lunch?"
Lia:
"Good, thank you! I did have lunch already, babe! Staying warm! So It's so cold today! What are you up to tonight?"
Joel:
"I'm indoors, I can't do anything now."
Lia:
"Enjoy the indoors! Be cozy! (Heart, kiss)"
Joel:
"I want you here, nothing makes me more cozy the more!"
Lia:
"OK, I'll be there. Can we get jobs in North Cyprus? Maybe we can live there and work ourselves out or not!" (Crazy face)
Joel:
"I can never subject you to a life here."
Lia:
"Why did you go there? Lol…"

March 18, 2018, 3:56 PM

Joel:
"My task is to remove myself from this place and get back to you!".
Lia:
"Ok Honey! Best thing I've heard so far!"
Joel:
"I love you. What are you doing?"
Lia:
"Working on the laptop!" (Kiss, heart)
Joel:
"How is it going? You've been quiet about it! No news means good, Yes?"

Lia:
"Nothing to tell. I am doing revisions and testing. Nothing interesting!"
Joel:
"I love you!"
Lia:
"(Heart)"

March 19, 2018, 7:34 AM

Joel:
"Woke up to the sound of wedding bells ringing in my head! You're the reason I ever have a sound like that ringing to me. I love you! (heart) Baby!!"

March 19, 2018, 8:51 AM

Lia:
"Being on an island for long can make you lose your mind sometimes! Despite your good thoughts you are not able to propose marriage to me. Have a wonderful day and enjoy! May it all go well. I love you!! Actions speak louder than words even though I love all your words!" (Heart, kiss)

March 20, 2018, 10:13 AM

Joel:
"How are you baby cats?" (heart)
Lia:
"Good Darling! How was your day?" (Kiss, kiss)
Joel:
"I'm okay my Love, I'm out in town tonight. I'm getting my energy up!"
Lia:
"Good! Enjoy! (Heart, kiss)"

Joel:
"What are you up to my Love?"

March 20, 2018, 12:37 PM

Lia:
"Just got out of exercise class. Going to have some lunch now! Did you have a nice day babe?" (flower)

March 20, 2018, 2:42 PM

Lia:
"(Love cat, heart, moneybag, lucky fly, sunflower)"
Joel:
"Honey! (Love cat)"
Lia:
"What are you up to my Love cat?"
Joel:
"I'm just relaxing, I took a walk down today to ease my mind. I came back this evening to take a nap and sleep again!"
Lia:
"Good. Feeling good? But it's evening there now? Did you have dinner yet?"
Joel:
"Yes my Love. Before coming back in for a nap. Pretty sure that's what weighed me down."
Lia:
"Glad you feel better now!" (Kiss face)

LIA:

"Joel had surprisingly received a wire transfer from his source, but it was held up by the bank and it took a long time before it came in and he was able to use it for payment, so he said."

"He was short and needed 40K in addition to the wire he received, and he was hinting that I was the one that had to get it.

I was spent and borrowed out and was paying back the notes with high interest and I was not able to even think of coming up with more money.

I was seriously considering getting a job myself and going back to work as an employee because my online businesses were brand new and I was not certain how it was going to go.

I had a credit line at the bank which we used to complete my work and run ads and we had used it all up and now it had to be paid back on top of all the notes I had borrowed for Joel.

I knew that somehow, I needed to restructure, or he needed to come back fast and pay me back.
I was not sure what was going to happen first.

Joel was being sweet and saying amorous words but I was beginning to tire of the repetitive pattern which always led to him needing more of my money.

I just wanted him back so that we could be free of all this money hunting and be together."

QUEEN ELIZABETH ENAHORO:

"Since Queen Elizbeth Enahoro had seized all the ownership paperwork and Joel could not provide the bank with the required documents for transfer, his transfer was rejected several times until Joel agreed to have it deposited into the business account that Queen Elizabeth Enahoro had taken over while Joel was in her jail cell."

"Joel had no choice but to iron things out with her and hope that she would use the transfer money to pay off the contract taxes and fees which required payment.

He was at her mercy and his entire business project depended on how things would proceed between them. He was so upset and hated the situation he was in and was trying his hardest to figure out a way to change the impossible circumstances he had put himself into.

As usual, he never said a word to me about any of this, and I only knew what he told me to be true."

JOEL AND LIA:

Joel:
"What are you doing? Hope it's not as busy as it was yesterday for you? Hope you've had lunch?"
Lia:
"I had a manufacturer call me today who is stuck with cotton pants. Lol…why me?
Joel:
"Wow, you've got a handful of work to deal with."
Lia:
"I don't want to do this or talk to these people, this just diverts me to nowhere.
I have my own stuff which I need to concentrate on. But you asked if my day was less busy than yesterday, and the answer may be no, yesterday was worse!!
But tomorrow! Lol…will be having fun if we get the promised 6-8" of snow! Lunch was very good!"
Joel:
"Lol…8? Wow!! Can you stay indoors tomorrow?"
Lia:
"Let's see if it happens! Sure!"

Joel:
"Please! Thank you. I worry about you!"
Lia:
"Why baby! I have to go out to play at some point! But I appreciate your concern Love!!"
Joel:
"I wish I could get to play with you, my Love!"
Lia:
"Hurry up!! I am beginning to think you are glued to that island!"
Joel:
"Lol… nope! My ass is glued to you alone!"
Lia:
"Better be!"
Joel:
"(Wondering face)"
Lia:
"I love you! (Laughing face)"
Joel:
"My star! You make me feel great every time!"
Lia:
"I am glad you feel good! No more headaches!"
Joel:
"No, No more headaches, baby!"
Lia:
"Ok Good!"
Joel:
"Are you home, though?"
Lia:
"Yes"
Joel:
"Okay, did you get to do the shopping, you said you would do today?"
Lia:
"Yes darling, all done. Now I am making dinner! Thank you for reminding me!"

Joel:
"Okay, Honey! You're welcome! What are you making for dinner?"
Lia:
"Quiche and meat pie, one for today and the other for tomorrow. You are welcome for dinner!"
Joel:
"I like meat pies, so we've got to have that tonight."
Lia:
"This one is delicious".
Joel:
"Is it dinner time yet?"
Lia:
"Not yet, sweets! Has to bake in the oven."
Joel:
"(Cannot believe it face)"
Lia:
"Are you hungry?"
Joel:
"For what you are cooking? I'm starving!"
Lia:
"(Kisses)"

March 21, 2018, 8:51 AM

Joel:
"Good morning, sugar, hope you had a wonderful night!"
Lia:
"I did have a very nice night, thank you! Now the snow blizzard has begun, and we are all home enjoying the vision from indoors! How is your day? Productive I hope?"
Joel:
"Yes, it is baby. I'm glad you're Okay. What are you doing, how is the storm and snow baby?"

Lia:
"It's a big storm, snow is coming down heavily and it's only 9:20 AM. Lol…it will be fun in the park later!! It's going to be a Spring winter wonderland!!"

March 21, 2018, 10:28 AM

Joel:
"Hehe...Take pictures, Honey!"
Lia:
"I will, darling! It's an exciting storm!"
Joel:
"Ha-ha! And be safe!"
Lia:
"Will do, thank you! Have a good one!"

March 21, 2018, 1:27 PM

Lia:
SENDS PICTURE TO JOEL OF THE SNOW IN NYC
Lia:
"Still snowing, but it's not so bad yet! Will see what happens tonight. Lol…" (Love cat)
Joel:
"Too much…Too fucking much!!"
Lia:
"Baby Cat! How are you doing? What is new?"

March 21, 2018, 5:12 PM

Joel:
"(Heart) He's not answering his phone now, my translator. I don't know why?"
Lia:
"Who is your translator?"

Joel:
"I needed him to get information for a previous man that who helped us with a payment we had made before baby. Hassan! Tried reaching him all day today, but no answer."
Lia:
"He does not answer his phone and my number was blocked from his phone!"
Joel:
"He blocked you?"
Lia:
"Why do you want to go back to a man who sold you off?"
Joel:
"Ah, forget him. I don't need him. I need details from a man I had met sometime back.
 I gave him that contact to keep safe, and I need it!"
Lia:
"Why did you give safe safe-keeping things to him?"
Joel:
"We were working, he was with me all the time, it only felt right to give him a phone number to keep for me."
Lia:
"E-mail anything you want stored, and I will resend it to you! Lol..."
Joel:
"Sure. Okay, my Love!"
Lia:
"Is there another way to find this man?"
Joel:
"I don't need him as much, baby! Don't worry! I'll check through my own emails and all."
Lia:
"Ok! I called Hassan 100 times when you were away, and the calls were rejected!
It made me go out of my mind!! Ok, Honey! Stay safe. Are you making progress in your case?"

Joel:
"It's been a day! Progress is slow, but I'll push on! Don't have no choice but me, right?"
Lia:
"Funny I heard. I heard about a similar situation from another friend's friend who is trying to get out of Portugal. Interesting!"
Lia:
SENDS JOEL A PICTURE OF THE SNOW IN CENTRAL PARK
Joel:
"What were you doing all day through the storm, Honey?"
Lia:
"Thinking about you and me!"
Joel:
"What thoughts?? I want to know! Oh...these pictures are wonderful! Makes me feel like I'm right inside the snow with you. I see now why you're thinking of me and you both!"
Lia:
"I went to the park just for your eyes only! Yes baby, I told you, you are always with me!"
Joel:
"It's come through twice. There's nothing stopping it. It's just having the fucking man to go all the way to the bank and have it sent again! He claims he's working with other clients!"
Lia:
"What does this mean?"
Joel:
"I'm pressuring him to go do it for me, but he does not seem to be bothered. He's insisting he's booked until Monday. So, I have to wait baby!"
Lia:
"Something fishy about this, you better check tomorrow! Where is the money from the transfer now?"

Joel:
"No, it's in safe hands, I am certain of it! Don't worry about that 100K, I'll have to kill someone before I let anyone get to it!"
Lia:
"I thought it was for 120K on the transfer?"
Joel:
"It is, I'm rounding up. 120K"
Lia:
"You are losing money on the exchange of the money. Lol...maybe you'll gain on the Turkish lira?"
Joel:
"Yes, I know. And right now, the Turkish lira is gaining on the dollar!"
Lia:
"I had a lot of bills which went out this month and I have to see if I can divert the accountant but will send a small amount to tie you over for the weekend. You do need help from an angel. Please find the angel!!"
Joel:
"If you don't have much, please hold on to it. I can manage the weekend, my Love!"
Lia:
"Whatever you want, Darling!"
Joel:
"I love you!"
Lia:
"I love you too!"
Joel:
"What are you doing? I can't sleep. Have you had dinner yet?"
Lia:
"Skipping dinner tonight! I just came back from exercise class, so I am not hungry!"
Joel:
"Are you sure baby?"

Lia:
"I'm sure. Tomorrow is another day and there are plenty of calories waiting for me!"
Joel:
"Baby, you know how I feel about skipping dinner!"
Lia:
"You are my dinner tonight! I just want you! It's so funny, Tara cleaned her room and wanted to get the vacuum but she doesn't know how the vacuum works and forgot the hose that attaches to the vacuum, so she vacuumed on her hands and knees with the smaller hose. I was dying!
Let the housekeeper teach her to vacuum! He…heh..."
Joel:
"(Laughing faces). No way! It's 2018, h. How does she not know how it works? I'm dead! This just made my night!"
Lia:
"She is like a Princess! She has no interest in anything domestic. No cooking, cleaning, nothing! Just works and goes out! Her boyfriend has to do everything for her! Hysterics!!"
Joel:
"I'm blown! I want to be like her!!"
Lia:
"Will get you a housekeeper and you'll have me. That should do it! At least she vacuumed and cleaned up! Looks nice now!"
Joel:
"Thank you but I'll not be King, at least not like her."
Lia:
"Why not?"
Joel:
"Well, it comes naturally to her as you can see. Her Mother is of Royal blood baby! I'm just a man!"

Lia:
"Why, you like to vacuum? You are a good man Joel, and don't you forget that I know it. My heart turns every day and I wish I could do everything for you!" (Heart, kiss)

Joel:
"(Hearts), What aches me the most is the fact I have drawn you to this. My life, I feel crashed the moment I got the one wish I had always prayed for, I want to show you the world Lia! I am sorry it's taking this long and this much hurt!"

Lia:
"Baby, please try to free yourself from this unending chain. I have your heart and will stand by you always!"

Joel:
"I love you. You're the best!"

Lia:
"I love you too and we will see the world together! (Heart, roses), Our world, with our eyes!"

Joel:
"Thank you Honey. You're so comforting!"

Lia:
"(Kisses), Try to rest my Darling! It's so late for you. Sleep is your escape, indulge in it!"

Joel:
"Alright my Love. Thank you!"

Lia:
"Smooch and hug and hold! All three at once!" (King)

March 22, 2018, 6:59 AM

Joel:
"With you I feel only completeness, it takes me to a point where I can feel the slow individual beats to your heart. It's so hard to conceal the weakness caused by you but if I told you just how deep my love really goes for you and that you got all my trust, if you knew, tell me what you would do?"

"If I told you that you're worth the world and it's love to me, if I told you that I wanna continue a family with you someday, if I told you that I wanna grow old together with you, what would you say? If I was to let you know I wanna see forever with you, would you run away? If I told you I wanna be your drive, your strength and courage when you're weak, if I said that I send my angels out every night to protect you in your sleep, I'll I'd do anything for your happiness.

All I ever want to do is to love you, everything I have is yours and only yours and nothing like you has ever touched my soul like this before, it just feels so right. I love you!"
Lia:
"You are my Man and I am ready to take on and be everything with you! I love you! (heart)"
Joel:
"This is what I live for, your love, the whole of it. I love you!"

March 22, 2018, 5:07 PM

Joel:
"Hi, Honey!"
Lia:
"Hey babe! How do you feel?"
Joel:
"My head hurts baby, other than that I'm Okay. It hurts, I can't sleep!"
Lia:
"Take some aspirin and relax! You have to get some sleep or you will get sick! Love you baby!"
Joel:
"I love you more."
Lia:
"(Kisses)"

Joel:
"I have no more aspirins left so I'm just trying to relax. It's the stress I know, so I'll be alright tomorrow!"
Lia:
"Lol...why are you tense...nothing is happening till Monday, so why stress? Calm down and relax. Rest, you were up all night last night, tonight the same, you are going to drop! Go to sleep, you will feel better and drink water!"
Joel:
"Hmm... Okay, baby!"
Lia:
"(King figure), Do you like him?"
Joel:
"Who's him, Honey?"
Lia:
"King with a crown on the head!"
Joel:
"I had a feeling you were talking about him."
Lia:
"I'm looking for some new ones!"
Joel:
'Ha-he. Are there any? I doubt there'd be any better! This fits perfectly!"
Lia:
"This is perfect but I wish they made them a little bigger!"
Joel:
"(Hysterical face) I've got the bigger one!"
Lia:
"How do you get the bigger ones?"
Joel:
"Lol...It comes factory fitted with the King my love! "ME."
Lia:
"You better find the Queen one and send it here! We are talking about emojis, No?"
Joel:
"You're the Queen silly!! "(Confused face)

Lia:
"Are you up? Close your eyes my Man and rest that head of yours! Your Queen orders you to do so!!"

March 23, 2018, 7:35 AM

Lia:
"Baby cat!! How are you? How is your head feeling?"
Joel:
"My Love! I'm okay, how are you, baby?"
Lia:
"Good!"
Joel:
"Good morning, did you sleep well, Honey?"
Lia:
"I did, Darling. Good morning!" (kiss)."

March 23, 2018, 11:18 AM

Lia:
"Honey cakes, (Love cat)"

March 23, 2018, 2:04 PM

Joel:
"Hi baby, I've been away all day!"
Lia:
"Where have you been? (Love cat)"

March 23, 2018, 5:29 PM

Joel:
"I'm sorry I disappeared again!

LIA:

"Joel's business partner Queen Elizabeth Enahoro had surmised that Joel's amorous affections were not for her and in a jealous rage decided to commit herself to doing everything possible to keep Joel where he is and detain him so that he never gets to meet Lia and he remains in her grasp and mercy and she vows that he will be hers one day soon!

She did not tell Joel of her plot, and he did not know her plan, of trying to ruin everything he had worked for on his contract.

She held all his ownership documents and his passport, and without these in a foreign country and without money access, his contract and vision were being erased."

CHAPTER 13

JOEL AND LIA:

March 23, 2018, 9:36 PM

Lia:
SENDS JOEL A PRAYER

March 24, 2018, 7:33 AM

Joel:
"I cannot get the money baby, not yet at least! I'll have to provide an invoice as requested by the government. I'll try to sort that out this week and see what happens. It's why the money has been returned twice!"
Lia:
"I told you that! You need the amount of payment requested in writing. It's the way to do it. It will protect you in the end. They should have given you the invoice in the first place. Most important."

March 24, 2018, 9:33 AM

Joel:
"Baby, baby..."

March 24, 2018, 5:26 PM

Joel:
"Honey, (Wondering face)"
Lia:
"(Kisses)"
Joel:
"I miss you! How are you, my Queen?"

Lia:
"Wonderful! (Butterfly, heart) I miss you, my King!"
Joel:
"Honey, it will be over soon. I need your body and touch also, and I'm so craving you!"
(Queen, Butterfly, heart).
Lia:
"I'm so craving you too!"
Joel:
"What are you doing, Honey?"
Lia:
"In the car going back to Manhattan!"
Joel:
"(Puzzled face)"

March 24, 2018, 7:34 PM

Lia:
"My cousin had a birthday party in New Jersey!"
(Sends Joel a song," Happy" by Ferrell, on youtube.com)

March 25, 2018, 11:12 AM

Joel:
"Hey baby"
Lia:
"How was your weekend?"
Joel:
"It's going alright, Honey, nothing exciting, the weather is good and mild, perfect for taking walks and reflecting on a lot of things. How was your weekend, my love?"
Lia:
"Very fun birthday dinner celebration on Saturday. Today a funeral for Harriette. Sweet and sour all in one weekend. I'm torn in half! Glad you had a reflecting weekend! What did you reflect on?"

Joel:
"Lost time... (broken heart)"
Lia:
"Yes, heart breaking! But the good note is that we still have each other!" (heart)
Joel:
"(Heartbroken, cry face), We do, I do, You do!"
Lia:
"(Heart, kiss) I wish I can wrap myself around you!"
Joel:
"I love you more with every passing day!"
Lia:
"(Heart, kiss)"

March 25, 2018, 8:23 PM

Joel:
"I miss you terribly, my Love. My nights and days are filled with the wonders of your love.
You are simply the stars of my dream! Thank you, baby, for being that special woman for me!"
Lia:
"You are welcome, but I miss you more! (Heart, kisses)"

March 26, 2018, 8:06 AM

Lia:
SENDS JOEL A FUNNY PICTURE OF A CAT

March 26, 2018, 1:53 PM

Joel:
"Honey!"
Lia:
"What is doing Love?"

Joel:
"I'll call you."
Lia:
"Ok. Call me tomorrow at 10 AM, and I will be out tonight!"
Joel:
"Okay, you're fine?"
Lia:
"Yes baby, I am in class now and then going to dinner. Not I'm not sure when I will be back, and I don't want to hold you up. Kisses (heart)"
Joel:
"I figured., it's okay, baby, just enjoy!"

March 27, 7:50 AM

Lia:
"Thank you, baby! (kiss)

March 27, 11:43 AM

Joel:
"My love!"
Lia:
"I love you and miss you to pieces!" (heart)

March 27, 2018, 1:35 PM

Joel:
"I honestly am trying all my best to get this money over. Sad but I feel I have offended G-d and I need to ask for forgiveness! I feel terrible coming to you like this! I want to be independent of you financially. Give breathing space that you've totally expected and not expect so much of you.
I love you so much baby!"
Lia:
"How did you offend G-d?"

Joel:
"Everything just keeps breaking me."
Lia:
"Maybe G-d is trying to point you in another direction?"
Joel:
"Simply transferring my own money has now become a thing to stress baby. I have nothing on me and my world keeps crushing! A week since I've heard from my own daughter. Nothing is in place. Do you see why I feel I have offended Him? So much just keeps putting me at a disadvantage."
Lia:
"I feel you! Try to keep your emotions intact. There is always a reason why things work out the way they do. Small money is not your problem but the big bucks that you need is virtually impossible for you unless you release some of your own money. You may be able to receive one transfer, if this one is real, but two, I have to see it to believe it!"
Joel:
"One transfer still hasn't gone through, not to talk of the second. I'm still stressing on having one come through. I am losing my mind!"
Lia:
"Look, let's be adults here, the one transfer is nothing without the second. The first is not enough and how long can you hold on to it until the rest comes in! It's unending! The rest which you have no promise of ever getting? So, what is the solution here? You need to do something else besides waiting and asking others for funds. Do you have funds of your own?"
Joel:
"I've been here too long with nothing to show. I need at least one transfer to show I'm serious about it. I can't unlimitedly stay here on their land, a land that isn't mine?"

"No one would permit me to, and I also honestly am tired of playing the waiting game. I would ask you to get me the other 40K, I need for this to end, but you'll say you are tied up!

If we had paid this since I was in jail, we would've possibly gotten me out of here by now, but we got distracted and chased the most irrelevant of thoughts. I honestly am so disappointed and so ashamed Lia, my heart breaks every night at our misfortune.

So many other nights I take long walks into the dark thinking to only jump off a cliff or drown myself and have this sad, sad story end."

Lia:
"Baby, what are you saying to me? Show you are serious to whom for what? You want to pay it off, find me the funds? I gave you all that I have. But why can't you release some of yours?

I cannot give you what I don't have! And please answer my question!"

Joel:
"You know that I would never go through this or let you go through this if I had a way of freeing my funds from here. Both banks have me tied down. My bank won't even respond to me now and the one form my employers still just has our details running. They're not approved or functional so we can't even tap into that until this is cleared. Waiting and asking others for funds from others though ...."

Lia:
"If you jump off a cliff the story would be much sadder for me. You have not been in this game alone. Don't forget who has funded who here. Do not be angry with the wrong source even if you don't feel good about things!"

Joel:
"Wow, Lia, wow, baby! This is all so wrong!"

Lia:
"Do you have funds in Wells Fargo?"

Joel:
"Now this is how I get spoken to! Yes, I do, you know I do!"
Lia:
"You are speaking that way to me!"
Joel:
"That's the account that got frozen in the first place to start with. My money!! And I have no access to it!! I'm shocked you think that all this while I would have an option to release funds but decided to pressure you, Donald and even go to jail before. It's silly to think I could do all this while I never did!"

March 27, 2018, 4:13 PM

Lia:
"Can you get a statement from your bank stating that the money required is there but needs you to go get it?"

March 27, 2018, 5:20 PM

Lia:
"(Hearts), please contact shlomo33@gmail.com and see if he can find the rest of your money!"

March 28, 2018, 8:12 AM

Joel:
"Good morning my Love (heart), Sleeping well my Love?"
Lia:
"Yes, thank you! Having a good day? This unusual situation which you are in is one which you will have the responsibility to guide and get out of on your own, it's very complicated and only you understand it.
When your heart wants to find mine nothing in the world will stop you from doing that."

"If you choose not to, no magic wand will force you to do otherwise! I leave you in G-ds hands, he is the master of these kinds of events. His plan for us will come to be if we do our part and we wish it to be.
Godspeed with you, I love you so much, never you forget that, and my heart hurts every minute you are away from me. I wish I had a magic wand to make it easier for you, but I am just a simple girl with a heart tattooed with your name!" (hearts)
Joel:
"I don't know how to respond to this!"

LIA:

"Queen Elizabeth Enahoros restrictions and document seizures had gotten to Joel in a big way once he found out about her deceptive plan to keep him in her grasp. He was furious but had his hands tied and was left without resources which meant that somehow he had to agree and give into her ploy without saying anything to me!"

JOEL AND LIA:

March 28, 2018, 11:59 AM

Joel:
"Babe"
Lia:
"Hi honey! In the car going to another funeral. Our friend Jeff died. Please come home soon. I am so sad!!"
Joel:
"I am so sad. This is such bad news. I'm sorry!"
Lia:
"Thank you! (Heart)"

Joel:
"Please accept my condolences. May his soul rest in peace. I am so sorry my Love!"
Lia:
"Thank you."
Joel:
"Are you okay?"
Lia:
"Just sad! I am OK Honey! Thank you for your support!"
Joel:
"Hey, let me know when you're okay and can talk, I'll call you. (heart) I love you!!"
Lia:
"Ok baby!"

March 28, 2018, 1:49 PM

Joel:
"(Hearts), I'll always be here for you. Remember this!"

March 28, 2018, 4:15 PM

Lia:
"Thank you! But here is too far away, I want you beside me."
Joel:
"You know what I mean. You're harsh on me today. Watch it babe!"

March 28, 2018, 6:13 PM

Lia:
"You know what I mean too. Why are you so harsh today?"
Joel:
"Okay baby let's calm down. Who got you mad today??"
Lia:
"I don't want to fight with you!"

Joel:
"Me? I'm not harsh babe, I'm scared to talk to you for not knowing what else you'd say to me. You see what I mean?"
Lia:
"Tomorrow, I will send you some money if you need it! (Kiss), I am sorry to write so late to you. I am still at the funeral. Long day!"
Joel:
"Just call me when you're done with everything and rested at home. I would love to hear you talk. It's the one thing that calms me regardless of what wreck I'm in!"
Lia:
"I love you!"
Joel:
"(Heart)"

March 29, 2018, 7:36 AM

Joel:
"Hey, baby!"
Lia:
"Hi, Honey!"
Joel:
"I miss you!
Lia:
"Same"
Joel:
"You slept well? How was your night?"
Lia:
"I was exhausted, so I slept well. Just waking up to another busy day! How is your day today?"
Joel:
"I know, I figured my Love! I was exhausted. I'm still exhausted. There's an e-mail address you sent me that I want to look into today. I'm indoors and it's raining outside. Cold weather so my mind is constantly on you".

Lia:
"Stay warm my Love. Try and see if he can fix you up with the rest of the money!
I told him I have a note that needs to be paid and is looking for 100K. Try, he is connected with a lot of investors and may be able to get you financing or a financier.
He asked a lot of questions which I did not know the answers to, you will give, so you will sort it out! If he does not respond right away it will be because Passover starts tomorrow, and he is away until the Holiday ends so do not be discouraged."

Joel:
"Okay my Love, thank you so much! (hearts), I won't be discouraged. Baby, I have nothing else I haven't tried. Fingers crossed something comes out of this. I'm being positive."

Lia:
"Yes."

Joel:
"How was your day, Honey?"

Lia:
"The whole day yesterday was very sad. Jeff was the kindest, sweetest, most intelligent, successful man with an amazing wife and two beautiful daughters who had everything to live for. His golden life was cut so short by cancer. We buried him and went back to their home for the family's comfort. Saw a lot of people and it was a long day and evening!
I think of you during this time because it makes me realize how short life is and how much we need to make the most of life since we never know how it goes."

Joel:
"(Broken heart), I am so, so sorry!"

Lia:
"We need to live! Thank you."

Joel:
"Are my calls going through to you, baby? Honey!"
Lia:
"No!! It's very hard to understand your words on the phone. Crackling sound all the time!
I'll call you in a bit. Just give me a moment Love."
Joel:
"My network is horrible because of the local where I am."
Lia:
"It's OK, I will try."
Joel:
"Okay, baby"
Lia:
"Let's talk by text, easier. But it's always good to hear your voice!"
Joel:
"Phone died, I got a little too excited."
Lia:
"Heart, kiss!"
Joel:
"I do miss your voice already! Oh, you always make me laugh! You always get me excited!"
Lia:
"I like that! Same!"
Joel:
"It's stopped raining here. The weather is just beautiful! Air smells nice!"
Lia:
"Wonderful!"
Joel:
"Lol...I don't know what my obsession with fresh smelling air is. It's so nice and relaxing.
Might give into your idea of just imagining my vacation and taking a chill day!"

Lia:
"I noticed the smell of fresh air yesterday in the country. It is very relaxing and pleasant.
Have a nice vacation! Relax and enjoy!"
Joel:
"Thank you, Love."
Lia:
"(Kisses)"
Joel:
"I've got the name here for the transfer, whenever you're ready.
Surname: Sibanda
First name: Heather
North Cyprus
I'm starving, babe, everything is becoming harder by the day. I'll go try to get something I can eat. (heart)"
Lia:
"Just sent it. You should get a copy of your passport so you can pick up your money. I told you I have a restriction on third parties."
Joel:
"Yes. You do. You have told me before, but we've been good ever since, until Hassan!"
Lia:
"Just try to do it the way I am asking because I will get restricted and will not be able to do anything more for you!"
Joel:
"What restrictions do you mean, babe?"
Lia:
"FBI monitoring restrictions."
Joel:
"Okay, I understand, I love you! Don't worry about the FBI. I'm sure those are only threats."
Lia:
"Who is Heather?"

Joel:
"She works at the WU office; I don't have a passport, nor do I have Hassan anymore. I had to plead for help, and she came through."
Joel:
"How much is it, baby? There's no amount on the slip."
Lia:
"$1000."
Joel:
"Alright, thank you. Thank you so much!"
Joel:
"(Calls and asks if Lia can give him another $500 on top of the $1000, she just sent.)"
Lia:
"You are welcome, please understand that I can do a lot of other things with the money I send you. I am not required to send you any if I don't want to. Asking for more only makes me feel inadequate, and I don't want to have that feeling in my soul. I understand how it may be for you, but I do have a choice."
Joel:
"Why do you say this? I'm so grateful to you. There's no need for this, honey really.
I love you, and I thank you. This shouldn't come up between us again, baby cats!"
Lia:
"OK (heart)."

March 29, 2018, 1:47 PM

Joel:
"How's it going, Honey?"
Lia:
"(Heart)"

March 29, 2018, 3:54 PM

Lia:
"Are you occupied with something important?"
Joel:
"Dinner and a conversation with Faruk."
Lia:
"Lol…"
Joel:
"You done cooking?"
Lia:
"Not yet!"
Joel:
"Shlomo hasn't left my mind, don't worry!!"
Lia:
"Yes, but if you miss him today you may not get him for another week if you miss him today."
Joel:
"I have sent him a short e-mail."
Lia:
"Good, Let's see what happens next! (heart)"

March 29, 2018, 9:30 PM

Joel:
"Chag Sameach, baby!!"
Lia:
"Thank you, same to you! Happy Passover. Wish I wish you were here." (Heart, flower)
Joel:
"Happy Passover Darling!" (hearts)

Joel writes an Email to Lia:

"Put aside the negatives that's happened in the past week or so, our life together is already amazing, and I have no doubts that together, it will only get better and better.

I will forever be grateful that you came into my life and have since been making my dreams brighter. Baby, together, we're perfect, and I also have no doubts that I know we will enjoy spending the rest of our lives together.

You are a charming, gorgeous, sincere, caring, loving woman, and I wouldn't trade you for the world baby, all the words in the world cannot describe how I feel about you!

I use the word "love" only for the lack a better word to describe how I feel for you. Honey, I am so thankful and blessed that you love me as equally as I love you and maybe even more, I'm sorry that you miss me and I promise again that I'll do all I can today to get this sorted out, I will not disrespect that you made me your Man. I love you with my whole heart.

I trust you and Lia, honestly since my mother, I have not trusted anyone the way I trust you. You are my true love and you've given me no reason not to love you, you've been positive with me through everything and I thank you for that,

I thank you for your love and support both physically and emotionally my Darling, I know deep down inside that you will never break my heart or let me down in any way and I'll soon come to you, I'll find a way of getting out of this mess baby though I can't be home in time for Passover!"

"I know, I really am looking forward to spending the Amazing rest of my life with you.
Every day I love you more,
Joel."

March 30, 2018, 9:13 AM

Lia:
"I love you!" (Love cat)

March 30, 2018, 11:55 AM

Joel:
"My baby! How are you?" (Love cats)
Lia:
"Real good Honey! It's all coming together. Will take a shot and send it later when done!
Love you!" (Heart)
Joel:
"Okay, my Love. I love you!" (Heart, flower)

March 30, 2018, 4:34 PM

Lia:
SENDS JOEL A PICTURE OF HER PASSOVER TABLE
Joel:
"Hi, Honey! (Hearts, love faces) you're magnificent! It is set so gorgeous! Has your touch and taste all over it. Oh, my G-d! "
Lia:
"Thank you! It was a little tricky because the Passover set of dishes was for 8 and I have 9 coming. How do you get another soup bowl? I found one mug in ceramic and will have to do this time. I thought I had 11 coming and I hope I did, and I hope I will not forget them. Lol…"

Joel:
"Lol…these things happen, Love! Don't sweat it! You're well known for this type of hosting and you're always efficient and more than capable."

Lia:
"I am not! Just laughing at it all! Now comes the hard part. What to wear?? I wish I had someone to dress me!"

Joel:
"What are your options? Show me. I'll be your stylist!"

Lia:
SENDS JOEL A PICTURE OF CHOICE OF DRESSES FOR DINNER

Lia:
"Which one? I don't know whether to be casual or put on a dress?"

Joel:
"Hmm... tough choice. Casual seems to be a wonderful option but the setup of how your table is and the fact that you're the host my love prompts towards you wearing a dress. I'll say "dress" my Love."

Lia:
"Okay, which one do you like?"

Joel:
"I want to see the grey one on you."

Lia:
"Somehow Passover reminds me of your trip. Perhaps with some reflection and prayer we can make your passage to freedom a reality this year. Will miss you so much at the table. Will save you some food and desert. (Heart, flower, kiss)".

Joel:
"(Love faces), Oh my Darling! You are the best and you deserve the world!"

Lia:
"With the crazy silver skirt! It's a fun one!"

Joel:
"I love you dearly!"
Lia:
"I love you so much!"
Joel:
"Ha-ha... Yup, I just did another look at it and thought it was."
Lia:
"You cannot imagine how cold it is. House is freezing!"
Joel:
"Wear something warm then."
Lia:
"Ok, Honey, Thank you! What are you up to?"
Joel:
"Lying down staring at the ceiling and talking to you, my Love. There isn't much to do and I don't move around much at night, so I don't wake the house owners. You baby?"
Lia:
"You can go and have dinner with the Rabbis Family! You never know what happens, you might get much more than dinner. Another opportunity to meet people."
Joel:
"Okay, I'll try to search for it, my Love."
Lia:
"Ph: 90-533-8-770-888"
Joel:
"I love you!"
Lia:
"(Love cat), The only man who came to look for you while you were in the Hospital, The one who gave me the lawyer who searched for you, called me several times if he can do something! Very, very nice."

March 31, 2018, 8:50 AM

Joel:
"(Heart,) Baby!"
Lia:
"Hi baby, I cannot move!
It was wonderful, delicious, and fun! Lots of beautiful flowers. Amazing cake, just the Best!
I wore a grey sweatshirt with a silver pleated skirt, very cute on!"
Joel:
"Ha-ha... Why?"
Lia:
"So tired!"
Joel:
"This is when you need me the most."
Lia:
"Yes!"
Joel:
"I'm at your service!"
Lia:
"(Butterfly, kisses)"
Joel:
"(Kiss faces, heart)"
Lia:
"All for you, my Love!"
SENDS JOEL A PICTURE OF THE FLOWERS AT PASSOVER
Joel:
"And did you take pictures of yourself, baby?"
Lia:
"No, Honey!"
Joel:
"Oh... these are beautiful! Oh, my G-d. You're the most amazing!" (hearts)

Lia:
"You want to laugh now, it's 11 AM, everyone is sleeping. I'm up! They are exhausted! Imagine!"
Joel:
"Lol… (laughing faces), thank you for this baby! "
Lia:
"(Heart, kiss face)"

March 31, 2018, 2:35 PM

Lia:
"My gorgeous Man! (Heart, kiss)."
Joel:
"My Love! You're, OK?"
Lia:
"Yes babe! What a gorgeous day today, I must say what a difference a day makes. Beautiful outside!! Had a nice walk in the park. It's getting busy there though because they are hunting for rabbits and eggs, carrots! Lol…"
Joel:
"(Flowers) I want to be with you!"
Lia:
"You are with me".

March 31, 2018, 5:38 PM

Joel:
"How's your day been my Love?"
Lia:
"Very nice day, Honey!"

April 1, 2018, 9:42 AM

Joel:
"Good morning, my Love! Happy Easter!"

Lia:
"I miss you more than ever!" (hearts)

LIA:

"Joel and I were conversing lightly. Text and long telephone conversations were done almost every day. We talked about everything and everyone we both knew but not so much of what was happening with his contract and money and not a mention of him making any plans to come home.

I was disillusioned with his entire mayhem but wanted him and hoped that one day he would succeed and surprise me. It looked to me as if it would never happen. He kept asking for more money and time was just passing by!"

JOEL AND LIA:

April 1, 2018, 1:52 PM

Joel:
"(Flower, smile face), a flower to boost your smile on this wonderful day!"
Lia:
"Kisses and hugs to you. Thank you! Good Holidays to inspire you!
No matter what obstacles they had they found a way to cross the Red Sea and find freedom and even death could not keep Jesus in a tomb! They found a way to escape their state of being!
Be inspired and think…think until you figure it out. Ask the bunny!"
Joel:
"You're my bunny! You bring me joy!!"
Lia:
"(Heart, kiss, love cat)"

April 1, 2018, 4:45 PM

Joel:
"My Queen?"
Lia:
"Baby boy! How can I live without my King?"
Joel:
"You're not going to live without your King my Love!"
Lia:
"Kisses all over. Kisses..."
Joel:
"I want more baby!"
Lia:
"I want a lot more, too!"
Joel:
"(Hundred kiss faces in rows), "My Queen!"
Lia:
"Very clever! But I had many more naughty needs in mind! Shhhhh….
Sleep well, my Love, and have an amazing day tomorrow! Miss you to pieces!" (Heart)
Joel:
"Thank you, my Love. You're everything to me. You have a wonderful night too!"
Lia:
"Thank you, baby!"

April 2, 2018, 7:06 AM

Joel:
"(Hearts) You especially are the greatest woman in the world, unarguably the best mother with the sweetest love. With you, I do hope for nothing but your continual love through this world and the next. I wish to be side by side with you until I breathe my last. I love you forever!"

Lia:
"Wow! Thank you. Woke up to a great text and more snow!"

April 2, 2018, 11:25 AM

Joel:
"(Love cat) So beautiful baby! I want in."
Lia:
"I went to the park on Saturday, the trees are blooming with beautiful flowers. Yesterday was so nice, but today it snowed and was cold! Wearing a ski jacket in April! Lol… How was your day baby?" (flower)
Joel:
"I'm just missing you!"
Lia:
"How are we going to solve the mutual missing issue?" (heart)
Joel:
"Lol…Love that line! I wish you had a broomstick!"
Lia:
"I don't have a broomstick, I'm not a witch! But several airlines go where you are!"
Joel:
"Ones I can't get on!"
Lia:
"Oh… OK! I thought you were talking about me! Maybe you should start looking for that flying broom yourself, I am not sure how much more waiting I can do before I explode!" (Kiss face)
Joel:
"(Hearts), Don't explode, keep that fire for me."
Lia:
"My fire is always for you only!" (heart)
Joel:
"So poetic, I love you so much!"

Lia:
"I love you so much!"

April 4, 9:42 AM

Joel:
"Good morning, Sweetheart!" (Heart)
Lia:
"Hello, Darling, how are you?"
Joel:
"I'm not bad today, I had a horrible day yesterday"!
Lia:
"What happened, Dear?"
Joel:
"I was upset, it was a long day Honey! It's nothing. I love you! I miss you how are you?"
Lia:
"Baby, open up to me, I long for you, my Man, I miss you!" (Heart, love cat)
Joel:
"I miss you so much. I am out now for an appointment to get a loan again. I'll let you know how it goes."
Lia:
"Good luck, my Love!"
Joel:
"Luck doesn't live on this side of the world."
Lia:
"I hope it does for you today!" (Heart, kiss, flower)

April 4, 2018, 11:16 AM

Joel:
Thank you, my Love!"
SENDS LIA A PICTURE OF A SIGN:
"THANK YOU, I LOVE YOU"

Lia:
"Tell me, is there oil in the tanker at the port? Is it sold or can you sell it?"
Joel:
"There's no oil my Love. My job was to bring the tankers here for delivery."

LIA:

"He had endless surprises! Who brings in oil tankers into a foreign port with no oil in them?

I was having a very hard time understanding exactly what kind of cargo Joel had delivered in port and why he would have to pay anything for empty tankers?

I just did not understand and he was not explaining either. I began to question everything and moved very slowly going forward.

There was a lot that I did not know or understand and I couldn't figure out what impacted Joel's contract and work.

I do think, all and all, I did manage quite well considering I knew nothing of the existence of Queen Elizabeth Enahoros role in his mess and all that she had done to slow down the process of Joel clearing his contract and collecting his money."

CHAPTER 14

JOEL AND LIA:

Joel:
"I've just had dinner, how are you, my Love?"
Lia:
"Fine, thank you. What did you have for dinner? Did you deliver all the cargo?"
Joel:
"Honestly just a kebab. Couldn't finish it so it's still just sitting looking at me! Did you have lunch?"
Lia:
"Say hello to it!"
Joel:
"Low. Another way to get me smiling!"
Lia:
"I'm asking about the oil cargo because Bert has people who buy this commodity and maybe you can get the money this way!"
Joel:
"Oh my Love, you're so sweet to me. It never worked with Bert because we did not align properly. He wanted oil and I only had tankers."
Lia:
"Do the tankers have oil in it? He always gives me conflicting answers, I can never understand exactly what he can do.
He told me he had a gold buyer, all kinds of quantities and discounts, I connected him with a gold seller and he said the buyer moved.
The stupidest thing I ever heard. Lol… You know I'm just trying to help you."

Joel:
"No baby, there's no oil in the tankers from whence I brought them."
Lia:
"What's in the tankers?"
Joel:
"Forget Bert, he's complicated baby. I know you're trying to help!"
Lia:
"OK"
Joel:
"They're empty, they've got nothing in them."
Lia:
"So what are you doing there? Delivering empty tankers? Lol…I have a tanker receipt, it that says oil! Anything happened with Shlomo?'"
Joel:
"You think there'd be any oil in them until now? Come on, babe!"
Lia:
"What happened to it?"
Joel:
"The Company has possession of them only. I cannot hold them off from getting their claws on them. It's been theirs for a long time now."
Lia:
"Lol…"
Joel:
"I was just used, since I'm still here, I can't go back and sign off to get my money given to me. I've stopped thinking about all that, I only want to come home."
Lia:
"Why can't the Company send you your money and then they can have their oil. "

"What is the purpose of them using you? Maybe you need a lawyer from here to put pressure on the Company to release your money to you!"

Joel:

"Babe, the contract expressly says expressly to go back home to report when I'm done and submit all necessary documents before I get my money."

Lia:

"Ok, it has to be in person then, can it not be sent to you?"

Joel:

"Lol…No baby."

Lia:

"Very airtight this entire game. This Company cannot lend you the money to get out based on the amount they owe you?"

LIA:

"Now I heard everything! What was I not understanding? The tankers that he was to pay the tax for were empty? I was just lost as to what kind of contract this was and what he wanted to pay for with the money he was looking to get from other sources.

I kept repeating the same conversation with him on different days just to understand what he was doing. They were using him? What did all of that mean? He was not going to get his money?

I realized that I just did not know enough about the shipping business to be able to completely understand what Joel was doing. I could feel that there was a lot I did not know on all ends."

"He was keeping in touch in a minimal conversation. He would call and we would be on the phone forever, but it was the same mission and how much could we talk until we came back to the same thing!

How can we get the additional money he needed to pay for the tankers which had no oil so he could come home?"

April 4, 2018, 5:35 PM

Joel:
"It's in an account already. Remember they opened the account and put the money there? I need to come home for all this to be sorted right, baby, please do something to help me. I beg you now!" (Broken heart)
Lia:
"I remember! Is there a time limit on the contract? I am trying to help you! Can someone like Faruk give credit for your fine and then come home with you to receive it back or a family member? You should email me the contract so the lawyer can read it.
We went through all this already, no one will give me this amount of money without something as collateral!"
Joel:
"Baby my documents are all confiscated, what can I do? I myself do not have any collateral! Please get me out of this hell! Baby do something, baby!!"

JOEL:

"Joel was the only one who knew what Queen Elizabeth Enahoros intentions and plans were regarding their Company and how it would affect his contract.

His dream of achieving a life changing income and having the woman of his dream had shifted to a new plateau."

"He had been punished by his jealous business Partner and had been kept in a facility unknown to anyone and he did not know the extent and reasons of my search for him and my doubts about his whole situation.

I did not know the existence nor the intention of Queen Elizabeth Enahoro and her relationship with Joel.

He didn't understand my mistrust and constant questioning because I had been searching all over the island and had found nothing and my efforts to find the truth had failed because no one knew what the truth actually was on either side."

JOEL AND LIA:

Lia:
"Did you read what I wrote to you? You need someone with collateral that is willing to put it up for you so you can retrieve what you have and compensate them back. Did you receive your wire transfer?"
Joel:
"I only have my head to place down for compensation."
Lia:
"Not bad, how much is your head worth?"
Joel:
"5-8K Max, low. What do you think it's worth?"
Lia:
"The amount you claim you need requires an equal amount or more collateral. If you cannot come up with it maybe you need help from a source that can negotiate a return for you with payment due on arrival. I don't know any other way or if you find someone who can post credit or money for you that knows you!"

April 4, 2018, 9:05 PM

Joel:
"Go and find who can give us the remainder we need for this. I'll make sure the 120K comes through if it's the last thing I do."

Lia:
"You need another 100K. Who is going to give me that? Who?"

Joel:
"Baby, let's try please, do not think negatively or negativity will be all that we see.

Have faith and take the step, let's walk more by faith in these good times and I swear good will come to us. I have tried to secure 120K. The rest will surely come because G-d will not let us suffer in vain."

Lia:
"I am positive but do not have money sources. When will you have 120K?"

Joel:
"Let's search again for money sources. Loans, financiers, and Donald cannot be our only source."

Lia:
"I will dream about this all night!"

Joel:
"You're going to bed?"

Lia:
"I am in bed!"

Joel:
"I love you baby and I love that you're putting up all you can to get this through. I appreciate you and all that you do baby, we are at out last lap with this, so I want you to stand with me and we use all our might to fight this and get this money."

"Honey, 100K sure sounds like much in this situation, but it's not when we're hitting the right sources, try one person or two people if we can get say 30K from each well be so far gone my Dear. Do dream about this too... Well, talk in the morning!"

Lia:
"Make good sense. Get some sleep yourself!!"

LIA:

"Again!! I was in a rage already!! The same thing! I told him a million times that I have no money to give, no borrowing power left and no one I knew would give him a loan without collateral and he was asking me for money!

Which part did he not understand? I was beginning to be so uncomfortable with him again.
Just as we heated up and got to a good point, he would have a breakdown and start asking me to get the rest of the money he needed.

It was very one sided. He asked for money, and I just gave it. What did I ever get from him? Not even a postcard!! I couldn't get out of this as well since I had invested so much in him already!"

April 5, 2018, 8:05 AM

Joel:
"(Heart, flower)"
Lia:
"(Handwave, butterfly, kiss)"

April 5, 2018, 1:44 PM

Joel:
"How are you today, my Love?"
Lia:
"Good Honey, how is it by you?"
Joel:
"I'm not as frustrated as I was last night so I'm guessing that's good, yeah? I miss you babe!"
Lia:
"You are good most of the time considering things. I miss you too, my Love!" (Heart)
Joel:
"How's your day?"
Lia:
"Busy. Yours?"
Joel:
"Even more so. I've just refused to let it get to me today!"
Lia:
"Good attitude, Darling! Proud of you!"
Joel:
"How's your project going?"

April 5, 2018, 3:11 PM

Lia:
"Going ok, have a few more corrections but it looks good!"
Joel:
"Sounds promising!"
Lia:
"Yes"
Joel:
"Great work you're doing, Honey!" (Kiss face, Heart)
Lia:
"Thank you, Honey!"

April 5, 2018, 9:13 PM

Joel:
"Lia baby!" (Heart)"
Lia:
"(Love cat, heart)"
Joel:
"I love you!"
Lia:
"You are up so late, or you just woke up?"
Joel:
"Yes! I did, just woke up thinking about you!"
Lia:
"Because I was thinking of you at the same time?"
Joel:
"We're synced, you and I!"
Lia:
"I don't want to text you, not to wake you! You must be tired!"
Joel:
"You possess power over me I cannot explain! You must text me whenever you feel you need me. Don't be silly!"
Lia:
"You and I are rare and unique commodities."
Joel:
"It doesn't matter, you're my life and you deserve all of my time. You're more than a commodity to me. You're my world!"
Lia:
"Oh baby, you are so sweet. Thank you. It's just an expression!"
Joel:
"I miss you!"
Lia:
"I miss you too! And tired of texting. Lol...I am visual...Why can't the world understand that!"

Joel:
JOEL SENDS A POST:
"BE WITH SOMEONE WHO IS PROUD OF YOU."
Lia:
"This is so nice!"
Joel:
"It's torture to us both. I need to feel you in my arms."
Lia:
"Yes baby! Same here!"
Joel:
"I need you!"
Lia:
"I need you more than you know!"
Joel:
JOEL SENDS A PICTURE OF A SIGN:
"I WANT TO HAVE MORE SEX, TRAVEL MORE, DRINK MORE WINE AND LOVE LIFE."
Lia:
"More sex? How much are you having now?" (Laughing face)
Joel:
"I never wrote it, lol…it followed the package."
Lia:
"Cute!"
Joel:
"No, I'm serious baby, I need your love!"
Lia:
"You better start looking for an apartment in North Cyprus, you will just have to live there by the beach. Which do you like better? Baby, where did you go?"
LIA SEND SENDS JOEL TWO PICTURES:
ONE OF A COUPLE OTHER OF TWO DOGS
Joel:
"Caught me off guard again! Oh, I love the last photo more. Everything about you is just unique and amazing!"

Joel Sends an email to Lia:

"Absence is the highest form of being present, the feeling of completeness is what I'm after with you as my partner, I so don't need the feeling of empty and alone.
I long to touch your skin, to trace across the plains of your beautiful body and just familiarize myself with every curve.

I tend to spend a lot of time thinking lately, thinking about necessary solutions of how to save us from this nightmare that's life apart from each other. All my life I honestly never really had anyone who stood by me and supported me the way you have, which begs to think everyone is blessed with a guardian angel, some of whom might not even know of their angelic characters, but you are my angel.

You have given me the brightest stage of my life and upon knowing you I've begun seeing everything in a different light from how it's always been. I have become a different person after knowing you, the love of my life.

Every time I think of you my heart misses a beat so much that I begin to wonder how I even stay living from all the skip beats, baby you're constantly the theme for my dream, my love with you, every moment we share together we grow closer.

 I'm simply hanging by a moment, waiting to see you, so you can hold me so tight I don't feel the pressure mounted around us.

Each day I wake up dreaming of our time together and all the good time we would share together, the laughs we have and will have, oh, I miss you so much my love, these things should be emphasized that the kind of love existing in our relationship is void of fantasy or a whirlwind romance."

"If you don't know, my love for you isn't the comparative analysis of "M&B" stories or any other fictional romance stories, this is the love that is enveloped with the seal of reality without any shadow of doubt or mistrust.

All my adult life all I've wanted was a life partner who loves me with such generosity at heart, not the makeup to break up love you see at every corner you turn to for love, I want a hand that meets my own with a grasp that causes all the sensation in the world to be felt by us, I've found this love within you, sensation only you possess and can transmit through to me across distances, I love you not only because of beauty but for your sense of decency, delicacy, kindness and other complementary qualities baby, you drive me so crazy that I lose myself, but in all I face, all my gestures of love towards you come straight from the bottom of my heart.

You've always had this special place, a special spot in my heart so special that I have you in my mind, no matter where I go, I carry you in me no matter what I do honey, I'm never leaving you, never losing you and all I do pray for every night before I lay to sleep is that you feel the same way for me as I do for you, Remember, I love you!

When I look at your photos, I look in your eyes and I feel you because of the bond between us that no one can break, you're the one for me and when I look in your eyes, I see the love that abides deep within your soul, I know you love me because your loving heart and I speak in language only we would know, lol.

My love, you are my life. I love you more than anything, more than I have loved anyone before. I see myself being with you for eternity and being eternally happy."

"When you are happy and you smile for me, my heart melts and I wonder how I could be so lucky as to find someone so wonderful to love and be loved by.
When you are sad, my heart breaks and I want to do whatever is in my power to make your beautiful smile return.

I desperately need your love and your affection, and I feel that without it I would shrivel up into nothing and disappear. All night I sit, and I stare in the mirror and wonder how you could want me. You are all that I could ever want, partner, friend, and lover. You are amazing, wonderful, sexy, beautiful, playful, alluring, sensual, loving, caring, undeniably the perfect person for me.

I can't imagine where I would be or what I would do without you in my life.
This is fate and we're meant for each other, We are meant to be for each other for now and forever, we belong to each other after having tasted you, I could never want another.

You and I, we'll happily travel through our lives until we are that perfect elderly couple who sits on the porch, having good time naturally picking at each other only to smile and hold hands and go upstairs and make happy fucking love.

I really mean my words to you and say things I think of in my heart because my heart is all you and I'm full of joy despite all that's been happening.

Achieving a happy ending often depends on how you decide to end a story, I fell in love with the world in you and I do think you still love me, but we can't escape the fact that I'm not enough for you.
I guess in life each of us humans at some time, find one person with whom we are compelled toward absolute honesty."

"There is nothing as cruel in this world as the desolation of having nothing to hope for and thankfully I have you. I'd wish to remind you that being with you and not being with you are the only way I know how to measure time."

Remember though, that the best relationship is one in which your love for each other exceeds your need for each other as well as anything else!

Know that you are always the highest priority in my life. All I want to do is love you, you're all I have to live for, I pray you will be able to see just how much I love you and how much you mean to me when I'm home, I'm soon coming home, and we'll live our beautiful life together. I love you so much baby! Please be strong for us and always keep me updated, it's very important for me to hear from you please!!

I'm sure I've told you this before but If I had to give you one piece of advice it would be that baby, don't give up. Remember, it's always the last key on the key ring that opens the door.

It all begins and ends in your mind. What you give power to has dominion over you, so I need you to calm down and don't be scared baby, we will work together and find this money and get me home. I have so much faith in you and our union together.

I'm your Man and every day I love you so much."
Joel

April 6, 2018, 8:05 AM

Lia:
"Thank you, babe!"

Lia writes an email to Joel:

"My Dearest,

These words you write are so beautiful and I appreciate everything you are saying to me!

Remember that you are more than enough for me, sometimes too much for me, since all that you are dealing with is sometimes difficult and frustrating for me!

I have a Man who keeps me positive, inspired, pushes me to the limit, loves me and wants a life in my arms, it's my dream come true!

I know that your strength and faith will find a way to get you out of your situation and you will be back! The excitement and beauty of that moment keeps me going!

I do get antsy because sometimes I long for you so much that I just go wild! I wish for the magic wand all of the time!

You and I love to live life, drink wine, embrace love and have plenty of sex, I just can't wait to kiss and hold you and mold my body around yours! I want to experience and spend all my moments with you until my last breath!

I do have a world of my own but so do you and our joint combination of them will make our lives stronger and better! I cannot wait to see you! I love you so much!"

Lia.

LIA:

"Joel wrote very elaborate and long e-mails full of loving and exotic sayings. I sometimes thought he was either a writer or had a place to copy and paste love sayings.

I was a much simple writer, and I was always reserved because I was not sure where it would lead me, I had past memories which made me feel disappointed. I wanted to be happy with him, I wanted him!"

April 7, 2018, 9:36 AM

Joel:
"Hi, my Love"
Lia:
"Hi baby, how are you?"
Joel:
"Missing you, that's how I feel! You?"
Lia:
"Same, you know that!" (Heart, kisses, flower)
Joel:
"How was your night, my Love?"
Lia:
"Good, I slept very well. What are you doing today, Honey?"
Joel:
"He...he, I am up!"
Lia:
"You are the only one allowed to wake me!" (Love cats)
Joel:
"Lol, you're always so sweet my Love. What's up for today? It's beautiful here, and I'm really
considering getting a house here, as you said, lol, I wish you were here."
Lia:
"If you get a house, I am coming!"

Joel:
"Well?!!" I mean if they hold me like this they might as well claim me!"
Lia:
"What? Are you going to stay in a house?"
Joel:
"Lol...I'm just playing with you, Honey!"
Lia:
"Why did you not know the outcome of this situation all the way back in the Hospital?
Did you not read the contract? Why would you get deserted by a Company you do business with? How does this happen? Why?"
Joel:
"I have delivered to them, which is my own end of the business, they've paid their part and the rest will be paid back after I've signed with them back home where it all started.
They have no problem doing these things, I just have to do my own part."
Lia:
"Ok, Honey! I miss you so much and if you do get a house, I'll come and stay with you for as long as it takes. At least we'll be together. More fun that way!"
Joel:
"I love you!"
Lia:
"I love you!" (Heart, flower)

April 7, 2018, 12:58 PM

Joel:
"Lia! Baby, where are you? It's hot here, I need to talk to you!"
Lia:
"Here! What do you want to talk about?"

Joel:
"Hold On!!" (Joel calls and lets Lia listen to a fighting screaming conversation between Mr. & Mrs. Faruk, in the house where Joel is staying.)

Lia:
"Just stay put for a minute and see what happens! Let them work it out, it may have nothing to do with you! Tomorrow you can decide what to do, it's too late now! Tell me what's happening?"

Joel:
"Honey, I'm out of it and leaving, before they ask me to!"

Lia:
"Where do you want to go? What's going on? Try to wait it out for a couple of days! Talk to him. Maybe he can help find you something. Why is the woman so upset? Does she have to do extra work for you?"

Joel:
"I don't know my Love! I have to get something by myself. I got one for $400 per month."

Lia:
"That's good."

Joel:
"I'm speaking with the owner to reduce the rent for me, he's demanding I pay in advance, and I don't have the money for the advance. He's agreed to consider but hasn't gotten back to me. I'll have to call him tonight!"

Lia:
"How much advance does he want?"

Joel:
"$400 for 9 months. I'm not here for 9 months. I want the least time he can give me, maybe one month! Hold on! The wife is at it again!"

Lia:
"Take it month by month!"

Joel:
"That's only if he agrees!"

Lia:
"Lol…make sure she does not kill you! What did you do to her?"
Joel:
"One month would be tough but he says he has to run it through his wife first. I did not do anything!! She complained the last time that she can't have her house to herself. I can't blame her, it's hers!"
Lia:
"You have to be out of the house every day from morning to evening! Women don't like men hanging around! Lol…lol…hysterics... what else is going to happen?"
Joel:
"I have been, except when I fell sick. I'm leaving, it's the best thing."
Lia:
"OK"
Joel:
"OK"
Lia:
"Of course, a conversation about all of this should have been sufficient for you to understand what was expected from you, as their guest!"
Joel:
"I will have that either way!"
Lia:
"You should find out what she wants and do it!"
Joel:
"(Heart, kiss face)"
Lia:
"Poor Faruk, he has to go to bed with her tonight! Lol…"
Joel:
"Stop laughing! This is serious!"
Lia:
"OK, OK."

Joel:
"I'm trying to get the landlord on the phone but he's ignoring the calls, lol…Just my night!"
Lia:
"It's late now babe! Maybe in the morning. People go out on the weekend. He is not ignoring you Love! Calm yourself. What a night for you! Sorry!"
Joel:
"Mind blown tonight!"
Lia:
"How old is Faruk and his wife? The weather must be nice today? Tomorrow will rain
maybe for a couple of days?"

LIA:

"Just as we had settled somewhat in our relationship, he called and let me listen to a frightful conversation of screaming and yelling between Mr. & Mrs. Faruk about Joel's overstay as a guest in their house. Who knew if it was true or who was actually yelling, but it sounded dreadful and frightening!

Joel said he left the same night trying to find himself an affordable place to live on a moment's notice. I am not sure how it was possible, but he managed to get something and I had to immediately spring into action and come up with the money for his move and survival.

I of course would help him, but I was starting to resent the fact that he demanded my money on a minute's notice, without even asking if I had it, or if I could spare it. My money was his and he proceeded to treat it that way, but, in my mind, it was very one sided."

"I didn't even know if this episode was real or not. It was just a conversation on the phone with Joel and there was a lot of yelling in the background. It could have been anyone and an opportunity for him to collect more money from me. He wanted a house, of course, with my money! I was livid and so upset, but I had to help him in his hour of need."

April 7, 2018, 3:44 PM

Lia:
"Did your transfer come in, Babe?"
Joel:
"No baby, (broken heart)"
Lia:
"You must have some money if you are thinking of getting your own apartment?"
Joel:
"I have $850 saved from the last one you sent, that's why I'm hoping he takes one or two months from me. I have pleaded again. I don't have money, Honey, but what can I do? I am breaking this union and I cannot stand it!"
Lia:
"I hope that you are able to make a deal with the landlord soon."
Joel:
"I'll be calm and try him again tomorrow."
Lia:
"I look so gorgeous now. I am trying on my dress which I am wearing to Jonathan Coles wedding!
Joel:
"Honey, I miss you! Jonathan Coles?
Lia:
"I miss you more."
Joel:
"When's the wedding?"

April 7, 2018, 4:37 PM

Lia:
"April 10th. I cannot get good pictures to send you! Ok, let's see what happens with the landlord and then we take it from there! Don't worry Honey, it will be OK. Someday, maybe, but it will be ok! I miss you so much, wish you were here, I have to go to weddings with my son! Lol... lol...
Let me ask the famous question. Out of the bank account which you need to show up in person to release in Maryland, how much of it is yours to keep exactly?"

SENDS JOEL A PICTURE OF LIA WEARING A PRETTY DRESS

Joel:
"I love the photo, what do you mean you can't get photos? You look Dashing, my Love!"

Lia:
"It comes out cropped and the sunlight is coming through the blinds but I am glad you like it. Thank you!"

Joel:
"All of it is mine of course, that's why I can't let these evil people get their claws on it, sugar.
Yes, I have no help but I'll do all I can to get all I want. Oh, it's not the light I see my Love, it's you that I see all day, my Love!"

Lia:
"That's why you don't have interested parties to want to get you out! Sorry (love cat), tough spot! Is there a time limit on this contract?"

Joel:
"You're my only interested party! Time limit has been exhausted, long time before I had left the Hospital, which again I thank you for helping me through! I owe you my life!"

Lia:
"Lol…can you still claim your money? That is the contract I am asking about?"
Joel:
"Oh yes, my money is my money! I can claim it once I sign off. That's my struggle, I want to come back home, sign off and then have what's mine as mine."
Lia:
"Then you need serious help."
Joel:
"I thought we could play them by putting your name as well as mine on the account so you get access, but I'll have to first be given control before we have access. I've been crying to you and you don't know the extent of why we need this final 100K and why we need it so desperately!! Have you thought of any leads? Any way we can get this? Please tell me you have Lia! Please, baby please! At this wedding? Or after? Please see who can help us with the money."
Lia:
"I am going to inquire about this. I will ask what to do?"
Joel:
"100K from someone you know there or even half of it would take us a long way. It would at least pay off my debt here if added to what I have."
Lia:
"It all has to come in all at once so you can pay and get out. I will inquire!"
Joel:
"What inquiry? What are you talking about here? Allow that we've spent a year trying those options my Love. I can't spend another year trying to open that account while I know exactly why we can't access it. Well, I haven't paid and I can't get out! Help me at least clear one section!"
Lia:
"What did Shlomo offer you? How are you given control of the account?"

Joel:
"Oh baby, I have to come back home with the final report for the project! Shlomo stopped responding to me after I explained to him what I wanted. He asked what I wanted and I told him I needed funds for family problems. Then he said he had not gotten enough info. from you! I told you that whenever you mention me, (third party) no one will accept. That's why no one had helped. Think about it! I know you're scared and worried but you see that this is the end now. We have to please do our very best baby!

Tell them you need it to cover a debt or help with a friend in dire medical help. Anything you feel will encourage them. Please Lia, you've done everything for me!

Let's finish this, I beg you, I need you now! You know how to get this, you can get this despite how hard it feels for us!"

Lia:
"Ok, I will talk to him again. He said something about getting money from loan sharks and you had offered him 20% return, but he was not satisfied! I told him it was a very good return and not to be a pig! He got very mad!

I cannot get involved with a loan shark! I am not from that world. That is why I left him to make a deal with you! I might have someone else. I will find out next week."

Joel:
"Okay, what will you do Honey? Tell me. Find out and let me know."

Lia:
"When I know, I will tell you!"

Joel:
"I will give him up to 50% if he does come through for me, I just fear he asks for things I can't provide or documents the police won't release.

I love you! Next week is close but remember to have it in mind as you party.

I still can't get you off my mind you know, I told you black dresses do look so great on you all the time."

Lia:
"I am going to a wedding in Great Neck, all Persian Businessmen, before they give you a dime you have to offer an excellent explanation and a secured collateral. What do you want me to do?" "Shlomo, he told me, sell the oil in the tankers and you'll have the money! That is why I was asking about the oil. You cannot fax the project report to me so I can go and get the money?"

Joel:
"Lol, fool...sell the oil though! I wish. I'm the one in this baby, by myself, I think if I had a partner, I would have sold my partner for ransom and gotten myself out of here."

Lia:
"That's what he said to me. I couldn't understand it. That's why I was asking you! 50% is a lot but what timeframe for return?"

Joel:
"Placing me in the picture disrupts everything because they stop seeing you who they're ready to do business with and start looking at me, an alien!

They'd prefer doing business with you more than they'd do me. 50%, you gauge the time frame for return. Two weeks, three weeks should be enough time to get the money ready from the US, get it down here and pay for this. Then get my documents and my flight out of here."

Lia:
"I see."

Joel:
"My 120K should be done this week. I had given them one week to have it here or else I'm not paying for their work. Had to take control!"

Lia:
"Lol baby, be careful not to lose it! (heart)"

Joel:
"Just see what you can do from your end."

Lia:
"Will do all I can, Honey!"
Joel:
"I love you so much that I can't stand to think about not having you!"
Lia:
"Why would you be thinking that?"
Joel:
"I'm scared."
Lia:
"I am your Love and an invested partner in your crazy adventure, how can I live without this excitement? The major problem is how to convince them that you will pay back what you are asking for?"
Joel:
"What leverage do we have? What assurance will they request?"
Lia:
"You need to compose a letter with notarized, signature, name, address, ss etc. something, in your case it may not be enough."
Joel:
"I'll write something up!"
Lia:
"Let's see what the requirement is?"
Joel:
"But Honey, again why tell them it's me who wants this? It will never work Lia. It will never work, why do we keep doing the same thing for this long? "
"Think about it? If you mention I need it, they will say no! Take my word for it! If you doubt me, go then, and see if the impossible finally works in your favor."

Lia:
"Do you remember who borrowed 50K last year for one of your payments? Did you pay it back yet? Who has the ability to borrow? It's not personal Joel, I am working all the logistics in a circle for you! Don't be getting angry at me. I heard your point and it's valid ok, but I have nothing in my hand to feed them!
I need things too. I am trying more than you know.
I think that the lone wolf thing is beneficial to you in what you receive but it's not in the situation you are in. Will cost you an arm and a leg to get out of this mess but if you can somehow configure to add me as a partner it will expedite things, and in the end, will be better all-around for you and me."

April 8, 8:19 AM

Joel:
"Good morning, my Love! (Hearts), all day, you've been on my mind!"
Lia:
"You've been on my mind all night! I don't want to tell.... (Heart, kiss)"
Joel:
"Shush, only the two of us know this... (Love face, heart, queen, crazy face)."
Lia:
"Kisses, how far is the Syrian capital from you? Chemical attack there!"
Joel:
"My island is quite far from Syria, next door neighbors but the sea separates us."
Lia:
"OK"

Joel:
"My G-d! These people are losing their minds. A chemical attack? Please let it end there!"

Lia:
"Yes, it's on the news this morning. How are you doing babe?"

Joel:
"I never checked the news today! Now I'm getting anxious! But I'm okay, Love".

Lia:
"Good!"

Joel:
"I'm out of Faruk's hair, I left his house this morning!"

Lia:
"Are you out for the day or have you found another place?"

Joel:
"We talked and discussed, and just as we had suspected, his wife wasn't fond with having me around."

LIA:

"The stars had aligned! Joel came up with wanting a new apartment and I had to pay for it.

Also, the burden of getting the rest of his contract money fell into my lap! My stress factor was out of control.

First, I had no more money and I had to borrow to give now. Getting $100K from anywhere required collateral and paperwork and Joel had none of it.

Also, without explaining the entire business relationship between Queen Elizabeth Enahoro and Joel and their situation and status, no one understood how this business calamity could take place and everyone I told said it was some kind of scam and I should refrain from being in it."

"How was I going to love him and have a normal relationship with a man whose total dependency on money, which I did not have, was on my shoulders? I did not know what to do."

CHAPTER 15

JOEL AND LIA:

Joel:
"The fight last night was shameful and I cannot bear being the cause of that. I am out, I've not found a place yet and the landlord from last night has still not responded to me. I'm still hoping though, frankly I have no option!"
Lia:
"Jolie, your money is online and you are the only one who can get the access code to use it.
Why don't you find a way, since my name is on it, to go with the project paperwork and release payment for you from here and then you can use it to pay everything and you'll be done? Where are you going to stay tonight?"
Joel:
"I'm at a Church now. I'll spend the night here tonight."
Lia:
"Church?"
Joel:
"Place of worship, yes!"
Lia:
"Enjoy!"
Joel:
"I'm only here until the landlord responds to me Honey!"
Lia:
"Ok Honey!"
Joel:
"I know that landlord got back to me. I'm meeting him in an hour, thankfully."
Lia:
"Good!"
Joel:
"Had breakfast? Have you? I'm asking you Honey!"

Lia:
"Lots of coffee! I am good Honey. Miss you!"
Joel:
"I miss you, I'm horny"! (Crazy face)
Lia:
"Come right over then! Who says I'm horny to a woman that's across the world from you?" Hmm…."
Joel:
"I'm letting you know of my current condition! I'm thinking about you all the time my Love, this is a result of that. Lol… I love you!"
Lia:
"I know Love, (heart), (Kisses)…If you had been here last night…you would be 3" longer today!"
Joel:
"Honey, just finished with the man."
Lia:
"You have a place to stay?"
Joel:
"No! He's insisting I pay advance for three months and a 600 pound deposit. It's the only deal I can get, I'll sublet the room so I can have the extra cash as you advised. I paid him the 600 Pounds for the deposit because I'm really interested, and I have nowhere to go tonight. It's getting dark and the temperature is getting lower."
Lia:
"Ok babe. Everything is going to be ok. Don't worry. How much is the 3 months? It's 400 pounds for one month, 1200 pounds total."
Lia:
"How much is that in dollars?"
Joel:
"I've considered leveraging 200 pounds off the 600 I've given him already to pay over for rent."
Lia:
"Why are they not charging in Turkish liras?"

Joel:
"I was the one who mistook his rent payment for dollars. They charge whatever they want to charge, believe me! Some stores will refuse your dollars saying it's old or give an excuse the exchange rate is low. Ridiculous, if I pay him in Turkish liras, I'll have to convert it first from the desired currency to Turkish liras."

Lia:
"Turkish lira is .25 to $1 dollar. That is a big difference. Their lira is worth .25 of the dollar! Should be much cheaper."

Joel:
"Correct, it's cheaper and that's why they prefer to use GBP instead of the lira. Tried to have him take $ instead but he refused. Honestly, I think it's better to pay in $."

Lia:
"I'd say so. He is ripping you off. BP is $1.41 to $1. Lol…you should insist they use
local currency. That is what they are fighting for! No? You need to take a breath and think. We cannot keep up with this at this stage. We are losing money on a daily basis. I just hope he lets you share your place with someone else. Lol…just rest. Will work it out. But I really hate that British Pound exchange rate!"

Joel:
"This whole fucking place is a rip-off! If I pay with local currency now, he'll just change it and demand about 7000 Turkish liras Honey! He'll gain either way! But I will try! Oh, he has to let me share, where am I going to get money for food? I'll have to generate some for myself, and I'll also charge in the British pound. (Little devil)"

Lia:

"I like the way everybody will suck you dry and lick you all over when you have money. I always remember this in my head! It will be Ok. You have a place now."

"Where is it located?' They are so ridiculous, they are fighting for independence and using someone else's currency to gain financial advantage! Blah..."

Joel:

"Honestly, I just pray for an opportunity to pay these people back. They've taken so much from us baby, spiritually, emotionally, physically, it's bad! All their kids are in parts of Briton, they're all talking about paying fees in London, oh taking care of there, even Faruk wants his kids to go there. It's all a load of bullshit!"

Lia:

"I know Honey, that's why I said to you about trying to release your funds. I am not sure we can keep up with this insanity and your health and wellbeing may be endangered as well!"

Joel:
"It's not far off from Famagusta, I don't have the address yet, everything is in a rush, I'm waiting for him here at the property. I want to see if he lets me spend the night there tonight."

Lia:
"Lol...you don't know yet?"

Joel:
"I have no escape and so has he, he was insisting on full payment tonight, but I held him off telling him it's a weekend and he should give me till tomorrow morning."

Lia:
"You need to buy more time!"

Joel:
"The proper address? It's in Turkish babe, who has time to remember the whole thing!
I don't know about more time baby, but I am doing all I can!"

Lia:
"Please send it to me when you remember."
Joel:
"Yes, sure I will my Love, it's not about remembering, when I pay the whole thing, I'll obviously get a payment confirmation that I'll make him out down the address on. Well, he has to show the address on a receipt, right?"
Lia:
"Ok no problem, let's figure out how you will pay? Give him half of the deposit and one months' rent. Buy one week and we'll work on the rest!"

April 8, 2018, 1:07PM

Lia:
"You OK?"
Joel:
"No baby, I've only got enough to pay for one deposit and half a month's rent which I am afraid isn't enough to buy him for a week. If he had one month rent complete and one deposit he says. I'm exhausted just from trying to convince him."
Lia:
"Tell him I'll send you $1000. Tomorrow."
Joel:
"Okay Honey!"
Lia:
"Tell me where to send it"
Joel:
"I'm stationed up here convincing him. Let me talk to him first. If he accepts this plea, then we can go further."
Lia:
"OK"
Joel:
"But you can send it to the last person we sent it to, then I can go pick it up early tomorrow."

Lia:
"Heather? Why don't you send it to him directly!"
Joel:
"Yes, Heather."
Lia:
"Ok. He has to take dollars. Are you in?"
Joel:
"Nope, still insisting on the full amount."
Lia:
"How much is the total amount? I am sure there is another apartment in town. This guy is never going to let you live!"
Joel:
"1400 pounds my Dear. Trust me, this is the cheapest! The rest I've seen want 1 year rent and a guarantor. This amount is easy, it's 10 PM and I have him outside with his wife talking about this.
He's doing me a favor. Hold on baby, his wife I'm sure will talk to him."
Lia:
"I don't have this amount now. You straddled me with this in one day! He can take $1000 and then next week will send more."
Joel:
"Albright, I'll push more on this. I'm sorry. Thank you, Love!"
Lia:
"It amounts to $1972.19. I have to go and arrange this with the Bank, so I need the week."
Joel:
"Alright my Love, yes there about. I still have about $40. on me. I can do much with that."
Lia:
"Do you have a deal then?"
Joel:
"He's a son of a bitch! Hold on baby, we're talking. 2 minutes please."

Lia:
"I will get more but I have to do transfers etc. Lol... He is getting 80% tomorrow.
What is the matter with him?"
Joel:
"Okay. They've agreed, I'll stay the night, but I'll pay tomorrow."
Lia:
"Ok Honey! Perfect! I will send it to Heather then?"
Joel:
"Contract would be signed once I'm done paying the full amount. Oh, I'm so thirsty! Haven't had a drink in forever, like 12 hours!"
Lia:
"Send it to Heather, correct?"
Joel:
"Yes, Heather."
Lia:
"Go drink water! Bottled!"
Joel:
"I'll contact her to let her know."
Lia:
"Should I wait until she OKS?"
Joel:
"Water is cheap, I really only take healthy water. It's fine, she's going to be at work either way."
Lia:
"Feel good! It will be OK."
Joel:
"Hmm...they're so funny, OMG!! They're keeping the keys until I come with 1K! You see honey? This is how Turkish men deal business! So strict."
Lia:
"Lol... So, you'll sleep there with the door open all night?"
Joel:
"It locks from the outside."

Lia:
"Is it furnished?"
Joel:
"Slightly, it's got the basics couch, bed, oven and sink but what else can I ask for?"
Lia:
"Towels and sheets, pillow, blanket, me?"
Joel:
"No, no, I'll have to get those myself if I need mine."
Lia:
"Lol...ask her."
Joel:
"I did, don't worry I have a cover with me from Faruk's, I'll get the rest with time. I'm glad I have a roof over me right now. Thank you so very much my love."
Lia:
"Ok babe. Glad we got over this hurdle".
Joel:
"Thank you babe, I'm so glad myself. I just went around the place and it's not bad, still a rip off but it will do."
Lia:
"Wonderful"
Joel:
"Thank you again Honey! I have a gruesome headache coming up!"
Lia:
"No Honey it's from lack of water and fluids. Drink please! Love you (heart)"
Joel:
"I love you so much! (heart) Thank you for everything!"
Lia:
"You are welcome! Don't worry"!
Joel:
"I'm feeling better now but I think I should sleep now and see what tomorrow brings."
(Flower, hearts)

Lia:
"Ok, have a good sleep!" (Heat, kisses)
Joel:
Okay. You had dinner?"
Lia:
"Not yet, I'm out shopping with my friend Jan. As soon as I get home, I will take care of you!
Go to sleep, rest up. Tomorrow is another day(heart)"
Joel:
"Ah, Jan. Okay my Love. Tomorrow is another day! Yes! My regards to Jan! Okay?"
Lia:
"Thank you Dear! (heart)"

April 9, 2018, 8:00 AM

Joel:
"(Hearts) keep me in your heart, thoughts and prayers please!" (heart)
Lia:
"(Heart)"
SENDS PICTURE OF $1000 TRANSFER FOR JOEL

April 9, 2018, 11:44 AM

Lia:
"Everything OK?" (flower)

LIA:

"The entire move from Faruk's house fiasco took place very quickly. He made several phone calls to me and was hysterical at the fact that he was being thrown out by Faruk's wife."

"I was a little surprised, I didn't know what Joel had done to bring this onto him, he said he didn't do anything to instigate this but I knew that no one throws someone out at night if they did not do something.

I didn't know what the truth was actually. I only responded to him and tried to help him but this whole incident might not have been real at all. I had no way of knowing what was true.

I was furious that I was still in this equation. I wanted out! I did not want to give him any more money. He had shown me money he had in accounts, and it was huge. Why did he expect me to be the giver of money when he had so much of it himself?

After all this time he never gave me anything and had not paid back any of the money I had lent him. I was so invested in him and was staying in hoping to find a way to get my money back but I began to feel that it may never happen. I just wanted him and the relationship without the banking and money asking episodes. I also started questioning myself as to why I wanted a man like Joel?"

JOEL AND LIA:

April 9, 2018, 4:51 PM

Joel:
"Jesus, Lia! How are you, my Love?"
Lia:
"Jesus and I are from the same place!" (Crazy face) (Love cats)

April 9, 2018, 10:19 PM

Joel:
"You know you're related by blood. It's the only way you can have the power to work such miracles my Love!"
Lia:
"Like walking on water?"
Joel:
"And turn water to wine?"
Lia:
"Yes! That one too. How is it being in your own apartment?"
Joel:
"Lonely…"
Lia:
"What would it take to make you happy? Interesting how money and honey are one letter apart! Hmm…"

April 10, 11:04 AM

Joel:
"(Hearts) My Love?"

April 10, 2018, 1:29 PM

Lia:
"Hello (love cat) My blanket! Kiss…"
Joel:
"He…he… Blanket she said. How are you, my love?"
Lia:
"Good! Missing you!" (Heart)
Joel:
"Me more my Love, what are you up to?"
Lia:
"Resting a little then going downtown. My friends exhibit opening tonight!"

Joel:
"What do you think? I'm listening to Turkish music, lol...I apparently have a thing for it now. Exhibit? You are having fun baby!"
Lia:
"Oh, the life you are having...peace and quiet and Turkish music... All you need is coffee and baklava! I'm always trying to have as much fun as I want to handle! "
Joel:
"Ha-ha... That's why your life is so easy! Must be good being you! Lol... Coffee, yes!
Baklava? Not really sure! I know I need you though!"
Lia:
"Not exactly! It's a life full of responsibility! I know I need you too and that is the best part of all! Can you send a postcard?"
Joel:
"Postcard? Lol...well yes! You read my mind Lia!"
Lia:
"Adorably sweet and so smart. Lol…. I have to keep up!"
Joel:
"Ha-he. Well, I'm proud baby!"
Lia:
"I don't know what you do all day? Where are the hamsas, postcards, letters, anything?
I'm picking on you! (Crazy faces)"
Joel:
"Lol...trust me times come when even those emails become a luxury for me."
Lia:
"Tell me what you need?"
Joel:
"Just you in all your glory!"
Lia:
"Ok, perfect! Will they let you out of the country to go on a yoga retreat in Ibiza for a few days for your health?"

"Baby cat, I wish you were here to go with me! My friend is married to an artist from a prominent old art Family, I'm gathering this as the reason for her exhibit tonight! Will be next to you the whole night." (heart)

Joel:
"Ibiza is right next door, I heard but, they won't permit me to. I wish they could. I love you and I wish too that I did go with you, my sweet angel.
I love you, I really do. Hurts that we cannot do the things we wish to do as we wish to do them."

Lia:
"I love you! I can only dream, imagine and pretend. Save more for later (kiss!)"

Joel:
"My reception the past two days had been crappy for some reason."

Lia:
"What do you think it's from?"

April 10, 2018, 6:56 PM

Lia:
"Real is Rare! Mostly everyone is Fake! Blah…"

April 11, 10:09 AM

Joel:
"(Kiss face, flower, heart), Morning my Real Angel!"

Lia:
"Hi Honey!" (Love cat)

Joel:
"I miss you! Are you OK?"

Lia:
"Yes babe! I am good! What are you up to? How was your day?"

Joel:
"I'm sorry if my messages don't deliver! My day isn't bad at all Honey! I've been thinking about you. I send it multiple times in order for them to deliver."

Lia:
"I get them, no problem!" (Heart, kiss)

Joel:
"Okay, so how are you Honey, what are you up to? I wish you could be with me here, it's peaceful!"

Lia:
"I am coming next month!"

Joel:
"(Love cats)"

Lia:
"Kiss face, love cat."

Joel:
"So, I should hold off letting half the place for rent? Lol because there's no way I'll have anyone around the first time I get to host you baby! WE have so much to catch upon! "

Lia:
"You do what's good for you. I will manage when I get there!"

Joel:
"I had spoken to the owner informing him about share room decision we made.
I'll not move further with the plans though until next week when all is settled with him.
I don't want to complicate things with him. He's not a nice fellow."

Lia:
"How much do you owe him? You should be able to keep it for yourself for the 3 months.
Then you can maybe do something!"

April 11, 2018, 1:59 PM

Joel:
"I owe him $980. Baby! I paid him $1000."
Lia:
"Ok, let me see. I have to find it from somewhere. Will let you know. When do you have to pay him?"

April 11, 2018, 3:16 PM

Joel:
"Okay my Love. Had agreed on the coming week. I understand!"
Lia:
"Have a good night"
Joel:
"Thank you, Darling!" (heart)

CHAPTER 16

JOEL:

April 12, 2018, 6:30 AM

Joel:
Sends Lia an Email:

"I've been thinking lately and obviously always feel inclined to share some with you, my Rock, my everything, you're always with me and always in my thoughts, I've secretly always wished we shared thoughts lol! Going through life I've learned to understand though how unpredictable things are.

Honestly, you're the only consistent thing in my now messy universe. The person you really are that I hope to live forever with, you make me feel good despite everything that's happened to me, I think of you and my whole world breaks with joy! I receive so much joy to hear from you and these might be the little things you say to me. I know there's a magic that makes you so special and I'm bound to discover what it is, you're just such a rare combination of so many special things honey, you are really amazing to me, no wonder I find that you're on my mind more often than any other thought.

So much has been happening, there's so much tension Lia, maybe not between us but between everything. This life can be, with so many ups and downs twists and turns, changes always come along, in big or small ways. "

"I still don't know why this happened to me and why G-d chose to punish me, but baby, this change has turned my world upside down. I don't know exactly what it is, I can't place a finger on it and honestly it just hurts and I know it hurts to be in this like we are. We've done so much and we deserve to be done with this whole mess, I pray every day for this to end and I pray every day for you.

Here I have with me a chunk from one of my writings, lol I have this feeling I had sent it to you before now, I don't know so maybe you'd recognize it instantly. Reading it made me feel good, energized and I really hope that you feel the same way I felt as I read it. I thought that it was important to reflect back on it.

A walk in the park becomes a reality based metaphor where we're together living through our journey together hand in hand forever where even in our moods, regardless of the irritations of daily life we manage to make each other laugh.

Our banter that may seem odd to others makes us giggle to no end when we start, the difference between you and I are very few or should I say non-existent, yet we accept those differences with no question, embracing them because they are part of something we love about one another. This, Us, it isn't about looks nor money or possessions nor even a social status but the simplicity in life that we find so attractive.

Knowing we could survive anywhere as long as we were together that's what makes "Us" so lovable and desirable, so beautiful baby, this Love is not a job, but Unconditional love is what I offer you and as a Man with so many flaws currently in my life, I only wish and hope that this unconditional love is all that gets reciprocated to me."

"My Love, you are in my heart, you're my soulmate, friend, lover, and partner for life.

You've shown me what it feels like to love and be loved again, I don't want to lose or forget this feeling baby I want to grow old with and live happily with you my significant other half.

I am with so many flaws and am far from perfect, but I want you more than anything in the world. I deserve your love, your love so perfect so wonderful, the most amazing thing my G-d has given to me.

G-d is the most perfect and having created us in his own image there's no reason why he's being us here to suffer my love, I want you to trust me and keep praying, I know a miracle is on the corner somewhere!

Honey let's take things easy, this is beautiful, we are beautiful, always keep in mind that good things can be so easily destroyed but creating a good thing on the other hand takes time, we've created this beauty that is Us, I'm not about to let anything come between you and I, I'm reassuring you this today! Take care of yourself Darling.

I hope that every day you wake up with a smile on your face and you read from me, please keep in mind that Everything is going to be just fine, I promise, this situation is temporary.

I am so, so sorry to have put us in this since you feel it's I who's the single cause of this, I terribly need you feeling at your best always my love, even though I know how hard it is. "

"I'm out again trying my best, I don't want to encounter a situation where this situation turns worse, if it does then it would be bad for everyone, I try so hard so this all goes away, I can't wait to come home to you, my Darling.
I love you so much."
Joel

LIA:

"After all my agitation with Joel's situation he would write a beautiful email which melted my heart and made me continue to give into whatever he wanted. I wanted us to be together."

April 12, 2018, 11:23 AM

Lia:
"I just want to kiss you now! (kisses)"

April 12, 2018, 12:45 PM

Joel:
"But I want that too!" (kiss) What are you up to my Love? How is your day going?"
Lia:
"I am fortunate to live the life I have! Sometimes it's tough but I can handle it!
Have you been able to secure the funding you need Love? You've got to play all your cards right! Otherwise, you may never get to see me. You've got to be tough now, you can handle it, scary but try to do it anyway you can!"
Joel:
"Lol...well, I'm happy baby. My funding is soon going to get sent. It's being worked on now and what necessary documents are being prepared. Don't you worry my Love.
I understand what you mean." (Heart, kiss)

Lia:
"Today I want to kiss you all over".
Joel:
"You always make me feel deeply. I love you! Kiss me!"
Lia:
"Kiss..."
Joel:
"(Kiss faces)" You'll give me a heart attack!"
Lia:
"With Love."
Joel:
"What are you up to? I want to be laying with you playing with your hair!
Gosh, that would be the most amazing feeling! I'm having a kebab for dinner, come eat with me!"
Lia:
"You love kebabs. Enjoy! Yum...I am starving...for every part of you!"
Joel:
"Oh you! (Hearts) Every part of me yearns for you! It's come to a point I can't take it anymore. You know what I've always asked myself?"
Lia:
"What?"
Joel:
"Every night I ask, you're a wonderful woman Lia. Why on earth have you been all alone all this while? You're Gorgeous, beautiful, very energetic, such a passionate lover, the list goes on!!
Why has no one come forth before me to take you away? Truly! We are destined for each other."
Lia:
"I had the same thought about you!"

Joel:
"Well, I was working all the time. And of course, preserving myself for only the best! I'm not big on many women. I like my own to be just for me."
Lia:
"I certainly hope so, why would you want to share your woman with someone else?"
Joel:
"I've never wanted to, but I hear some men want to. Some want theirs to amount to more.
My friend Faruk had mentioned having more for himself."
Lia:
"I try to always be positive. Love for me is Love, I never doubt my plan with you, you are my strength and rock, my Man!"
Joel:
"He was so blown away with the Love we share."
Lia:
"I would never downgrade myself to Faruk's misery!"
Joel:
"Never subject you to such. You are Royale"
Lia:
"I love you babe! (Heart, kiss)"
Joel:
"I love you babe. Thank you for your Love! I am sorry I demand too much of it!"
Lia:
"Just remember the reason for this statement "Misery loves company", don't forget it! Don't allow anyone to choose what you do!"
Joel:
"Honey, did you call me? I can't receive calls or make them anymore!"
Lia:
"Why?"

Joel:
"My subscription ended couldn't bother you with that there's already much you're handling."
Lia:
"Tomorrow I am sending you some money! How much do you need for the phone? Bert found some money for me."
Joel:
"I don't know how much we're talking here but out of it I'd also want you to have some for yourself!"
Lia:
"What are you saying to me? How much do you need?"
Joel:
"You always send me all of your money, this time I want you to keep it for yourself."
Lia:
"Ok, fine!"
Joel:
"100K, lol...baby you know!"
Lia:
"I don't have 100K, you have to work on this yourself!"
Joel:
"I know, I'm just pulling your legs (kiss face), I am, I am, You know I am!"
Lia:
"OK, but my legs are long and beautiful already!"
Joel:
"Lol...I've always been fascinated by them. I love them. You're the one who said we should joke sometimes! It eases the mind baby!"
Lia:
"I am not happy! I like to hear your voice!"
Joel:
"100K, I know, I'm just pulling your legs (Kiss face). And frankly you know I need a lot of money. "

"Jokes apart now baby, I love to hear your voice too, but I don't know how much you have to send. Whether I'm working this myself or not.

Somehow sometimes, I do have people around who with money can influence and with some money in hand things would move a lot faster, I would have leverage too. So, 8-10K will take us a long way honestly. I'll love you to have something for yourself also baby!"
Lia:
"Now I feel like you've lost your mind and have reverted to being someone else. I cannot text anymore. Got to go. Talk tomorrow."
Joel:
"I asked how much are we talking about here, I was making a suggestion and also, I've got a lot of problems. As for myself, a thousand dollars will take me a long way. You asked how much I needed, I told you and you say I've lost my mind? Don't be like this baby. We should be able to talk at all times no matter what."
Lia:
"I am going to send you $1500. So you have some extra."
Joel:
"Ok. The extra will give me the food and telephone. Thank you!"
Lia:
"Let me know where to send it."
Joel:
"I'll need to get in touch with Heather, get back to you!'
Lia:
"Ok Darling. Have a good night!" (Heart, kiss)
Joel:
"It's fine to send it to Heather tomorrow. I've messaged for confirmation."

April 13, 2018, 6:21 AM

Lia:
"I want to kiss you today too all over now!" (kisses)
Joel:
"I love this about you! How are you sweetie?"
Lia:
"Good. What's happening?"
Joel:
"Love that you kiss me every morning! I need you so much right now being alone is unbearable. The part of the story that I hate is where I can't see you every day as I wish. I can't kiss you every day as I wish.
I'm doing good Honey, I just finished paying an email, it's for my money, I want them to send it by next week hopefully but everything is fine, there's no problem with that as well and I'm sorry it's taken this long, but it's this new procedure receiving money or something and I don't belong to a company account it's just confusing even to me as well but I started it and I'm sure I'm gonna get through with it. I love you. How was your night?"
Lia:
"But you were alone all along. What's this discomfort now? Why are you not enjoying being by yourself? I will kiss you every day as I wake. (heart)!"
Joel:
"(Heart) you mean that?"
Lia:
"Every chance I get that you will give me, I will! I might want to kiss you even when you least expect it!"
Joel:
"Well, I want that reality! Honestly, I love you! I just feel like such a screwup!"
Lia:
"I love you and I want you to feel happy and lucky! (Heart, kisses)"

Joel:
"Oh, I already feel these things, these emotions. I miss you so much, I'm just not living life until I meet you! I feel very happy and lucky that I have you, you're making me feel like a King and I have not felt that in a while honestly. You know that!"

Lia:
"Yes Dear!"

Joel:
"I may never understand how deeply my heart feels for you, a life without you will decimate me entirely.

You bring me to climax without sex, I love you! You are my soul in human form. Never Part from me, I won't ever let you out of my sight, I will never stop fighting for you because you're my life and life is effort, I'll stop when I die."

Lia:
"That's my Man I've been waiting for all my life!" (Kiss, hearts)

Joel:
"He's never stopped being your Man. I'll never stop loving you!"

Lia:
"Why would you ever stop loving your Queen? It's through my love that you become King!" (Heart, butterfly) (Kisses)

Joel:
"I cannot, what good am I to the heavens and earth if I don't have a Queen to love and serve. You're my everything! (Heart, love cat) What are you doing baby?"

Lia:
"Waiting for Bert to wake up and make the cash transfer so I can send it to you!"

Joel:
"Ha-ha! Bert is a big man still asleep? Does anyone wake up at these times at all? Lol, its NYC Bert!"

Lia:
"He is in Staten Island, otherwise I would be knocking on his door! All these stockbrokers drive me crazy. I am trying to cultivate patience but it's very hard for me."

Joel:
"Baby, patience is a virtue you possess in abundance."

Lia:
"I am trying my Love!" (Heart)

Joel:
"Always your patience is being tested and when finally have had enough that's when you pull the wooden spoon out!"

Lia:
"Lol…I'm cooking right now! Making stuffed peppers!"

Joel:
"Ha-ha! Please, please I want some".

Lia:
"You should tell me about the fact that you cannot call or receive calls before it happens.
What if I need to talk to you?"

Joel:
"Yes, I'll do but only when we don't have all too much to worry about."

Lia:
"I want to ride the horse with you and me on it together!" (Butterfly)

Joel:
"Ride me instead! I will be your horse! Ride me until tomorrow!!"

Lia:
"Now you want to be a horse?"

Joel:
"I should be the only thing you'd be riding, baby!"

Lia:
"You are correct that's why you need to get yourself here!"

"You've done so well today, you've been a King, you've climaxed, you've been a horse, you've been kissed all over! Amazing!
Now be careful and watch out for the donkeys! I hear they are plenty lingering about!"

April 14, 2018, 11:41 AM

Joel:
"Honey, I love you all my life!"
Lia:
"Bert is such a puts, he just called and we made the transfer. Is WU open now?"
Joel:
"WU closed until Monday sadly!"
Lia:
"Lol…I am sorry!"
Lia sends Joel $1500, to Heather Sibanda for pick up at WU on 4/16/2018 (MTCN)8251193978)
Joel:
"But it's fine, I figured it was going to come to this. Hey, don't you ever be sorry to me for such.
It's fine, I'm good with you. You don't need to apologize."
Lia:
"Ok then wait till it hits the bank and I'll send it then."
Joel:
"Okay honey cakes(heart), Thank you!"
Lia:
"(Kiss, heart)"
Joel:
"What has your day been like?"
Lia:
"Hyper drive!"
Joel:
"Ha-ha! Oh please!"

Lia:
"Today it's 65 degrees and tomorrow 70!"
Joel:
"I know when you're in a hot hyperactive mood!"
Lia:
"I've been up since 5AM. Lol…I feel like taking a nap already!"
Joel:
"You can take a nap! It's totally fine. Don't you think?"
Lia:
"I know. With you? Did you have dinner yet baby?"
Joel:
"I'm about to. Still thinking about what to have. Have you had lunch my Lady?

For hours now I've got you running through my mind causing total and complete awareness for the loneliness around me. I crave intimacy in many forms with you. From you, I want honesty as a Crown, as the one I carry on my head.

I long for soulful conversations with you, my love full of gutted truths, we are so good with each other, and we deserve a connection so telepathic it requires a soul like only ours to reach, a soul who can feel for the world. I need you to touch my skin, so I feel all the emotions I'm starved off, the oceans and the wildfire.

Ultimately Lia, I am happy to find a person who knows how to love me into freedom."
Lia:
"Same here. I'm so lucky we want the same thing with each other. (kiss) By the way, I touch your face every day!"
Joel:
"Oh, yes you do, you kiss me every day, my face and all over, but you know me, I'm quite a greedy one when it comes to you baby!"
Lia:
"Yes, baby my favorite. I'm excited now!"

Joel:
"Are you? I don't know I could still get you excited?"
Lia:
"Yes, the quite greedy part is exciting! I miss you so much my soul!"
Joel:
"I hope a day will disappear from the time I have to spend longing for you! I am desperate, so desperate!"
Lia:
"Me too my Love!"
Joel:
"I do miss you so much more my Love!"
Lia:
"(Hearts, kisses)" Maybe you need a camera, and you can go and take photographs of the island. I would like that!"
Joel:
"That's going to become a recreational hobby! I would love that too!"
Lia:
"Fabulous! You are going to write a book one day, you need to document your journey!"
Joel:
"(Thinking faces, little devil face)"
Lia:
"You are using that little devil mojo a lot lately! (Halo face) I love you so much! (Love cat)"
Joel:
"Don't put so many thoughts into it babe. You are okay?"
Lia:
"Yes, why?"
SENDS JOEL A PICTURE OF THE FIRST BUD OF SPRING IN THE PARK
Lia:
"Almost there... How was your day, baby?"

April 14, 2018, 12:53 PM

Joel:
"Oh stressing, I feel like a zombie! Tired and grumpy, my knees and joints all feel horribly in pain Honey! I can walk though, I only feel pain when I'm resting!"
Lia:
"What? How did this happen?"
Joel:
"It's nothing Honey! I probably only need to exercise and massage them. It's just that age has caught up with me."
Lia:
"You are a young stallion and must take care of yourself Honey! Take some calcium and drink water! Tara has gone to London, I sent Dion an Email if she wants to meet up with her!"

April 14, 2018, 6:04 PM

Lia:
"How do you feel Sunshine?" (Love cat and sun)
Joel:
"Hello baby!"

LIA:

"Joel answered questions if he wanted to. If he didn't, he would start a new conversation of some polite small chit chat. I hated this habit and couldn't figure out why he was doing it.

Sometimes it aggravated me and made me mistrust what he was trying to tell me. After all, why would a man do that if he is trying to get me to help him?"

JOEL AND LIA:

April 15, 2018, 8:46 AM

Lia:
"(Love cat), How are you feeling Darling?"
Joel:
"I'm not better baby, there's nothing fascinating happening over here and every day I wake to find that my money's not been sent already, I feel like strangling someone. Really!!"
Lia:
"Just shine anyway my Love. It will all come to be soon. Feel better, I love you!"
Joel:
"Thank you for this, ever wonderful, I love you. How's your day going my Darling?"
Lia:
"Very busy! Getting ready to go to the wedding and I cannot find my stockings. Yesterday was 70 degrees and today it's 40! Lol… Ha…I found them!"
Joel:
"Lol…make sure they're the right ones! Please we wouldn't want a wardrobe malfunction at a wedding now."
Lia:
"Now you got me going! If nothing works, I'll go naked!"
Joel:
"Ha-ha... No way!! Your nakedness is for my eyes only!"
Lia:
"Since Preston will be taking pictures, you will only get fully clothed ones!"
Joel:
"Ha-ha!! Oh Preston, you've never made me jealous of being him, like you just did!"
Lia:
"Please, you think Preston wants to take pictures of me and hang here?"

Joel:
"I know baby, I know, I also don't want to hang here alone."
Lia:
SENDE JOEL A PICTURE OF LIA GOING TO THE WEDDING ALL DRESSED UP

April 15, 2018, 4:48 PM

Lia:
"You cannot believe how beautiful this wedding venue is. On the water with spectacular views. Lol…so nice! Miss you!"

April 17, 2018, 7:54 AM

Joel:
"My Love"
Lia:
"How are you doing Joel? Did you pick up the money?"
Joel:
"Hi my Love. I'm doing okay Honey!"

April 17, 2018, 9:27 PM

Lia:
SENDS PICTURE OF A GIANT SUNFLOWER TO JOEL

April 19, 2018, 2:35 PM

Lia:
Sends Joel $1500 to Victor Mandy for pick up at WU(MTCN) 4480983346, cancelling the one for Heather Siban 8251193978 on 4/16/18 due to Heather not being able to pick up.

April 20, 2018, 11:38 AM

Lia:
"Why don't you answer your phone?"
Joel:
"I didn't know you called. When did you call? You know I wouldn't pass your phone call.
I've just got reconnected, you know!"
Lia:
"Ok good. You got reconnected! Hope you are feeling well and in good shape!" (Heart)
Joel:
"No, I'm not feeling okay, since knowing you honestly, I've not been myself, not until I've met my Queen. I swear not to be by myself. I miss you Honey! I'll have some cheese and chips with fish for dinner."
Lia:
"Sounds yummy. Enjoy!"
Joel:
Thank you, my Love!"

April 20, 2018, 2:53 PM

Lia:
"Are you satisfied with your dinner my Love?"
Joel:
"Hi my Love!"
Lia:
"How was your yummy dinner, Honey?"
Joel:
"Done and digested, I'm feeling good now Honey!"
Lia:
"Wonderful! What is going on?"
Joel:
"Getting the whole place in order, trying to do laundry."

Lia:
"You do laundry? I'm sure it will look amazing when you are done. You have a washer
and a dryer?"

Joel:
"Ha-ha! I'm in my own place now, I have to do the little I can. Washer no dryer baby!
Lol…"

Lia:
"Good! So why are you doing laundry at midnight? They have a clothesline to hang laundry with pins? In the dark! Lol…"

Joel:
"Lol. Yes baby, old ways."

Lia:
"I am dying laughing! Don't let anyone kidnap or arrest you for hanging clothes out in the middle of the night! I remember once upon time, my father liked the smell of his laundry drying on the clothesline which he remembered from his childhood. He asked me if I would not mind doing this for him.

My Mom went to the back yard with a pair of scissors and cut the rope and told him the line was broken and we had to use the dryer. This was the end of laundry in the sun!"

LIA:

"While Joel was waiting for his money to come in, Queen Elizabeth Enahoro had put the deposit on hold without his knowledge, Joel moved to a new apartment and was asking constantly for money for his personal expenses, such as rent, food and extras which he needed."

It was really getting hard for me to constantly give him money while I attended to my own bills and had to start paying the loans for previous money I had given him."

"In all this time he did not come back as he stated, nor did he attempt in any way to pay me back and ease my burden. I was starting to become resentful of all his actions and did not know the extent of problems he had.

He did not know the evil plans of his partner and we were both battling each other for our own survival!"

CHAPTER 17

JOEL AND LIA:

April 21, 2018, 12:11 PM

Joel:
"(hearts)"
Lia:
"Sends Joel "Love"-Gianluca Vacchi/ Sebastian Yatra on Youtube.com

April 21, 2018, 5:18 PM

Lia:
"Love cat, how are you? "

April 23, 2018, 5:30 PM

Lia:
"Where are you baby cat?"

May 5, 2018, 11:35 AM

Lia:
Lia does not hear from Joel in a while, and she writes him an Email:

"Hello Darling, how are you? I do hope that you are getting your Emails and you are well! I feel like somehow, I've lost you, have no idea what's happening with you! Where are you living now?

Are you OK? I want to know what the strategy is now? How do we get you off this island? "

"How do we get the money you need? What have you been doing all this time? What is the trouble with your phone? Do you want me to send you a phone? I am so busy my head is in multiple directions!

I have until July 15th of this month to finish all my sites but I recon I will be ready sooner! Trying to sign up advertising going forward, now we are going into summer and the world is not shopping, they are traveling!

Would be fun to do some traveling! Lol...did you hear about the volcano in Hawaii? Will not be going there any time soon, which means I have another lifetime to complete! Kisses to you, miss you! "

May 10, 2018, 7:53 AM

JOEL:

"Hi baby I'm very well thank you, how are you? I miss you so much. You would never lose me baby, I am yours forever. I do get your emails, but I have to take quite a long walk to the cafe where I can have access to the internet.

It's been a really stressful week for me as I've been trying to put things in place and the situation of not having a phone makes it quite difficult.

I've settled into the new apartment I was able to pay for. I'm now keeping my fingers crossed waiting until Tuesday to get the money I've been expecting.

Meanwhile, sending me a phone wouldn't be a bad idea as it'll really take me a long way and ease up a lot of my stress."

"How is it going with your sites? I'm hoping there's a lot of progress? No, I didn't hear about the volcano in Hawaii, I feel like I've been shut out of the world, ha-ha, I'm happy things are finally coming together. I look forward to traveling the world with you and laying on your thighs everyday my woman. Please take good care of yourself for me. All my love! Joel"

Lia:
"Baby Cat how are you! What is happening? I feel like you are all alone and I am sending you a prayer that G-d watches over you and gives you an Angel to assist you in this time!"
"I know it will be a success if you can endure the uncertainty! Manage well my love and tell me all as soon as you can! I cannot believe that you don't have a phone yet!! Kisses and love your way!!"

Joel:
"Hi my love,

Thank you for your prayers, I feel the angels touching my heart and making me well again.

G-d had already planned all our futures, we just have to trust him today, you have so much joy and love in you baby and I hope the joyful spirit keeps glowing in your heart, I wish all the negative stress, anxiety and difficulties also end.

I might need an aspirin before I can leave the room, I've been avoiding taking any form of medication for this stress but if I don't, I might just collapse, just like the phone, food is scarce for me but I do all I can when I can go get something to eat. I've had potatoes and fruits I bought over a month ago, I don't know because it's all I have to eat.

Shit is hard Lia baby, but it's all going to end soon I have a feeling. I love you too much to miss you like this."

"I've just made payments of $120k to the Police today I tell you, the hardest thing I had been tasked with in my life for so long. I'm starved, depressed, and stressed out, longing to leave this place but I couldn't touch not one cent from that money, having to collect it from me turned out to be a battle yesterday because they claimed it was not the stated amount from the Courts, luckily, I was able to pay it off and hold them off on the rest of the money.

I have too many problems and my mind cannot contain it all. I need a phone so we can talk to each other more and find a way of solving this ongoing mess. Baby do you think we could find a way to solve this problem I face my love? The issue with my phone is that it is broken and does not work anymore.

The bill is okay on it. It's the phone itself that I don't have and that's why I thought you could send me one but if it's too much hassle I could manage here.
Right now, food and the phone are my only problems and are the only thing I need baby.

I'm working on the whole money thing. There's no need for the embassy though, I'll give my best and go to them, since you my love have suggested it.

Beyond the edge of the world there's a space where emptiness and substance neatly overlap, where past and future form a continuous, endless loop. And, hovering about, there are signs no one has ever read, chords no one has ever heard, beauty no one has ever been graced with except you, my Darling.

The world has nothing on you, I wish to see you, so you grace your gorgeousness on me. Good morning loveliness, I miss you! "

May 11, 2018, at 9:00 AM

Lia:
(Sends Joel $1500. To Kennedy Main Anson Mkama for pick up at WU (MTCN) 2393703646)

May 11, 2018, at 9:36 AM

Lia:
"Money you said is for your phone and food! You have received a lot of money since Feb!
In 3 1/2 months you have gone through $6000! You are in a Turkish lira zone, what the heck are you doing with all the money? I don't spend this money in NYC! Please watch what you are doing and hurry up and end this situation! I am losing my patience and understanding of this drama!"
Joel:
"Those stormy nights are the best but only when spent together. Thank you, my love, I see the tracking. I've gotten it my love, thank you so much, I'm headed to go get some food, do I get a phone from this as well? Let me know if you want to so I know our plans. I love you so much. All my love every day!"
Lia:
"Whose ID did you use to get your 120k transfer and whose ID do you use to pay it!
All these receipts and payment require ID! Why are you telling me to send you money via third parties? "
Joel:
"120k came through a bank account and not western union my Dear, I did not need an ID but rather an account and I paid using my name since they already have my docs and passport."
Lia:
"All the severity of our actions and behavior stem from deep longing to love the one we are served with."

"Love is what we all need, and longing is what fuels us to express and be understood in order to conquer our actions! Kisses.."

Joel:
"Dream? Epiphany? Does it matter? Every day since I fell in love with you baby, you've been nothing but a wonderful lover to me. You've been with no flaw. I love you, how are you?"

May 12, 2018, 3:05 PM

Joel:
Writes an email to Lia:

"To be beautiful means to be yourself. You don't need to be accepted by others. You need to accept yourself. When you are born a lotus flower, be a beautiful lotus flower, don't try to be a magnolia flower. If you crave acceptance and recognition and try to change yourself to fit what other people want you to be, you will suffer all your life.

True happiness and true power lie in understanding yourself, accepting yourself, having confidence in yourself. I'm fine now and I'm Ok, I'm sorry for having put your heart through this all but I couldn't reach out to you and that's why I wasn't able to reach you.

I've come now miles from my newly rented apartment in order to get to this café I used to communicate with you. Yes, again newly rented because I got kicked out the other because I had apparently failed to adhere to our agreement with the landlord to pay him. I was able to retrace my steps around, retrieved my money and used it to rent a new apartment I could find. I had slept two days on the worship center pavement here."

"I don't have a phone anymore because the one I had obviously got wrecked, getting a new one without any money isn't easy as well but I've tried and with what I have I was able to pay for a secondhand phone and should be able to get it by tomorrow when the merchant I got it from arrives back here.

You can contact me for a while here my love, I'll be around the cafe waiting for your responses. I love you so much. PS my 120k should be delivered to me on Tuesday and I just got the message, so I guess that's good news."

May 12, 2018, 12:35 AM

Joel:
"All my dreams of color start from here and end on you right in your bed like a rainbow.
I love you my dear, I hope you sleep extra peaceful tonight as I have two angels watching you tonight. "
Lia:
"I miss our conversations on the weekends! I don't know how you could give up your phone!
I don't understand!"

May 15, 2018, 2:37 AM

Joel:
"Hi my love, good morning! I'm back at the cafe now and you can email me until 4-5pm. I've paid for a phone and I'm collecting it today, sorry I wasn't able to write much yesterday as I was in a hurry, I only popped in and out of the Cafe quickly to settle the phone. I love you baby, sleep tight."

May 18, 2018, 10:53 AM

Lia:
"(Butterfly heart)"
Joel:
"Hold on, I'm still setting up the phone love, I'll text you once I'm done!"
Lia:
"OK"

May 19, 2018, 10:47 AM

Joel:
"Hey pumpkin! How are you this morning? You don't enjoy my poetic messages anymore?"
Lia:
"You know how I feel about you, my Love! (heart)"

LIA:

"I had no idea what to do with Joel. I wanted him to feel good and receive his money and get out of his predicament but with all his needs and demands for money I was starting to feel like I was his mother instead of his woman.

I couldn't show any vulnerability or need to him. My money which I had saved was all gone now and I had no one to share my fear about not having any money for myself.

He was running his business on his own and I felt that I just did not know the entire story and was privy to just minimal information.

I wanted the relationship to go forward but each step forward made us go back again and his coming back home was delayed again."

"I kept asking the same questions over and over again hoping the conversation would lead to when he was coming home but it never happened. The illusion of it followed our daily deeds but the reality of it never came to be."

QUEEN ELIZABETH ENAHORO:

"Queen Elizabeth Enahoro had allowed Joel to go live on his own on the island, but she and her spies were watching him carefully.

She knew that he had gotten a huge amount from a former employer, whom she knew well, and made it her business to contact him and sway him her way and have him delay and complicate the transfer so Joel would have to wait.

She also asked him to give Joel less than the amount he needed because she wanted Joel not to be able to leave.

She wanted Joel to realize that she was the only way out and no matter what he did, unless he agreed to stay with her, he would never pay up his fees and be freed to leave.

I did not know any of this and I think that Joel did not know this as well and even if he did know, there was nothing he could do to change it. As a result of this, Joel did not know what to say to me or how to plan his situation or what was going to happen to him in the end."

May 19, 10:15 PM

Joel:
"Kiss faces, hearts."

May 20, 2018, 9:52 AM

Lia:
"What has happened to you?"
Joel:
"Hi baby!"
Lia:
"Hi Honey! How are you?"
Joel:
"I'm okay baby, thank you, how are you? Been so long, so, so long!"
Lia:
"I am missing you. Why so long, babe? Can you talk on the phone?"
Joel:
"I'm holding on because of the connection."
Lia:
"We need the connection of the phone! No one can get anything to you if they cannot connect with you! Keep me posted on things you need! (Heart, kiss)"

May 20, 2018, 6:03 PM

Joel:
"I love you so deeply! It's terrible, honestly, maybe it's because I've been off for so long baby!
Do you think?"
Lia:
"Baby, you and I have an amazing bond, I don't think anyone can break it no matter what happens because my heart is yours. I love you so much. I cannot live without you Honey!"

May 22, 2018, 12:02 PM

Lia:
"Are you Ok babe? (heart)"

May 24, 2018, 7:37 AM

Lia:
"Where oh where has my Love gone! Do I dream or do I fly to find the kiss of my beloved! (Butterfly, flower)"

LIA:

"Joel had become a constant in my life. I would do anything for him and not expect anything in return. I knew that it was wrong to be that way. A relationship should be a two-way street and both parties should have equal amounts of attention and need, but his was always more needed than mine.

I always managed to take care of my own needs and did not depend on someone to take care of me. Deep down I really wanted someone who would take care of me, sweep me off my feet and take me into his arms and make me feel safe and wanted. I wanted to believe in this relationship, and I longed for it to be real…but the "why, how and when" was always in my head."

May 25, 2018, 5:08 AM

Joel:
"(Hearts), Before you wake my Darling, I love you!"
Lia:
"I made money to send to you by being a host for Airbnb. My building management found out and issued a notice of eviction to us. If the Staten Island house exists, now is a good time to send the key and its address. I love you too! (Heart)"
Joel:
"I will be with you through this, I promise. I love you and we will overcome everything."

"Can you not talk to management? Have them re-consider? You've been with them for long. They must have a pardon for loyal occupants?"

Lia:

"My heart is very heavy! I don't want to be broken but my tears keep coming! I am sorry to have to tell you and add burden to your life!"

Joel:

"I understand how you feel my Darling! But honestly, it's fine that you burden me."

Lia:

"I am today! I've had a very tough week!"

Joel:

"Who else have you got? I'm your all and you're mine too. I'm sorry!"

Lia:

"Thank you!"

Joel:

"I had returned the phone for another. It had more problems than both of us combined so I switched and complained to them. This one is fine. I'm sorry you had a bad and tough week my Darling! I only wish I was with you to hold you and wipe your tears. I am so sad."

Lia:

"You are so wonderful and perfect for me. Thank you for being in my life! (heart)"

Joel:

"Thank you for being in mine. (heart) I love you so much! Waited all my life to meet you. It's you I should thank for being in my life!"

Lia:

"I love you so much Love! Life is so interesting! How are you doing? What does the future hold for you?"

Joel:

"I am freaking out because of our situation."

Lia:
Sends Joel a slogan:
"NOTHING IS SEXIER THAN A MAN WHO ADMITS HE WANTS YOU AND DOES ANYTHING HE CAN TO HAVE YOU AND KEEP YOU."

May 25, 2018, 12:37 PM

Lia:
"My Building Manager said that we must answer the petition and meet next week. They will work on an amicable solution. Let's see what happens. It already smells expensive!"

Joel:
"Honey, keep a positive mindset towards this. Please, I beg of you! Things will work in our favor."

Lia:
"I am! This is why I became your angel! Are you ok with yourself my Darling?"

Joel:
"And the kids? Are they alright baby?"

Lia:
"Yes. Tell me about yourself?"

Joel:
"It's prayer time, the masques here use high volume loudspeakers. It's always a nuisance."

Lia:
"Lol..."

Joel:
"That alone always reminds me to leave this place. It's horrible. How's your day going?
Tell me about this Airbnb thing Honey? How long have you been doing it?"

Lia:
"Since I met you?"

Joel:
"It's been so long!"
Lia:
"Yes babe, it has!"
Joel:
"Oh my, It's alright. Everything will be fine. I thought you owned the apartment.?
Lia:
"I do with restriction."
Joel:
"Well, that's BS if you asked me. What they are saying is BS."
Lia:
"Building is owned by the City of NY and has a 5yr note due on the Mortgage. When it's paid ownership is deeded. It's beside the point, they will resolve it with lawyers on both sides and it will be my tab!"
Joel:
"I can't log in to the bank babe?"
Lia:
"You have the account number and routing."
Joel:
"Yes, but it did not work?"
Lia:
"You entered the passwords?'
Joel:
"Yes. Still does not."
Lia:
"Ok, let me check."
Joel:
"Okay Honey."
Lia:
"I went to the Bank and unlocked the block on the account and gave Joel the new password."
Joel:
"Did you get your code?"

Lia:
"Yes, 147656."
Joel:
"Thank you, Honey!"
Lia:
"My lawyer said that the building lawyers are sending a stipulated agreement next week or so and it looks like a settlement if all parties will agree!"
Joel:
"Oh, Honey! Though a settlement is better than eviction. If this is what it's going to take let them proceed."
Lia:
"He told me to breathe so I'm guessing it will be OK!"
Joel:
"I wished things worked this way in Cyprus."
Lia:
"They are the worst in the world! Maybe you need to find a business which will loan you the money and you will submit a receipt of goods paid by them for the amount loaned. They can then generate an invoice to justify the payment and can deduct it from their taxes. This way they don't have to worry if you ever pay it back, they get the money back one way or another!"
Joel:
"I love you baby!"

May 26, 2018, 9:54 AM

Joel:
"Good morning my Love, how are you?"
Lia:
"Hi Honey! I am fine thank you! I am in Long Island with my friend going to the beach today! How do you feel my Love?"

Joel:
"Ha-ha! Take pictures, those legs, mmm...hmmm in daydreaming already!"
Lia:
"Will do!"
Joel:
"I miss you, how are you?"
Lia:
"I miss you too! When are you coming to NYC?"
Joel:
"Ha-he. Next Tuesday! Then we could have that dinner I have forever owed you!"
(heart)
Lia:
"Ok, I cannot wait!" (Heart, kiss)
Joel:
"When are you leaving baby?"
Lia:
"I am here! Miss you so much! "(heart)
LIA SEDS JOEL A PICTURE OF THE BOATS IN THE WATER

May 26, 2018, 1:29 PM

Joel:
"My life! (hearts)"
Lia:
"(Kisses, crazy face) My new Bo!"
SENDS JOEL A PICTURE OF LIA WITH A FRIEND'S DOG
Joel:
"Ha-ha! so sweet. When did you two meet? "
Lia:
"Some time ago!" (Hearts)

Joel:
"So sweet, now I'm jealous. Ha-ha...I think you should really get a dog! I know you said no more pets but maybe one more? You deserve all the happiness in the world".
Lia:
"Thank you, I will think about it!"
Joel:
"Today was a Big Saturday for me, I was out putting a few things around in order, tried to get some money myself, so in case you need any with your situation, I would be able to chip in. I care so much about you. I try to keep positive. "Energy begets energy," I love that, it's my new motto."
Lia:
"You are my Love! I appreciate you so much! Thank you!" (Heat, Rose)
Joel:
"Thank you baby! How are you? You having a good day?"
Lia:
"Always babe. So far so good. Miss you, my babe! What are you up to? Go find me a dog with the purple hair that we both like." (Crazy face)
Joel:
"(Hearts), you know I still have that on my mind baby!"
Lia:
"I love you Jolie!" (Hears)
Joel:
"So lovely!"
Lia:
"Lia sends Joel Tina Turner's song, "Simply the Best "on youtube.com"

May 27, 2018, 6:32 AM

Joel:
"Good morning My Love!"

Lia:
"Good morning my Darling, how is your day?"
Joel:
"My Love, it's mild and cloudy, (heart, flower), I love it!"
Lia:
"Wonderful! (butterfly)Enjoy!"

May 27, 2018, 10:24 AM

Lia:
"First time I heard you say you love it in North Cyprus".

May 28, 2018, 6:51 AM

Joel:
"I feel having you makes me a lucky man. I really am looking forward to our union, physical and spiritual. I must admit to you honestly that the thoughts of you brings me so much joy to my heart like nothing else does. I love you!"
Lia:
"Same! You sweet, sweet Man, I'm so happy you are mine!" (Kisses, hearts)
Joel:
"See why you make me so happy!"
Lia:
"Most important Darling!" (hearts)
Joel:
"How was your night my Dear?"
Lia:
"Wonderful! My bed is very comfy! What are you up to today? Swimming?"
Joel:
"I need to feel that bed with you in it!"
Lia:
"Hmmm…it's so comfy! But with you in it…it will be Fantastic! I miss you!" (Flowers)

Joel:
"Wonderful time to go swimming, right? Ha-ha...I'm not going close to the ocean for fear of having gotten tempted to use a boat! If I ever get to spend time with you on a bed, I doubt I'll ever get off! I've longed for this my entire life!"
Lia:
"We have so many things to do together my Love and whichever we do longer so be it! (Crazy face) I remember when you were so excited about sailing, I thought you would get the excitement of your life, and now it offers you fear every time you think of it!
Don't worry, there will come a time when all the fear will disappear and new excitement will be all around, you and happiness will return!"

May 28, 2018, 12:44 PM

Joel:
"You are my happiness, my happiness had always existed in you and that's why when you're sad then I'm devastated and when you're in so much joy, I have all your grace around me! "
Lia:
"You and me, is my happiness! (hearts)"
Joel:
"How are you feeling?"
Lia:
"Good Honey! Enjoying Memorial Day. Very quiet in the City. I love it!"

May 28, 2018, 2:57 PM

Joel:
"My Love, My everything! I have a strong headache!"

Lia:
"Baby! Drink water! Rest and dream…dream big!! (Kisses)!"
Joel:
"I want nothing on earth but you and to make all your dreams come true!! You're my knightess in shining Armor, do you know that?"
Lia:
"My dreams came true because of you! Never you forget that my Love! (Heart, kiss)"
Joel:
"I shan't! Thank you for your Love! I just had a glass of water. I'll have another in 20 min."
Lia:
"Feel good my Man! Going to exercise class! (Heart, kisses)"

May 29, 2018, 7:46 AM

Lia:
"(Love cat, Heart), How do you feel my Darling?"

May 29, 2018, 3:43 PM

Joel:
"Hello beautiful, how are you? How was your day today my Love?"
Lia:
"Splendid Darling! What are you up to tonight?"
Joel:
"What I'm up to is never of importance. I'm always usually trying to live or survive, which I get through by thinking about you constantly, you give me hope! Babe, how is your apartment situation?"

Lia:
"Everything about you is important to me. I am always thinking about you!"
"Apartment situation will be resolved next week. Will keep you posted. Thank you for asking my Love! (Flower, heart)"
Joel:
"Like it's a duty to care about me, it is duty for me to care about you as well my Love!
I pray for you every day, success and peace of mind."
Lia:
"I know that my Love and I appreciate you so much! (Flowers) However, trying to live and survive is only partial, you must gather a plan of action which includes a ticket to NYC, before you and I turn 100! Very important Darling!"

May 30, 2018, 9:33 PM

Joel:
"My love!"
Lia:
"I love you so much!" (Heart)"

May 31, 2018, 5:24 PM

Lia:
"My Sunshine! (Sun)"

May 31, 2018, 6:25 PM

Joel:
"Your feelings towards me are so surreal, I feel sometimes I can reach out to you!
Darling, I can't sleep, I can't think. I don't have a well clear way of expressing myself and how I feel because of the problems."

"I am glad you're with me because no one will be with anyone that causes them such heartbreak, you and I feel the emotions that run deep within each other, you've inspired me and guided me through my sadness.
Honey, I will not do you bad, I promise, I promise whole heartedly to only do good to make everything right by you. Living every day without you is like further punishment to me."
Lia:
"Thank you for expressing your feelings Honey, believe me it's no picnic living without you here as well! The wish for a magic wand is eternal and I miss you enormously!
I just hope that sometime very soon I will hear your voice! What is going on with you and what is the plan?"

May 31, 2018, 8:34 PM

Joel:
"I'm hiding in shame, that's why you've not heard my voice. I have to admit, I don't lie to you and I can't lie now!"
Lia:
"Baby, what shame? Because you are in a difficult situation? Please, I am not a child and you have nothing to be shameful about! We are both alive and love each other, there is no shame.
We are responsible for clearing up our own mess, that is why we are adults! You are my Man and that is the end of it! When you hide from me you hurt me, make me worthy to be trusted and respected as equal! Then I can love you completely!"

June 1, 2018, 9:28 AM

Lia:
"Sorry I missed your calls baby! Will be home at 11:30 AM my time.!!" (Heart, kisses)

June 1, 2018, 11:04 AM

Joel:
"Okay my Dear!"

June 2, 2018, 1:52 PM

Lia:
"(Love cats)"
Joel:
"Hey pumpkin! The one that lights up my soul with fire and joy!"
Lia:
"What are you doing without me?"
Joel:
"Surfing the waves of Cyprus shirtless with lots of sun. What do you think I'm doing?"
Lia:
"Sounds amazing! Can you send me a picture? I love surfing, standing up! Fun!!"
Joel:
"Okie dokie! For you, you'll get anything!"
Lia:
"Why are you angry?"
Joel:
"I'm not Darling, not at you! (Butterfly, heart)"
Lia:
"Sends Joel, Maddie Poppes "Brand new key" by Melanie-on youtube.com)"
Joel:
"Baby, thank you! What are you doing my Love? I'm just in bed at home lying down.
Had some bread for dinner and I am so grateful it's all from you!"

Lia:
"I am getting ready to go out for a walk. I think you should go surfing without a shirt and get me some good selfies and send them to me. Bread is not enough for dinner, what else are you having?"

Joel:
"It's what I have that I'll eat, I couldn't go surf if I wanted to, the beach is quite far from where I am and I have no board darling!"

Lia:
"You do know that I am kidding! But I still like that shirtless idea!"

Joel:
"I know baby, trust me. You're only trying to make me feel better! Naughty girl, I love you, now you're giving me the shirtless idea as well!"

Lia:
"Yea baby! Forget everything else!!"

Joel:
"I just want you! You're so important to me!"

Lia:
"I feel like a Dentist every time I want you. Pulling teeth with force!"

Joel:
"Ha-ha...Well, you don't need to pull so strong this time around!"

Lia:
"Well, at least I got the Ha-ha out of you!" (heart)

Joel:
"Lol...You're my woman. You always get the best out of me! No matter what day it is or what I feel, I know I've always been thinking all day about you since you captured my heart. I love you despite everything!"

Lia:
"Kiss, heart!"

June 2, 2018, 5:10 PM

Lia:
"I am interested in knowing what "despite everything" is?"

June 3, 2018, 8:36 AM

Joel:
"Hi my Love!"
Lia:
"Hi baby! How are you?"
Joel:
"Woke feeling sad today."
Lia:
"Why honey?"
Joel:
"I've been managing to get myself up and feeling like myself but nothing seems to be doing it for me."
Lia:
'What is happening?"
Joel:
"I miss you though! Last night I got a rejection from a company I had asked for loan assistance. I've been asking for financial aid since your home management fiasco.
You know, I hoped they would approve it for me, you know. In case you needed it!"
Lia:
"Baby! Are you my hero or what? Don't stress or be sad my Darling! You look for a company which will give you the money for your fees so you will get out! Like I suggested where they write it off on their taxes. I have a very good Lawyer who has dealt with most of my life's nonsense. He will make it ok for me! I appreciate your effort so much and thank you! I love you! (Heart)"

Joel:
"How am I a hero when I had failed in procuring what it was I wanted? Okay, I love you.
How are you today? How did you sleep?"
Lia:
"You did not fail, the company you selected did not give you the funds. Can you try someone else? It's a nice day today! Lots happening!"
Joel:
"I'll try someone else."
Lia:
"Honey, try to get the funds for yourself, I want you out of there, otherwise I will be subjected to living with you in North Cyprus forever!"

June 3, 2018, 5:52 PM

Lia:
"(Heart, butterfly), heart, kisses"
Joel:
"Thinking about you!"
Lia:
"I hope I am shirtless?"
Joel:
"My Love, you would've been making my year, (Heart, love face)"
Lia:
"How?"
Joel:
"Having you shirtless with me."
Lia:
"I thought I should be completely naked when you are thinking of me at this hour, but I don't want to push it! What are you thinking about?"

Joel:
"Lol...I like it slow and steady, one step at a time sometimes...what am I getting now?"
Lia:
"You know I am a wild girl with a huge imagination who likes interesting things and therefore, slow and steady or else it's something different each time!
You did not tell me what you are thinking so I wait to see where you are going!"
Joel:
"I love the sound of the other, (love face), "something different each time."
Lia:
"Yeah!" (Kiss face, love cat)
Joel:
"My girl."
Lia:
"When you call me a girl you make me feel 20 years younger!"
Joel:
"My Wonder Woman, I want you coming half covered so I have so much of you to strip!!
I will tear each garment off piece by piece to reveal what it is you've kept from me."
Lia:
"Ahh...this I love! (Love cat)"
Joel:
"But you've always been my girl, you've always been that girl for me, young and glamorous, looking like you just walked off the runway!"
Lia:
"We all have our moment in the Sun! I cherish every moment in your eyes!"
Joel:
"I want to be with you in a garden!"

Lia:
"Bringing the garden to you!" (Flowers)

SENDS JOEL A PICTURE OF THE FLOWERS IN CENTRAL PARK

Joel:
"It's beautiful my Love!"
Lia:
"Yes, very lush, you are up late Love?"
Joel:
"I know baby, I had to talk with you a little before I slept."
Lia:
"You are so sweet! Thank you. I enjoy it so much! "
Joel:
"I do too, they are the only comfort I have in these lonely days."
Lia:
"Baby...try hard to find money to pay and get out. I don't want you there forever!
Lol... (upside-down) I will lose my Soul if I lose you!"
Joel:
"You will never lose me baby!"
Lia:
"(Heart, kiss)"

June 4, 2018, 6:49 AM

Joel:
"Good morning Dearest Woman (Butterfly)"
Lia:
"Good morning Darling!"

June 4, 2018, 10:07 AM

Joel:
"Hey baby, how are you? How was your night?"
Lia:
"Celebrating Leslie's birthday today. We are in Chinatown waiting for her parents to arrive. What are you up to love?"
Joel:
"Oh Leslie, how is she? My very well heartfelt regards to her on this day!"
Lia:
"Thank you Darling. She is a wonderful friend, like a sister!"
Joel:
"She is a sister. You've gone back years. It's wonderful that she has you around."
Lia:
"Yes babe. It's all good. Thank you!"
Joel:
"I'm hungry! I have so much appetite for you though!"
Lia:
"Well said! Enjoy lunch!"

June 4, 2018, 3:44 PM

Lia:
"Kiss face."
Joel:
" Love you."

DION AND LIA:

Dion:

Joel's daughter Dion, E-mails Lia:

"Hello Lia,

"I'm sorry this is coming late, as I only just saw this email now. I've had a lot going on with me and it's really not been easy, especially with the situation with Dad.

It's funny how sometimes I want to scream so Out loud, because I can't deal with being in his situation, he has refused to let me come see him, he isn't sending me any money for upkeep or anything and it's not been easy and I honestly feel so lost, as though he's not my father.

I shouldn't bother you with any of that, I know he's your lover and you are going to be mum, and I don't want us to be as distant as we've been, so I thought I should send you an email, little did I know that you had sent me one already. I hope your daughter is well, my regards to the family.
I hope to hear back from you."

Best Wishes,
Dion

Lia:

Sends Dion an E-mail:

"My Darling Dion,
I am so happy to hear from you! Thank you for letting me know your frustration in this matter!

I think so highly of your dad, he is a very good man, just got himself in a difficult situation and you must try very hard to do everything possible to make his life as easy as possible, so that he will have all of his strength and good mind to get himself sorted and get himself out of this. "

"What do you do in London? Do you work, live alone or with relatives, friends?

You are welcome to come and live here with us if you like! I will make space for you and you can take your time getting sorted out, I will take care of you! Please do all you can to cheer up your dad and make him feel loved, he loves you more than anything!

I know it is difficult to understand now, but he will explain everything to you when all of this is over! Be patient Darling and strong! You always have me if you need anything!

Hugs and love your way!"
Best,
Lia

JOEL AND LIA:

June 5, 2018, 6:27 AM

Joel:
"Hey baby!"
Lia:
"Kisses!"

Joel:
"How are you my love?"
Lia:
"Good Honey! How are you doing?"
Joel:
"I'm staying strong, how are you?"
Lia:
"Tired! Yesterday was an all-day affair, very fun and very long."

"We had lunch with Leslie's parents in Chinatown, very good food, we went to the MET to see the Catholic Influence on Fashion, interesting show but my opinion on the Catholic wealth accumulated by the Vatican is going to be severe, cannot believe so much wealth is wasted for the gathering of power of oneself. I was distraught the whole way! Lol… then dinner in the park by the pond, very lovely and calming!"

Joel:
"I just want to see you, all this is great, yes! But Honey, I miss you, I wish it was me with you at the park, or at the MET! All these great places, all these great things, none of them interests me but you!"

Lia:
"I miss you too! How is everything going by you? I wish for the same baby! Dion emailed me."

Joel:
"My Dion? When? Today?"

Lia:
"Which other Dion? Yesterday I think!"

Joel:
"Oh, my G-d! How is she? This is amazing, she has not emailed or called me you know, my e-mails to her remain unresponsive. Oh my! I miss her so much! I miss my baby. Please tell her to email or call me, I need to speak to her, find out how she is doing? I miss her and tell her I love her so much!"

Lia:
"She is good, but frustrated with your situation, and she said she has no money, is this possible? I don't know her situation, what she does, who she lives with, etc. but I told her if she is strapped, she is welcome to come live here with us! I will take care of her.

I certainly tried to assure her that things are Ok with you and you love her and all that!"

"I did tell her to be patient and understanding and she misses you as well. You are a lucky man!" (heart)

June 5, 2018, 8:25 AM

Joel:
"I love you so much! You know, I can't stop crying my Love!"
Lia:
"Do not cry my Love, figure out how to solve this situation! Everything else will be OK! I love you so much!"
Joel:
"She still hasn't emailed me."
Lia:
"She will when she is ready! It took her about two and a half weeks to e-mail me back!"

June 5, 2018, 12:27 PM

Joel:
"Like Father, like Daughter."
Lia:
"Well, she expressed frustration over not being able to visit you, which means she wants to be with you, an e-mail is not much to ask of her. She should be alerted to needs that arise and check daily all her emails. And ignoring someone Dear should not be on anyone's agender!"
Joel:
"Please don't feel as though I don't care about my daughter, I speak to you often but don't mention her as often because of how the situation is. I send messages daily caring if she answers or not.
It's been a nightmare for me being there and having this all happen to me. Now I am short of 40K before it's coming."

"I'm topped out and don't know what to do anymore. You speak of 100k, we need, as if we could get it. 40K is what we need and let's work towards that.

Honey, I know so much is going on and there's so much pressure on us, but it's another summer here and I can't just stay here any longer. Go out and see who can give us any money at any cost. 10-15-30K however much from whoever so we don't scare them.

See what you can find this week please, if you love me, you'll do this. I'm done with this, if I can't come home, I'd rather hang than keep suffering like this. NO Lia!! You'll only try to talk to me."

You know something has to be done. Bert screwed up, so did Donald and everyone. I am tired of this, and I know you are too. I have dragged your heart into this and look how we've become.

Ending this is the only way to go in my head, no more sorrows for you all, Period!!"

Lia:
"Please don't be angry at me! I will not take it! All that you got comes from me and you don't want to talk to me!! Thank you! Calm yourself and let's find a solution! How did it become 40K now?"

Joel:
"I'm not angry at you my Love, you know I would never be angry at you or upset! It's me who's got the problems here, you should live comfortably but look what I bring to you, honestly!"

Lia:
"I am not complaining! But if you think of some ideas that I can help implement, it may work!"

Joel:
"What good ideas? I've just given you some read up, honey we've been one year at this? "

"Is this the longest relationship or what? And it's 40K because 160K-120K, I paid earlier from my financier. Did you forget that happened baby?"

Lia:
"I already said this to you! You want to break up? You said you cannot live without me!
How does the need of this money fall on my shoulders? Who gives you this privilege to talk and test my love for you now! With Money!! Lol...Give me a break!!

Joel:
"What money? I just want to go home! This money means nothing to me and has meant nothing to me. I want to leave this place, I want to hold you and kiss you, I remember the face of my daughter and the relationship we have is crushed completely, so you understand what I'm talking about? Are you actually paying attention here?

Baby, I love you and I love my daughter, you two are the one thing that keeps me alive but living through this merciless life for longer without having seen any of you. Resting on your shoulders?

Baby, it's all on me baby and you know that I'll show my face and pay back all these expenses I've not forgotten not one of them, I'm here living the nightmare and you're home sweet home with your loves around you no matter what and you really think to say that this all rests on you like we aren't in this together?"

Lia:
"Why are you fighting with me? You just came up with this new figure! I know all of this that you are saying to me! What happened to the financing and money you had sorted?"

Joel:
"But I never just came up with this new figure!"

Lia:
"Lol... send me a receipt for this payment, I can show it to a business owner! And I could have deducted the 50K as well if someone sent me a receipt!"

Joel:
"Plus, who is this business owner? Why do they need it?"

Lia:
"Because if they can deduct the payment from their taxes, it is getting the money back! I have to find out how much my fiasco is going to cost. I will try to work on things tomorrow. Be calm and it will be OK soon! You need $46,864.48 to pay 40000 euros. What currency do you have to pay in?"

Joel:
"I'll have to pay in Euros, but I keep my calculations in USD which I am more familiar with. I try to stay off the pounds because it fluctuates worse than the USD."

June 5, 2018, 5:31 PM

Lia:
"Then you need 50K, 40 is not enough, so why do you ask for it?"

Joel:
"What can I do? Do I bite more than I can chew? Conversion did not ruin me when I paid 120K and I intentionally paid them in USD though I'm not sure how it would work out again. I've learned to play them at their own game and no more will they take advantage of me like they did the last time. This is the last payment I make with my Passport, or I sue, they've accepted that it is, I just need to provide it."

Lia:
"Exhausting!"

Joel:
"Let's work it out while I still have the strength in me to live! I am sorry!"

Lia:
"What are you sorry about? I don't like these scenarios! I don't like to argue!"

LIA:

"Joel called hysterically complaining that he needs to get the rest of his payment money and since there is no one else I must try to find it. He was cynical and crazed and made me feel as if it's my fault that he was not able to leave his situation and come home.

He was driving me crazy with phone calls and text and the insistence of finding the money without collateral from anyone I could find! Like whom was I going to find to give me 40K?

I couldn't believe it and didn't really know how to help him. We started arguing a lot about this and my frustration was enormous with his situation, and I talked about anything else but money with him!"

June 5, 2018, 8:04 PM

Joel:
"I can't sleep, I've been up, I'm sad and concerned about you, I love you, I don't like this, I hate tonight, and I hate myself for having put us in this situation.

This is me at my lowest and in my years, I've known that honestly, the most intimate thing we can really do as humans is to allow the people, we love the most, to see us at our worst, at our lowest, at our weakest because true intimacy happens when nothing is perfect."

"You must be feeling sad and disappointed but hey, hold onto me, I love you, I'm doing this for us honestly, this is big and believe that I'm not playing around with you.

You are my soul, and I cannot live without you, look how we feel because we're apart from each other, I cannot, and I refuse to subject neither you nor I to a life without the other. Bear with me Love, until I'm done with this, trust me, it's nothing and this time will fly by, I promise to be in your arms before you blink again.

I'm just a man pure in heart and I've come to meet you with an open heart, my Love and my words are all I have, and those words are what I fear the most. Truly, honestly, I'm sorry and I will make this all up to you!"

Lia:
"(Heart, kiss)"

June 6, 2018, 6:19 AM

Joel:
"Distance is not for the fearful, it is for the bold. It's for those who are willing to spend a lot of time alone in exchange for a little time with the one they love. It's for those knowing a good thing when they see it, even if they don't see it nearly enough..."

June 6, 2018, 7:58 AM

Lia:
"Bold, Bipolar, Stupid, they all apply!"
Joel:
"I agree. How are you?

"I was waiting for when you'd wake so I could once more remind you that until my last breath you would be my woman and the only woman beside me, my wife, girlfriend and confidant, the only person I would share everything with for the rest of my life baby, what's mine is yours.

Our bond, my Love, our love is stronger than anything we are or would face in this life, no weakness, fear, or anxiety should make us feel different about how we feel for each other, I am your home, and you are my home, your arms are where I will sleep in for the rest of my life and heart too should be your home of comfort, safety, and security.

How did you sleep without me, my Love?"
Lia:
"I agree, without you I would lose my Soul!"

June 6, 2018, 11:55 AM

Joel:
"Honey, how are you feeling?"

June 6, 2018, 1:20 PM

Lia:
"Let me see here, I have a Man who teases me with a shirtless look but will not take a picture of himself for me to see, he lives in a place, which I gave him money to pay for, but did he did not say where it is, I have not heard his voice in two months, even though I gave him money for the phone payment, and he put me through a bipolar night of hysteria which now he wants to make up for, I am not sure, I need a day at the spa to reflect and relax, which I need to pay for as well. How do you think I feel? How would you feel?"
Joel:
"What do you want? (Puzzled face)"

Lia:
"Everything"
Joel:
"I give you everything, I have nothing more. I am nothing Lia."
Lia:
"I don't understand what you mean?"
Joel:
"OK Darling, you will have it all!"
Lia:
"I want you the most!" (Heart)

June 7, 2018, 8:09 AM

Lia:
"Are you having a good day babe?" (Kiss face)
Joel:
"Hey my Love! Just one of those days, how are you?"
Lia:
"Good!"
Joel:
"Did you hear back from Dion?"
Lia:
"No Honey! I will tell you if I do. I love that girl already. She is going to be my best friend.
I wish she wrote sooner. My lost child, she is. I want her back!"
Joel:
"Oh my, I love that you love her! Your lost child indeed. She is very stubborn though. Very, very, she's such a goal getter and once she sets her mind on something she must achieve it! It's really difficult to change her mind."
Lia:
"I don't know what she is doing and what her life is like, but I told her I would buy her a ticket if she wanted to come over!"

Joel:
"I wonder if that's a good thing or a bad thing? I hope she decides to come over. She must be going through a lot."
Lia:
"It's a good thing! She will get to relax and not be stressed!"
Joel:
"How is Tara? I know baby!"
Lia:
"She is young, and she might like Preston? Tara is good. Tara went to London, and I emailed Dion if she wanted to meet up with her, but she saw the email too late."
Joel:
"That would have been wonderful!"
Lia:
"Yes"
Joel:
"I just can't wait for all of this to pass. There's a lot I need to put in place."
Lia:
"Yes."
Joel:
'What do you have planned for today?"
Lia:
"Talk to my lawyer, talk to the loan lender, set up Amazon shipping, cook dinner and have a friend over, go to exercise class, hope it all goes well!"

June 7, 2018, 1:16 PM

Lia:
"You can kill yourself with the Banks here. They are not giving personal loans, only business based on performance! Lol... (sad face)"

June 7, 2018, 4:20 PM

Lia:
"Love cat, heart, kiss. There is always a light at the end of the tunnel!"

June 7, 2018, 6:34 PM

Joel:
"I believe you! It's just heart breaking that after all the efforts you had put into this situation, we still can't get past it. I feel caged with my rights and my life stolen from me, I don't want to imagine how you feel having gone through the stress you have and what I'm putting you through.
I am sorry!"
Lia:
"Just hold on! Something will happen soon! I can feel it! Be Positive!!"
Joel:
"I can feel you. Always!"
Lia:
"I know babe, same here, you are my Soul!"
Joel:
"I love you so much! How did it go with your lawyer baby?"
Lia:
"I love you!"

June 8, 2018, 7:53 AM

Joel:
"Hi my Queen!"
Lia:
"Hi my King! How are you, baby! (Heart, kiss), Lost you in the middle!" (After a phone call)
Joel:
"I know, I'm trying again!"

Lia:
"Ok"

June 8, 2018, 10:28 AM

Joel:
"Never give up hope. Things can change overnight, and problems can dissolve in the light of a new day's sun!"

Lia:
"I am with you baby! "
Joel:
"Thank you baby. Having a good day?"
Lia:
"Yes Darling! So far, the best day since I heard your voice!" (kiss)
Joel:
"You are so cute. You always try to make me feel the best! I am still with a shine on my face because I heard you speak, your laugh is still a charm to me and will forever be. Thank you for your Love!"
Lia:
"You are the Best for me! Always will be! I love you! (heart)"
Joel:
Joel sends Lia text for Ruth by mistake:
"Hello Ruth, how are you? I hope you are well. I have asked for the rest of the food from last night to be delivered but still have seen no one come to my door!"
Lia:
"You are sending Ruth's message to me! She will never deliver your food this way!"

Joel:
"(laughing faces)
Lol...Excuse me!! My bad!! But you're hilarious, Ruth has a shop down where I live, I had paid for some fresh food stuff to be delivered last night but I'm still waiting with nothing! My fridge is empty, lol... I thought to message wondering where my stuff is, lol...she apologized just now. They are sending it over!"
Lia:
"Good now you'll have something good to eat! Enjoy!!"
Joel:
"I'm starving!"
Lia:
"I'm starving for you! Even better! (Kisses)"
Joel:
"I confess the love I have for you is undying. It is as strong and enduring and will stand the test of time, I promise. I truly feel blessed that you have become part of my Soul and I cannot wait for the day that we join our lives together. I want to fall asleep in your arms, to wake to your beautiful smile.

I want to share in your joys and sorrows. Make love and grow old with you, I want to be your everything!

I pledge to always love you and always hold you in my heart, I pledge my loyalty to you, and I will always be for you when you need me, I will love you no matter what life brings us.

You are everything to me, and I vow to love you all eternity, I love you more every day! You are my eternity!"
Lia:
"(Kisses), same you with me!"
Joel:
"(Royal heart)"

June 8, 2018, 3:57 PM

Lia:
"Love cat and Heart"
Joel:
"Thinking about me?"
Lia:
"Always."
Joel:
"Good, keep it this way!"
Lia:
"You bet."
Joel:
"Having a peaceful time?"
Lia:
"I am making eggplant now!"
Joel:
"(Smiling faces), Well, I'm just lying down, since I'm doing nothing, can I join?"
Lia:
"Yes! This is your place setting. You sit at one end of the table, I sit on the other end!"
Joel:
"(Hearts), for me? You're Divine, thank you!"
Lia:
"Yes, thank you!"
Joel:
"I would wink often at you, making you giggle! You may be too far to kiss and touch when I want to, sitting from the opposite side of the bed!"
Lia:
"You mean the table? My side is close to the kitchen, your side is far from the kitchen, a much better seat for service."

Joel:
"Whenever you are creating beauty, you are restoring your Soul. Your Soul should've been fully restored because you've got so much beauty being crafted in everything you touch. What will we do in the room though? Can't talk about it!"

Lia:
"My Soul is always trying to reach the Higher Power! Is my trust that has some flaws, which I am working on. Long stories, too long to tell. No longer important or relevant!
Ahhh.... the bedroom, with my comfy bed, it's all mine now!!" (Crazy face)

Joel:
"Only for now! What stories are you implying aren't important?"

Lia:
"Don't muddle your head with this Darling! Obstacles which we overcome are all in the past and long gone! Thank you for your concern. It's all good now!"

Joel:
"Okay, I trust you my Dear! You are my Soul and my Spirit! I love you!!"

Lia:
"Same, (heart, kiss)"

Joel:
"Are you done now?"

Lia:
"Yes! Dressed all good and ready to head out. Thank you!"

Joel:
"Can't be thinking about what we're going to do to each other in the bedroom baby!
That conversation isn't for now!"

Lia:
"I know! I am not saying anything! You know I have one favorite word...Everything! (Kiss faces)! Sleep well my Honey! Enjoy!" (Heart, butterfly)

June 9, 2018, 9:11 AM

Joel:
"I love you my Dear, good Morning!"
Lia:
"Good morning my Love! How are you doing? Are you having a nice day?"
Joel:
"I'm missing you baby, did you just wake up?"
Lia:
"Just woke up Honey! Sorry the phone was off! Don't worry it will be OK. I miss you so much.
I want to tickle you!
I heard from my lawyer late yesterday! They are looking for over 3K in their attorney fees which should be in the same ballpark if not more, so it will be around 7K when done!"
Joel:
"Will you be able to pay the 7K? Honestly, the justice system globally needs an overhaul. We will get through this too. I only wish I had money to send you now, that you're in need. I am so sorry!!"
Lia:
"It will get sorted out! They pushed the date to 6/26, Lol…I told him to close the case ASAP. Who needs to drag out attorney fees? It's life I guess, one step forward, one step back, I'm going to take dancing lessons, so I get better at dancing."

June 9, 2018, 1:01 PM

Joel:
"I hate lawyers, I don't see how you like them. Dance? Hah, ha…are you getting ready for me?"

June 9, 2018, 2:05 PM

Lia:
"I don't like them either, but they protect me when I need them. I want to be ready for you!
This is how some people dance for a living!"
LIA SEND JOEL PICTURE OF THE NAKED COWBOY DANCING IN TIMES SQUARE

June 9, 2018, 6:32 PM

Joel:
"Hi Honey!"
Lia:
"Hi baby, how is it going?"
Joel:
"I'm Ok Love, I'm sorry I have had an absent day, though I hope it would please you to know you've been in my thoughts all day!"
Lia:
"That's all I need!" (Heart, flower)
Joel:
"I love you!"
Lia:
"I love you! Did you have a nice night? What did you eat Love? I sent you some e-mails.
One is from Dion, forward, the other is a transfer, which I cannot figure out!"

June 10, 2018, 7:43 AM

Joel:
"My Love! Good morning baby!
Ignore the transfer as they're trying to take advantage of our desperation. Ignore, okay?"

Lia:
"OK", (heart, kiss)"
Joel:
"Baby, are you Ok? How did you sleep last night?"
Lia:
"Yes Honey, just woke up. Thank you! How are you?"
Joel:
"I'm ok baby! It's so hot and I'm so tense and stressed! I may need some money, Please baby by tomorrow, please if you can! I have utilities I need to settle for, I just came from the office."
Lia:
"I can send you $1500, where do I send it?"
Joel:
"I haven't paid for two months plus I think there had been incurred bills from a previous tenant, but I couldn't argue because if it's not paid, I get cut off by Tuesday.

It's sudden, I'm sorry knowing I just told you I need no money, plus I know you have problems to solve baby!"
Lia:
"You need to get yourself a job!"
Joel:
"Hold on, I'll ask who I can use that's close to me?"
Lia:
"Who is living in your house in Staten Island?"
Joel:
"I've got a neighbor here, a kind man as well, he agreed to help me this time around!
Convenient because he's so close, we'll go together tomorrow."
Lia:
"Ok, what's his name? "

June 10, 2018, 10:59 AM

Lia:
"Did you fall asleep?"
Joel:
"No, my battery died my Love"
Lia:
"OK Honey!"
Joel:
"I'm sorry!"
Lia:
"I am out now, will be back in a couple hours. Please give me the correct information for your money transfer!"
Joel:
"Okay my Love, Enjoy your day!" (Heart, rose)"
Here's the details my Love:
Surname: Faena
First name: Alhaji Mustapha
Location: North Cyprus
Lia:
"Lol..."
Joel:
"Lol"
Lia:
"Who lives in the Staten Island House?"

June 10, 2018, 9:28 PM

Joel:
"I love you so much, this amazing woman!"
Lia:
"I love you so much my amazing Man!"

Sends Joel a song on youtube.com:
"The Phantom of the Opera, "All I ask of you",

Lia sends Joel $1500.
For pickup to Alhaji Mustapha Faena at WU (MTCN) 6681421310 ON 6/10/18)

June 11, 2018, 6:54 AM

Joel:
"(heart, royal heart, rose)"
Lia:
"(Kisses)", I just want to kiss you all day long!!"

LIA:

"Our conversation was loving, and time was passing without a solution to any of his problems.
Joel always had this situation as our problem, but I didn't see it that way. I saw everything as his problem and was resentful that I was his money source.

He was the one who came to North Cyprus and got a Contract to make a lot of money. But I guess that is why I was here to help him find funds and remedy his situation.

I was not part of it nor of any of his other involvements which he would spring up on a minute's notice. I was just so invested in him already and he did not let me get out of the situation. I know that it was all up to me. I did not have to give him anything!

I should have been more vigilant and had larger boundaries and made them known and stuck with them. I should have gotten out of his situation long ago and maybe never started to begin with.

I was lost, and he meant so much to me now. He had become my everything!"

June 11, 2018, 12:12 PM

Joel:
"My Love, how are you? Thank you, I was able to get the money"
Lia:
"You are welcome! Having a good night?"
Joel:
"It's not nighttime yet Honey boo boo!"
Lia:
"7 PM? Enjoy the light then! I am sitting with IT here…lol…tomorrow too… I want to get this going, I am bored to death with all this!"
Joel:
"Lia, maybe he does this just to spend time with you?"
Lia:
"I am getting an assessment from another company and after we go over it, I will see if this is true or not! Are you doing OK Sunshine? (Love cat), Going to have a little lunch now and take a breath. Lightning strikes all at once!!"

June 11, 2018, 3:14 PM

Lia:
"Miss you baby! (Love cats)"

June 11, 2018, 4:46 PM

Joel:
"Hi Honey! How's your day so far?"

Lia:
"Wonderful, thank you!"
Joel:
"What did you do? I'm exhausted and my feet are killing me, I don't know why? I am massaging with a cold rag though!"

Lia:
"Just came out of class! Feel good. Lol...your toes? Do you have salt, you can soak them. Poor baby! I'll massage your feet! (Kiss faces) What did you do today? Are you wearing flip flops on your feet?"
Joel:
"Lol...I remember you always complaining about class Honey. I have a runner shoe I got that I use more often than most!"
Lia:
"Well not today! No more complaining! I only enjoy everything now! I cannot wear closed shoe in the spring or summer, my feet are too hot! I only wear flip flops in the heat! Sneakers are the hottest shoe ever! I cannot even run in them in the winter. So hot!!"
Joel:
"Lol, I want to see you run!"
Lia:
"You will soon! Running to North Cyprus to see you!"
Joel:
"Ha-ha! You joke too much my Love!"
Lia:
"Angel face"

June 12, 2018, 6:34 AM

Joel:
"Hello runner" (heart, little devil)"
Lia:
"Hello, how are your feet feeling today? (Kisses, kiss faces), Enjoy my Love!"
Joel:
"This is the most thoughtful thing my Love. Thank you for loving me unconditionally my Love!"

Lia:
"You are the sweetest man, and I am so happy that you are mine! (kiss)"
Joel:
"(Kiss faces)"

June 12, 2018, 12:49 PM

Lia:
"(Love cat)"
Joel:
"Friendly reminder that till my last breath you would be the woman beside me, my wife, and the only person I would share everything with for the rest of my life.

Our bond, our love is stronger than anything we are or would face in this life, we should not let or even let any weakness, fear or anxiety attack us back or make us feel different about ourselves, I am your home and you're my home baby!"
Lia:
"I know baby, I agree, I have this in my head!"
Joel:
"And in your heart baby?"
Lia:
"You are tattooed in my heart so it's a deposit box for all that is in my head as well my Angel!" (Kiss face)
Joel:
"You have my heart baby, always! I imagined you laughing your cute laugh!"
Lia:
"You like that laugh, ha?"
Joel:
"Ha-ha!! I've always loved it! You're so adorable!"
Lia:
"Thank you! What's for dinner?"

LIA:

"We were chatting and complimenting each other every day. The conversation was light and just a chat. It was not going anywhere except when it got to Joel needing more money it escalated and he repeated his pattern of caressing me in order to receive money from me.

I was busy creating my business and was spending all my time with the IT man, who was putting it together. I was spending a ton of money on ads which the IT man ran on Instagram and Facebook. They cost a fortune and brought in a small amount of orders.

As I started to develop my business, I realized that I had a lot of problems that needed to change.
I also realized that I needed much more money behind the business if I was to succeed.

I had money saved but it all went to Joel, and he was delayed in coming back by a year and a half by now and it was not going well with funding everything I had on my plate.

My building eviction issue got settled but it cost me over 7K, and I could not do Airbnb any longer. This took a big chunk of income from me.

I also had borrowed money for Joel and that had to be paid back. I just ran out of money! That was the real truth. I had to get a job or find a backer to back me up with a substantial amount of money.

I was engulfed with too many issues and did not step back to sit and think things carefully, get help and assess my needs first, then his and then everything else."

CHAPER 18

June 13, 2018, 7:07 AM

Joel:
"I love you Dear woman! Good night and G-d bless (Heart)"
Lia:
"(Heart, kiss face)"

June 14, 2018, 9:07 AM

Joel:
"You can't touch Love, but you can feel the sweetness that it pours into your heart. I hope you can feel it right now as I sent you my warmest hugs and kisses to make your day more beautiful and worthwhile. Good morning to the most precious gem of my life.
Good morning my dearest Woman ...."
Lia:
"Good morning my Love! Thank you! How is your day babe?"
Joel:
"Hot and slow!"
Lia:
"Baby, what are you doing to expedite and solve your situation?"
Joel:
"Hi my Love. I Wish I had a magic wand! Do you happen to have one yourself?"
Lia:
"Are you telling me that you will be there forever?"
Joel:
"Why say so? Believe me I want you with me now!"

Lia:
"What does your answer mean? Am I ever going to see you? The fact that we both want to does not tell me yes or no. I cannot continue to support you and I cannot continue to be without you. What is your situation and how soon do you foresee that you may be able to get out?"

June 14, 2018, 4:20 PM

Lia:
"Permit yourself to be human! Never let a good crisis go to waste, we learn from hardship! Stress is not the problem, lack of recovery is! The best predictor of happiness is a relationship that is real!" (heart)

June 15, 2018, 8:59 AM

Joel:
"My love!"
It made my day to hear from you. I love you so much. I know it's hard but try to stay positive. "
"Not long and we will be together. We have an amazing future ahead of us as long as we are together. "(Kiss face, hearts)
Lia:
"I will stay positive and hopeful!" (heart)

June 15, 2018, 6:38 PM

Joel:
"My love!"

June 15, 2018, 9:06 PM

Lia:
"Baby!"

Joel:
"I don't need anything other than your love for me from you, your heart is what I desire!"
Lia:
"My heart is Tattooed with you and is therefore always going to be yours! I am sorry I woke you!"
Joel:
"It's alright, I love to be awake for you! How are you?"
Lia:
"Good baby. Why are you up so late?"
Joel:
"My heart is all yours baby. No doubt in my mind. I am all yours! Reading our conversations.
The heat woke me up! How's your day? Had dinner yet?"
Lia:
"Yes, had a wonderful dinner, salmon, beef and rice, salad, desert, I am a stuffed chicken now!" (Love cat, rabbit, kiss, heart)
Joel:
"Okay my Love, I really have to retire now, I love you and I'll do everything to make You happy. And I know getting out will make you happy!"
Lia:
"I love you Jolie! So much!" (Heart, Kisses)
Joel:
"Sleep tight my Queen, every day I love you!" (butterfly)
Lia:
"You too, my King! Sweet, sweet dreams!!"

June 16, 2018, 8:13 AM

Joel:
"Except for this life, we don't have any other time. You want something, you go after it.
Not for physical reasons, to influence our steps to measure the world."

"Good Love is No. 1 and everything else is secondary, I love you Honey!"
Lia:
"So sweet. I love you too Honey!" (heart)

June 16, 2018, 10:30 AM

Joel:
"My soulmate, my Love. Your words serve as a breather, your voice like a lullaby.
Your laughter comes as a beautiful symphony. Darling, you bring the best out of me, just a man when I feel I have certain limitations.
You support me and push me harder, further you ask me to break the barriers, you make me come forward a step ahead, you are the shore I wish to return to after a hectic and tiring day to satiate my life. Darling, you are the reason I have learned that not all days are going to be the same. Staying still won't do any good, remaining in motion through this love we share my love and fully trusting each other's as partners will bring happiness and more fulfilment into our lives. I miss you baby!!"
Lia:
"Real love begins with romance, candlelight dinners and walks along the beach. But it's based on care, compromise, respect, and trust." (Kisses)
Joel:
"You are Gold, baby! Solid Gold!"
Lia:
"(Heart), How has your day been? Did you get to cool off?"
Joel:
"Nope, had told you the city was down. I just took a shower and cooled off at home. How about you Honey Cakes? What's up? Any news?"

Lia:
"Walking through the park! It's a beautiful day!"

LIA SENDS JOEL A PICTURE OF CENTRAL PARK
Lol...what city are you in?"
Joel:
"This is great! It looks so wonderful! Famagusta, there's water yes, but scary water!"
Lia:
"Stay away from scary water! You drink water from there?"

June 16, 2018, 4:52 PM

Joel:
"My Darling!"
Lia:
SENDS JOEL A PICTURE OF FLOWERS IN THE PARK

June 16, 11:51 PM

Lia:
"My Darling Man, I wish you a beautiful day filled with delight and warmth, happy Father's Day to you, enjoy and dream and be happy! I love you!"

June 17, 2018, 5:40 PM

Joel:
"My Darling! How are you my Angel?"
Lia:
"Where have you been? I am very good, thank you! "

June 18, 2018, 7:20 AM

Joel:
"(Heart) Good Morning my Love!"
Lia:
"Good morning!" (Kiss)
Joel:
"How are you? Thank you for your Father's Day message yesterday my Love!
Did make me really happy getting it!"
Lia:
"I'm good. Glad to hear. How was your Day?"
Joel:
"Felt so meaningful! My girl never sent me anything! Not a text or call or email."
Lia:
"I'm sorry Dion is behaving this way!"
Joel:
"It's okay, I'm just so happy and lucky I have you and her in my life my Love"
Lia:
"You do Honey, and you hold it dear to your heart! I went to Brooklyn over the weekend. I cannot even describe the torture the MTA puts you to get there and back. They have constant construction on different train lines. But the weather was nice and hot and the festivities went on as planned. Had the best pizza under the Brooklyn bridge. Flea market was nice too."

June 18, 2018, 12:29 PM

Lia:
"Dion, Joel's daughter, wanted to speak to me since Joel had told her about me. She finally got the courage and reached out to me by email."

DION AND LIA:

Dion:
Sends Lia an Email:

"Hello Lia,
First, I'd love to apologize for always replying to your mails late. I have a lot going on and things skip my mind very often. How are you and the family? I understand that you have things to do lol, we all do so it's okay that you can't come over.

I would not want to put such responsibility on you anyways. I'm hoping I get vacation from work really but then again, my bills won't pay themselves, so I have to do what I have to do; Notwithstanding, if I get a vacation, I'll sure let you know, I really need one anyways.

Please say Hi to Daddy for me, I'll try to send him a message when I can.
Thank you for caring and checking in on me. Please extend my greetings to the family."

Warm Regards,
Dion

Lia:

Replies to Dion's E-mail:

Dear Dion,
"How are you Dear girl? Now it is the summer, do you get vacation from your job? Come over and spend some time in NYC! Would love to have you and see you! Your Dad misses you so much!"

"I would come to London to see you, but I am working on my project and cannot go anywhere until next year perhaps!

My daughter goes to London periodically, I will let you know when next time, she is your age and a very nice girl! I do hope that all is well with you! Please let me know if you need anything!"
All the best, Lia.

JOEL AND LIA:

Lia:
"Dion said hello to you! (Heart, love face)"
Joel:
"Thank you, Darling."

June 19, 2018, 11:58 AM

Joel:
"Are you okay? I'm here for dinner and I'm thinking about you!"
Lia:
"Where is here?"
Joel:
"The restaurant sweety!"
Lia:
"Nice, enjoy!"
Joel:
"I do hope it's nice, what I ordered. How are you my Darling?"
Lia:
"Good."
SENDS JOEL A PICTURE OF A LOVE POST ON A GARAGE DOOR

Joel:
"You're upset about something again. If you are then I'll let you cool off baby. I'll call you when I'm home. Thank you!" (Heart, butterfly)
Lia:
"I am not upset sweets. Enjoy your dinner babe!" (heart)

June 20, 2018, 3:41 PM

Lia:
"Hi baby cats! I was looking forward to hearing your voice but the reception was bad. Anyway, hope all is well, today is Tara's Birthday, so we are going to Central Park to celebrate with a few friends. Will be out late and I will send you a picture if you want it. Miss you much! Kisses to you, all over! Hugs too!" (Heart, kiss)
Joel:
"Okay my Love, enjoy and have a wonderful time with your daughter."
Lia:
"Thank you, sweets! How are you?"
Joel:
"Missing you!"
Lia:
"Missing you too! How was your dinner last night, did you like what you ordered?"
Joel:
"That's how I am. Oh dinner, yes, I did. I wasn't having too much appetite being at home really that's why I had gone out for food baby! It gets lonely here."
Lia:
"I know that! Wish I was there with you!" (kisses)
Joel:
"It's fine my Love. We'll soon be united together. Thank you for your hope and faith in me.
I love you!!"

Lia:
"Wonderful to hear, Dear! I thought you were going to tell me that you wanted to be here with me! I love you so much!" (Kisses, hearts)

June 20, 2018, 8:15 PM

Joel:
"One last thought I would leave you with would be my only regret if this was the last day of the rest of my life is I would not have the pleasure of your company. I mean what I say. Until we meet again, luscious kisses filled with what you have taste for your partner in pleasure. I shake with thoughts of Divine Blessings for us, my only wish is that I wish I could be with you, I will see you soon I hope!"

Lia:
"Baby...the sooner the better!" (Heart, kiss)

June 21, 2018, 9:15 AM

Lia:
"Baby, if you need money, tell me, do not wait, and lapse the phone or your apartment! I mean it!"

Joel:
"Yes, my Love, maybe next week! But don't hurt yourself. I love you. You are so great for me! (Heart) I don't know what I'd do without you!"

Lia:
"Have someone take a picture of you and send it to me! I need it please!"

June 21, 2018. 12:32 PM

Joel:
"Okay love!"

June 21, 2018, 1:34 PM

Joel:
"I managed to get someone to give me their phone without thinking I'll run away with it!
Lia:
"Don't get arrested with stupid stuff! Phones are traceable!"
Joel:
"No, no. That was a joke baby!" I'm not going to run with someone's phone, I'm no thief!
I mean they agreed to give me their phone for one picture".
Lia:
"OK, take it and send it!"

June 21, 2018, 3:41 PM

Joel:
"I look so old now, unlike when we started talking, I'm old now!"
JOEL SEND LIA A PICTURE GIANLUCA VACCHI AS HIM
Lia:
"Well, now you've done it! Unless you are an unknown twin of Gianluca Vacchi, you must think me to be the stupidest woman on earth to think that this is a picture of you! I am glad I asked and happy you replied because all that this was, is no longer!
My heart is shattered but I feel so much worse for you, living a fake life of deception as a thief, liar, cheat, absolutely disgusting! Don't worry, Karma has a way of bringing you to a high mountain where you will stand before G-d and have to answer for what you've done one day! Too bad you will never know what real love feels like!"

Joel:
"What is this? You're back at this again? Lia?? Who is this man you always confuse me to be? What's all this you're telling me? I'm not ready for this, not tonight please! Goodnight, we'll talk tomorrow!"

Lia:
"Stop playing this song! I know the cousin of Gianluca and I know him. Stop being someone else! Unless you are his lost twin you are not this person!"

Joel:
"What has gotten into you! You don't know a man you've been in love with? You don't know who you share your heart with?"

Lia:
"I would like that, I would respect it better. But you are not Gianluca! Understand!"

Joel:
"I am not and have not claimed to be, why would I claim to be someone else? What then will I say if I come to you as another man? I am one man."

Lia:
"Exactly my question!"

Joel:
"I honored your request today and this is what I get in return from you, you must now wonder why I ignore you when you come up with these allegations."

Lia:
"I'm going to send your picture to Gianluca and Arneso and will confirm!"

Joel:
"What's that nonsense! Why are you sending my pictures to anyone? Why are you disgracing me like this? I forbid it. This is mediocrity Lia."

Lia:
"It's a $600 shirt you are wearing, I want to know who made it?"

Joel:
"This wasn't how we started this day! "Baker'" that's the maker of the shirt. Fuck $600. Its 30 euros here, stop it! Please! What $600?? Who's feeding you these?
I have two black pants I have worn since I got out, got me a set of shirts for the summer and a few tees to wear at home. I told you before, I could do all my laundry in one night with no sweat and that's why I don't care that I have no washing machine. Jesus Lia, what's wrong with you?'
"When will you ever give up? Do you want to keep this up? Let's fucking get me home, that's what we talk about all day but this is what you're actually doing? I trust you and you only, don't squash that please, I beg you!"
Lia:
"It must be very lonely not to be able to trust anyone!"
Joel:
"Tell me about it!"
Lia:
"That's why we get along so well, we are in the same place! Except I have proven my trust and you have not!"
Joel:
"Have not? Now you discredit me and what love and trust I have for you? Okay baby!"
Lia:
"$200K you've received! OK!! I don't even have your address!"
Joel:
"What good will having my address do for us? Sending me flowers when I'm away? I've given you everything you've asked for as well my Darling!
I understand what this is, it's anxiety from not ever meeting, the stress builds and builds in us until it covers in and pours out like lava. Won't stop until all is out!"
"I'm tensed up myself and I don't want to leave you upset tonight or ever! "

"You know that regardless of everything I do have the best interest for you at heart. I'd never fade from you even if you leave me.

$200K, I'll pay back when I eventually find my way home. It's not money taken by force nor is it stolen from you my Dear, you speak of Karma as if I'm here to leave you somehow behind.

You are my Soul and you and I believe it, or not, are intertwined.

Why are you ignoring me? You come up with these allegations and ignore me? Really baby?"

LIA:

"This was the point when I lost my cool with the man whom I had interwoven my Soul with. I did not understand why he would be hiding his identity from me after all we had gone through together.

This tapestry was a picture of something that I did not want to see. I at least had to tell him that I knew that he was not the man in all the pictures he had sent.

My heart cringed because he was confirming that he did not want to be found and even if he ever made it back to the USA, how was I going to recognize him anyway? What was the point of this entire relationship if he was hiding behind the pictures of a famous model?

I did not know that his contract would become null and void if a picture of him was released to anyone in the world. He did not tell me.

My soul was taken by him and my heart was shattered as well but he was correct, I had allowed it to take place. Everything that I had given to him was all of my free will."

"He had just professionally guided me in receiving everything he wanted and I innocently was not sure how and if I could stop."

QUEEN ELIZABETH ENAHORO:

"Queen Elizabeth Enahoro had made a provision in Joels contract that if he revealed an image of himself, his contract with her would become null and void and he would lose all his investment and not be able to collect his contract money.

He never told me this and my reaction was always one of betrayal and disappointment!
How can I love a man whom I did not know what he looked like? How can I find a man whose picture and ID I did not have?

Queen Elizabeth Enahoro was aware of this event and was taking great pleasure in seeing Joel arguing with me all the time. What woman would love a man who will not show himself to her?
It would be impossible, and she would finally get Joel to be hers. It was a great plan and it worked."

JOEL:

"Joel was offended by my outburst and reaction to him sending me pictures of someone else.

He did not explain his contract dilemma and I mistrusted everything he said, but it was too late!

I had fallen emotionally for him and had invested so much that the only choice left was to make up and stay with him in the hope of something working out and him being able to pay me back my money."

June 21, 2018, 6:28 PM

Lia:
SENDS MANY PICTURES OF GIANLUCA VACCHI TO JOEL, ALL OF THESE ARE YOU?
"These too?" Lol…and I wear the masks! I am not leaving you, you are my Soul, we are interwoven and whatever will be now, will be! But I think it's best if the masks come off, they are only for entertainment! And Karma will find you. She has been looking for you for a long time."

June 22, 2018, 1:14 PM

Joel:
"Hello Lia, how are you today?"
Lia:
"I am fine, how is your day going?"
Joel:
"I'm alright, I guess having a bad day, as today it's so hot everywhere!"
Lia:
"Try to stay cool and have a nice night!"
Joel:
"I am not a priority to you but I love you so I will let go of my sadness and embrace you because even after all, there's none like you. You show more love than anyone else on earth. I'm not happy with you, but I love you."
Lia:
"It's very well said and unfortunately for me I feel the same about you!"

June 22, 2018, 3:00 PM

Lia:
"But you have always been a priority to me! Your situation is too complex!"

Joel:
"Too complex, Yes! But solvable! I'm tired myself. But what must we do?"

Lia:
"Look, Preston could have been driving his car and I my Ranger by now, but you got the money. I trusted you with my money and with my heart and your word! You are sending me pictures of Gianluca Vacchi! What would you do if you were me?"

Joel:
"You're still on this, huh? I don't know what to say to you about this."

Lia:
"Ok. Think about it and when you have the answer to what you would do, let me know."

Joel:
"I love you with all of my heart and I have never for once betrayed you, I wouldn't start now.

I still am the same person you've fallen in love with. I assure you, you have not been dupped, I am real and so is my situation.

This isn't the first time you've come up with this and I know through this it won't be the last, we'll not until we meet, and you finally agree to what I'm saying.

Now I won't have you treat me like some secondhand lowlife you may be thinking in your head, answering me as you wish and saying whatever you like. I have respect for you, and I expect the same from you regardless of the situation."

Lia:
"I am not sure what all this is, the reality is that there is no more money to go around.

I got you out of the Hospital, I sent you on the boat and now I cannot find any more funds."

"The financiers want collateral and I have none. I have a good heart to do everything for you but this time around I need help. That is where it is. My Love is not related to the amount of money I can come up with! I just don't have any more!"

June 22, 2018, 4:52 PM

Joel:
"Your love and my love have never been based on money! I've never ever been bad to you because of money and my love for you is totally dependent on your love and compassion.
You need to trust me!"
Lia:
"I do and I love you!"

Joel:
"I love you so much! I'm sorry! I won't hurt you, I can't hurt you!" (Heart)
Lia:
"Same babe" (heart), (kisses, flower, butterfly)

CHAPTER 19

June 25, 2018, 10:39 AM

Joel:
"My darling! My woman, seeing you wake next to me would make me full of joy and gladness you see, right now all I feel is my heart racing as I long for nothing but your embrace. While I sleep, it's you I miss and now it's time for our Good Morning kiss but I'm far, far away laying sick with a broken heart. In the evenings and the mornings.
When I close my eyes it's you, I see. (Rose, butterfly)"
Lia:
"I tried to book a Hotel in Famagusta, but they are sold out for the week I wanted, so I will have to reschedule!"

June 25, 2018, 12:53 PM

Joel:
"Oh really?? You should've told me about it, I would've been able to do something maybe!"
Lia:
"I know but I wanted to surprise you!"
Joel:
"So sweet, having you like this is my personal miracle. This thought is enough for me. Stay where you are. There's no need to come here, I've told you this time and again. I'm in a hole here that's hard for me to get out of and it's embarrassing to have you come join me here! Now what we should focus on is getting the necessary funds to get me out of here!! If you have any funds you have to spare for travels and hotel trips down to this Godforsaken place, please save it up or direct it into our cause for getting me out of here before I die here. That's the most reasonable and rational thing to do in this situation."

June 25, 2028, 3:13 PM

Lia:
"I'll think about it!" (Rose, kiss face)
Joel:
"Do that and inform me about your decisions, communicate with me and we can probably settle this mess together! Thank you my Love, you mean so much to me." (Butterfly, kiss face)
Lia:
"Remember Uncle Uri, who went to Nicosia to pay the non-existing Lawyer?
He has a very bad taste in his mouth from that incident. He is done with one of his projects and I will resume conversation with him again, but I am letting you know in advance that he will never wire transfer the money, he might agree to a meeting, or he may give it to me, but it will be hand delivered so prepare yourself to look your best!"

June 26, 2018, 9:05 AM

Joel:
"Hi baby! Good morning(heart), Call me, I do miss hearing from you."
Lia:
"Hi baby!" (Heart, kiss)

June 26, 11:55 AM

Joel:
'(Heart) Are you busy? How are you?"
Lia:
"Hi baby! Sorry, I'm very busy today!" (kiss)
Joel:
"I understand. I'm checking in on you wondering how you are?"

Lia:
"How are you doing my Love?"
Joel:
"I'm okay, woke up dreaming about you, now I'm here still thinking about you!"
Lia:
"You should be thinking of how to get yourself out of there!"
Joel:
"Like I can forget that bit!"
Lia:
"This is your journey, and you need to work on getting you out! We all have journeys which we need to complete it. Enjoy your night!" (Heart, kiss)

June 26, 2018, 4:27 PM

Lia:
("Sends Joel "La vie en Rose" on Youtube.com")

June 27, 2018, 6:29 AM

Joel:
"I have to confess, this is the most wonderful song. It's my new favorite! Thank you!
I have one for you as well!

(Sends Lia Phil Collins "Against all Odds" on youtube.com)
I've always loved songs by Phil, thinking you may as well, tell me what you think My Darling?"

Lia:
"You will always be my Darling as long as I live! (Hart, kiss)"

June 27, 2018, 12:17 PM

Joel:
"<3"

June 27, 2018, 2:24 PM

Lia:
"How are you doing love cat?'
Joel:
"I feel some type of way, nauseous and I've been puking all day."
Lia:
"Why Honey?"
Joel:
"I'm energy drained, I'm thinking it's something I ate?"
Lia:
"Lol…hate to say it again but drink water and flush it out!!"
Joel:
"I just need a day's rest maybe, I'm sure I've cleared everything in my stomach!
Lol, I do. I did. It's so hot so you bet I'm drinking enough water."
Lia:
"Rest well and feel better soon! I am well, thx."
Joel:
"Thank you, Sugar, (hearts, kiss face) How did your day go?"
Lia:
"I'm busy now every day, have to finish all of these websites and they go into advertising on July 15, so I have to go over everything and make sure they are presentable!"
Joel:
"15th is so close, it's crazy, what can I do to help my Darling? "

"Though I'm this far from you, I want to be involved in all you do day after day. It's not fair that you do this alone!"
Lia:
"Thank you so much but I have two IT's and that is all the men I want to handle while I work.
I have to download all the items I want to sell on each site and I'm the only one that can make the selection now. Later I'll decide if going forward they should do it as well."
Joel:
"How far have you gone? Do you think you can reach the deadline?"
Lia:
"Deadline will be met! I am a little ahead of schedule, but I have a few days to review etc."
Joel:
"This is so much, too much for you! When would you ever rest?"
Lia:
"Thank you for being so sweet while you are not even feeling well my Love! I just want you better! Kisses!! I rest with you only! You know that already!!"
Joel:
"I'll be better thanks to you. You've shown me so much love, honestly you are my reason for existing! I hope you find time to eat with all the ups and downs my Love!"
Lia:
"I hope to always be the reason for existence and be able to eat together with you! Kiss!"
Joel:
"I still owe you a magnificent rooftop dinner date, <3!"
Lia:
"Thank you!"
Joel:
"No, thank you, you shouldn't be thanking me!"
Lia:
"I want to! (flower)"

Joel:
"I love you Lia, <3, so freaking much!! I adore you and it's why I cannot stay upset with you.
You really are tattooed in my heart, you are just there controlling what I do and the feeling of having you in there is just magnificent!"
Lia:
"Same for you Dear!"
Joel:
"You might call it spiritual logistics, or you might just call it weird.
Baby, sometimes you have to move away to get closer. Either way, it helps to remember it from time to time that our union is blessed by G-d Himself!"
Lia:
"From your mouth to G-d's ears!"
Joel:
"Amen"
Lia:
"Going to exercise class."
Joel:
"Sends Lia a song: "Time to say goodbye" by Andrea Bocelli and Sarah Brightman. Enjoy!"
Lia:
"Thank you, my Darling! Rest and feel better! (Kiss face)"
Joel:
"Thank you, my Love! Shalom <3, Chaim Sheli. I love you to bits and nothing can take my love for you anyway, nothing can take you from me, not this job, not distance, not death, I will be with you forever!
Lia:
"I love you!"

June 27, 2018, 7:44 PM

Joel:
"Everything about the future is uncertain, but one thing is for sure that G-d has already planned all our tomorrows. We just have to trust him today. I hope the joyful spirit keeps glowing in your heart, I hope all the negative stress, anxiety and difficulties also end tonight."
Lia:
"OK Love!" (Heart)

June 28, 2018, 9:49 AM

Lia:
"Hi, are you feeling, better?"
Joel:
"Hi my Love, how are you today? Yes, I'm feeling better now, glad to have sweet words from you yesterday. How was your night my Love?"
Lia:
"Stormy! But the sun is out now. Not that it matters, it's going to be one of the 3 hottest days and I have work to do in air conditioning!"

June 28, 2018, 11:15 AM

Joel:
"How did you sleep in the heat then? Did you know I had sent angels to cover you and make sure you're sound? Oh, my Love!"
Lia:
"I always know that my Love! It's why I sleep so well!!" (Heart, kiss)

June 28, 2018, 3:37 PM

Lia:
"Baby Cakes, when I am done with the sites, I will send them to you for your OK! Just hold on tight! Your opinion is the most important to me!" (kiss)

Joel:
"Heart, thank you! I've waited so long for this. How are you my Love?"

Lia:
"Having fun downloading a lot of cool stuff! Waiting for my IT to synchronize Chrome with my Mac so I can download from AliExpress too. I am going to take a break now and go exercise my butt off, I've got so much energy and excitement, must release!"

Joel:
"Lol...you've learned, yeah!! It's good, I'm impressed!! AliExpress too? You're a booming woman! I wish I was on you right now having you release all this energy in me!
I need you Lia, all the cells and atoms in me are calling for your touch, the feel of your fingers through my skin, my Love!"

Lia:
"Ahhh...my Love!"

Joel:
"I care so much for you!"

Lia:
"I have you! All I need!"

Joel:
"Hearts, I bow to you, Queen!"

Lia:
"We have to make the money which we need!"

Joel:
"Thank you for your Love! I'm all in with you, I know you have great ideas and things would've been better if I was with you! I'm so curious as to what the concept you had come up with looks like?"
Lia:
"Don't fret, I have unending ideas!"
Joel:
"I know you always have such amazing visualization."
Lia:
"I wish with all my might and desire that I was able to release all my energy with you!
My happiness level would reach the roof!" (Rose, heart, kiss)
Joel:
"Same here Angel!"
Lia:
"I started walking to the gym and it's raining so hard I got soaked and I am sitting in a café with tea! Flooding the streets, never seen it so strong! Lol…Now is such a good time to run in the rain together, get all wet and wild!! (Crazy face, heart)"
SENDS JOEL A PICTURE OF THE FLOODED STREET IN NYC

June 28, 2018, 6:03 PM

Joel:
"What better thing to do with you! But don't get sick as you're wet my Love!
I need you to feel better. Why's the weather this wet though? Lol…"
Lia:
"Does not matter! I can still rock and roll! (Crazy face) Thank you for your concern, Love".

Joel:
"Haha…You are my Angel, I care so much for you! (Heart, butterfly) Done downloading?"
Lia:
"Yes baby! Done for the day. Thank you!"

June 28, 2018, 7:58 PM

Joel:
"My Love!"
Lia:
"Baby Cat!"

June 29, 2018, 8:21 PM

Joel:
"Are you Okay? Just say yes at least, I'm so worried."
Lia:
"Yes baby! All good!"
Joel:
"Aright (heart), please let me know you're good daily (heart) I love you!"
Lia:
"I've had a good day and I've missed you the whole time!" (heart)
Joel:
"(Heart, clover), okay my Love! Now I'm glad I've heard that. I'm glad you're well!
Thank you, my Love. Now let me go back to sleep. I love you!"
Lia:
"I love you!" (Heart, kiss)

June 30, 2018, 7:37 AM

Joel:
"Good morning, hope you have a good day my Love! Woke to chirping birds and thought of you!"
Lia:
"Good morning! Woke up to you in color! (Kiss face) Enjoy your day!"

SENDS JOEL A PICTURE OF A MAN WALKING IN THE STREET

Joel:
"This is so beautiful, so colorful!"
Lia:
"By Lior Sela, my favorite Artist!"
Joel:
"May I save it baby? I'm still staring, it's spectacular really, I love it!"
Lia:
"I'll ask him to send it to me. I'll save it for you!"
Joel:
"It's a beautiful piece and the use of beautiful colors, that's just what lures me in!"
Lia:
"Glad you like it Dear!"
Joel:
"Thank you, I like anything you show me, the color hair dog, remember?"
The representation of your dreams in color, you in color! <3 everything my Lover! Are you okay?"
Lia:
"Thank you! Everything is good. Enjoy your day!"
Joel:
"Thank you, Darling, I will talk to you after dinner, should be around lunch where you are!"

Lia:
"(Heart)"
Joel:
"I don't know what's going on Honey?"
Lia:
"Are you Okay?"
Joel:
"I don't, I am okay my love, are you?"
Lia:
"Yes, did you pay for the phone?"
Joel:
"I tried and it got through but there was no confirmation message!
I concluded it would have gone through. I'm not sure what it is now."
Lia:
"Ok! It was nice to hear your voice even for a bit! Thank you. (heart) Have a good night!"
Joel:
"Thank you, my darling! I love you! Go do what you need to do and take it easy, Please, okay?"
Lia:
"Ok Honey! I'll be indoors all day tomorrow! Lol… (hearts and kisses)"
Joel:
"I believe G-d sent you through to me. I intend to keep you! <3"
Lia:
"Ok, but I get to keep you and you get to love and protect me!"
Joel:
"As your Man and Royal King, that's all my heart desires!"
Lia:
"(Hearts, Kisses)"

June 30, 2018, 8:21 PM

Joel:
Sends Lia an Email:

"I intend to keep you my Darling as my Wife, to love and grow old with, in sickness and good health, I love you with my dear heart and I shan't let anything happen to you so long as I live.

Already concerning this final stage collecting the shipment from the port, I feel I've graced you into this and now I'm worried that you're stressed and it's because of me, I never intended to stress you or burden you with any of this honey, yes now I'm in need and truly who better to turn to this my partner?

We're capable of doing this between us, I represent you and it's vice versa. I have to be able to appear rigid and strong, so you look good and you get your respect.

I don't want to appear weak, I only want to make you proud my darling. I love you and I want you, I also want you to understand that to understand I've never been in the position to need someone and now being here in this situation makes me nervous.

Baby I have you now as my partner and you're the number one person in my life now and there's no one above you, you're my Queen. Baby, it's me and you against the world, and I love that I'm able to say that about us, my baby girl and I, we'll do this together.

Baby do you know my translator is a good man, he's also tried for me and I really, I owe him huge, he's but an employee of mine but he's putting it in for me too."

"You on the other hand, lol, I think I should owe you my life as you always are around to encourage and support me daily, you strengthen me and you have been here for me, you've shown me so much love and happiness I never knew existed and you continue to show me and I'm so grateful for that honey, you're a great woman and I know you'd be an even better wife to me because I know what is in your heart and your heart is pure.

I've tickled your right brain! You've put butterflies in my yoni... And fire in my soul so thank you for rekindling the light in my soul, in you I've found what I had been searching for all this while, I love you and I have nothing to hide, I am your open book.

You have express rights over everything I own and possess, my banks and its details are available to you upon request, the keys to my house and so are the keys to my heart.
I wanted to touch on some things you had mentioned in one of your messages to me, something you mentioned about having money problems and what nots, I want to be clear that I have no money problems, I have more than enough in my account even after this shipment and project is done.

All this while I've gotten into problems that would require consulting you or asking you for help and understanding our situation and also, as a man I should stand strong and not let my weakness show. I find my way through, I'm resourceful but helpless in this situation and depend on you to bring me out, you know how you're resourceful too.

I have no one helping me, but you! You've done so much for me already I cannot say thank you enough and I thank you."

"Everything is alright and will be under control, I'll hold on to the lion masculinity you know and trust me with, I have you in my mind and I want to come back to you so bad, I miss you.

Please don't be anxious my love, because anxiety will bring and jinx bad luck to me, I can't jeopardize everything we've worked hard together for to go to waste, and I need you to understand that, I implore you to stand beside me as my warrior, soldier, wife, girlfriend, and best friend.

On my team there's just you, we need to work together to come out of this, please, who better equipped with the knowledge and intelligence to advise and support me on this?

None but you baby, you're my everything and I mean it when I said it, I will never say I love you if I didn't mean it and since you know how much I love you, the question of coming home in time shouldn't exist, all I want in this miserable world is you, my shining light.

I'm here to protect you from everything and I will take care of you, sadly baby this money shouldn't be a problem to you as I have so much of it saved up entirely for you, see I have been searching for you my whole life and I know I have you.

I don't want to fight with you concerning nothing worst of all money, when I have it, I'll give you to sort yourself out and go shopping and when you do have yours you take me out and spoil me and I believe that's how it should be done, and in terms of pain and sorrow too I'll do the same as well, I'll never leave you in trouble and I pray you honor me and never let me go stray or fall into evil hands, I hope you have it in your heart to be there for me when it counts. I'll stand for you if my life depends on it, I love you."

"Don't be afraid my love, for we have everything under control, even if it does not appear so. I want to go on a vacation with you, or we could go on Virgin Galactic with me to explore space for $200k per person once they begin traveling, I can afford it and you're more than worth a trip like that, to the stars and the heavens above us. I have so much to do with you. We need a house of our own to stay and live together in which you won't flip, lol, but live and make love with me, you'll be my Queen and I your King in our kingdom.

I may never understand how deeply my heart feels for you, a life without you will decimate me entirely. You bring me to climax without sex, I love you, you are my soul in human form.
Never part from me, I won't ever let you out of my sight, I will never stop fighting for you because you're my life and life is effort, I'll stop only when I die!"
I love you, Joel.

Lia:

Writes back an email to Joel:

"My Darling,

I am so honored that you trust me to express your feelings in this way! I admire and respect your courage! You know that I've loved you from the start and trusted your word despite all sorts of advice!

Your situation is still complex and confusing to me and sometimes I feel that I must explode and dictate but, in my heart, I feel only love for you, and the confusion is with my own feelings because they are strong, and I don't understand their reality sometimes."

"I cannot imagine myself in your position, but my Soul is bound with you forever and that is how it is. My ring, which I wear, is for my soul which I have found in you, and I search and wait for you every day. I cannot part from you my Love, I strive to be your Queen and seek unending happiness for both of us! "

LIA:

"No matter what happened and how confusing his situation was, even the unbelievable parts, Joel became a constant in my life and parting from him became an impossibility in my brain.

Anything that he needed became my need, anything that hurt him, hurt me, we became one for all and all for one."

QUEEN ELIZABETH ENAHORO:

"Queen Elizabeth Enahoro was keeping a very close watch on Joel's every move. Their conversations and meetings became more frequent because Joel wanted to settle his business dealings and leave but her intentions changed to sheer determination to do anything to make Joel stay with her forever!"

CHAPTER 20

July 1, 2018, 8:44 AM

Joel:
"Love, your smiles, so gorgeous, you're the reason for my survival, I've seen now, you are simply my everything, my love and desire, no other Man shall replace me in your heart because I will possess the throne which resides within your heart, for you are my Queen and I am your King.
I love you so much and thank you for your Love, care, and protection.
Good morning my Darling!"
Lia:
"You are incredible! Totally amazing!" (Heart, kisses)
Joel:
"Those are words often used to describe you, I am not yet worthy of such praise my Darling!"
Lia:
"I share all my praises equally with you!" (Love cat)
Joel:
"My Queen, you've never failed to make me smile! Even in the darkest time and the worst nights! I'm incredibly lucky to have found you and I really do mean this, I am yours!"
Lia:
SENDS JOEL A PICTURE OF A COUPLE WALKING TOGETHER
Joel:
"How did you sleep baby?"
Lia:
"Very good and very late! How is your day my Love? What are you doing today?"

Joel:
"It's so hot, it's burning here today, the weather here is incredibly annoying to me, it gets on my nerves, but I don't have anything to say about it! I have to go do what I need to do if I can have anything out, I can do.

It's Sunday today so all I've done was to go get some drinking water from the market which is far and now I'm resting on the patio thinking, talking to you, and watching the laundry dry. Lol...quite a way to spend my day, right?"

Lia:
"Same here baby! So hot and humid! Please take care to stay cool anywhere you can find! Rest and yes...think of good thoughts!" "Smooching on the patio with me!! (Kisses) Very good time to have some ice cream!"

Joel:
"I know baby, I wish I could bathe you every ten minutes or even take you vacationing elsewhere around the world to enjoy and escape this uncomfortable heat! Ha...ha...well I'm having fresh bananas! Got them on my way back. Ha-ha...Goodluck making me eat ice cream after my lung procedure!"

Lia:
"Ice cream is too cold for the throat?

Joel:
"Well, it's not easy when it goes past the throat but with you around, I'll manage!"

Lia:
"Will handle you with care then!" (Flower)

Joel:
"You already do, what more can I ask for? You give me refuge at a time no one wants me, and you think I'll forget that? No baby, you're my life and the only reason I exist! Thank you! Have you had breakfast yet? I know it's late, almost midday, lol..."

Lia:
"Good breakfast today! Scramble of eggs with feta cheese and tomato with olive oil. It was yummy! I miss you, Love!" (Flower)

Joel:
"I miss you too, my Baby! Thank you for your love and care, you will forever remain in my heart. I don't want you to ever think I can do you bad my Love!"

Lia:
"These are not the concerns I question!"

Joel:
"Whatever they are, I will conquer them and prove my legitimate love for you!"

Lia:
"I love you baby Boy! You are my Soul!" (Love cat)

Joel:
"Thank you sugar Love. I love you, thank you! Okay, go enjoy your day my Love!"

Lia:
"I will be here Honey! The AC is my lover today! Do not fret. I'll be working. I love you!"

Joel:
"Love you more my Darling! I'll try to call again later to see if this phone thing goes through."

Lia:
"I have news for you! Check to make sure, but I heard that Palestine will be establishing a port in Cyprus. Maybe they are all moving?"

Joel:
"What? Palestine? New port? Where's this? North or South? Baby, we can't live in this agony all this while until they build a New Port before I get out! Please help me get the remainder for this payment my Dear!"

Lia:
"I am trying, but this is what I heard. Don't get frazzled, it may not be true!"

Joel:
"The earth shall tremble, and tear and I will not shake for you! Thank you for all you've done for me, but I really need to get out!"
Lia:
"I have to go to work now. Talk later!" (heart)
Joel:
"To start this life we've envisioned together, my dinner date for you on the rooftop, your Range, I'll keep trying, it's appreciation Sunday!"

LIA:

"The pressure was on again. With every sentence he said the last word was to get the remainder of the money and get him out. It was the usual pattern of all fun and then the dagger. It was all up to me again.

The whole sadness was that I had no more money to give, and I prolonged all our conversations for as long as I could on any subject because I did not want to break his heart and hopes of coming to me. I wanted that magic wand to appear in my hand."

JOEL AND LIA:

Joel:
"You are lovely, and you have a beautiful mind, nothing rivals you! (Heart, rose), I close my eyes so I can lock in the dreams I have of us both on an island of our own with none of this before us and all of it behind us, this dream will come true."
Lia:
"It will! I know it! Make sure the island has a hospital on it!"
Joel:
"Lol...what for?"

Lia:
"You have a lung disease. In case you over sex on the island and you need help?"
Joel:
"Lol, nah, nothing will phase me at all! I'm with you, remember? Having you, having a best friend to share life with, the good things and the hard things of life is the key to a good life."
Lia:
"Yes. Very true! You are incredible!"

July 1, 2018, 3:02 PM

Joel:
"Hi my love."
Lia:
"Heart!"

July 1, 2018, 5:12 PM

Joel:
"My Darling!"
(Joel calls Lia and they speak on the phone for a long time.)
Lia:
"Sleep and relax my dear, it will be OK!" (Heart, rose)
Joel:
"Thank you for your consoling words. I love you!"
Lia:
"I love you!" (Love cat)

July 2, 2018, 7:33 AM

Joel:
"Good morning my Darling, up, up, get up and have a productive day today!"

Lia:
"Kisses and my warmest embrace!" (Kiss faces)
Joel:
"Coldest! Right now, it's the cool hugs I need. The warm ones will burn, it's like 90 degrees."
Lia:
"Same here. ACs are working overtime! Take the bus and go swimming. Take some pictures for me! Stay cool!" (heart)
Joel:
"<3 the fan here working triple time, I tell you, I am in control of its destiny right here it dies or lives with me this thing! If I ever make it out of here, I'm taking it with me!"
Lia:
"Sounds like you have a best friend! "

July 2, 2018, 2:41 PM

Joel:
"Hello my Darling!"
Lia:
"Hello baby! Did you have dinner, Love?"

July 3, 2018, 6:57 AM

Joel:
"Good morning, Love! Sending you "not letting go" hugs and kisses!! Enjoy this day!"
Lia:
"Enjoy your day!" (Hearts, kisses)
Joel:
"Thank you, my Darling! Inspiring!"
Lia:
"Glad you are in a good spirit. Hugs and so many kisses, I cannot count!"
Joel:
"Just as I want them. Thank you!"

Lia:
"You are welcome!"

July 3, 2018, 1:30 PM

Lia:
"(heart, love cat)"

July 3, 2018, 3:30 PM

Joel:
"Hi my Love!"
Lia:
"Hi (Love cat)"
Joel:
"That's how I'm feeling now!" (hearts)
Lia:
"I'm always feeling this way toward you!" (kiss)
Joel:
"It's a good feeling to have, to be lost in someone!"
Lia:
"Indeed."
Joel:
"I love being lost in you!"
Lia:
"Best place baby! You and me!"
Joel:
"What have you been up to?" (heart)
Lia:
"I now have to download as many products as possible and on the 15th, they go into advertising on the web. It has been a busy few day. Now I can relax and go to a barbecue tomorrow, see some fireworks and enjoy! The heat is supposed to cool down a bit by tomorrow!
How is it by you? Did you have something for dinner?"

Joel:
"Hope it does. You're making such a break with your work and I'm so happy!"
"You should see me smiling as if it's my project moving as scheduled. I'm so happy baby, you deserve the rest for tomorrow."
Lia:
"Thank you for your support and smile, it's so appreciated!"
Joel:
"The fireworks should be for your valor!"
Lia:
"As long as I find a spot from where I can see them. Thank you!"
Joel:
"I wished I was able to support you through better!"
Lia:
"Like wrap yourself around me and watch the fireworks together?"
Joel:
"That thought is so in the right direction, Yes my Love, just like that!"
Lia:
"I know, I would like nothing better!"
Joel:
"I love the mood you've just set for us, I love that you consider being wrapped around each other is the greatest form of support we can give ourselves. Right now baby, the thoughts of it comes really close to the real thing for me."
Lia:
"Bliss!" (Heart, kiss)
Joel:
"I cannot live in a world without you, I don't know how I've done it all those years."
Lia:
"I was thinking the same but then I felt like the now is so much better than anything of the past, as if it never was!"

Joel:
"I need a cruise with you and a massage on board!" (Queen, King)
Lia:
"Yes!"
Joel:
"Right? Lol... I'm starting to think nothing would be better!"
Lia:
"The sooner the better!"
Joel:
"Does not have to be a big boat! Small yacht would do. I want our own privacy so the less people the better."
Lia:
"No small yachts for me. I saw a movie where they go on a romantic trip and then the weather turns and he gets lost and she's alone and she goes to find him and must get him to safety! Lol...never!!"
Joel:
"Lol...Wow, that escalated really quickly!"
Lia:
"Think of something else!"
Joel:
"Okay Honey, no small yachts, ones with hundreds of people on board. Whatever makes you happy works for me. Whatever rocks your boat!"
Lia:
"Love you! (heart) You have a good idea, I appreciate it, but I am scared after seeing the movie!"
Joel:
"Lol...it's fine baby! What movie was it you watched?"
Lia:
"Adrift" is the name of the movie. I will have dinner soon without you! Blah..."
Joel:
"I've seen it before but I'm not sure I remember the whole thing. Must watch it again."

Lia:
"You go ahead. I'm still scared! Same story as us but in a different venue! How was your day, baby cats?"
"All I know is that I CRAVE you! On the boat, off the boat, on land, at sea, in the mountains, on an island, with people, without, at home, in the store, in the shower, the supermarket, you name it, same craving!"

July 4, 2018, 9:33 AM

Joel:
"Good morning my sweet (heart) hope you slept well my Darling!"
Lia:
"Hi, it is a good morning indeed!" (Heart, kiss)

July 4, 2018, 10:59 AM

Joel:
"I miss you dearly."
Lia:
"I miss you dearly too!"
Joel:
"I'll be better, I just need to be with you. I'm not good my Darling! (heart)"
Lia:
"What's happening?"
Joel:
"I'm dying here! I want to be home! I want to be away from this!"
Lia:
"I know, working on this! Stay calm!"
Joel:
"I want to be with you!"
Lia:
"I know."

Joel:
"I haven't been with you since the minute you captured my heart, I love you, I really do, you make it so easy to love you but this complication makes it seem so hard for us.
We're not these people, we're so simple and desire so little."
(heart)
Lia:
"I know baby! It will be soon. We'll be together!"
Joel:
"(heart, boat, Jewish fag) Thank you my Darling!"

LIA:

"Joel was sweet talking me to death. I was getting really tired from being under such pressure. I couldn't be myself. I had to play him every day and sweet talk him back.

It was not that I did not want to or because I didn't feel amorous toward him, it was that I couldn't relax, and I didn't know if he was that way and meant it, or was sweet because he wanted the money from me.

He had decided that I am the one to get him the rest of the money he needed, and we were going to go at it until I came up with it. He did not understand or accept that my money had run out.

I couldn't help him no matter what I did. I was overspent and overcharged and no good intentions on my side was going to help him. I didn't know anything about his mayhem with his business."

QUEEN ELIZABET ENAHORO:

"Queen Elizabeth Enahoro was swarming with delight at Joel's misery and desperation.

She drew delight at the fact that he would not be able to pay his fees and was living like a beggar by himself on the island. She was delighted that she might have him forever soon."

JOEL AND LIA:

July 4, 2018, 2:38 PM

Joel:
"Are you okay Honey?"
Lia:
"Yes baby! At a barbecue, thinking of you! (Love cat)"

July 5, 2018, 11:21 AM

Joel:
"You can't touch love, but you can feel the sweetness that it pours into your heart. I hope you can feel it right now as I sent you my warmest hugs and kisses to make your day more beautiful and worthwhile. Good morning my beloved!" (Flower)
Lia:
"How did you know I was just thinking of you! Hugs and kisses back to you! "(Hear, kiss)
Joel:
"I have my moments! I miss you all the time, I think about you all the time. You're my Love, how are you?"
Lia:
"I am your beloved and you are mine! Ani L'Dodi!
(Heart, Love cat)"

Joel:
"(Heart), Ani L'Dodi." Love that, is that what it means?"
Lia:
"Ani L'Dodi, V'Dodi Li", "I am my beloved's, and my beloved is mine."
Joel:
"(Love face), learn a word a day? I'm still learning from you!"

July 5, 2018, 6:09 PM

Joel:
"Baby, are you OK? (Hearts), Okay, let me know when you can talk my Love!"
Lia:
"I love you baby! Everything is good! Just out for dinner. Have a good night!"
Joel:
"Okay my baby, I was checking in on you. I love you!"

July 5, 2018, 9:15 PM

Joel:
"(Heart)"
Lia:
"(Kiss)"

July 6, 2018, 8:51 AM

Joel:
JOEL SENDS A QUOTE TO LIA: "YOU MADE FLOWERS GROW IN MY LUNGS AND ALTHOUGH THEY ARE BEAUTIFUL, I CAN'T BREATHE."
Lia:
"What does this mean? It's a very disturbing first thing in the morning. Are you OK?"

Joel:
"Did not mean to disturb you, it's supposed to be a reference to how you make me feel, Darling, so good and soft, full of wonderful smells of beautiful flowers within!
I can't breathe refers to how much you've consumed me through and through, I love you!"

Lia:
"Ok Honey, I love you!" (Heart, love cat)

Joel:
"Good morning my lover, how are you?"

Lia:
"Good morning baby! I am good. Very busy and working hard! How is your day, Love?"

Joel:
"I know, the time I get to miss you is when you're working my love, but I know I got you!
My heart forever remains with you! I just pray we both survive this."

Lia:
"We have to overcome and survive! We must constantly search for L'chaim-Life, our sacred mission!"

Joel:
"(Queen, heart), Yes my Queen! You are my everything. Thank you for your love!"

Lia:
"(Heart, kisses)"

July 6, 2018, 11:46 AM

Lia:
"How are you (love cat)? You gave me such a scare this morning! Lol...sorry!"

Joel:
"Shouldn't be, I'm all yours and I'll forever be, you make me whole and keep me checked."

Lia:
"It was the part about I cannot breathe! I think I am traumatized from the hospital! "
Joel:
"There is no need to be scared for me now, I promised you I'll stay safe and take care of myself for you, the only redemption for me is to come home to you. See myself lying with you in your apartment!"
Lia:
"And my comfy bed!"
Joel:
"Not excluding that."
Lia:
"Lol...would be wonderful!" (Heart, Kiss face)
Joel:
"Hehe...What are you doing? How is it going?"
Lia:
"One headache gives more headaches...but I am moving forward!"
Joel:
"Share your aches, there's enough head here with me to take the stress."
Lia:
"Can you write a customer trust story page for each web site?"
Joel:
"Wait? What? Each Website?"
Lia:
"Yes, our wonderful customers are the secret to our success".
Joel:
"Okay! I didn't see that coming. Lol...you know I never really thought who wrote those
things on websites I visit!"

Lia:
"That is why I said, one headache makes another! Etc....etc..."
Joel:
"Lol...I'm sorry my Love", I understand more elaborately. You're right baby and please do understand that I know what you're doing and how demanding it can be on you, I believe, and I trust you. I love you!"

July 6, 2018, 3:52 PM

Lia:
"Thank you baby!" (Heart, kiss)

July 6, 2018, 9:59 PM

Joel:
"Are you Ok my Love?"
Lia:
"Thinking about you!" (Kiss)

July 7, 2018, 7:46 AM

Joel:
"(Heart, jewel), You meet thousands of people and none of them really mean anything to you.
And then you meet one person, and your life is changed forever! I have survived. I am here. Confused, screwed up, but here with you, for You!"
Lia:
"Hi Honey! You are my Hero!" (Hearts)

July 7, 2018, 8:58 AM

Lia:
SENDS PICTURE OF HEARTS TO JOEL

July 7, 2018, 11:25 AM

Joel:
"How did you sleep my Love?"

July 7, 2018, 6:28 PM

Joel:
"I just prayed for you my Dear!"
Lia:
"Baby cat, how are you my love? Thank you! Why are you praying for me?
You need it more than me! I appreciate it! Miss you…"
Joel:
"I don't, you need it as well. You are my pride and my Love!"
Lia:
"(Heart, rose, love cat)"
Joel:
"I was praying for your security and that G-d should bless you immensely!
Thank you for your love and support, those I can never repay you! I am eternally in your debt!"
Lia:
"Thank you Darling!" (Heart, love cat)
Joel:
"You are welcome my Dear! What are you doing baby? How is work going?"
Lia:
"Eating Chinese food! Why are you up so late?"
Joel:
"Oh, that's nice, I want some."
Lia:
"Ok, you are most welcome to have it!"

Joel:
"I just woke up not quite long ago but don't worry about me, I'm barely awake anyway!
(Heart) Keep an extra plate, I'm in the elevator!"
Lia:
"You are so sweet and cute I want to eat you up!"
Joel:
"Careful now, I'm not like Chinese food. Darling, I bite back!"
Lia:
"I am expecting it from you!" (Crazy face)

SENDS PICTURE OF FLOWERS TO JOEL AND ALSO SENDS HIM A PICTURE OF LIA

Lia:
(Sends Joel Gianluca Vacchi, Sebastian Yatra- "Love" on youtube.com)

July 8, 2018, 6:52 AM

Joel:
"Who's this gorgeous Girl? (Heart, love faces) I'm always blooming whenever I get a picture of you! "
Lia:
"(Heart, kiss face)"

July 8, 2018, 7:57 AM

Joel:
"Good morning my Love! How did you sleep?"

"It's asexual you still go to bed without me, but I am positive this would be over soon so bear with me and hold on tightly!" (Heart)

Lia:
"Some dreams are absolutely fantastic sometimes! Baby, you and me in bed would be a dream to behold!! (Love cat)!! Doing anything exciting today? (Hearts)"

Joel:
"Yup, I'm taking a 5 mile walk today, this evening! I do that to help me relax, I might call you to walk with me, <3 on the phone of course, I love you baby! Too much to express over the internet or lines. With all my heart I do! I want you in my arms all day and night. I'll show you how much you mean to me, how much of a "Goddess" you are to me."

Lia:
"Wow! Amazing! Enjoy! Wish I was there with you walking! I love you my Man! So proud of you!! You make me excited and I am burning now!" (Heart, kisses)

Joel:
"Thank you, baby cats! Hoping you have a fabulous day as well, I wish you were here though, would be an even more fabulous day with you! You know I'd never leave your side and we'll never leave the bedroom either!"

Lia:
"I want to come and be with you!" (Butterfly)

Joel:
"Too many adventures to be had, too many dreams and wishes to fulfil. I love you and I want to be with you too. You are the very backbone that supports me!"

Lia:
"Yes baby! So many with you!"

Joel:
"I truly need you to survive!"

Lia:
"I will baby, it's difficult but I will handle it! You are my constant inspiration and the fuel to my desires! (Love cat), Kisses as many as you can handle on your 5-mile walk. Breathe and intake the experience!" (Flower)

Joel:
"Okay baby! Thank you for your encouraging words my Love! I would walk the distance to you if I could. Since this started up until now, I'm sure I would have reached where you are right now, honestly!"

Lia:
"Love you! How did the walking thing begin?"

Joel:
"Well, I've always walked. Sometimes in the nighttime, it's quiet and I can think. I've told you before!"

Lia:
"I love walking! You are just like I am! Stay on safe paths, don't be a roaming lunatic like me!"

Joel:
"You're my psychic twin (heart), my essential half that completes me and that's why I cannot live in this world or any other without you!" (Heart, flower)

Lia:
"Where is this walk taking place, around the beach, mountains, city? Be sure your phone is fully charged and or you have a charging source! Is it cooler at night? Be safe and happy on this walk!" (Hearts)

Joel:
"We'll be together no matter what, I think the universe keeps us together and sometimes I feel the further the distance the stronger the love, I love you regardless, you're an amazing woman and a fighter, I admire you, I am glad that you're on my side.

Yes, I'm so proud of you regarding all the help you've done to me, you're not a selfish woman, you have a beautiful heart. I really want to be with you forever. I appreciate you!"

Lia:
"Same here my Man! (Heart), Enjoy the walk!"

Joel:
"(Hearts)"

July 8, 2018, 2:59 PM

Lia:
"How was your walk, Love?"

July 8, 2018, 4:29 PM

Joel:
"My Love, how are you? I did enjoy my walk, thank you very much, I had just come back and I'm about to jump in the shower! What are you doing?"
Lia:
"I'm so glad you enjoyed it! I love the shower, can I come in as well?" (Heart, kisses)
Joel:
"Needless to ask, my doors are open, leave your robe in your room, I need you naked when I'm naked so I can kiss and hold you and feel the electricity flow between us!"
Lia:
"Then I'm there babe! Will soap you up but watch out, I am very clever! And very needy for your touch!"
Joel:
"I know you are, I'll slip right into you, so you'd better watch out my Baby!"
Lia:
"Enjoy your shower my Dearest!" (Heart, kisses)
Joel:
"Can't get you wet, can I?" (hearts)
Lia:
"I am already wet and hungry!" (Kiss faces)

July 9, 2018, 8:16 AM

Joel:
"(Hearts), Hi my Darling! Good morning Angel, how are you?"

Lia:
"Just woke up, Love! Getting ready for the day! Very busy and crazy! All good. How is your day, Love?"
Joel:
"Hot, sun is shining, all good! I wish you a wonderful and prosperous day Darling!"
Lia:
"(Heart, rose, love cat), You as well Love!"
Joel:
"Thank you, baby, I'll check back at you later on, go get ready for the day! (heart). Honey, I beg for you to be blessed and your choice to be at peace. It's not what happens around you, or to you, it is what happens in you. You are Priceless!!"

July 10, 2018, 5:17 PM

Joel:
"Baby? This is an emergency? Are you OK? Call me! Now I'm worried, I'm very worried!
Are you ok baby?"
Lia:
"What is the matter with you? I am fine. I am on a long distance call and you are calling me like a mad man during my call. What is it?"
Joel:
"Nothing! G-d, I saw 5 missed calls from you!"
Lia:
"I am going to send you glasses so you see better!"
Joel:
"Back to back! And I shouldn't FREAK OUT OR WORRY? I don't even know what to think. Ah! This woman…You really have me dancing to your music!"
Lia:
"That's why you Love me! I don't want you to worry about me."

"I want you to find your financiers and get your life together. I will be fine! When and if you ever show up, we will deal with it then!"

JOEL:

"Joel had discovered that his financier was consorting with Queen Elizabeth Enahoro and quickly realized that he would not give him the full amount necessary to pay off his debt.

Not only that but Joel was afraid that the Queen would step in and seize all the money he received from his financier and then Joel would have to pay him back without being able to pay his tax.

He was going crazy trying to figure out how to get rid of Queen Elizabeth Enahoro and how to get a partner who would be able to help him get out of this hopeless dilemma.

The whole time he was sweet talking to me, he was trying to have me be engaged in his mission for not losing his mind and having me stay and be by his side so he will have motivation and a purpose. I did not know any of this again because he did not tell me the whole story."

JOEL AND LIA:

Joel:
"Lol...I love you though, I really do, and I will never deny that."
Lia:
"Remember that most tattoos can be removed but not the one in the heart! That is all you need to remember!"

Joel:
"If? Lol...I know I'm not dying here my Love. Not that one, no one else has that but you and I. We're infused together, I love you!"
Lia:
"And it will always be that way!"
Joel:
"I trust you, my whole heart is yours, I love you."
Lia:
"I just told you, you never have to worry about my Love or trust, my heart tattooed with you are always in me and my body!"
Joel:
"Thank you for really making me feel as I feel."
Lia:
"I love you my Love!"
Joel:
"Love, love how that sounds to me! So, are you going to call me?"
Lia:
"No baby, I cannot now!"
Joel:
"(heart) Okay."
Lia:
"You go to sleep, I will call you in the morning!"
Joel:
"Aright Love!"

Lia:
"(kisses)"
Joel:
"I love you so much and I'm thinking about you!"

July 11, 2018, 6:28 AM

LIA:
"The pressure and demands from Joel were starting to wear me out. He was expecting me to find the money which he needed again for his business expenses. I could not come up with the money.
I had asked him for a picture of himself and he sent me a picture of a model that he had sent me before.
I was livid and did not understand, and Joel did not explain his situation with Queen Elizabeth Enahoro, and I decided that I just couldn't deal with all of it and despite my losses needed to pull out.
I didn't want to, I loved him and wanted us to be together, but I felt I had no choice left.
I hoped that I would have the emotional strength to actually break up and be without him!"

JOEL AND LIA:

Lia:
"I have decided, even though my heart is shattered, that I cannot love an illusion!
Hiding behind someone else's face makes you an illusion and there is nothing in an illusion that you can love!
There must be a real person behind the illusion and there is a reason for the illusion but that is yours to bear. I want a real man with body and soul to love. When and if you are ready for this you let me know, and if my Soul is free to merge with you, we will take it from there. There is nothing but good blessings that I wish for you!"

Joel:
"The strain is too much to handle, I know. I've always had high respect and high regards for you, is this why you did not answer when I called?"

Lia:
"Strain I can handle, illusions I don't want to! No baby, you did call me during an important call and then I had to go to dinner with a friend!"

Joel:
"We have plans to get me out of here, how are we living an illusion reality? You can say it's complicated but an illusion?"

Lia:
"Illusion is not reality, when you hide behind someone else's face it's creating an illusion of being that person when you are not!"

Joel:
"Personally, I don't know where you come to me with these notions, and why you come to me with them, but I know they're solidly in your heart and it worries you, I care about you so much to never ignore you or anything that hurts you. I know though that you are the one for me, because if not? How do we feel as we feel for each other, I ask?

Look what you've done to me. How do you make all these wonders come out, how you've impacted me so, you've made me come alive, I am a mess without you and I've told you countless times, how you have become the very essence of my living.

How do you see an illusion out of me when you're what comforts my soul so? How so?
We fit together so well with nothing a little as argument between us for months now, going so long.

No my baby, we are matched from the heavens, thank G-d. You and I are cut from the same fabric, and are aligned in all that we do, the passion for what we want out of life. The distance between us is devastating, yes!"

"Don't give in to it, you and I have worked so hard to get to this point, we cannot let go, I am flesh and I am yours.

There's none better for me and I couldn't have done better babe, I am no illusion so think if this were what a dream would feel like then I can only wonder what being together would feel like my Love!"

Lia:
"I am in agreement with everything you said here, therefore even more confused as to why you would hide from me behind the face of another.

If your face is hidden and you are an illusion, then your situation is the same. Can my head override this? My heart cannot give you up but until you come forward as your true self my head cannot accept this."

LIA:

"I knew that he would not let me go and I was too weak. I just couldn't be without him!"

July 11, 2018, 12:57 PM

Joel:
"(Heart, flowers) You're on my mind!"
Lia:
"I like that! Nothing will make me happier if you prove me wrong on the illusion issue!"
Joel:
"I love you, your words to me are so pure and heartfelt, I still humbly implore you to care for me in this situation. I love you and I want to come to you.
You're my life and nothing is worth more than what you do to me.!"

Lia:
"I feel the same for you and will have to wait patiently until you take care of your situation and come back and make your words come to action!" (Heart)
Joel:
"I've made so many promises. I'm bound to prove them all. You know what type of a man I am! (Kiss faces, tulips), hey, calm down, everything is okay, I promise you. You'll see, I told you. You'll shock everyone and put shame to their faces.

This torture is long, and we don't want no trouble now that we've come to the end.
We can do this! We can get me out of this situation. I need to talk to you so when you're ready please call me."
Lia:
"Are you available now?"
Joel:
"Yes my Love, I am now!"

CHAPTER 21

LIA:

"Joel told me that he met a businessman on the island that was willing to lend him half of the rest of the money he needed. He did not know him very well and was a bit hesitant, but I said take it, since he was willing to give it.

We needed someone else for the rest of the money. I was still in the same predicament since it was not enough to cover the entire payment and someone else had to get the rest! It was getting impossible to talk and be with Joel and not talk about the money he needed to get out.

My hesitancy was that I wasn't sure he would actually get out since we tried so many times and he was still there"

JOEL AND LIA:

July 11, 2018, 6:43 PM

Joel:
"I love you so much my Dear!"
Lia:
"I love you so much my dear too!" (heart)
SENDS JOEL A PICTURE OF LIA IN THE PARK
Joel:
"(Sunflowers) If you're not the most beautiful woman I've ever had the pleasure of seeing!
Thank you for this. You'd be surprised to know this really got me excited! I love you! I'll hold this to my heart!"
Lia:
"Wonderful!" (heart)

July 12, 2018, 7:17 AM

Joel:
"My Love!"
Lia:
"(Heart, kisses)"
Joel:
"You okay? It's early, too early!" Try to rest more, I love you!"
Lia:
"Just waking up! (Kiss), How is your day going, Honey?"
Joel:
"(Hearts), Just logged off? (Laughing faces), Lol Baby!"
Lia:
"Send me an email explaining the money thing exactly!"
Joel:
"Okay, Little lost, but tell me what you need explained and I will." (Heart)
Lia:
"Tell me what you need exactly, how much you will be getting from your friend and where the money will be going!"
Joel:
"OK"

July 12, 2018, 8:53 AM

Lia:
SENDS JOEL A SPIRITUAL REMINDER
Joel:
"You're spiritual (Heart), Thank you!"
Lia:
"Please accept your friends' money and go looking for more! Go to the beach and encounter the guys who rent out jet skis etc. they have a huge cash business!"

Joel:
"I have been doing that, I've struggled so hard for this. Do not let the two week time frame get to you, this is doable. I have faith and I believe."
Lia:
"Ok baby!"
Joel:
"Two weeks is a long time for us, trust me on this. Try and see what we can come up with by then, I myself will continue to scout and search. G-d is in our favor my Love, I can feel his work on our Family."
Lia:
"If I come up with money this time it will be hand delivered to you! No one will let me wire transfer to third parties anymore!"
Joel:
"What do you mean no one will let you transfer to third parties anymore? We shouldn't begin with this! Let's focus on what's important please! We've gone through this with you and I've told you many times I don't want anyone's involvement in this anymore. Everything I'm doing, I'm watching it! Spearheading everything! Stop this instant! Okay?"
Lia:
"I only have one source that maybe will give the money from Israel. They will not wire transfer. They will send a messenger!"
Joel:
"Honey! Let them transfer it to you! I don't want any complications."
Lia:
"They don't transfer to anyone."
Joel:
"?? What's that?' Please I don't want to hear that."
Lia:
"OK"

Joel:
"You know me well, I've said this!"
Lia:
"OK"
Joel:
"Have them transfer it. Let someone else collect it. There are many ways, find one out.
We've worked so hard to get here."
Lia:
"OK"

July 12, 2018, 10:39 PM

Joel:
"Hey Honey! Can I call you?"
Sends Lia a quote: "I truly respect the people who stay strong even when they have every right to break down."
Lia:
"(Heart, kiss)"
Joel:
"I have an angel in my life, her name is Lia. I love you!"
Lia:
"Call me!"

July 13, 2018, 11:04 AM

Lia:
"The saddest thing will be if we never meet, if you never feel my kiss on your lips, if you never feel my embrace on your body, it would be a karmic payment into this life and the next!"
Joel:
"There's no version of this where I come out of here and not come straight to you. I don't want money, I don't want no drama or cosmic relief, I just want you (heart)."

Lia:
"I love you Jolie!" (Kisses)

July 14, 2018, 10:41 AM

Joel:
"Good morning Lover!"
Lia:
"I pray for you and bless you today and anoint you with frangipani oil to save you!"
Joel:
"There's none like you, your love to me (heart), Thank you for your wishes and prayer! (Heart, butterfly), Enjoy!"
Lia:
"Enjoy as well!"
Joel:
"Thank you, my Darling. Though there's nothing quite to enjoy here."
Lia:
"I am certain that a man of your ability can always find something to enjoy!"

July 14, 2018, 2:50 PM

Joel:
"Hearts, You okay, right?"
Lia:
"(Kisses), I get so excited when you check on me, you cannot even imagine how much I love it!"
Joel:
"(Heart, lovely face), But you know I do have to! I get sick and grumpy when we don't talk for a while! Sick for you!
I always have a craving for you and you've known my Love!"

Lia:
"I expect nothing less because I can feel you across the continent and crave you at the same time! G-d it's exciting!" (Kiss)
Joel:
"It's only you that's ever made me feel this way. I'm quite blown you're human in flesh and blood. (Love cat, heart) Thank you for your Love."
Lia:
"You are welcome, Love! Thank you for your Love!"
Joel:
"You deserve to be cared for and loved so much my Love!"
Lia:
"I know! I want it to be you!" (Heart)
Joel:
"My Love, I want to be with you forever from now. Never part from you, I love you! You're liberating, your love is thrilling!!"
Lia:
"Kisses! Hugs! My heart!!"
Joel:
"You're the sweetest my Darling! We will soon be united, we've come to the end of this already, I cannot wait for our fingers to touch!"
Lia:
"Thank you Love, me too!"
Joel:
"Lips meet and we kiss!"
Lia:
"Absolutely! "(Kisses)
Joel:
"This money has held us apart for so long I'm embarrassed!"
Lia:
"Money comes and goes! Love once found can be eternal!"
Joel:
"I have found you! Thank you for not letting me go!" (heart)

Lia:
"And I you."
Joel:
"I'll never let you go. I've always told you I'll be here for you! I've always meant it.
Every word."
Lia:
"I wait patiently when" here" is the same place for you and me. To me it doesn't matter where that is, home is where we are both together." (Love cat, hearts)
Joel:
"Heart, G-d you're such a Good Writer!!"
Lia:
"(Kiss face)"
Joel:
"What are you doing baby?"
Lia:
"Getting ready to go to the movies."
Joel:
"Something I really want to do with you! Believe me. So, do you have time?
We could talk for 5 min, if you have time?"
Lia:
"Ok! I didn't think of it, but we can do it. Will call you in half an hour, my hair is being done, cannot talk on the phone!" (heart)
Joel:
"Gorgeous!" (Heart, face)
Lia:
"Kiss! I did explain to you that I have no more money left! There was a maybe from one source but now that has changed as well! I know that you are anxious but please do not take it out on me. You told me you were going to scout and look for more yourself!"

July 15, 2018, 8:02 AM

Joel:
"I have faith in you. Together we can overcome anything! I love John Legend, his music is truly romantic but tonight, Pharrell Williams- "Happy"!
You should listen to it! How am I so lucky to find you? It's an absolutely beautiful dream! I cannot even imagine! Dream of me as you sleep for every night that goes by, I get closer to being with you! I love you!"
Lia:
"My favorite music and song! Thank you, my Love!"

July 15, 2018, 10:37 AM

Joel:
"Good morning, Sweetheart!"
Lia:
"Thank you, baby cat! How is your day?"

July 15, 2018, 1:25 PM

Joel:
"Hot and painful but it's become a norm to me, it's sundown now and I'm feeling better though. I'm dreading tomorrow however! It's the day I have to go meet this guy for the money $18,000, I don't know what to do, where to keep it safe until we find the rest, I'm so pressured, I need money, we all do! It's all too stressful to begin to think about!"
Lia:
"Hi baby, glad you are feeling better! Why do you have to keep the money? Why don't you go pay for it? Go get cargo shorts with a big pocket with zipper and roll the money with a rubber band and keep it zipped up in your shorts. No one will know! Or you can wire transfer it to the Bank account!"

Joel:
"Not easy my Love, I cannot go pay the 18K, no, no. I'll need the complete funds with these people. I cannot give space for a negotiation or give them time to think, I want to pay all 40K one instalment and get my passport.
Oh dear, I need to get the hell out of this fucking island!"
Lia:
"Then the cargo short pocket may work."
Joel:
"Lol...I won't sleep. My eyes will stay fixed day and night on it. I love you. You cheer me up!"
Lia:
"That is how they told me. They roll the money in a roll as tight as they can get it and they put a rubber band on it. Then they put it in a pocket with a zipper closing! If you don't lose the pants, you always know where the money is!"
Joel:
"I'll end up feeling and having extra lumps down there you know! More than I already have and it's not easy dealing with the ones hanging there already!" (Laughing faces)
Lia:
"Poker is on the side of the short!" (Laughing face)
Joel:
"I love you baby! I still don't understand baby, I have never been treated with kindness as such before, I don't understand why a noble like you would ever consider coming to my aid in this? Why would you want to help me this much? Is there something you expect me to do in return?"
Lia:
"You must be writing to several different women because this does not apply to me!"
Joel:
"It does not apply to you my Dear, to think I would write for none other than yourself is completely out of order. I was simply thinking about all the kindness you've offered to me in all the time you've known me."

"Coming from something you mentioned yesterday on the phone about being the one who's always been on the giving side between us.

You've sacrificed so much of your time, love, and money to my aid, escape and survival in this very short time we've known each other, relatively short compared to how long we've been alive for, I can only imagine the next 10-20 years with you. It will be nothing short of amazing.

So, I don't know where you got that thought you'd just presented to me, but I guess it shows me exactly where your heart is and what you probably think of me honestly. You're amazing and I'll forever be appreciative of you in my life, you're a Noble to me, look how I now live, like a slave in Cyprus.

All you've done to me means so much to me, this type of kindness does not come for free! Baby cat (Heart)! Don't ever think about it, sometimes I do get in my feelings.

Good night my Dearest. I love you so much!"

Lia:
"Baby cats, Sleep well! The correct answer is that I can be your wife! I will do anything for you!" (Heart, kiss)
Joel:
"I will never forget. (Heart), Do you think then that I will ever be unfaithful to you or lie?"
Lia:
"You must never be because Karma is watching you!" (Love cat)
Joel:
"I never forget that also (Heart), You shouldn't either my Love!"

Lia:
"I only expect and want you to come to me soon! My heart is tattooed with you, I can never cheat or lie to you baby cats! Something you have to live with wherever you are!" (Flower)

July 16, 2018, 7:34 AM

Joel:
"Lia, you make me so happy, and you empower me, thank you my Love!" (Kiss faces)
Lia:
"You are welcome my Love! (Love cat), You can do it baby, you can get yourself out of there! I cannot wait!"
Joel:
"But I cannot get the rest of the money by myself, I've told you and you know this. Miracles happen but I don't know how far I can take this, I need your assistance, please!"
Lia:
"I know this!"
Joel:
"I really do wish I could do this myself, get myself out of this. I need you, it's been so tough for us through this!"
Lia:
"I know this too, Love!"
Joel:
"I love you! I guess you know that too!"
Lia:
"Yes Darling!"
Joel:
"What you don't know is how much I want to fuck the life out of you! I've needed a way to de-stress for so long, you don't even know!"
Lia:
"I know my baby!"

Joel:
"Walking stopped cutting it for me 9 months ago!"
Lia:
"What started happening?"
Joel:
"I feel on fire, please keep your strength for me and see what can be done about this baby, let's get me home already!
Oh, nothing, I just kept walking because it's the only other way I had, you're too far from me simply thinking about it stresses me the most!"
Lia:
"That is why I want to come to you and have a few days with you!"
Joel:
"We've gone over this for well over 9 months, I cannot have you here my Darling no matter the circumstance!"
Lia:
"Why?"
Joel:
"I feel lost and disoriented, I feel submerged underwater starting to feel that I don't know what's up! I cannot allow us both to fall into this abyss. Plus, I will never forgive myself if anything happens!"
Lia:
"Will stay in a Hotel, I am a tourist, nothing will happen!"
Joel:
"I'm living this reality baby girl, we cannot lose focus of what our goal here is no matter what we want. I stayed in a hotel. When I came, I walked myself through the airport. Now I cannot leave.
How do you think that happened? You think I planned for this? You cannot see it coming, take it from me who's in it! Why waste time, money, and resources we both are desperately in need of?"

"Why make me defend this point always? It always does sound bad as if I don't want you to come, don't you get it? Do you not believe me? Lia…baby, I hear you but you don't want this my Love! Getting my passport from these guys is the goal here, let's do just that Dear!"
Lia:
"OK my Honey! Have a good day baby! (heart)"

LIA:

"Being desired and needed brings out the biggest emotions in you! Joel had the ability to use his words in such a way that you always felt desired and the demands for his neediness got answered."

July 16, 2018, 11:59 AM

Joel:
"I love you!"
Lia:
"(Heart, love cat)"
Joel:
"Give me an update Darling!"
Lia:
"I have to work forever! Can you verify your account at Fargo Bank?"
Joel:
"My Love, I have not had access to it since the incident, I have nothing with the Bank until I come back because that's when they reinstate me."
Lia:
"It's unbelievable that you cannot verify anything about yourself!"
Joel:
"I'm a slave to the world now!"

Lia:
"I want you to come home so we can solve all of that. Don't you think I want to take this off you?"
Lia:
"Baby cats, you think I have time and energy to be praying to you with all kinds of questions. I just don't have anyone who will give me 22K without something to satisfy them! Please!
I am trying too! I cannot talk on the phone, I have no more time today, sorry!"
Joel:
"Okay, please help me get this, please don't throw what little faith I have left, things seem to be going well for us here, if this does not work out I don't know what else to do!"
Lia:
"Will try!"

CHAPTER 22

LIA:

"I had invested so much time, effort, and money into what I believed was helping this man get out of a miserable and unfortunate situation, but I was beginning to realize that something was off center in how it was progressing.

My friend did tell me that a contractor on a contract job is prohibited from showing pictures of himself during his project to anyone and if found his contract would be null and void. Who knew?

I then decided that despite anything "Love had to win" and I had to step up and be the one who would finish this story in a positive way and if he was an illusion, it was all on him.

Karma always knows who to look for and I decided the Universe will answer the outcome."

JOEL AND LIA:

Joel:
"How are you, baby? Can we talk? Can you send me please as little as $200-300?
Please, if you have any to spare, I know it's a rough time with work, but you shouldn't worry if it's hard, I know you don't have any money left. G-d I did not want to ask for this, it's heart breaking!"
Lia:
"Did you get the money from your friend? Ok, I will send you!"

Joel:
"Not yet, we aren't meeting until sundown. But this is different. Thank you, I have a few utilities I want to take care of and some food, that's all!"
Lia:
"Tell me where to send it!"
Joel:
"Ok, trying to contact Mr. Kennedy to see if he could help me."
Lia:
"Ok baby, tell me when ready! I will send you $500."
Joel:
"Last name-Kama, Given names: Kennedy Main Anson."
Lia:
"I'm working on getting you out. Make sure you get your friends money!"
Joel:
"(Heart) Thank you very much, Love! Yes! Yes, I will. I told you I'm not going to fuck up this unlike I had done with Donald!"
Lia:
(Sends Joel $500. At WU to Kennedy Main Anson Kama, to pick up. MTCN/ 6684882058 ON 7/17/18)
Joel:
"I LOVE YOU."
Lia:
"I love you too! You know that already!"
Joel:
"Let's rush before the day ends!"
Lia:
"Be careful my Love!"
Joel:
"Okay Baby did not make it, but I'll try again tomorrow. I'll make my way to my friend's shop right away!"
Lia:
"Ok Honey! Get as much as you can from him, Please!!"

July 17, 2018, 12:03 PM

Joel:
"Good news! The $19K total sum has been secured in $100 bills. My man is efficient! I am overjoyed!! Our G-d is living!!"

Lia:
"Wonderful Love! Lay the money on your bed and swim in it! Take a selfie and send it! Let me enjoy it!"

Joel:
"(Heart, smiling face), Okay! Just got home now! Doors locked and sealed, I cannot take chances, I will always have it tucked in me, it's in my bag now wrapped round my waist."

Lia:
"Throw it on your bed and swim in it! You will feel amazing!"

Joel:
"Ha-ha!! Come on, it's just 20K! Nothing compared to the room of money you would have swum in your 30s? Or the pool you'd swim in when I get home!"

Lia:
"I always wanted to do that, you know! I've had that dream for a long time! Enjoy your night, Love and be careful!"

Joel:
"I love you!"

Lia:
"I love you!"

Joel:
"What are you doing? How's your day going? I'm ecstatic!"

Lia:
"Thinking of how lucky you are!"

July 18, 2018, 7:50 AM

Joel:
"(Hearts, Sunshine), I'm wishing you a wonderful day my Love! Be full of life and love!"
Lia:
"Thank you! You as well!"
Joel:
"I just got the money you sent my Love, thank you so much! So, so much! You're my life and my love. Thank you for your care and protection!"

July 18, 2018, 1:24 PM

Lia:
"(Love cat, kiss face)"

July 18, 2018, 3:34 PM

Joel:
"Are you okay baby?"
Lia:
"Yes honey! How are you doing?"
Joel:
"I'm okay, sitting in the dark. Reflecting on the past year and how it has been so far. You?"
Lia:
"Going over every style on one of the sights! My behind is flat as a pancake! Why are you sitting in the dark? You have no lights?"
Joel:
"It doesn't matter if I have the lights on or off"
Lia:
"Ok"

Joel:
"It's okay! I'm alright, I'm just tired, I love you though, you're always on my mind.
You've never disappointed me, I love you dearly!"
Lia:
"Ok baby, rest up and feel better! Kisses and hugs! (Heart, kiss)"
Joel:
"I felt it all over me. Little blue butterflies all around me and I know they're from you my Dear! You are my sunshine!"
Lia:
"Yes, they are my Love."
Joel:
"I'll move rocks and boulders to show you my vision for us, to show you why I love you so!"
Lia:
"You said you are tired now, wait until tomorrow. Having a vision is the first step.
Thank you, my Darling!"
Joel:
"Thank you for sticking with me and being with me. Have a productive evening my Love!"
Lia:
"Have a nice peaceful and lovely night with big visions of many butterflies taking you on an endless flight!"
Joel:
"Okay baby!"

LIA:

"I wanted Joel to love me for me, just the way I was. He kept saying "I love you" every day and I appreciated it but there was always a money condition that had to be met along the way.
I couldn't understand why it was "me" that had to meet his condition!"

July 19, 2018, 2:17 PM

Joel:
"How are you today? (Hearts), I hope you are well, I'm thinking of you."
Lia:
"Same here! (heart)"
Joel:
"How are you my Love?"
Lia:
"Beach day today!"
Joel:
"Oh, I should join. But you beat me to it! I love you baby!"
Lia:
"I love you!"
Joel:
"I know this, enjoy it, and don't get too carried away by the old man in his speedo. I know you like the finer things.!"
Lia:
"Okay Honey!"
SENDS JOEL A PICTURE OF A MAN LYING ON THE BEACH IN A SPEEDO SUIT
Joel:
"Wow, wow, there you go now!"
Lia:
"Lol...Hysterical!"
Joel:
"I know, I'm dying here, tears running out of my eyes, did not know this was what you meant!"
Lia:
"I'll leave you with just this view, I don't want to kill you with the rest. Enjoying the beach,
very pleasant!"
Joel:
"Hah...it's well thought I love it! I should see you through! I love you so much!"

Lia:
"Okay baby! (Heart, kisses)"
SENDS JOEL A PICTURE OF LIA AT THE BEACH
Joel:
"My heart! I will treasure you forever in my heart. You look 20 years younger. I'm obsessed!!"
Lia:
"Thank you, Love!"
Joel:
"Every time I blow a kiss this happens! I'm only trying to kiss you my Love!"
Lia:
"That means the kiss went through and I have it on my face now! (Kisses, flower)"
Joel:
"Another coming to your heart!"
Lia:
"(Kisses)"
Joel:
"(Hearts), Keep shining! Shush, I'm still watching you!"
Lia:
"You are the only one who likes to watch me! (Love cat)"
Joel:
"Oh, I watch you all day. You just don't know it, how you think I survive through these lonely times!"
Lia:
SENDS JOEL A PICTURE OF LIA WATCHING THE BEACH

July 20, 2018, 8:48 AM

Joel:
"My Love!"
Lia:
"Hi"

July 20, 2018, 3:02 PM

Joel:
"Are you okay your Majesty?"
Lia:
"Yes Dear but missing you!"
Joel:
"Can I call you?"

July 20, 2018, 4:43 PM

LIA:

"Joel wanted me to get him the rest of the money but he was being difficult. He was giving nothing as far as information needed to secure a loan. He wanted me to assume the responsibility for the loan and then give him the money. What was going on here?

It was bothering me that he was not telling me what I needed to know and was being impossible!
He said that he had secured 20K from his friend and needed 24K more to get his payment done."

I had decided that I would do whatever I could to help him out and did not expect his resistance and withholding of information from me when I needed it most. It was for him and his release after all!

Who knew that Queen Elizabeth Enahoro was watching his moves very carefully and he did not want anything done that she could trace or snatch away from him! He wanted to leave and be rid of her!"

JOEL AND LIA:

Lia:
"Why, why are you making me crazy? What is it that you cannot tell your address, phone number and passport no? Why? This money is coming from somewhere else! It has to be wire transferred! They need this information at the bank."

Joel:
"Baby, I'm not trying to get you crazy. They should wire you! This is easy, I'm not making it hard, you have most of the details I have and I don't have the rest of them. I cannot forge false details and send them to you, G-d forbids it, I cannot lie to you. I love you with all my heart!"

Lia:
"I love you too baby! Will see what can be done my Darling! Will see…Kiss!"

Joel:
"I will never hurt you, I promise."

Lia:
"You have already! All my spare money has gone to you and now your unwillingness to provide basic information is preventing you from coming home and honoring all that you promised.
What do you think, you've made me happy?"

Joel:
"My Love!"

July 20, 2018, 8:56 PM

Joel:
"I love you my Angel, you're everything to me, you mean the world to me, and I need you to believe me Lia, I really do love you. "

"I exist to make you happy, and I'll do what I can to make sure you're happy. Don't be upset at me, please if I had these details, I would send them to you."
Lia:
"My eyes will not lose sight of you even though you are a magician!"
Joel:
"<3 a magician with no tricks in his sleeves is no magician baby"
Lia:
"The Magician's skill is to make the illusion seem real."
Joel:
"You've seen enough in your lifetime to fall for just an illusion my Dear!"
Lia:
"I fell for you! What am I going to do now?"
Joel:
"I am not an illusion nor am I an illusionist!"
Lia:
"I said you are a Magician."
Joel:
"If I were, I would have a magic wand!"
Lia:
"Which I want! You already have it?"
Joel:
"I love you! My magic wand is yours!"
Lia:
" I said I would not joke anymore and I am going on again!"
Joel:
"Laugh a little, is good you do! You can use my condition too occasionally if it pleases you,
it would make you smile."
Lia:
"Why are you angry?"
Joel:
"I'm not. Honestly, I cannot be angry at you anymore!"

Lia:
"Find your driver license, give me your address and I can move on! Please!"
Joel:
"Now you really want me doing magic baby, I really don't have these details which you require. It hurts my heart, I am sorry!"
Lia: "You don't know your address?"
SENDS JOEL A PICTURE OF LIA GOING OUT FOR A WALK

Lia:
"Off for a walk!"
Joel:
"You look great my Love!"

July 21, 2018, 2:30 PM

Joel:
"I make this promise to you my Dear, I now look to the future and forget the past. My life is yours and we will make it last. I love you more today than I did yesterday, and I'll love you more tomorrow than I do today, I will forever have love and respect for you my Dear.

Judging from the shit we've gone through between us, nothing can come between us, nothing can break us apart, I love you more than anything in the world so there's no need to lie to you, I know you're mad at me, but I want you to please believe me, I'll do anything to help you because you're in turn helping me.

Please believe me. I love you!"

July 21, 2018, 7:51 PM

Joel:
"Right now, You're on my mind my Love!"
(Sends Willie Nelson- "Always on my Mind" on youtube.com)

July 22, 2018, 7:56 PM

Joel:
"(Sends, "I choose you"-The wedding Song-Ryann Darling on youtube.com)
Lia:
"Thank you, baby! I Choose you too!"

July 23, 208, 6:52 AM

Joel:
"(Heart) It's nice falling asleep knowing that you think so much about me!"

July 23, 2018, 9:42 AM

Joel:
"Good morning, how are you, my Love? How did you sleep baby?"
Lia:
"Good babe. All is well. Starting my IT meeting this morning! Hope you've had a nice day!"
Joel:
"Okay my Love. Please let me know when you're okay to talk. I miss you!"

July 24, 2018, 12:37 PM

Joel:
"Hi baby!"
Lia:
"Hi honey cakes! How are you, sweets?"
Joel:
"I'm ok, are you better? I hope you are better than me!"
Lia:
"I'm fine."
Joel:
"Are you having a productive day?"
Lia:
"My family from Israel is here, we are eating now."
Joel:
"(Heart, happy face) Enjoy! I wish I was sitting across from you! I don't want to be alone!"
Lia:
"Me too baby!"
Joel:
"I hope this works out, I'm drained of all energy, but you give me hope."

July 25, 2018, 1:49 PM

Joel:
"Hello Lia, how are you? How are you faring today?"
Lia:
"I'm good baby! Where did you go all day without your phone?"
Joel:
"I was with it all day. I visited my landlord to see if I can talk him into helping me out since this is taking so long, I cannot leave everything in your hands."

"I've been a good tenant and I hope he'll listen to me with a good heart. Maybe he can point me in the right direction too. I miss you!"

Lia:
"(Heart, kiss) Lol…you should hear what's happening in South America, over the year.

My friend's son went to Columbia on a tour, his best friend was kidnapped for 200K ransom, the tour guides wife said she had the money and they released him, when she couldn't come up with the money, they killed her! In Mexico the Police came up to them, robbed and took their wallets, asked for all the money or they would be arrested and jailed…disgusting!"

Joel:
"What?"

Lia:
"Don't be looking to stay! Let's get you out but cover all holes this time. There is no room for any more mishaps to happen!

Joel:
"How do you respond to this?"

Lia:
"He is lucky to be here! They are doing it to American tourists in South America. It will spread very quickly!"

Joel:
"This is really terrifying, and I am extremely heartbroken. Tourists and foreigners are targets, and I cannot let this happen to me, we've worked so hard to get here I cannot allow this to get more complicated."

Lia:
"Yup."

July 25, 2018, 6:36 PM

Joel:
"**(Sends a picture of a pear-shaped diamond ring)**, I've just been thinking about you and I as married couples. Officially married couples! It's a sudden thought that gave my heart the jolt it needed."

Lia:
"You make me so happy my Darling! I wish you were here for me to wrap myself around you!" (Heart)

Joel:
"I need you in my life, permanently! No fears or scars, doubts, or problems. I'll cry to you like a river, but I want to hold what little pride I've got as your Man!"

Lia:
"You are my Man! Pride gets in the way of reason many times. I just want to get this done and get you out, I hope you understand me and help me do it. I love you and want you here in my embrace!"

Joel:
"I just need you to believe me! I trust you!"

Lia:
"There is no reason not to trust me, I am a fully invested partner in your journey!"

Joel:
"I need you to trust me as well! You're so good Lia, anyone else would say screw it and run but you haven't. I love you, and I want my life with you.

You will eventually meet me, and we'll be together hopefully forever. I love you!"

Lia:
"(Heart, love cat)"

Joel:
"Can't sleep, thinking again!"

Lia:
"What are you thinking about my Love?"

Joel:
"Well, I'm thinking of you! I need you, it's you I am thinking about! I need to move on from here."
Lia:
"I know baby! I will gather all this I can find and try for you, my Love! It's so hard to convince them you are real without anything!"
Joel:
"We wouldn't have made it this far if I wasn't real, the illusion would've washed off by now!"
Lia:
"That's between me and you sweets! Unfortunately, the rest of the world is tough!"
Joel:
"You need to convince them, please don't make me suffer more. I can't stand any more, please!"
Lia:
"I will do what I can!"
Joel:
"This is why I trust you! Get me home, I need you!"
Lia:
"Try to sleep, Dear! Tomorrow is another day. Will see what I can do. I just don't understand why you cannot give me your basics, address, and deposit info! Will make it so much easier for me?"
Joel:
"We have awakened this energy of attraction within us and harness its power to bring our desires to fulfilment!"

July 25, 2018, 11:49 PM

Lia:
"The most expensive thing in this world is trust."

July 26, 2018, 8:19 AM

Joel:
"Good morning my Love, how was your night? Did you rest well my darling? How did you sleep without me? Love, I want to kiss you every morning as I wake, I know I wouldn't want to leave our home without kissing you, my Love!"

Lia:
"Never imagine you will go out without a kiss!"

Joel:
"You're so sweet to me! Okay, tell me what's up for today?"

Lia:
"You'll have to cook too! To get the Kiss! "

Joel:
"Ha...ha! I'll wake up with an apron!"

Lia:
"And nothing underneath?"

Joel:
"(Little devil face), Oh...That's where you're going with this.!"

Lia:
"Today will be a day of begging, borrowing, and stealing. It isn't the amount of funds that is hard to get, it's the lack of validation from you! No one including me can comprehend it. They are all protecting me now and have refused to budge. They say that a man who cannot issue a picture is not worth my effort no matter what he says!"

Joel:
"A picture of what, this woman? What do you want me to do???? Please tell me! Don't be like this, I am suffering here, you don't know! Day to Day! Why do you give these people the right to say this Rubbish to me? They all come and insult me because I am begging?? Lol...Lia, its fine! I am not worth your time. Follow them, they're your protection. I am exhausted, everything, every day, you don't know the half of it."

Lia:
"You asked me, and I am telling you! I will make the rounds again, but it will be a hard and humiliating time for me. I will try everything and everyone. Don't be down. Something will come through! Warrior Lia with her magic wand is out today!" (Kiss)
Joel:
"G-d bless you."
Lia:
"I want to know half of it, tell me! All personal loans are at 20.87%. I might be able to get one for 12K. And they charge you a fee of $720. The rest I have to find elsewhere! What's the total amount you need?"
Joel:
"Funny story, you'll love it, but I'll save it for when we meet! I am dying here every day and facing my own share of the humiliation and heartbreak and I really cannot take anymore from you, (they), friends, my Love. I physically cannot. They can sit in their fancy chairs and talk shit because they're not living my reality, our reality, they've not suffered as we have! As I have been suffering here daily for months and months!
So, no one should talk about validation! I am validated! If anyone wants any, he or she should just get me home and have their validation in flesh. I'm sorry but this is not meant to hurt or demoralize you, it's simply the truth to what's in my heart."
Lia:
"I lost you again. Have a good night, eat something good!"
Joel:
"You're the most important person in my life right now, I love you and I am so thankful that you're in my life Honey, the things you have done for me, things you are doing for me, your Man!"

"I mean no one would ever see this or experience love, care, and compassion like this. You're my warrior and my heroine, your place is reserved in heaven. I love you so much my Love. Thank you!"

Lia:

SENDS JOEL A PICTURE OF THE LOAN APPLICATION

Lia:

"This is the loan form for review. What do you say on the loan? Yes or no?"

Joel:

"Still can't get over the insane interest. I'm sorry, but we don't have a choice here. So Yes!"

Lia:

"OK"

Joel:

"I had checked the 35-60 months but that's super high 25%! That's not an option."

Lia:

"Yes."

Joel:

"Okay I'm researching about them."

Lia:

"Please!"

Joel:

"You know how uneasy I get about these online loan companies. Let's proceed with the 20%, its more rational option of the two."

Lia:

"We just need money, it's not the end of the world and I told you no one is giving personal loans, that's why they care so much!"

Joel:

"Thank you Love (heart). I know, I understand they're all rip-offs. But we'll stay out of their way!"

July 27, 2018, 11:44 AM

Joel:
"My Love, how are you, Darling? Any good news?"
Lia:
"I'm good. How is your day? Will let you know of good news the moment it happens!"

July 27, 2018, 6:44 PM

Joel:
"Thank you, my Love! I need you to know just how much I love you, I believe in you, I trust you and to know that I'm your partner for life!" (Heart)
Lia:
"Thank you, my love, I always want to feel the same towards you. I love you!" (Heart, kiss)
Joel:
"This is all a test. And you're still here. My partner, I love you so much! Hashem Himself has blessed this Union!"
Lia:
"Hashem knows best!" (Flower)

July 28, 2018, 9:08 AM

Joel:
"When You read this message, remember You have been in my thoughts all night long.
If I was there in your thoughts too, smile and send me a Good Morning Kiss!
Wish you a beautiful morning, Good Morning!"
Lia:
"(Kisses) Thank you my Darling, Good Morning!"
Joel:
"I love you! So many kisses, I like this. You're beautiful!"

Lia:
"How did I find the only person I cannot live without!" (Love cat, Heart)

Joel:
"(Smiley face, upside-down face), What are you up to this morning sweet Woman?"

Lia:
"Just working. Had a friend over for dinner last night, went past midnight, tired this morning!"

Joel:
"I know, that's why I don't bother. Did you cook? What did you make? I can't wait to spend these Friday days and nights with you and your Family!"

Lia:
"I made salmon, meatloaf, schnitzel, salad, carrots, peas, Persian rice, lol… Joel, my dream come true for you and me to be at the same table on Shabbat!"

Joel:
"I know, I want to have my own space on your table, I'll light candles and I'll pray with you.
I care about you. I want to completely become a part of your life. Genuinely!"

Lia:
"I miss you!" (Hand sign, kiss face)

Joel:
"That's such a sign, I love it! I can't wait to be with you! Ha-ha! This is new to me. Ha-ha!
I need to spend a good day like today with you! Sunny and warm, on the beach relaxing and talking about our success."

Lia:
"Wonderful. You are out enjoying the beach? I love it. Have a great time."

Joel:
"(Big heart), I love you! Thank you my dear!"

Lia:
"I love you!" (Kiss face)

July 28, 2018, 6:45 PM

Joel:
"My Life (heart), You are always on my mind, you're stuck there!"
Lia:
"Same here. Stuck!!"
Joel:
"It's the best feeling though, nothing but this should last forever."
Lia:
"I agree!"
Joel:
"You're my agenda and I will stop at nothing to be with you. You need to know this!"
Lia:
"I want to fling my arms around your neck and smooch the life out of you! (Kisses) You've had SOOO many kisses today!"
Joel:
"(Hearts)<3, and you've had all of my heart today. You deserve so much and more!
He...he, careful you will remain lonely if you smooch the life out of me. That is until you arrive in heaven where there too I shall sit waiting for you, my Angel!"
Lia:
"No, I will be waiting for you!"
Joel:
"We will arrive together. I love you! Are you alright?"
Lia:
"Best deal!" (Star)
Joel:
"Ha-ha! You're on fire baby. I miss you! Missed having this fun with you! It's you! All you.
You brought the light into my life when you stepped in!"

Lia:
"I miss you! How was the beach? The light must have been there somewhere inside all along! Did you go swimming?"
Joel:
"It was beautiful. I had the green shorts on and it was great there. Was talking about the green shorts you had given me from last year. It's got rubber fittings. So, it will fit regardless, I always have it on me that one, treasure it!"
Lia:
"Amazing they still fit! I should have sent you more stuff!"
Joel:
"Too late for that now and it's okay Love. You've done more than enough!"
Lia:
"OK"

July 29, 2018, 9:46 AM

Joel:
"How are you, my Love?" (heart)
Lia:
SENDS JOEL A PICTURE OF LIA AT THE BEACH
Lia:
"Wonderful! You, my Darling? At the beach today. How is your day?"
Joel:
"You are my love forever." (Palm tree, love face)

July 29, 2018, 1:44 PM

Joel:
"I prayed for you today. Pray for your success so we can have a blessed life together!
I want to be featured in everyday life from now on."

Lia:
"It's exactly what we need. Lots of praying! Thank you." (heart)
Joel:
"How was your day? Still at the beach my Love?"
Lia:
"Yes baby! We are in Westhampton today visiting a friend. Coming home very late!
It's so beautiful here. The Internet stinks, I will send pictures later."
Joel:
"My Darling okay, I will be waiting! And let me know when you can call. I miss your voice my Dear. "
Lia:
"I miss you my Man. I am crazy for you!"
Joel:
"I miss you ever more! Don't go crazy just yet, I need you, we're so close."
Lia:
"Don't lose sight of what's really important!"
Joel:
"I will never lose sight of you! Not in a million years."
Lia:
"(Heart. Love cat)"

July 29, 2018, 10:10 PM

Joel:
"Thank you, my Love who fills my heart, like no other. It's good to be loved by you, can't wait to have a happy and colorful life together for the years to come.
I am with you forever. (heart) Got to go back to sleep now, You okay baby?"
Lia:
"(Kiss, heart), Yes baby, Go sleep!"

July 30, 2018, 7:03 AM

Joel:
"I love you Darling and I can't wait to build our forever…I'm here as your partner for life.
I thank Hashem every day for the past months of having such an amazing woman brought into my life for me to love and support until the end of time. Every day I love you!"
Lia:
SENDS JOEL PICTURES OF THE VIEWS IN WEST HAMPTON
"Day in the Hamptons! Really beautiful!"
Joel:
"My woman I cannot think of anything more beautiful! You're so good, everything just fits with you, myself inclusive, I love these photos. Love the ones of you more, I have the feeling there's so much you have in store waiting for me baby!"
Lia:
"You bet baby! (Heat, love cat)"

July 30, 2018, 1:12 PM

Joel:
"Hi baby! Sorry I missed your calls!"
Lia:
"This is my constant fear with you!"
Joel:
"What is? I'm always here, always going to be here. I was taking a nap my Love, wasn't dead and I'm not dying, I'm actually okay baby. Anticipating every little thing!"
Lia:
"No problem!"
Joel:
"I'm sorry. I did not mean to make you worry my Darling."

Lia:
"No worries!"
Joel:
"Are you okay?"
Lia:
"Busy, sorry!"
Joel:
"OK"

July 30, 2018, 4:39 PM

Joel:
"(Large hearts)'
Lia:
"Baby, love cat! I miss you my (Heart)"

July 30, 2018, 8:17 PM

Joel:
"My Love"
Lia:
"Hi baby! Unbelievable but I just received a strange Email from either Donald or a friend of his who has found my email. Will let you know the rest when I find out myself!"
Joel:
"Okay, when can you show me the Email?"
Lia:
"I also forwarded it to you Honey."

Jul 30, 2018, at 7:31 PM

Lia:
E-mail Lia got from Donald's server:

Donald W <dowoo003@gmail.com> wrote:

"Hello Lia, how are you doing? I really haven't been so free myself and I don't get in this email myself. I saw your last email a couple of days ago.

You know it's been a while now that I gave Donald some money and he hasn't sent me any yet nor did I hear from him.

However, he is my best friend, and I didn't know he still had all his struggles out there since I proposed how much I had but he refused.

I will love you to explain what's really going on now with him to me in a much better way so I can understand it all. Have a great night."

Joel:
"That's weird, it's not Donald but probably somebody Donald collected money from.
From the looks of things, he's needing his money back and that's going to be a bigger bill on our heads. So, let's sort me out before listening to any other stories. There's no time for this."

Lia:
"OK"

Joel:
"Are you okay?"

Lia:
"Yes. Resting a bit! How do you feel?"

Joel:
"Still anxious but I'm finding ways to calm my mind and the anxiety. I don't want to result
to medication for that yet. I feel so close. Did our application for the loan pass through?"

Lia:
"Stay nice and calm. Why don't you sleep? I spoke to them today, and they keep asking for this and that. I told them to hurry up! Holding my fingers crossed."

Joel:
"Well, every time I close my eyes, I get nightmares and it's never good rest, but I know it's all fear grown to accommodate my heart."

Lia:
"Why fear? What's going on?"

Joel:
"Over time I've built up fears of staying here forever. Not finding a possible way out was by far my biggest fear. I am terrified of this."

Lia:
"It will work out. Be positive with a good outlook. Don't look for trouble to yourself!"

Joel:
"I love you so much! Thank you for your love."

Lia:
"Honey, calm yourself and rest! You will kill yourself from anxiety and stress!
Concentrate on good things to come! I love you!" (Hearts, flowers, kisses)

Joel:
"Okay my Love."

Lia:
"What passport do you have, USA or UK?"

Joel:
"UK, my Love!"

Lia:
"Maybe it may be a good idea that you walk yourself over to the British embassy and befriend someone who will escort you out of there once you have paid the full amount who will assure that no further harm can come to you and you will come back with no problems. What do you think?"

July 31, 2018, 8:12 AM

Lia:
"(Sends Fontella Bass- "Rescue me" on youtube.com)

July 31, 2018, 9:46 AM

Joel:
"Hello Love!"
Lia:
LIA SENDS AN INSPIRATION QUOTE TO JOEL

Joel:
"I kiss you, thank you very much. I will get something to eat pretty soon. I mean it's just about dinner time, so you enjoy your exercise class and let me know when you're done."
Lia:
"Ok sweets!"
Joel:
(Calls Lia and they talk for a very long time.)

July 31, 2018, 2:12 PM

Lia:
"I'm so glad you are enjoying the beach. Do you go by yourself or with a friend? It was so nice to hear your voice, my Love!"
Joel:
"You got me over joyous. I love you every day and your voice just calms me, neither the walks nor the beaches do what you do to me. You're always there when I reach out."

August 1, 2018, 9:11 AM

Lia:
"Start packing! (Love cat)"

August 1, 2018, 10:50 AM

Joel:
"The most joyous thing I've heard. I'm packing! What's the occasion? Ha-ha! I love you so much this is so intense. You'd be shocked, I'm done packing!"
Lia:
"Good"
Joel:
"What? Are you busy?
Lia:
"Have you told me everything about this situation? Is this the final fiasco or is there the chance of more drama? Please give me the entire scope of how this will go down."
Joel:
"No baby, I'm afraid I may need a little more."
Lia:
"What do you mean? What is a little more?"
Joel:
"About $4K more actually!"
Lia:
"I think you have to find another financier! What is the matter with you? Who can put up with this? Lol…"
Joel:
"Calm down sugar! Don't want you to blow open your cap!"
Lia:
"You did the same thing last time! This is like a patterned progression! It's making me angry!
You have to ask your friend for extra, I don't have it!"

Joel:
"I'm not trying to make you angry! However, nothing we cannot handle with His grace to help us."
Lia:
"I am serious!"

LIA:

"The loan for Joel, which I applied for, came in. I was so relieved that he will have the money to pay and be done. What happens? He asks for more money!! OMG!! I wanted to strangle him.

He was creating a situation which postponed his exit every time! It was almost the last straw!!

The strange Email sent to me from Donald's server was a bit disturbing as well since it was not Donald but the person who had given him money to give to Joel and he had my email and contact information now!"

August 2, 2018, 10:48AM

Joel:
"My Love!"
Lia:
"Kisses and more, much more…Why am I not feeling excitement from you?"
Joel:
"What do you mean? I'm sorry but I am. The frustration within maybe has crept in too far?
My exhaustion may finally be exposing itself, but it's nothing to worry about me dearest Wife,
I am ecstatic nonetheless!!"

Lia:
"Hmm...Please get yourself hydrated and rest so you feel better! Don't fall apart at your triumph! You can do it!"
Joel:
"My triumph, he...he, like the ring to it! Though I think it better suits our triumph!! (Heart), you're every bit as important!"
Lia:
"Yes baby! It's exciting!"
Joel:
"Let me know when you can talk, I just got done with my meal, it was delicious. After our text, I took a cab with the last money I had on me and went on into a hotel restaurant here in Famagusta! I had the chef make me salmon, meatloaf, schnitzel, salad, carrot, peas, Persian rice as I believe it would be the last proper meal I'd have here. I want it to be my last, but we have a weekend plus ahead."
Lia:
"And the whole island will be asking why you ate so much in one meal!"
Joel:
"I did not care, it cost like $80. But in my mind, I had a huge grin while eating, I only wished for one thing tonight!"
Lia:
"You will be comparing this meal to my cooking, but I make all of these very well and tasty!"
Joel:
"(Heart) Your cooking is everything!"
Lia:
"You make me crave you! So much!" (Kisses)
Joel:
"No, I'm the one who's craving. I need you, you're the essence of what makes my soul glow."
Lia:
"But it's the same here my Love!"

Joel:
"I want you!"
Lia:
"I want you too!"
Joel:
"Empty dinners are nothing enjoyable. I need you either with me or as my dinner. In any case, I'll be glad to have it all!"
Lia:
"Sounds yummy either way!"
Joel:
"Baby, you know I'm still so upset at how things turned out entirely for us from the beginning and I felt every day that if I made you wait any longer, I was afraid I was going to lose you but I want to let you know you will never lose me, true Love is hard to find and I am ready to pay the fine. I love you and I'm so glad I am able to connect with you.

Lia, we've been so caught up, but I promise you will never be alone or lonely for as long as I am alive. I love you and I will love you for the rest of my life. Thank you for this and everything!"
Lia:
"Baby, Love is a very rare gift, I embrace you with all my warmth and look forward to all the fun that is left to live for us! Sharing it with you will be my delight! I love you and trust you and I know that you will do all that is honorable and true! The Best is yet to come!"

August 3, 2018, 9:18 AM

Joel:
"(Heart, sunrise), Good Morning Baby. May your day be blessed and calm!"
Lia:
"Thank you my sweet! (Heart, kiss) Have a good day!" (hearts)

Joel:
"(Heart, happy man), you more! I love you!"
Lia:
"(Kisses)"
Joel:
"I'm going to be getting the account transfer details soon, assuming you aren't busy and if we have it today being Friday then we can work this out before Monday, He...eh kisses too (kiss faces), all over your soft face and neck, maybe down lower too."
Lia:
"I need the recipient, his address, phone, bank account number and routing.
Make sure please all the addresses match, the bank requires all of this for wire transfer!
It all depends on when the bank clears the money. I am waiting too!"

August 3, 2018, 10:33 AM

Lia:
"Takes 3 days to hit international transfer now, it's for $25K. Wednesday at the earliest!"
Joel:
"Okay Lovie (Heart)"
ACCOUNT NAME: SUDORE TEKSTIL SANAYI LTD.STI
ACCOUNT NUMBER: 74238913-5002
IBAN NUMBER: TR51-0001-0007-5774-2389-13-5002
BANK NAME:
TC. ZIRAAT BANKASI/MECIDIYEKOY SUBESI
BANK ADDRESS:
MECIDIYEKOY MAH. BUYUK DERE CAD NO: 83 SISLI/ISTANBUL
BENEFICIARY ADDRESS:
HALIDE EDIP ADIVAR MH.

BALCI SK. NO:20/4 SISLI-ISTANBUL
US DOLLAR SWIFT CODE: TCZBTR2AXXX

"It's a company address so everything is fine and should be there, (I can hold the company responsible if anything), not that anything would happen but to have you confident in everything I'm doing here. I'll get the cell number and attach it to you."
Lia:
"OK"
Joel:
"I love you and I'll keep you updated. Come Monday, I'll also go to the shop to collect the 18K I had deposited."
Lia:
"Who is the person receiving?"
Joel:
"Some man who had given me the 18k loan. I personally chose to use him as he's shown his faith and willingness to help my cause. He's a renewed businessman and he's reliable to me. Now my eyes are hooked on him because I don't trust these people but again, nothing will happen!"
Lia:
"Okay baby! You have a bank address and then address. Is this address the beneficiary address?"
Joel:
"Yes, Bank Address, and beneficiary address as requested."
Lia:
"I am going to send you 25K, so you have some extra for yourself."
Joel:
"Oh wow, thank you! Immensely!"
Lia:
"You are welcome!"
Joel:
"WOW Baby!" (hearts)

Lia:
"I need you to promise me something!"
Joel:
"Thank you for the extra, I will make ample use of it. You're my life! Hashem blesses you for me! You've mended my broken heart!"
Lia:
"I want you to keep your phone and answer it when I call you!"
Joel:
"I promise!"
Lia:
"OK"
Joel:
"He...he, I love you baby cats!"
Lia:
"I love you too (Love cat)"

August 3, 2018, 3:37 PM

Lia:
"Everything is ok, spending time with my Family from Israel all day! Hope you had a nice day!" (Kiss face)
Joel:
"Honey, you're my world and my partner for life. I always wish for the best things for you, only the best things! (Heart) When I come, everything will be alright, I'll love and take care of you, we will fall in love over and over again until eternity. I care so much about you!"
Lia:
"I love it! I'm so excited!"
Joel:
"My self, lol...you make me feel like this! (Rose)<3, I love you!"
Lia:
"Hee, hee, I love you! (Kisses, hearts)"

Joel:
"Are you okay? I want to try to sleep now, I love you! So much! And I wanted to say
Good night before leaving."
Lia:
"Good night my Love! Precious sweet dreams of chasing me around all the trees on the beach! (Crazy face, heart)"

CHAPTER 23

LIA:

"I sent Joel 25K and he assured me that this was his final payment, and he would be leaving as soon as it was done.

I trusted the Universe to deliver this man out of his misery and I prayed and hoped that his story and journey was real, and our union would come to be.

Little did I know of all the other elements and players in this game that Joel had put himself into."

JOEL AND LIA:

Lia:
"Where did you go?"
Joel:
"On the beach, one last time! I had lunch there! Rested, walked for a bit now I'm back."
Lia:
"Very nice."
Joel:
"And do you believe I'm feeling so happy now!"
Lia:
"Pouring rain here all day! So depressing and dark! Glad you are happy my Love!"

August 4, 2018, 1:23PM

Joel:
"I wouldn't mind a little transfer thinking about it to sustain before it's time to leave."

Lia:
"I will send you, tell me who to send it to?"

August 5, 2018, 6:16 AM

Joel:
"I've dreamed to be blessed by Hashem with an intelligent woman, a loving woman, a woman who teaches by being. Now I have you and every day I wake, I pray, and I appreciate having you. I love you!"
I got the name for the transfer Honey,
First name: Alhaji Mustapha
Last Name: Faena
Starting my morning with a light jog, I feel so happy and revitalized. I wish you were here."
Lia:

Sends $300. To Joel to Alhaji Mustapha Faena to pick up at WU MTCN 3284069890 on 8/5/18)

August 5, 2018, 10:55 AM

Joel:
"Hi baby cats, how are you?"
Lia:
"Please have the phone on you and answer my calls if I need you at the bank!"
Joel:
"Alright my Dear, I love you!"
Lia:
"Are you okay?"
Joel:
"I am my Dear, I am. Everything will be okay! <3"
Lia:
"I'm at the Bank waiting here all by myself. Miss you! (heart)"

Joel:
"(Heart), this is perfect. I wish you were here at this moment. I'm here with you my Dear, never leaving, never going away!"
Lia:
"Ok Honey!" (Love cat)
Joel:
"Keep me updated!"
Lia:
"I am here with the guy processing so stay close."
Joel:
"Okay Love."
Lia:
"What kind of account does the company have, US or other or unknown?"
Joel:
"I'm here!"
Lia:
"Answer my question!"
Joel:
"You have all the details secure? It is a USD account my Dear!"
Lia:
"Got it. Thank you!"
Joel:
"The wait is over, <3, this is about the most amazing day of my life, I cannot wait to kiss you!"
Lia:
"(Kisses)"
Joel:
"I LOVE YOU SO MUCH."
Lia:
"SAME HERE."
Joel:
I'm so filled with excitement here, I'm dancing by myself!"

Lia:
"Dance?"
Joel:
"Lol, <3
Lia:
SENDS PICTURE OF TRANSFER RECEIPT FROM THE BANK FOR 25K
"Is it ok on the phone or you want an email?"
Joel:
"Email my Darling, this way I can move it to the phone and have a secure copy of the email."
Lia:
"OK"
Joel:
"<3, I'm over joyous! You need to be here!"
Lia:
"No my Love, you need to be here, free at last!"
Joel:
"<3 I'm waving a flag with your name all through the airport!"
Lia:
"No Honey, please keep it quiet over there, you can do it when you land here!"
Joel:
"(Happy faces) < 3, Okay, I was getting a little over myself there. Got it, You're the Greatest!"
This feels as heavy as my passport will as held in my hands. Bet they have the same weight!
This must be the world's most expensive passport. Lol...
I admire your hard work Darling! You've done your part, I'll do mine. Now is time to rest and watch it rain down the goodness on you."
Lia:
"I will make no comment on the passport issue until it is in your hand!"

"I wanted to tell you this before but perhaps I feel as if now you must pull yourself together and use all of your might carefully and diplomatically in the quietest way possible to attain your passport and get yourself out. Once you are out, we will have all the time and desire to celebrate and be happy with the outcome.

The same way I worked long and hard to attain this money for you, now you need to work hard to make it come true. I trust and believe in you my Man that you will triumph!
I love you! (Kiss face), we said the same thing at the same time! Lol! (Heart, love cat)"
Joel:
"We're of the same Soul my Love."
Lia:
"I know my Love!"
Joel:
"I adore you!"
Lia:
"Thank you, baby! Kisses, a million kisses for you!"
Joel:
"X100, 000 for you! My Heroine!"
Lia:
"Thank you!"
Joel:
"Thank you, my Love, you are right, I will work long and hard to make sure we triumph!"
Lia:
LIA SENS JOEL A HER WISE QUOTE:
"ASPIRE TO EXTRAORDINARY"
Joel:
"Very powerful! Wow! Okay my Love, I have to shower now!"
Lia:
"Enjoy! I'll be soaping you galore! (heart)"

Joel:
"Ha-ha! You better!"
Lia:
"I will!"
Joel:
"But I'll be here so you don't think I've been kidnaped! Okay, I need to shower."
Lia:
"Do what you need, I am working all afternoon and may go to the beach later!"
Joel:
"I'm sweating from the running, dancing and all!"
Lia:
"Great sweat, I'm sure!"
Joel:
"Ha-ha! Soon we will be going to the beach finally, I'm going to wear those colorful reflective glasses you own>"
Lia:
"I have an entire collection baby! You will have all the crazy choices you want!"
Joel:
"Well, I wouldn't say Great though! Ha-ha! Yes!!"
Lia:
"Anything on you, even sweat is great!"
Joel:
"Lol... I'm sure you mean this, you're wonderful like this. Honestly, you're such a find.
Incredibly modest and very genuine." I am proud (heart)
Lia:
"Smooch!" (Heart, flower)
Joel:
"Ha-ha, you're getting excited. I love it!! (heart) You're significant in my life!"
Lia:
"I am your Queen, your Goddess Supreme!" (Butterfly, kiss)

Joel:
"Yes, you are! I love you immensely!"
Lia:
"I love you immensely too!" (Love cat)

August 5, 2018, 5:42 PM

Joel:
"Are you okay my Love?"
Lia:
"Yes baby! Taking a beautiful walk by the water! Lovely! You?"
Joel:
"Thinking of me I suppose?"
Lia:
"Always."
Joel:
"I love you so much!"
Lia:
"Kisses and hearts"
Joel:
"I've not stopped smiling since."
Lia:
"I like that!"
Joel:
"Yes my Love, I had made some spaghetti. It's quick and making a sauce from minced meat and olive oil is relatively easy as well Baby!"
Lia:
"Sounds delicious!"
Joel:
"Lol, you should wait until I make some for you!"
Lia:
"I am going to find an amazing apron for you. It will either say Capitan or it will be the Muscle Chest Man at his best! Or something else, I cannot wait to find!"

"I am also thinking, please be very nice and loving towards Donald! Whatever it is going on, he came through in a big way for you!"

Joel:

"Honey, I'll handle Donald as well. Don't respond to him, I'll tell you what to tell him and when to. I respect his comeback! Thank you for your advice, your words mean so much to me."

Lia:

"(Heart, kiss face)"

August 6, 2018, 5:06 AM

Joel:

"Sleep well my Darling, we'll talk when you wake. I'll make sure I have positive news about my day by the eve. You mean the world to me. Thank you! I love you!"

August 6, 2018, 7:39 AM

Joel:

"I got the WU to transfer my love. Thank you so much. How are you today my Love?"

Lia:

"Just waking up from my fantasy baby! (Kiss), You are welcome!"

Joel:

"Fantasy aha! I love it! You make me happy!"

Lia:

"I did, believe me!" (Kiss)

August 6, 2018, 11:16 AM

Joel:

"My Love, how's your day going?"

Lia:
"Going to a dance lesson! Are you having a good evening?"
Joel:
"Take pictures. I would love to see you dance. Yes, lovely evening!
It was warm and we got bright orange skies. It's so beautiful!"

August 6, 2018, 1:39 PM

Joel:
"I love you baby! Hey, your photo is my wallpaper! The one with you in a white shirt smiling. You got your glasses on too. You're always on my mind. Every day I wake, I wake with you on my mind. Every night I pick up your photos and sink myself in them, they are the closest I've been to you!"
Lia:
SENDS JOEL A PICTURE OF LIA WAITING
"Resting. We are on the same wavelength. (Kisses and hearts) Jolie baby, you will have to be very patient and careful dancing with me, making sure I don't step on your feet as well!"
Joel:
"Saucy! When do you take these? You're so creative, I love it! New wallpaper? You can step on me anytime, I love you! I know you are excited!"
Lia:
"You will have to forgive me many times, sometimes I am not sure why I go to the left when he goes to the right!" (Crazy face)
Joel:
"Well, you're already forgiven. I'll go left with you if ever you go left. You're my Soul.
We are on the same wavelength, Yes?"

Lia:
"(Kisses, heart)"
Joel:
"Don't worry baby. I'll have plenty of energy for you and Love."
Lia:
"Not worried, my Love! You know for me you are tops!"
Joel:
"Tops though, lol…and …My dirty mind interfered… (laughing face) I love you Honey!"
Lia:
"Dirty mind never asked what the fantasy was I woke up to this morning?"
Joel:
"I was threading light with you, you can be dangerous you know!"
Did you need to change your underwear after you woke up from dreaming about me?"
Lia:
"You know how much I love intensity! I had no underwear on!"
Joel:
"The heat! The tension within me now, I'm excited and already feeling thick between my thighs."
Lia:
"That's because my intensity allowed me to take advantage of you in that area last night, you have not recuperated from my lips!"
Joel:
"What's up with the no panties situation? You know it's about time I see you dripping, yes?
I cannot recuperate from you ever, we're intertwined."
Lia:
"I forgot to put them on!"

Joel:
"I have this feeling it was intended to happen like that. Seductress, I'm burning like wildfire for you! My G-d!"
Lia:
"You on the other hand were dressed to go out in this like James Bond suit with a white pleated shirt that you were tight in, and I saw you struggling, pulling it around, complaining about it being heavy, I just moved in and got hold of your waist and undid your pants.
The rest was intense and very good! Afterwards the shirt fit perfect, nice, and comfy!"
Joel:
"I was relaxed afterwards, maybe that's why it fit. Lol...I love you! Reading this, what you wrote."
Lia:
"Yes and I woke up! Everything was good!"
Joel:
"So poetic, so lovely so sexy but in a very mature way! (Love cat)
Now I know you got on your knees and gave me a blow job right after dropping my pants. I love you!"
Lia:
"I love you too."
Joel:
"And I need you to know I'll take you gently as you wish, you'll enjoy such nights with me, I may even leave you weak and sleeping for days.
Now remember I have not had this in a very, very, very long time my lover! Hmm..."
Lia:
"You can teach me all the positions you like, I learn fast."
Joel:
"I want to fuck you honestly, you don't even know how much I want to teach us so many positions, you're going to love it and I know you learn fast and you really want to get a piece of me, you're going to get everything."

Lia:
"Wonderful! I have so much to look forward to. Just make sure I am home when you get here."
Joel:
"You make me feel right. You make everything feel right. Ha-ha! Where else would you be? Wherever I'll come to you! I love you!"
Lia:
"Thank you, baby!"
Joel:
"Hmmm…What are you doing?"
Lia:
"Reading and talking to you!"
Joel:
"Love that, you're so reliable, which I think is among your most important quality. Always here for me, you're a real wife. Honestly, your ex had made his biggest mistake already.
The only way I'd lose you is if I die. I would fight for you through the storm and rains."
Lia:
"I divorced my ex."
Joel:
"Lol, his loss really."
Lia:
"I have many wonderful qualities. I have fought for you like no other. I know you are worth it! My heart tells me! Life is so much more fun with you, my Love!"

Joel:

"You're my one and my only one, I love you!"
Lia:
"Thank you, baby! Mine as well! Have you made any return plans?"
Joel:
"Yes, I'll be collecting the money on Wednesday from the safe and adding it to the balance you'd sent to me, pay up to collect my passport, I've been in talks with an agent about tickets, I paid him $100. bribe to have him on my side so when the time comes, he'll get a ticket for cheap for me. They're expensive but he's an agent and you know how they are. I don't have luggage, so I'll carry the bag I've got, say goodbye to my neighbors and get my ass on the way home."
Lia:
"Which is the airport?"
Joel:
"Only one, Erkan, Turkish Airlines."
Lia:
"Turkish airlines and maybe Delta?"

Joel:
"I'll have to buy a ticket from them here. Delta would fly to Turkey. Then Turkish airlines comes down here. You know North Cyprus isn't officially recognized, Yes?"
Lia:
"I thought you could lose the Turks, but I guess not! Sorry."
Joel:
"Hey, it's alright! G-d is going to get me through."
Lia:
"Hashem rules the world! May he be with you on your journey! I heard the food is not bad on Turkish Air!"
Joel:
"It's not? Wouldn't know., Honey, Hashem will guide me through."
Lia:
"I know baby! Why don't you go to the Greek side with your passport?"
Joel:
"They have a 30-year feud between them, Honey. You could read about it sometime. Apparently if you come through the South then you have access to both sides but when you're in the North there's no access for you."
Lia:
"Ok! That's why you don't want anyone to visit you! You are afraid of getting stuck!
You've been protecting us all along you sweet Dear! Thank you!"
Joel:
"I cannot express enough my concern for your safety. (heart), You're my Love. I love you so much!"
Lia:
"I love you so much!" (Kiss, heart)

Joel:
"You know I still feel like my heart is bursting from your love! Since the first time I fell for you! (Kiss faces)" This is what you've caused! (Heart, flowers) I love it though. The feeling is phenomenal!"
Lia:
"I love it too. Baby cats! (Kiss)"
Joel:
"Yes my Love, I care so much about you. Always remember that!"
Lia:
"Thank you, my Love!"
Joel:
"Are you alright?"
Lia:
"You are all set Dear and everything will go well between us. My heart will never leave
you!"
Joel:
"This is exactly what my heart wanted to feel. Your simple Divine touch!" (hearts)
Lia:
"I'm having watermelon! So good! Still very hot out. Sleep well my Darling!"

August 7, 2018, 10:04 AM

Joel:
"Hello baby, how are you my Love?"
Lia:
"Having fun. How is your day?"
Joel:
"I'm alright my Dear! Having a field day, I think the money should arrive tomorrow as stated. I've kept my eyes on it."
Lia:
"It's what the bank told me. Tomorrow!"

Joel:
"Ah-ah! My resolution day! I'll never forget and always make this day precious to me."
Lia:
"Yes, lucky day!"
Joel:
"I am so happy now. Wow, ha-ha!"
Lia:
"Yey! I have so much to tell you!"
Joel:
"My self too, everything!"
(Sends Ellie Goulding- "How Long will I love you" on youtube.com)
I listen over and over thinking about you and my heart melts for you! You have saved me Lia."
Lia:
"Such a beautiful song, my Love. Thank you!"

August 7, 208, 12:51 PM

Joel:
"(Happy face, Heart)"
Lia:
"Going to the Dentist!"
Joel:
"What for? Baby stop playing with your tooth? Are you growing new ones?"
Lia:
"Teeth cleaning!"
Joel:
"Oh, that's more impressive, better even, how are you, Honey?"
Lia:
"A day full of variety!"
Joel:
"I don't like variety, I want only you!"

Lia:
"Frequent Fantasies with you. I miss you!" (hearts)
Joel:
"Absence is truly the highest form of being present, all this while we reside halfway across the globe, I still feel you right in my heart whenever I think about you. You give me the feeling of completeness, which happens to be all I desire from a partner, I do not need the feeling of emptiness and aloneness."
Lia:
"You are so cute! Just so sweet!" (Kiss faces)
Joel:
"Your keen eye for things, I know, I love you and adore you, that's why!"
Lia:
"I am trained to read every word in order to understand content! I can spend the rest of my day kissing you!" (kisses)
Joel:
"You would! Told you I wouldn't stop once I begin."
Lia:
"I'm going to have your favorite tonight, Chinese food, will have you next to me tasting everything! Best of Luck tomorrow! I believe in you. I love you so much! (Heart, kisses)
My variety, my fantasy, my frequency, my intensity is with you only! Sweet dreams!"
Joel:
"Sweet dreams my Darling. I want to be inside you! Thank you so much, I really am so calm, but my insides are turning, lol...I hope you're alright!" (Heart)
Lia:
"Stay calm! Tomorrow will be most important for you! You will be alright, and everything will go well. You are always inside me!"
Joel:
"Honey, you'd feel me different if I had been inside you!"

Lia:
"I have a big imagination, Honey!"
Joel:
"Hmm...felt that right in my heart. I love your imagination!"
Lia:
"Thank you!"
Joel:
"But open up your doors for me to step in."
Lia:
"I will!"
Joel:
"Know this though, once I'm in I do not leave!"
Lia:
"Will give you a special key then!"
Joel:
"I already do have mine."
Lia:
"Are you OK?"
Joel:
"I am!"

LIA:

"I was doing it all, going to the bank, getting a loan, anticipating all sorts of emotions and feelings and uncertainties! I had no one else and he kept me busy with all of his needs. I was fascinated with the outcome of all this work.

The uncertainty was in every pore of my body, but I kept going forward because the most important thing was for him to be freed and to come home to me."

QUEEN ELIZABETH ENAHORO:

"Joel was behaving nicely with Queen Elizabeth Enahoro. He did not want her to find out that he had been able to secure the funds for his payment due. He wanted to outsmart her.

He wanted to go pay, get his papers stamped and grab his things then race to the airport before she could surmise his deed.

He was fed up with their partnership and had figured out that he was tricked by her all along and that he would have been done with his business much sooner if it wasn't for all her actions against him.

All of his money was tied up at the bank and he was dealing in cash for all of his payments.
Joel, an honorable man, did not want to leave without paying all of his obligations and to say goodbye to all the people who had supported and helped him during this horrible journey!"

CHAPTER 24

August 7, 2018, 7:28 PM

Joel:
"I love you!"
Lia:
"I love you."
Joel:
"I know baby cats!"
Lia:
"You cannot sleep?"
Joel:
"Well, I keep rolling and rolling. One thing on my mind."
Lia:
"Close your eyes and dream of something nice! Inhale deeply and put yourself to rest. Sleep next to me quietly!" (Kisses)
Joel:
"Ok my Love" (kiss face)

August 8, 2018, 7:22 AM

Lia:
"You can do it!" (Heart, kiss)
Joel:
"I know my love. (heart) I've been waiting, how are you, my Love?"
Lia:
"I am good. What are you waiting for?"
Joel:
"An alert my Love!"
Lia:
"What alert?"

Joel:
"With the bank my Love to let me know about the money. Why aren't you following? Lol... what are you doing?"
Lia:
"I am but you should have been able to pick up today and your day is done...Lol...I am going food shopping! I thought you picked it up already and we're done!"
Joel:
"I know, I thought so too."
Lia:
"What's holding it up?"
Joel:
"Nothing. There's nothing new come through yet, maybe just waiting to reflect. I'll inform you!"
Lia:
"Ok"

August 8, 2018, 10:41 AM

Lia:
"You are good Sunshine!"
Joel:
"Yes my love. I am alright. Everything will be okay!" (heart)

August 8, 2018, 2:32 PM

Joel:
"Your money smells so great!!" (Love faces)
Lia:
"Are you sleeping on it? When you give it back, I am throwing it all over the bed and we are making love!" (Crazy faces)
Joel:
"Ha-ha... No, I'm not sleeping on it, but I would very much want to sleep on it with you and make Love... "

"I want to make love with you! Now I know I can make love with you. I love you!"
Lia:
"(Kiss faces)"
Joel:
"Please write your complete house address for me my Love! I am kidnapping you!" (heart)
Lia:
"I wish you luck!" (heart)
Joel:
"Don't underestimate me."
Lia:
"Your eagerness fuels my desire! (Kiss)"
Joel:
"You're the catalyst to my eagerness, I love you! I'm still overwhelmed. I am finally coming home! You confirmed it for me and we will be forever. We will make our forever last as long as we want because normal forever's aren't long enough.
We'll make the best out of the life we have left and I promise we will be great Lia." (heart)
Lia:
"Wonderful Honey, I cannot wait!" (Heart, kiss)

August 8, 2018, 10:36 PM

Joel:
"(Sends Glen Campbell "Grow old with me", on youtube.com)
Lia:
"Baby... (love cat, heart)"
Joel:
"I dedicate them to you my Love!"
Lia:
"You are so sweet my Love. Thank you!"

Joel:
"Had them saved before I fell asleep on you, I'm sorry."
Lia:
"Cute" (Kisses)
Joel:
"Have a good night my Love!"
Lia:
"Thank you, Honey! You enjoy and have a successful day! I love you!"
Joel:
"(Heart)"
Lia:
Sends Joel a Quote:
"OPEN A DOOR FOR ANOTHER AND HEAVENS GATE WILL OPEN FOR YOU"

August 9, 2018, 6:07 AM

Joel:
"Wow! Very powerful!"
Lia:
"Kisses."

August 9, 2018, 7:50 AM

Joel:
"Good morning my Love. How are you?'
Lia:
"Good baby! How is your day going?"
Joel:
"Hot! But productive and hopeful. Suddenly there's more paperwork for me to sort out about myself than it takes to clear an entire army! But I'm doing great, I'm not melting down at least."

Lia:
"You can do it Honey! Be vigilant and careful filling in the blanks, I want you to get that passport in your hand! If you need the lawyer, I can give you the name again!"
Joel:
"Okay, No, I'll do it. I'm being vigilant, Very!"
Lia:
"Okay Baby!"
Joel:
"I have so many stamps to get and through it's crazy!"
Lia:
"I was figuring that, that's why I would tell you to have all the paperwork and stamps on you! They are so crazy there but once it's done it's over. Just check for correctness so they don't hold you up for nonsense!"
Joel:
"Okay, today has gone on quite well thankfully! I was praying and praying!"
Lia:
"I am as well. For many days!" (heart)
Joel:
"How are you? I missed you today!"
Lia:
"I cannot wait until you are done with all of this! I want to have you in my arms. That's all I want and miss!"
Joel:
"They tried to make hell for me but since I had no translator available. I requested that they give me an entire cache in English which was my written language. Bold move but I had to attack first to enforce my strength in this."
Lia:
"Be careful with their requirements. Seek advice and please don't mess up the paperwork. They will make hell for you. Can you imagine giving you the most important paperwork in a language you don't understand! Pigs!"

Joel:
"Okay my Love! I understand what you're saying, and I will not fail you."
Lia:
"Heart!"
Joel:
"They're obviously setting a trap or don't care about me."
Lia:
"How could you even think they care? They want to trap you further and get more money out of you! I really wish you would go to the UK Embassy and get someone on your side!"
Joel:
"That's where I'd go first if I smelled anything fishy, remember I still don't trust them.
I cannot believe them! I just wish I wasn't here in the first place.
Now I'm at the end and it's not fair for them to put any more pressure on me anymore."
Lia:
"You are correct Darling, but they will because they can! You must be the strongest now and overcome this to your advantage!"
Joel:
"I love you baby!"
Lia:
"I love you! You should find counsel and have them verify all that you do on this paperwork."
Joel:
"Yes I understand."
Lia:
"Is your release pending paperwork approval?"
Joel:
"Yes, it is, apparently "for my own safety", I have to clear everything involving Cyprus."

Lia:
"You will be there another year!"
Joel:
"Hence why I said it was apparently easier to bring an entire battalion through with much less work than it is to get me out of Cyprus."
Lia:
"You better get legal counsel! Did they get your money? Is this the only contract you've ever done?"

August 10, 2018, 7:08 AM

Joel:
"Good morning my Queen, I hope you're sleeping well tonight, I want you resting knowing Hashem is watching over you! I love you! I'm paying so many bribes it's coming out of my nose!"
Lia:
"Hi baby! (Heart, kiss), Please go to the embassy and work on regaining your passport. No one has money for bribes, and you don't want to be with those people anyway, they will prevent you from leaving! Lol…is the Embassy on the Greek or Turkish side?"
Joel:
"Turkish side, it's crazy! I haven't had my first meal today, can you imagine?"
Lia:
"Go get help! You will exhaust yourself! Call Donald too because it looks like you will need more money!"

August 10, 2018, 12:42 PM

Joel:
"Hmm! I don't know about Donald! But I'll do my best. I had promised you already!
How are you?"

Lia:
"Hi baby cats! I'm good! Getting ready to do a little work and then I'm going to the beach! Miss you clever cat!"

Joel:
"Look through the beach and see me standing and waving at you! Imagine having this sight, baby! I would lose my mind!"

Lia:
"I'd like to do better, but I will settle for the illusion of you at the beach!
I thought that you promised to be back and now it's turned into another drama on stage again!"

Joel:
"Drama though? No baby. No more Drama! I'm just telling you how my days go and what I face. You cannot deny we both knew these would arise. All the money I've paid is being complied and I'm just praying there's no lost payment somewhere, if they accuse me of anything else or ask me to pay more money that's where the problems are!"

Lia:
"If this does not put you on stage to await more drama, I cannot think of much worse, especially being alone and unprotected. Good Luck, I would be screaming!"

August 10, 2018, 3:58 PM

Lia:
"Where are you? I hope you can relax and have a nice sleep. My heart is screaming, and my head is praying that all goes well and you will win baby!"
(Kisses)

August 11, 2018, 10:12 AM

Joel:
"<3"

August 11, 2018, 11:32 AM

Joel:
"Are you okay?" <3, I miss you!

Sends Lia a Phone Message:

("I love you Honey, so much, I'm laying down, so hot, I'm thinking about you, and am thinking a lot about what I'm doing and how everything is going. I miss you though! KISS")
Lia:
"Baby cats, why can't I find you? Where are you? Miss you! Such a nice message you left me.
I adore it! (kisses)"

August 12, 2018, 11:24 AM

Lia:
"Can you call me?"
Joel:
"Certainly, just got home, give me a minute. Been a hot, hot day!"
Lia:
"Okay."
Joel:
"Journey to my Queen! (Heart, map, bike, boat, car, taxi, plane, flowers, queen)
Lia:
"It's the journey of my King!"

August 12, 2018, 3:43 PM

Lia:
"Baby cats are you good? (kiss)
LIA SENDS JOEL A PICTURE OF HER GLADIOLAS IN THE LIVING ROOM

August 12, 2018, 5:34 PM

Joel:
"My Love" (heart, love face) I love these flowers so much!"
Lia:
"As much as I love you!"

August 13, 2018, 7:14 AM

Lia:
"I cannot wait until you come home." (Hearts and kisses)

August 13, 2018, 2:05 PM

Joel:
"My love, how are you baby?"
Lia:
"I am good. How was your day?"
Joel:
"Progressive and productive, thank you!"
Lia:
"Interesting! So how is my love cat, whom I miss so much?"
Joel:
"I'm tired, I need you as my appetizer and my main course right this minute, I don't care which, I just want you!"

Lia:
"Take whichever you crave more. Satisfy your hunger! Do it! I have some good grapes, if you get closer and open your mouth, I can try to throw them in one at the time?" (Crazy face)

Joel:
"My mouth is open and you make my mouth watery with your approach. I don't want you throwing honey, slowly, glide it through my chest and chin into my mouth with it for me to grip, sexy!"

Lia:
"Must get closer then! Even more fun, I like it!"

Joel:
"(Love face, hearts) < My mouth is watery. You've given me the shivers."

Lia:
"Lick your lips because I have more than grapes!"

Joel:
"I've done it 5 times already!"

Lia:
"I love you so much!!" (Kisses)

Joel:
"I'm being real with you, you do amazing things in my heart!"

Lia:
"And you are tattooed in mine and are never coming out of it!"

Joel:
"I never want to, I never need to! I'm content with being tattooed in there!"

Lia:
"Never you forget that!"

Joel:
"Never! (Hearts) Are you okay my Love? I want to go to bed now. It's late!"

Lia:
"Sweet sleep to you my Love, I kiss you good night!" (Kisses, heart)

August 14, 2018, 10:58 AM

Joel:
"My Love, Are you Okay?"
Lia:
"Yes baby! How are you? Everything going well?"
Joel:
"I'm okay, yes so far. It's Tuesday and I've done almost everything they've required. But yes, everything else is fine. I miss you. I feel closer to you! How is your Morning? Tell me everything is going well?"
Lia:
"Everything is going well! My heart moves only for you!"
Joel:
"I love that it moves. That's such a powerful sentence honestly!" (heart)
Lia:
"(Kisses, love cat)"
Joel:
"My heart moves only for you! You have me completely. I swear it!"
Lia:
"Are you done for the day? What else do you have to do in order to get your passport
back?"

LIA:

"I had done the impossible for Joel. I had gotten the money he needed. I asked if there was anything else and he said no. Why did so much paperwork suddenly come up?"

"He made a fuss and wanted to do it all himself. I was insisting on legal help, but he refused.
I was praying that all will go well, and he will get to come home but it was getting delayed again and I knew what that meant. Just this once I was hoping that all of this would be over for real.

It was too much to bear and keep calm about. Every day was a guessing game and my anticipation of what was going to happen the next day kept me in a nervous stitch.

I had to be upbeat and help him get through the rough parts, but I did not understand why he did things the way he did and the only explanation in my head was that it was because of lack of money on his part.

But even though he claimed that this was the end, and it would all be ok I still felt as if something was going to happen and lead him into another mayhem."

JOEL AND LIA:

Joel:
"I'm waiting now for a stamp from the customs boss, here my Love, but she's in Turkey held up apparently! Hey, are you seeing the currency values going up lately? Do you know what is happening between Turkey and Cyprus? US?"
Lia:
"It was on the news this morning! Disgusting hate for the UK and US! This is why I am Screaming to hurry up!
The Turkish lira was devalued! It's very troubling and the Turks have imposed sanctions on US electronics! Lol...how can anyone do any business and the stock market is in the red for days! Lol..."

Joel:
"There's really no hope! Everyone is closing down. Shops and offices. This cannot be happening now.
Glad though I haven't paid the money now. Wondering why they're not pressuring me as much to pay up? I don't want to jinx it so I'm keeping quiet."

Lia:
"They are not pressuring you to pay because if your money gets converted you will lose a lot of it and not be able to pay! In this case it would have been better if you paid ASAP and been done!"

Joel:
"But that's not why they're feeding me these unnecessary documents and stamps. I would rather be done with this and end this bullshit really!"

Lia:
"Honey the only thing I want is to hold you and kiss you! All I wish is that Hashem sets you free and sends you home!"

Joel:
"Thank you for your prayers."

Lia:
"It's so ridiculous to make you do all that paperwork and not have the person there to approve it! Crazy Turks!"

Joel:
"Someone asked me for $5000. Today? For one of the stamps and documents for apparently overstaying what my initial contract states. I ignored him, it's silly and retorted, he's not serious!"

Lia:
"It may happen! Why are you not going to the UK embassy to get someone to enforce and move them?"

Joel:
"I've had no headaches yet as I've told you, why am I involving the Embassy to help me fill the docs?"

Lia:
"Try to be nice and not rude as much as you can. Let me use the retorted word! They are all freaked out with their situation, the Embassy personnel can back you into getting your passport! Ok, let's see how it goes. When is the stamper back?"

Joel:
"No idea as of today, I only realized now she was in Turkey! They couldn't communicate with me since yesterday. The language barrier."

Lia:
"No one else in her place? She has no Boss? It will be OK. She will be back soon and will stamp you. You just relax and enjoy till she is back!"

Joel:
"Well, she's to sign and not her Boss or her office. But I'll find out tomorrow, Darling. I've set it all out. Lol…enjoy though, I wish I could! I am anxious and nervous. I'm a wreck!" (Crazy face)

Lia:
"Now you got to be the strongest and wisest! They will be on your neck, and you have to take it just to be able to get out. Be serious with the lady, they are the toughest!"

Joel:
"I love you. Loving you is exciting! Thank you, baby, for your love baby!"

Lia:
"You can do this. I hold your trust in my hands and love you to the moon and back!
Can the stamper read your paperwork in English, or it needs to be translated in Turkish?"

Joel:
"I don't care! It's their documents anyway! I just walk in and pass it to them. They have their copies, I just assume the documents are familiar to the offices. Let's stay there, on the moon and don't come back!"

Lia:
"This is why I am asking this question because they might need translation themselves before they can stamp, and I certainly hope you made copies for yourself."
Joel:
"No, No! It's not! I've been doing this the whole week. Don't you trust that I can take care of this? Don't you think I put these processes through my thoughts?"
Lia:
"Lol...I am going to the Moon now...but will stay on your side of the street! "
Joel:
"I love you!"
Lia:
"(Heart, Kiss face)"

August 14, 2018, 4:14 PM

Lia:
"Did you check if Dion? Is she OK? They had another incident in London today!"
Joel:
"I have and she's fine, these guys just crave attention. I tell you! Honey, did you email her? Just got your email. Going through it Dear."
Lia:
"Long time ago I did but you said you spoke to her and I didn't want to disturb her further. Very glad to hear she is OK! Crazy world out there, maybe we'll all move to a small village to stay safe."
Joel:
"LOL... BABY"
Lia:
"Do you have the money in dollars in your hand?"

August 15, 2018, 10:35 AM

Joel:
"Hello my Love. I miss you! How are you doing today baby?"
Lia:
"Hi Honey! At a conference now. Talk soon. Did you have a nice day?"
Joel:
"(Heart)"

August 15, 2018, 12:02 PM

Lia:
"I do hope you've had a productive day. Tell me all! Miss you like crazy!" (Love cat, kisses)

August 15, 2018, 3:35 PM

Lia:
"Hi baby"

August 16, 2018, 5:32 AM

Joel:
"Now I truly call you mine. No external sign reminds me of my possession. Soon I shall call you mine.
When I hold you clasped tightly in my arms, when you enfold me in your embrace, then we shall need no ring to remind us that we belong to each other, is not us embracing, more of a ring than an actual physical one?
And the more tightly we embrace, the more inseparable we knit ourselves together, the greater the freedom consists in being mine as my freedom consists in being yours!"

Lia:
"It is said in legends that the highest form of blessing is bestowed upon the Queen by Hashem with Ani L'Dodi, "I am my beloved, and he is mine," a ring she gives to the one she loves and honors! As her man accepts, he becomes King! He cannot become King without the Queen and he cannot have the Kingdom without the ring!
We are everything to each other!"

August 16, 2018, 10:45 AM

Joel:
Sends Lia an email:

"My love,
I cannot send messages anymore, calls too! I got your messages earlier in the morning though I couldn't respond to them. How are you my dear? Got news that the woman would resume work on the 24th-Aug and that means I can't collect my papers and have them signed until she's back.
I'm fucking outraged at the whole thing now, it's fucking incompetence that's consumed these people!! Forgive my language but that exactly how I feel now. I hope you're better yourself and you're having a swell day. I love you. So much."

Lia:
Sends Joel an email back:

"Lol...Why can't you send phone messages? Do you need to pay for the phone? The 24th is a Friday, she comes back to work on Friday?
Are you OK? Don't be aggravated, I was expecting this, everyone takes vacation these last two weeks of August!
It will be OK, she will come back, and you will get your stamp. Just hold on to sweets, it will happen soon! "

"It will all be Ok soon, it's coming, I can feel it! Kisses and hugs and much more for you! I love you!"

LIA:

"Queen Elizabeth Enahoro, Joel's partner, found out that he had borrowed money from a businessman in Turkey and she had surmised that Joel would come up with enough money to release his passport and be able to leave the island.

The woman who was missing at the document office was one of her employees and had been sent away on vacation, so that Joel would not be able to get his final signature and stamp, and he would be missing a substantial document required to leave the country and retrieve his contract money.

He did not have any money left on him and since I had given him all I had, he took a chance and decided to try to get out without the final signature and without the vital document.

I did not know any of this and did not know why he stopped sending Emails or couldn't call.
He had disconnected all his service, thinking he was leaving and would not be needing it.

He had received a signature from one of the assistants, collected all his baggage and documents and headed for the airport to Istanbul.

He was uneasy about the whole thing, but he had no money left to stay and leaving this wretched island was the only thing he wanted to do."

August 29, 2018, 8:49 PM

LIA:

"Some time passed, and I did not hear anything from Joel.
I was starting to imagine all sorts of things but did not know for sure.

His friend Donald was the only one whose number and email I had and was the only link between us. I waited to hear from Joel until I couldn't wait any longer!"

September 7, 2018, 7:16 AM

Lia:
"Where are you? I'm not having any fun without you! I hear your voice and listen to your message every day!"

September 11, 2018, 8:20 PM

LIA:

"I had been patiently waiting to hear something from Joel.
I left him some emails and texts and I listened to my voicemail.

He had assured me that this was the very last step of meeting his obligation of his contract payment and his passport would be released and he will be able to leave North Cyprus.

The abrupt exit did not sit well with me. I had no idea what to actually do. I had no knowledge of his complex business partnership with Queen Elizabeth Enahoro and knew nothing of her demands and therefore everything was confusing and unresolved in my head."

"I should have just accepted the outcome and gone on with my daily existence. But I could not!
The man I loved had disappeared again!

I had all sorts of questions in my head, and I worried about what had caused his disappearance and if he was alright. Where could he have gone wrong now, what had happened?

I had no one to go back to, no one to ask, the only contact I had was his best friend, Donald.

I decided to contact Donald and see if he knew what had happened. He was the only connection I had to Joel.

Unknown to me, Donald had been involved with Joel in several business deals and had lent Joel a lot of money which he had borrowed from his friend contractor Scott Jasper.

Being that Joel's contract had taken so long to execute, Donald had fallen short on money and had not paid Scott back as agreed.

Donald was able to secure himself a long term job on a Marine Biological rig in the Pacific and left immediately, to escape paying back and to get out of Queen Elizabeth Enahoros clutches. He was lucky that he got out when he did.

Queen Elizabeth Enahoro had relieved Donald somewhat of his debt but required him to be on her payroll and instructed him to give me an impossible time and never allow me to get near Joel."

DONALD AND SCOTT JASPER:

"Scott Jasper did not know any of this and came back to Donald's home hoping to find him and get his money back.

Donald was not home at his arrival, but Scott knew where the spare key was and led himself inside the house.

He looked around to see if Donald was around and then found Donald's big computer on his desk, unlocked, and was able to go into his emails and retrieve and retrace all the information regarding Joel and Donald and all that had gone on.

He surmised that he may not be getting his money back any time soon, since Donald was gone on a long mission, and Joel was still in North Cyprus, waiting to exit, and so the only link he had was my email and he decided to play me, pretend that he was Donald and see how far he can get in order to get his money back.

He was angry that Donald had not kept his end of the bargain and he didn't care about Joel, since he did not know him, and the only appealing and intriguing person that he found was me.

I had all the motivation to find Joel. Scott wanted to get his money paid back to him. He just had to get to Queen Elizabeth Enahoro and figure out the best way to take care of this interesting situation.

I didn't know any of this, I didn't know who Scott was, nor that Donald had borrowed from him, nor that he had access to Donald's e-mails, and that he was able to get in touch with Queen Elizabeth Enahoro, who was most amused and surprised to hear from him."

September 12, 2018, 10:25 AM

Lia:
"I finally called and emailed Donald and asked him if he had heard from Joel."

FBI's Warning:

Thousands of people become victims of love related scams. This story portrays how someone can use their ability to narrate love words to capture a person who is vulnerable, who wants to find love, who is lonely, who wants to be with another, who is willing to do all to feel that there is hope for them in finding a soulmate, a love they can call their own.

Below is a letter from the FBI warning victims of the potential scam:

FBI Cautions Public to be Wary of Online Romance Scams:

The Federal Bureau of Investigation (FBI) is working to raise awareness about online romance scams, also called confidence fraud.

In this type of fraud, scammers take advantage of people looking for romantic partners on dating websites, apps, or social media by obtaining access to their financial or personal identifying information.

Romance scams are prevalent during any time of the year, and the FBI cautions everyone who may be romantically involved with a person online.

According to the FBI's Internet Crime Complaint Center (IC3), which provides the public with a means of reporting Internet-facilitated crimes, romance scams result in the highest amount of financial losses to victims when compared to other online crimes. If you suspect an online relationship is a scam, stop all contact immediately.

We recognize that it may be embarrassing for victims to report this type of fraud scheme because of the personal relationships that are developed, but we ask for victims to come forward so the FBI can ensure that these online imposters are brought to justice.

Thank you for reading **GOLDBRICKS WIFE** and for contributing to the struggle for Love.

We love it when our readers send us a review.

GODBRICKBOOKS@GMAIL.COM

www.ingramcontent.com/pod-product-compliance
Lightning Source LLC
LaVergne TN
LVHW021753060526
838201LV00058B/3078